Lincolnshire
COUNTY COUNCIL

discover libraries

This book should be returned on or before the last date shown below.

CM1

OSK 19.19

D0270339

GOLD COAST ANGELS

The hottest docs, the warmest hearts, the highest drama

Gold Coast City Hospital is located right in Australia's
Surfers Paradise, at the heart of the Gold Coast,
just a stone's throw away from the world-famous beach.
The hospital has a reputation for some of the
finest doctors in their field, kind-hearted nurses
and cutting-edge treatments.

With their 'work hard and play hard' motto,
the staff form a warm, vibrant community
where rumours, passion and drama are never far away.
Especially when there is a new arrival—
fresh from Angel Mendez Hospital, NYC!

**When utterly gorgeous bad-boy-with-a-heart
Cade rolls into town, trouble is definitely
coming to Surfers Paradise!**

If you loved **NYC Angels**, you'll love the high drama
and passion of this irresistible four-book series
from Mills & Boon® Medical Romance™.

GOLD COAST ANGELS:
A DOCTOR'S REDEMPTION
by Marion Lennox

GOLD COAST ANGELS:
TWO TINY HEARTBEATS
by Fiona McArthur

GOLD COAST ANGELS:
BUNDLE OF TROUBLE
by Fiona Lowe

GOLD COAST ANGELS:
HOW TO RESIST TEMPTATION
by Amy Andrews

GOLD COAST ANGELS: BUNDLE OF TROUBLE

BY
FIONA LOWE

MILLS & BOON

First published in Great Britain 2013
by Mills & Boon, an imprint of Harlequin (UK) Limited.
Harlequin (UK) Limited, Eton House, 18-24 Paradise Road,
Richmond, Surrey TW9 1SR

© Harlequin Books S.A. 2013

Special thanks and acknowledgement are given to Fiona Lowe for her contribution to the *Gold Coast Angels* series

ISBN: 978 0 263 89921 4

Dear Reader

Almost everyone in Australia would associate the Gold Coast, Queensland, with theme parks, beaches, holidays and fun. Everyone except, of course, the people who live there. For them it's just home. They get to enjoy the lovely beaches and the tranquillity of the rainforest in their own back gardens. Last year, when I was at a conference of romance writers on the Gold Coast, I wondered what it would be like to live in a tourist town—because everyday life isn't vacation...it's everyday life! How often do the residents get to the beach or the rainforest?

So, when my editor asked me if I would like to be part of the *Gold Coast Angels* series, I leaped at the chance—because this was my opportunity to explore living and working in a place that ticked 24/7 with a holiday vibe but was still home to so many people.

Chloe hasn't really ever had a vacation, even though she's lived on the Gold Coast for a decade. She's been too busy supporting her brother Nick and getting her own life back together after being abandoned by her parents at sixteen. Now she's just turned thirty, and she's reflecting on her life and where it's headed. Have the sacrifices she's been forced to make been worth it?

Luke loved the casual Gold Coast lifestyle in the huge house on the canal that he shared with his wife and daughter, but one moment in time stole all that from him. Now he's living in a town known for its fun, and yet he's cloaked in sadness and not able to see a way out of it.

I hope you enjoy Chloe and Luke's story, set against the backdrop of sun, surf and life lived to the full, and seeing how they manage against the odds to find their place in it and each other.

For photos of the Gold Coast, and tourist information to help you plan your next vacation, head over to my website: www.fionalowe.com. I love to hear from my readers, and you can find me on Facebook, Twitter, Goodreads, my website and blog, or e-mail me at fiona@fionalowe.com

Happy reading!

Fiona x

Always an avid reader, **Fiona Lowe** decided to combine her love of romance with her interest in all things medical, so writing Mills & Boon® Medical Romance™ was an obvious choice! She lives in a seaside town in southern Australia, where she juggles writing, reading, working and raising two gorgeous sons with the support of her own real-life hero!

Recent books by the same author:

LETTING GO WITH DR RODRIGUEZ
SYDNEY HARBOUR HOSPITAL: TOM'S REDEMPTION*
CAREER GIRL IN THE COUNTRY
SINGLE DAD'S TRIPLE TROUBLE
THE MOST MAGICAL GIFT OF ALL
HER BROODING ITALIAN SURGEON
MIRACLE: TWIN BABIES

*Sydney Harbour Hospital

**These books are also available in eBook format
from www.millsandboon.co.uk**

DEDICATION

To Kath for sharing her story
and to Christine for telling it.

Wishing you both good health and happiness.

CHAPTER ONE

'HAPPY BIRTHDAY!'

The cheers rained over Chloe Kefes and she didn't know if she wanted to laugh, cry or run. Truth be told, she wanted to do all three as she stared in shocked surprise at the smiling faces of her colleagues.

Somehow she managed to get her legs to move and as she stepped forward into the meeting room, the staff enthusiastically rushed her with balloons and hugs before pressing a polystyrene cup containing a small drop of champagne into her hand. So much for this being a vital patient review meeting on the busy Gold Coast City Hospital's plastic surgery ward—instead it was a well-meant ambush.

'To Chloe.' They raised their cups.

'Many happy returns, Clo.'

'Have a good one.'

Her shoulders were squeezed, she was patted on the back, and her arm was pummelled with birthday bumps as half the room—the afternoon shift—rushed past her, dashing back to work.

'Don't let Richard eat all the Tim Tams,' Julie, the radiographer, called out over her shoulder.

Their departure left behind the now off-duty day staff, which comprised a student nurse, a medical student and the plastics registrar, Richard, who had a reputation for eating all the chocolates.

Chloe finally found her voice. 'Oh, you guys, you didn't have to do this.' *Really, I wish you hadn't.*

Keri Letterman, the unit nurse manager, gave her a wide smile. 'You didn't think we'd let the big *three-oh* go past without acknowledging it, now, did you?'

'Wow,' muttered the barely twenty-year-old student nurse to the twenty-one-year-old med student, 'I didn't think she was that old.'

Chloe tried to give the bright and breezy smile she was known for but, despite her very best attempt, her 'I guess not' came out a tad strangled.

Up until a few minutes ago she'd really thought she'd managed to slip under the birthday police's radar, otherwise known as Keri and Kate. Given the fuss they'd made of Lizzie, the ward clerk, on her fiftieth birthday, Chloe probably should have known better. Except that, unlike the rest of the staff, she hadn't spent the preceding days giving a birthday countdown to anyone who'd listen.

In fact, she hadn't told anyone it was her birthday and she certainly hadn't told them it was the dreaded thirtieth.

'Lucky for you,' Keri continued, 'I met Nick, Lucy and those gorgeous twins in the cafeteria and they told me it was your special day. If we were depending on you to tell us, we'd never have known.'

That was the general idea. 'Who needs enemies when you've got a big brother, right?' Chloe joked, hearing the slight criticism in her boss's voice. She worked on letting it slide over her. Unlike many of her colleagues, she didn't bring her private life to work—mostly because she didn't have one.

Instead, she chatted about her new apartment with the

sea view—a ten-centimetre glimpse of the ocean from her kitchen sink—her bushwalks in the rainforest hinterland around Mt Warning, and her latest adventures with sea kayaking. All of it kept the conversation firmly off the very personal.

Her reticence to share stemmed from experience. She'd learned a long time ago that the more you told people about your life, the more questions they asked, and she was only prepared to talk about the last couple of years. Any further back didn't bear thinking about.

'So what did you get for your birthday, Chloe?' Richard asked, licking chocolate off his fingers.

She slid a photo out of her pocket and metaphorically crossed her fingers that the sheer cuteness factor of the photo would forestall the inevitable comments. 'Chester.'

'Oh, my God! He's just like the puppy on the toilet-paper ads,' Kate, a fellow nurse, gushed. 'How old is he?'

'Eight weeks.'

'That's little.' Kate frowned. 'Who's looking after him while you're at work?'

'He's at doggie daycare.'

'Doggie daycare?' Richard rolled his eyes. 'Showing us photos of a dog is a sure sign you need a man and a baby.'

Chloe tried unsuccessfully not to let his words slap her. Richard was a congenial guy who had no idea his off-the-cuff comment encapsulated everything she wanted in her life but could never have. 'Dogs are so much easier,' she tried to quip lightly, 'and, unlike you, my puppy will eventually be house-trained.'

Richard laughed good-naturedly as his pager beeped. Grabbing the last two Tim Tams before Kate could stop him, he called the students to follow him and he left with a wicked grin.

Keri looked at the photo of Chester. 'He *is* cute. Did I show you the photo of Tahlia dressed up as a cat?'

'You did.' Chloe tried to stop the smile on her face from freezing. She'd seen every photo of Tahlia from a wet, slippery newborn on her mother's chest right up to the most recent ones taken on her second birthday. Keri, like most proud parents, loved to spread her mother joy around, sharing every milestone with anyone and everyone who would listen. If they didn't want to listen, she told them anyway.

'Jack's off his training wheels.' Kate pulled out her phone and brought up a photo of her second son.

'He looks so grown up,' Keri said.

'I know, right? I remember the day he took his first step and now he's six and riding his own bike.' Kate scrolled to another photo. 'Chloe, you have to see this one.'

'Lovely,' Chloe said faintly. Chester's photo was supposed to be her weapon against this sort of thing but instead the cuteness of the puppy seemed to be reminding everyone else that their children were cute too.

'You okay, Chloe?' Keri asked

She renewed her smile, putting extra wattage into it. 'Fine, why?'

'You're shredding the rim of your cup.'

'I must need more champagne, then.' She picked up the bottle and sloshed in more of the straw-coloured liquid before gulping it down.

Kate held out her cup for a refill. 'What are your plans for tonight?'

A walk along the beach with Chester, followed by take-out Indian and then tucking up in bed and watching all four hours of North and South. Only Kate, who was married with young kids and had rose-coloured memories of being single, would be horrified at the thought. 'I'm hitting *The Bedroom* with some friends.' It wasn't strictly a lie.

Kate's eyes lit up. 'Oh, I remember nightclubs. Good for you, Chloe.'

'I bet Nick and Lucy have plans to spoil you,' Keri said as she started to tidy up the remains of the food.

She thought of her wonderful and loving brother, who'd been her sole supporter since she was sixteen. They'd been through a huge amount together and their joint determination to succeed had kept the other going during the tougher times.

Nick's recent marriage was wonderful and she'd been thrilled he'd found such a supportive life partner in Lucy but, as expected, the wedding and the arrival of the twins had changed things between them. His focus was now on his wife and children, not his sister, which was right and proper—and as much as she loved the twins she found it excruciatingly hard to be around them. All of it meant there were times she missed Nick very much.

'Nick organised for Café Sunset to open at six and we ate breakfast watching the sunrise—'

'Sorry to interrupt the party.'

Chloe swung around at the deep and slightly disdainful voice that didn't sound sorry at all.

'Luke?' Keri squealed with delight, and rushed forward, hugging him hard.

His body stiffened and he closed his eyes for a moment, as if he was seeking a way to endure the affection.

Chloe blinked and then gave her glasses a surreptitious polish and took another look. Was this gaunt man with a spray of silver at his temples really Luke Stanley? The eminent plastic surgeon who was known for his good humour and easygoing manner? She scanned her memory, barely recognising him.

She didn't know him personally—in fact she'd only ever had one brief encounter with him and that had been well over a year ago. Just thinking about it made her cheeks burn with embarrassment. It had been her first day on the ward.

Due to her age, everyone had assumed she'd been nursing for years, but her education had been truncated at sixteen and it had taken her a few years to return to study. Graduating from university at twenty-eight had meant she'd had to work doubly hard to appear totally competent compared with the younger nurses for whom other staff members automatically made allowances on account of their youth and inexperience.

With that in mind, back on her first day she'd been busy concentrating on preparing a dressing pack by a patient's bed, readying to check the skin edges, where his finger had been stitched back in place. As she had been mentally checking off all the items she required, she'd suddenly heard a deep and booming voice behind her saying, 'Hello, Mr Benjamin.'

Startled, she'd swung around fast, completely forgetting she'd been holding an open container of iodine. The sudden movement had propelled the brown liquid out of the bottle, sending it flying up into the air where it had paused for a perilous moment—mocking her and her total lack of control over its trajectory. Gravity had pulled it down fast and it had landed on Mr Stanley, plastic surgeon, and, to all intents and purposes, her new boss.

As the indelible dark stain had oozed down his striped shirt, his crystal-clear green eyes had widened in surprise.

'Oh, God, I'm s-so s-sorry,' she stammered. 'Of course

I'll replace it.' Juggling this month's bills to pay for what was probably a two-hundred-dollar shirt would involve robbing Peter to pay Paul—otherwise known as raiding her car fund yet again.

He raised his head—his neatly clipped and styled jet-black curls barely moving—and he smiled. 'This is the third hit this shirt's taken today. My wife frowns whenever I wear it as apparently it's not my colour and I shouldn't be trusted to shop alone,' he said with good humour. 'My baby daughter added her opinion by sicking up on it this morning just as I was racing out the door, and now this. I think you may have done me a favour... I'm sorry, I don't know your name.'

'Kefes. Chloe Kefes. I'm new today.'

Mr Benjamin, bless him, chimed in with, 'She's been taking excellent care of me, Doc.'

'I'm sure she has.' Luke tilted his head in contemplation. 'Our obstetrician's surname was Kefes. He works here at Gold Coast City and I think my wife secretly fell in love with him when he delivered Amber.' He laughed and pulled out his phone, showing her a photo of a new-born baby in a bath.

With huge, dark eyes and a thatch of black hair, the baby, like all newborns, looked unmistakably like her father. Chloe thought of a baby lost in the mists of time and she teetered on the edge of darkness.

'This is Amber an hour after Nick delivered her,' he said fondly. 'Believe me, I was in awe of him as well. I don't suppose he's any relation?'

She grabbed onto the lifeline of a conversation about her brother—one far removed from babies—and said, 'Actually, Nick's my brother and he is pretty awe-inspiring.'

Nick had sacrificed a lot and worked really hard to get

to where he was today and she loved hearing how well regarded he was in the community.

Luke's smile widened. 'Caring professions must run in your family. Did you grow up in a medical household?'

She shook her head, not wanting to go anywhere near that mess of tangled and fraught emotions. 'Are you sure you're okay about your shirt?'

Again his ready smile graced his tanned cheeks. 'Please don't worry about it. Chances are Anna will probably write you a thank-you note for making it unwearable.' He turned his attention to his patient. 'So, Mr Benjamin, I just want to have a look at your fingers and see if my handiwork has counteracted the impact of the circular saw.'

That was the last time she'd seen him until today. Soon after the iodine debacle, a memo had been sent out from medical administration stating that Luke Stanley was on sabbatical for a year. At the time she hadn't thought anything of it. Consultants came and went, and her job was all about the patients. But now, looking at him, she wondered if he'd been on sabbatical in a place that lacked sunshine. The man who once could have been glibly described as tall, dark, tanned, charming and with a ready smile looked pale, tired and tense.

Keri smiled as she stepped back from the hug. 'I saw your name was back on the surgery list and I was wondering when you'd come up and say hi.' She extended her arm. 'You remember Kate, but I don't think you've met Chloe.'

Kate raised her hand in greeting. 'Welcome back, Luke.'

'Thanks.' The gruff word lacked grace.

Then eyes that Chloe remembered as having been bright and full of fun swung a dull gaze at her. No sign of recognition registered in their mossy dark depths. He gave her a curt nod of acknowledgment and an unruly curl fell across a slanted black eyebrow, highlighting his general dishevelment.

The inky stubble on his jaw had passed the three-day requirement of fashionable growth and now cried out for the tidying touch of a razor. Instead of a crisp shirt tucked into a pair of tailored suit trousers, he wore a dark red polo shirt and crumpled chinos that looked as if he'd slept in them. Perhaps he was jet-lagged and had just got off the plane?

He swung his attention back to Keri. 'I've got a complicated surgery this week on a child the foundation's brought over from Bali. He's got shocking scarring on his neck and face due to the burn of hot oil and he can't close his mouth or move his head. He'll need one-on-one nursing and I want him nursed here by a plastics nurse, not in Paediatrics.'

Keri nodded. 'What day are we talking?'

'Thursday.'

The unit manager consulted the nursing roster on the notice-board. 'Chloe's rostered on through Sunday.'

'Good,' Luke said, sounding weary and resigned, as if everything was an effort but at least one job had been sorted out.

No, not good at all. A mild flutter of anxiety batted Chloe's chest. She nursed adults and she didn't like where this conversation was heading at all.

Luke's gaze raked her again—a desolate look in his eyes calling up a sadness in her that she knew only too well. A sadness she'd learned to avoid thinking about. As she tried to shake off the melancholy his glance had elicited, she caught a momentary flash of something in his eyes that lit up the brilliant green.

A tingle shot up her spine, leaving a trail of unsettling effervescence. A tingle she barely remembered and had only *ever* associated with pain and regret. A tingle that had absolutely no place in this situation. He was married with a child and she wasn't the sort of woman who would ever break up a marriage. Never. Ever.

She tried to throw off the sensation. Ethics aside, she didn't even know him, so why a flutter of attraction? Her body, unlike her brain, must have its wires utterly crossed. Empathy was the *only* thing she should be feeling for this man—empathy generated by the sadness in his eyes—nothing else. Definitely not lust.

'...at eight in the operating theatre, Chloe.'

The way his tongue rolled over her name shocked her back into the conversation and with her heart thumping hard she threw a beseeching look at Keri. 'Jackie has way more experience than I do working with children.'

'She does,' Keri agreed, 'but she's not rostered on and you are.'

Chloe thought of her empty social calendar. 'I can swap.'

Keri shook her head. 'She's got her sister's wedding, remember?'

She turned to Kate, trying to hold her desperation in check. 'How about you, Kate? As a birthday gift to me?'

'Sorry, Chloe, I've got a family thing on. You know how it is.'

She didn't know at all. Apart from meals with Nick, she hadn't had a *family thing* in fourteen years.

A sigh of frustration hissed from Luke's thinned lips and it bounced around the room, loud in its disapproval. He zeroed his glare onto her. The ominous, dark look made his high cheekbones sharp and stark, which emphasised the charcoal shadows under his eyes. 'I'm sorry if my plans are inconveniencing you.'

His sarcasm—so far removed from the friendly, smiling man she'd met a year ago—bit hard, ruffling her usually calm demeanour. Her chin shot up. 'Your plans are not inconveniencing *me* in the slightest, Mr Stanley. However, my expertise lies in nursing adults and therefore I may well inconvenience your patient.'

'For heaven's sake, I'm not asking you to play games with him.' He shoved his hand through his hair, the thick curls snagging at his fingers. 'Look, I need a plastics nurse who's good at her job. Either you fit the bill or you don't.'

'She definitely fits the bill,' Keri interrupted, her voice full of soothing tones as she threw Chloe a look that said, *What on earth is the matter with you?* 'Chloe will head up a team of three nurses to cover each block of twenty-four hours for as long as the child needs that level of care.'

Chloe gulped in a steadying breath to stop the simmer of panic that was threatening to take off into a full-blown boil. Nursing children wasn't something she did. Even as a student nurse she'd minimised her exposure with a bit of dumb luck. Rostered onto the children's ward during a flu epidemic, she'd ended up nursing more adults under the bright, owl-covered bedspreads than children. This time, however, her luck had run out.

Keri took Luke's arm and steered him towards the door. 'How are Anna and Amber? Happy to be back home in sunny Australia?'

Luke blanched, the little colour he had in his face completely draining away. 'You don't know?'

His quiet words sent a chill through Chloe.

'I don't think I do,' Keri said warily.

He looked out towards the ward, avoiding eye contact with the three of them. 'Anna died thirteen months ago.'

His pain jerked through Chloe and her fingers closed

around her cup so hard it crumpled in her hand. The successful surgeon who'd once had everything had lost it.

Keri sagged against the doorjamb. 'I'm so sorry, Luke, none of us had any idea…'

'Now you do.' His words scorched the air like the summer sun—harsh, burning and devoid of any compassion that he'd just delivered shocking news. He turned abruptly to face Chloe, his emotions masked by tight control. 'Don't be late on Thursday.' Just as abruptly, he strode out of the ward.

At that moment Chloe would have given anything to avoid Thursday. As she absently listened to Kate and Keri express their stunned sorrow for Luke, the ramifications of the next few days—weeks even—hit her. The man with the reputation of being fun, forgiving and easy to work with had totally vanished. In his place was a tortured and grieving soul with a personality as black as his jet hair.

It was a hell of a way to start her thirty-first year.

CHAPTER TWO

'How was she today?' Luke asked, sitting at his sister's outdoor table under the protective shadow of a huge shade sail and watching Amber running around the yard with her older cousins. He tried not to think about the fact he had to take her home to a quiet and empty house.

'The kids ran her ragged and she napped for three hours straight,' Steph said with an apologetic shrug. 'I guess that means she'll be hard to settle tonight. Sorry.'

He thought about the hard-fought routine he'd established with his toddler daughter, all of which was about to change now he was returning to full-time work. 'Hopefully, she's running off more energy now and will snuggle down at seven.'

His sister gave him a contemplative glance. 'So, how was it?'

'What?' He was being deliberately obtuse just in case his perceptive sister was having an off day.

'Being back at Gold Coast City?'

The memory of the shocked expression of the nurses slugged him. 'They didn't know.'

'Hell.' Her hand touched his arm.

'Yeah.' He stirred the ice at the bottom of his glass. 'I thought someone would have told them. I mean, hospitals are usually seething with gossip, rumour and innuendo, but just when I needed my personal life to be part of that mill, it wasn't.'

'I guess because it happened in France…'

'Maybe.' He drained his glass, trying not to think of that night when the gendarmes had told him his car had drifted onto the wrong side of the road. 'I had to tell them, Steph. I had to watch their horror and then their sympathy. God, I thought by now I was over having to tell people. I thought at least that part would be done.'

'It'll get easier.'

'Don't say that.' He glared at her, hating platitudes. He'd heard enough of them to know they only made the speaker feel better. Nothing was ever going to make him feel better. Nothing could erase the bald fact that he'd unwittingly killed his darling wife.

Steph's usually smiling mouth flattened. 'We'll *always* miss Anna. You know I meant walking into the hospital and talking with the staff will get easier. Try to look on the plus side. By the time you return on Thursday they'll have digested the news and be onto something else. Besides, given the turnover of staff, half of them probably don't even know you.'

The image of a pair of hazel eyes framed by black-rimmed glasses, followed by a mane of glossy, chestnut hair, pinged into his mind. Eyes that seemed familiar and yet he felt sure that he'd never met the nurse before. If they'd met, he'd have remembered that particular combination of khaki-green flecked with brown. He knew that grief screwed with memory and his had been bad lately but, even so, she hadn't shown any spark of recognition either. Hell, he really didn't know why he was even thinking about her.

He tried to stop the picture of her at those eyes but,

like a movie reel, his brain recalled way more. In vivid detail, it rolled over her round, smiling face, her ruby-red lips that peaked in a delectable bow and her lush curves that no uniform could hide. Natural curves that in a by-gone era women had embraced but which today so many tried to dominate into submission. Curves that said, *I am all woman.*

His mouth dried as the same short, sharp kick of arousal he'd experienced the first time he'd seen her stirred again. He rubbed the back of his neck. God, what was wrong with him? Anna had only been dead just over a year and he missed her every single day. He didn't want to look at other women, let alone lust after them.

'You okay, Luke?'

No. 'Yep.' He didn't like the inquiring look in his sister's eyes so he shifted conversational gears. 'The daycare centre called and they can take Amber for the extra days each week while you're away on your big trip.'

Relief flitted across Steph's face. 'That's good news. Of course, if you hadn't sold the house around the corner...'

He shook his head, thinking about the five-bedroom house with its indoor-outdoor living, swimming pool and a spectacular view of the tidal canal and its constant boat traffic.

He and Anna had bought the colonnaded home when he'd been appointed to Gold Coast City. It was the place they'd taken Amber home to from the hospital and settled her into her nursery with the crooked wallpaper frieze of pastel balloons that he'd put on the wall. Anna had taken one look at his dodgy handiwork and had teased him not to give up his day job.

'I couldn't live in that house, no matter how close it was to you, and besides...' he raked his hand through his hair '…it's moot in this instance because you're going to be gone for two months. I appreciate that you've been having Amber three days a week while I've been doing some private practice stuff, but I don't want you putting your life on hold for me. Marty's been talking about driving up the centre from Adelaide to Darwin for as long as I've known him, and it isn't fair to you, him or the girls to put it off again.'

'Luke, we're family and we help each other out. It's what families do. And the moment we get back I want to have Amber three days a week again.' She leaned closer to him and smiled. 'We love having her here, and the girls have stopped pestering me for a baby brother or sister so it's win-win.'

He tried to match her smile. 'No more baby plans, then?'

'No. Marty wanted two and I wanted four so we've compromised on three.'

Luke detected a wistfulness in his sister's voice, but before he could say anything Amber took a tumble on the grass and sent up a shriek of shocked surprise.

'Up you get, honey,' Luke called out as he rose to his feet and crossed the lawn. He swung his daughter into his arms and gave her knees and elbows a quick inspection for skin damage but could only see grass stains. He kissed her. 'Bath time for you, young lady.'

'Play ducky?' Amber asked hopefully.

'Play ducky in your bathtub,' Luke replied, bracing himself for a howl of disappointment that Amber had to leave her beloved cousins and come with him.

'Okay.'

'Okay.' He kissed her again, battling a surge of sadness for them both. 'Let's go…' He couldn't bring himself to say home because the cottage was just a house.

* * *

Chloe checked little Made's observations as the six-year-old slept. The white of the sheets and pillowcases made his black hair and deeply olive skin seem even darker, and in the big hospital bed he looked tiny and in need of protection. Her protection.

She bit her lip against the rush of emotions—some caring, some painful, most tinged with loss. She'd lost her baby and along with it her chance to be a mother. Self-preservation meant she'd chosen not to nurse children, and in her off-duty life, while she didn't technically avoid children, she didn't actively seek them out either.

She knew from bitter experience that letting her mind drift backwards was unwise and unhealthy so she drew on every ounce of her professionalism. *He's a patient, like all your other patients.*

She picked up the Bahasa-English dictionary she'd purchased and thumbed through the pages. Last night she'd recalled her basic Indonesian from primary school, and using the dictionary she'd looked up the words for pain and thirst, adding them to her small list of phrases. The little boy's mother spoke less English than Chloe spoke Bahasa, which wasn't saying much, so the dictionary was getting a good workout.

Between them, they were muddling along and Made was pain-free, which right now was the most important thing for his recovery.

Chloe stifled a yawn. It had been a long day and she still had an hour to go before her relief took over. She'd started her shift early due to Luke Stanley's request that she attend the operation. She'd arrived before him and had spent the time chatting with the anaesthetist about Made's post-operative pain relief while the rest of the theatre staff had scurried around, getting ready. The scout nurse had set up Mr Stanley's favourite playlist of music but the moment he'd walked briskly into Theatre he'd demanded it be turned off.

The mood of the room had instantly changed—people had become tentative and quiet. Eyes had flashed and flickered over the tops of surgical masks, sending coded messages to each other. Luke Stanley had operated almost silently, his only words being infrequent curt demands for instruments that the experienced scrub nurse had failed to anticipate, and as a result the air was thick with confused tension. People wanted to be sympathetic and understanding, but nothing about Luke Stanley's demeanour allowed it.

Initially, Chloe hadn't understood why Luke had insisted she be in the operating room, but it had been utterly hypnotic watching him in action and seeing how those long, strong and competent fingers had freed the thick, scarred adhesions on Made's neck. He deserved his reputation as a talented surgeon and his skills were restoring little Made's life to normality. The young boy would once again be able to turn his head, and in time he would once again enjoy playing childhood games.

Although it hadn't been absolutely necessary to attend the operation to be able to nurse Made effectively, knowing exactly what Luke Stanley had done, seeing from where the skin grafts had been taken and how they had been positioned, did help. She rechecked Made's analgesia drip and then set about her fifteen-minute routine of observing the skin grafts. Circulation was key and she wanted to see pink, warm skin, not white and cool skin.

'How's he doing?'

Surprised, Chloe spun around at the sound of Luke's

deep but curt voice. Just like their first encounter fifteen months ago, she hadn't heard him enter the ward—only this time her hands were thankfully empty. This time Luke's face wasn't open, smiling and cheerful. Instead, gaunt skin stretched over high cheekbones, giving him a haunted look.

'He's doing great,' she said, suppressing a shudder at the pain Luke wore like a greatcoat. Her brain sought for something she could say that could give them a shared connection, which might make him look less formidable and unapproachable. 'Do you always enter the room panther style?'

His dark brows drew down. 'What are you talking about?'

She ignored his brusqueness and tried a smile. 'You have a habit of entering a room silently and surprising me.'

He looked blank and utterly uncomprehending. 'This is the first time I've seen you with a patient.'

She shook her head. 'Just before you went to France, you walked into this same ward very quietly and gave me such a fright that I covered you in iodine.'

His vivid green eyes finally flashed with recognition. 'Chloe? Nick's sister?' He said the words as if he needed to hear them to cement them in his mind.

'That's right. Lucky for you that today my hands are empty,' she joked.

He glanced down at his scrubs, as if he couldn't re-member what he was wearing, and then shrugged his wide shoulders like it really didn't really matter anyway. 'If there's any change with Made's grafts, notify me imme-diately. You have my mobile number?'

She swallowed a sigh. So much for attempting a friendly

connection with the man. 'I do. Are you leaving the hospital now?'

He seemed to stiffen. 'Yes. I have to pick my daughter up from daycare. They don't like it when I'm late.'

'I don't suppose she likes it either.'

His eyes burned, emitting sparks of green. 'You think I want Amber in daycare ten hours a day? She doesn't have a choice and neither do I.'

The loud and terse words slammed into her like a punch to her solar plexus, making her heart race.

Made's mother startled from her nap in the chair. *'Apa yang salah?'* Mrs Putu asked anxiously.

Chloe didn't need to understand the words to know that the mother was stressing that Luke's raised voice meant something was wrong with her son. She reached out her hand to comfort and reassure the woman.

'Semuabaik,' Luke said softly. 'All is well.'

'Terimakasih, Dokter.' The woman visibly relaxed and sank back in her chair.

Chloe turned back to face Luke, surprised at the ease in which the foreign language had rolled off his tongue but furious with him for upsetting Mrs Putu. For deliberately misconstruing her own words. Adrenaline pelted through her, sending rafts of agitation jetting along her veins, and she needed to work extra-hard to appear calm.

Choosing her words carefully, she shepherded Luke towards the door. 'I'm not judging you about daycare,' she said, *sotto voce,* 'I was talking about the fact your daughter probably doesn't like it when you're late either.'

He stared down at her, his jaw tight, his height dwarfing her by a good thirty centimetres, and she caught the scent of his spicy cologne. His eyes, which at times could be bright green, were now a dark moss and filled with so many flickering emotions that it was hard to decode any of them over and above the dominant and glaring pain.

Tall, dark, gorgeous, brooding and tortured.

Her heart did a ridiculous leap, which had absolutely nothing to do with his indignation or her chagrin.

Oh, no, she told herself sternly. *The man is grieving and you do not need to rescue him. You've just got your own life back on track. You've got a dog to love and be loved by.*

Shimmering tingles taunted her, spinning through her with their intoxicating call. *But it's been so long...*

No way in hell, Chloe! her ever-vigilant internal guard yelled. *Keep it simple, remember?*

She sucked in a long, deep breath, trying desperately to banish the delicious buzz of addictive warmth. 'Everything's fine here, Mr Stanley. Go and get your daughter.'

His eyes widened at her dismissal of him, and he rubbed his forehead with his fingers and his temple with his thumb as if his head hurt. 'Goodnight, then.'

She watched him turn and leave without giving an apology and she tried not to let it rankle. After all, it shouldn't bother her one bit because she was used to working with surgeons who believed all should bow down before them and kiss their feet. She also knew that apologies for bad behaviour were few and far between. Only Luke Stanley had always been an exception to that rule.

His reputation for skill and good humour had always meant that people had fallen over themselves to work with him. The nursing and auxiliary staff, from cleaners to occupational therapists, had loved him, and whenever he'd put together a team to go to Asia or Africa for a six-week stint with the foundation, repairing cleft lips and palates, there had always been more applicants than positions.

That man had utterly disappeared when his wife had died.

She wasn't a stranger to grief, and she understood the pain of it all too well. She'd been lost in the midst of it once, for a year, floundering in the suffocating darkness that had become both enemy and friend. It had been her beloved brother Nick who'd hauled her unwilling teenage mind out of the black and treacherous morass and pushed her back into the light of life.

At the time it had hurt like nothing she'd ever experienced before or since and the battle not to let grief become a toxic legacy had been beyond hard, but she'd done it. Years later, when Jason had told her he wouldn't marry her because she couldn't give him a child, she'd teetered on the edge but she'd survived and learned. Today, she knew that even though her life now wasn't anything like that she'd imagined for herself as a naïve sixteen-year-old, and neither was it the life she truly wanted, it was a life worth living and living well.

You could show him how to do it.

The thought clanged loudly in her head like the penetrating sound of a fire alarm and she wished she could put noise-cancelling headphones over her brain.

Yes, she was a nurse, a member of a caring profession, and, yes, she had the ability to recognise when someone needed help. Luke Stanley definitely fell into that category—he needed help big-time—but she was also a survivor. Helping a grieving man with a child would be more harmful to her than helpful to him and she wasn't prepared to risk her hard-won stability.

No, it wasn't her job to do the 'hands-on' helping stuff with Luke Stanley, but she'd talk to Keri and Kate. After all, they knew Luke a hell of a lot better than she did.

CHAPTER THREE

'WANT BUNNY,' AMBER sobbed into Luke's shoulder, her tears making a damp patch on his cotton shirt.

'Hello, Amber, I'm Mr Clown,' Luke said in a voice he thought might sound like a clown's as he waggled the soft toy near his daughter's face.

Amber's hand knocked the clown sideways. 'Want bunny!'

Luke's head pounded with fury at himself and despair for Amber, which rumbled through him and reminded him he had so much to learn as a father. How had he forgotten to check that her beloved bunny had been in the backpack when he'd collected Amber from daycare?

Because you were thinking about Chloe Kefes.

His anger at himself was buried deep with sharp roots. How had he forgotten ever meeting her? Unlike most of his colleagues, he didn't forget names and faces, especially when there was another connection, like her being Nick's sister. But today he'd needed all her prompting to recall the iodine incident.

He hated that he'd forgotten as much as he hated the fact his mind kept repeating the way her plump lips curved into a smile. A generous, captivating smile, which dimpled her round cheeks and danced in her eyes. A smile that had

faded under the onslaught of his bitter words—words generated by his own self-loathing and hurled out to land on
the nearest target. It wasn't Chloe's fault that Amber was
motherless and in full-time daycare. No, that responsibility lay solely at his feet.

Amber's wails sounded even louder than before.

Damn it, he shouldn't still be thinking about Chloe.
What sort of a pathetic excuse for a father was he?

Poor Amber. She was rarely without her talisman
bunny—her security blanket in her ever-changing world.
Her one stable item in a confusing place, where her previously mostly at-home father was now absent during the
day, and her aunt, uncle and cousins were unexpectedly
gone too.

He'd telephoned the director of the daycare centre, who,
although sympathetic to his plight, had not been prepared
to make the twenty-minute drive to open the building to
retrieve the bunny, no matter what Luke had offered. The
doctor in him understood. The father with the hysterical
child wasn't quite so reasonable.

He lined up all Amber's cuddly toys. 'Look, honey,
Teddy's sad and needs a cuddle,' he tried, desperate to
turn the situation around.

Amber screamed.

Abandoning any attempts to try and settle her into
her cot, Luke carried her outside to the deck. The slow
and rhythmic roll of the waves hitting the sand boomed
around them and the silver rays of moonlight beamed
down through the streaks of cloud to sparkle on the
Pacific Ocean. He lowered himself onto the sun lounger
and settled Amber on his chest, his hand patting her sobbing and shuddering body and matching the beat to the
tempo of the waves.

Oh, so very slowly, as the inky darkness cloaked them both, Amber's frantic sobs turned into occasional, gulping hiccoughs until her breathing steadied and her body relaxed against his. Despair finally turned to sleep. He knew he should probably take her into her room and settle her into her cot, but after the last hour he didn't dare move in case she woke up, remembered the missing bunny and was again faced with having to go through the same trauma.

He knew all about that. Even now, living in a different house, he still woke occasionally expecting to find Anna there, only to have the realisation she was gone dump all over him. Over and over. Anna was gone because he'd made a critical error that couldn't be fixed. At least Amber was spared the memory of missing her mother, or at least he hoped she was. She'd only been six months old when Anna had died. Did she miss someone she couldn't remember?

He pulled a beach towel off the chair next to him and covered both of them with it to ward off the slight chill of the night air. Amber may not have a mother, but she had a loving extended family who smothered her in love. Were aunts, uncles and cousins enough?

The image of clear and honest hazel eyes beamed into his brain and he instantly shut them out. He'd only ever had eyes for one woman, and even though Anna was gone he had no desire to look elsewhere. The idea was abhorrent to him. Closing his eyes, he found himself battling random images of dimples and long, glossy chestnut hair. Desperate, he focused on the sound of the sea and willed sleep to come.

The elevator doors closed and Callie Richards, neonatal specialist, wished she could turn off her pager and hide in the steel box for an hour. She knew it was just an idle dream, however, because the NICU was full of sickies and Nick Kefes, Gold Coast City's beloved obstetrician, had just called her, flagging a possible case that might require her skills. She hoped Nick was being his usual overcautious self and that she might actually get home tonight to sleep in her own bed.

Who else's bed would you sleep in? Certainly not arrogant Cade Coleman's.

Shut up!

She hated how her conscience threw up unexpected reminders of her most stupid mistake to date—flirting outrageously with Cade Coleman. Just when she'd been convinced she'd successfully let go of the embarrassing memory, her brain did this to her. It made little sense because it wasn't like he was the only man she'd ever had practise forgetting. Truth be told, he was just one in a long line of men—men she rarely gave a second thought after she'd picked up her shoes and tiptoed quietly out their doors, never to see them again.

Correction—thinking about Cade made *no* sense because she hadn't even got to first base with him, thank God, let alone kissing and sex. But flirting with him had been a basic error—a rookie mistake she should be long past making.

Rule Number One: don't hit on the men you work with. Prior to Cade, she'd held fast to that rule like superglue because it meant she never had to deal with coming face to face with her folly on a daily basis.

Mind you, the man didn't seem perturbed by that fact so she shouldn't be either and, damn it, she wasn't. Just yesterday she'd given him a polite nod and not felt a moment's regret. Well, not very much of a moment, anyway.

Emotionally stunted men like Cade are not worth thinking about. She repeated the mantra to herself.

The elevator pinged, the doors opened and she stepped out to see Chloe Kefes standing and staring through the large windows of the special care nursery. On the other side of the glass were the cots that were home to the premature babies who were now almost full term. The staff affectionately called this part of the room the 'fattening-up' corner and when babies graduated here, they were close to being discharged home into the loving care of their parents.

'Hi, Chloe, you're a long way from Plastics.'

The nurse looked momentarily flustered and a pink flush stained her cheeks. 'I'm on my way back from Pathology.'

'You're taking the long way, then.' Callie laughed, understanding exactly, because sometimes in a fraught and busy hospital, taking a circuitous route gave a professional the only breathing space they got in a day. She followed Chloe's gaze. Twin boys had managed to each get a hand out from under their bunny rug and their little fingers were exploring the air.

'Those two were so sick and now look at them. They're just itching to explore life,' Callie said with a glow of satisfaction.

'Hmm.'

Callie glanced at Chloe, who was usually a lot chattier. 'Tough day?'

Chloe shrugged. 'I used to love coming to work but for the last few weeks the ward's been on tenterhooks. It seems no matter what we do, we can't do anything right.'

'Luke Stanley?'

She nodded. 'When the consultant's not happy…'

'No one is.' Although Callie didn't know Luke, she'd heard the news of his wife's death on the hospital grapevine. She touched Chloe's arm in an understanding gesture because nurses often took the brunt of a doctor's unhappiness.

'When my day sucks, I often come down here and look at the babies.' Callie smiled. 'There's something about them that makes you feel better and gives you hope, right?'

Chloe spun away from the window so fast that she almost knocked into her. 'I have to get back to work, Callie. Catch you later.'

She walked away before Callie had time to say another word. Astonished by the nurse's abrupt departure, she watched her disappear into the lift. Chloe was usually so upbeat—one of those people who seemed to be almost too bright, bubbly and good humoured to be real, although Callie knew her to be absolutely genuine. Chloe Kefes was one of the hospital's best nurses, with a perfect blend of professionalism, empathy and good cheer. For her to be so skittish, Luke Stanley must really be getting her down.

Men. Working with them should be straightforward but so often it was far from that. Thoughts of Cade threatened to rise but she cut them off at the knees. She'd made a fool of herself once and she had no plans to do it again. She was over and done with Cade Coleman.

She pushed open the door of the nursery and did a round of her little patients. The baby with bronchomalacia, who was being nursed in the open cot, was improving and she hoped that by tomorrow he'd be breathing without the assistance of continuous positive airway pressure. She took the time to reassure anxious parents about the standard procedure of using an apnoea mattress with all premature babies, and she was thrilled to be able to help a mother hold her premature baby for the very first time.

Callie loved her job. Unlike her private life, here at the hospital she was in control and she knew exactly what she was doing. After she'd completed the discharge papers for the twins, Nick still hadn't called back, so she decided to grab something to eat while she had the chance.

As she reached the tearoom door, laughter and conversation rolled out to meet her.

'Oh, my God, that Cade Coleman has to be the sexiest man ever to walk the floor of this hospital.'

Callie recognised the voice of Sara Hennessey, one of the NICU nurses, and she stopped short of entering the room.

'I know, right? And that accent! He only has to say *hello* and I'm a puddle of lust,' replied a voice Callie wasn't familiar with.

'He is without a doubt *the* best addition to Gold Coast City in a very long time. I heard from the theatre nurses that Callie Richards—'

Oh, God, no! Callie hastily spun on her heel, away from the tearoom, and punched open the nursery door. It took every ounce of control she had to keep her feet from breaking into a run. One dumb mistake. It was bad enough she'd plastered herself all over him when they'd danced and then gone on to suggest that she was open to more, but to have the nursing staff talking about her was more than she could bear. She'd worked so hard at keeping her private life exactly that—private.

Never again was she going to give anyone any excuse to talk about her. From this day forward she was marking Cade Coleman and every other red-blooded male in the hospital as *off limits*.

* * *

'What is the point of writing down clear instructions if no one reads them?'

As Luke's terse words broke over Chloe like jagged shards of glass, she counted slowly to five. Despite talking with Keri and Kate and outlining her concerns about Luke, and their meeting with staff in Theatre to try and work out the best way to handle him, not much had changed in two weeks. With Keri and Kate, with whom he'd worked before, he seemed to hold himself in check, but there were still moments when he was difficult, and on those occasions he took down everyone in his path.

Oh, why had Keri gone to a seminar today, leaving her in charge of the ward? Now she had to deal with the man she'd nicknamed *the panther*. Like the big black cat, he was a perfect specimen—sleek, muscular and strong. At times his emerald eyes would glow with ruthless keenness that made her shiver with delicious anticipation.

It unnerved her because she didn't want to be attracted to him. She didn't want to be attracted to *any* man, let alone one who had a neon 'excess-baggage' sticker plastered all over him. That would be like throwing herself under a truck—both dangerous and deadly to her peace of mind.

Stay strong. Remember, no man is for you, especially not this one.

A raft of heady need skipped through her, deaf to her entreaties, and she stomped on it hard. She didn't even like this version of Luke, so why was her body doing this to her? When he was in one of his moods, he pounced on any weakness, attacking first and pausing second. Yes, the man was grieving, and for the last couple of weeks the staff had been making allowances for him, but that didn't absolve him from basic manners.

Glancing up at his handsome but scowling face, she said, 'And hello to you, Mr Stanley. Welcome to Ward Six.'

'Chloe.' He gave her a stiff nod as if he recognised that he should have at least greeted her first before lobbing his complaint at her like a grenade. 'Mrs Wharton's drain tubes should have been removed today. The woman's been through breast cancer and the least she can expect is to be free of tubes so she can get an idea of how her new breasts are going to look.'

'I agree.'

'I don't need you to agree.' He rubbed his temple and squinted at her as if he was having trouble focusing. 'I just need the drain tubes out.'

'And they will come out.' In every encounter with the irascible consultant she'd needed to draw on her counselling skills. It was exhausting. 'As a result of your busy morning in the operating theatre, we're flat out here with post-op checks. Along with that, we're one nurse down and as I am sure you're aware you didn't specify an exact time for the removal. There's still a lot of today left.'

She smiled at him to reinforce her commitment. 'I guarantee you that the drain tubes will be out before I go off duty at three.'

'Good,' he said gruffly, scrawling an order on another patient's chart. 'Make sure they are.'

His response crossed her threshold of what she was prepared to have dished out to her. 'Mr Stanley...Luke.'

His silver pen stilled in his hand. 'Yes?'

'I may not be Keri and we may not have had a long working relationship but I'm good at my job. When I give you my word, know that it will be honoured. I'd appreciate being treated with the same professional respect that I accord you.'

Despite the semi-permanent dull ache behind his eyes, Luke felt Chloe's words strike him and strum a chord. God, when had he turned into such an ogre?

Since you killed your wife. The cancerous words spread their malignancy through him again, ramping up the hatred he held for himself—an abhorrence he shielded Amber from. Like a full reservoir, there were times when it spilled out at work, no matter how hard he tried to contain it.

'I have a headache.' He rubbed his eyes and hid behind an excuse because it was easier than telling Chloe the truth.

Her hazel eyes widened in disbelief at his justification for rudeness, which even sounded lame to his own ears.

'I'm sorry to hear that,' she said, her chin tilting up defiantly, 'but is there any need to inflict it on us? Here…' She fished a foil disc out of her pocket. 'Take some ibuprofen.'

He accepted the two white tablets along with the admonishment and tried a wry smile. 'Spoken like a true nurse.'

Her lush mouth softened into a smile and the stirrings of warmth that eddied in him each time he met her became waves of liquid heat. Then she laughed and the sound surfed on the heat, pulling up memories of the times he'd laughed easily. For a brief moment the constant reminders of why he didn't laugh much any more—why he didn't feel any more—faded away and he let the wondrous and glorious sensations of life surge through him.

Betrayer.

Guilt seared him like the dry heat from a furnace, sucking the oxygen from the joy until it shrivelled to nothing. He didn't deserve to feel happy. He wanted to turn and leave—march away from Chloe immediately. Away from the temptation that represented everything he could no longer have in his life.

You have to work with her.

He did, and it wasn't Chloe's fault that Anna was dead. It wasn't Chloe's fault that with one ill-timed action he'd screwed up his perfect life.

He stood facing her with his fingers clenched on his Swiss pen and tried to apologise. 'I do appreciate your work here, Chloe.'

'Thank you.'

This time her smile made her dimples and her eyes dance, and the treacherous heat flared again, filling him with longing before vanishing and leaving only bitterness. Hell, he couldn't cope with this roller-coaster ride of emotions every time he came to the ward, but he could hardly ask Administration to have her removed. A thought struck him—the perfect solution for six weeks or more.

'You did a great job with Made, so great, in fact, that I think you should sign up for the foundation's cleft palate tour that leaves next week.' He tried for what he hoped was a reassuring smile. 'Jenny Patrick's looking for people and you're a natural with kids.'

She flinched as if he'd struck her. 'I appreciate the compliment but that won't be possible.'

No. 'Why not?' He heard the bark in his voice and wished he could snatch the words back because, damn it, his fear sounded the same as anger.

She blinked at him as if she couldn't believe he'd asked her the question. 'Because…' Her cheeks flamed red and she twirled her ponytail tightly around her forefinger as if she was struggling to give a reason. 'Because it's just *not* possible.' She picked up Glenda Wharton's drug chart and slapped it against his chest. 'Please write up some milder analgesia for her and I'll take out the drain tubes now.'

Her expression—a combination of defiance and pain—

was all too familiar and it silenced him. As much as he didn't want to have to see Chloe every day, he didn't want to hurt her either. While he quickly wrote the order across the page, neither of them said another word.

He got the distinct feeling both of them were battling demons they wanted to keep secret.

CHAPTER FOUR

'HE SHOULD SLEEP all afternoon because I ran him halfway to Burleigh Heads this morning,' Chloe told Nick as she settled Chester into his basket inside a playpen.

Even though Lucy had taken the twins to visit a friend, Chloe didn't want the puppy to escape and cause her sister-in-law any more work. Being the mother of twins was enough to exhaust her, without adding anything extra. Despite today being Chloe's weekend off, the hospital had called, asking if she could come in for three hours. She was happy to work but her puppy was still too small to be on his own for more than an hour.

'You'll be fine with your uncle, won't you?' Nick fondled the pup's golden ears.

'Enjoy him, because he's as close to a nephew as you're ever going to get.'

The acrid words spewed out of her, shocking her. For years she'd kept a tight lid on her sorrow, and she wasn't sure why today it had momentarily lifted, especially with her brother. He was the *one* person who knew the details of what had happened to her all those years ago at sixteen. If it hadn't been for Nick and his quick actions, she'd be dead.

Nick's eyes, the identical colour to hers, darkened with concern. 'You okay?'

'I will be.' She forced a smile. 'I think turning thirty was harder than I thought.'

'It can be a tough birthday,' Nick said, still patting the dog.

'Oh, yeah.' It had been a tough couple of weeks in so many ways—her birthday, working with Luke Stanley and nursing the little Balinese boy. She'd even added to it by walking past the special care nursery, instead of avoiding it like she normally did. For an extra dose of agony she'd paused, gazing at the babies. Reminding herself of what she could never have.

'You know, Chester reminds me of Cerberus,' Nick said, his voice filled with surprise.

'Sorry.' Chloe bit her lip, thinking about their child-hood dog. When their strict Greek father had discovered she'd broken his draconian rules and had snuck out of the house to meet a boy, he'd punished her by having the dog put down. Her actions had cost Nick his beloved dog. 'I think that's why I chose him.'

'Don't let your mind go back to that toxic place, sis. *Baba* just wanted an excuse to get rid of the dog, and if it hadn't happened then it would have happened another time.' Nick rose to his feet and gave her a hug. 'You really are having a tough time, aren't you?'

'Just a bit.' She pulled back from her brother. 'I'd better get going. At least Luke Stanley won't be in today to upset everyone, so that's something.'

'Give the guy a break, Chloe,' Nick admonished gently.

She slung her leather backpack over her shoulder with a jerk. 'He's mostly fine with Keri and Kate and I've done my best to be understanding, but there are times when he's tough to work with.'

'There's no time limit on grief.'

'You're preaching to the converted, Nick. Say *hi* to Lucy and the twins for me.'

He grinned at the mention of his wife and children. 'Will do. And, Chloe...'

She paused at the door. 'Yes?'

'Keep looking forward. Promise?'

She nodded at their old mantra—the cluster of words that had kept them strong through difficult times. 'Will do.'

Closing the door behind her, she walked the short distance to the hospital. Accident and Emergency was seething with humanity on this fine and sunny Saturday afternoon and she signed in, introducing herself to the staff.

'There are two rugby players with concussion and head lacerations who've just arrived,' said Greg Lindall, the nurse-in-charge. 'I've called Plastics and someone will be down.'

'I'm on it.' She pushed her arms into a gown, grabbed some dressing packs and made her way to the cubicles. Two burly men, their toned and buff bodies dwarfing the hospital trolleys, sat holding icepacks to their heads.

'Hi, I'm Chloe.'

'Finn Hudson,' replied one of the men.

'Harry Jameson,' said the other.

Chloe flicked through the head-injury charts that the ambulance officers had commenced and saw their ages. 'So, guys, your chart says you've both had concussion twice before. Isn't it time to give up the game?' She flicked on her pencil torch and checked Harry's pupils.

'We're thirty-two, not dead,' he said, flinching as she inspected the nasty gash on his head.

'That may be, but serial concussions are serious. You

don't want to be forty and suffering from memory loss. What about taking up tennis?'

The guys stared at her as if she'd just suggested they take up floristry. She laughed. 'Okay, then, maybe not tennis, but there are plenty of other non-contact sports to challenge you. Cycling or kayaking. I do sea kayaking and it's fabulous.'

'If you're offering a lesson I might just consider it,' Finn said, his face breaking into a flirty grin.

She laughed, comfortable with the banter. She was used to male patients flirting with her, and she enjoyed the safety of it because it never led anywhere, which was just how she liked it.

'I'm going to stitch up the gash on your head now, Harry, but the cut close to your eye needs the expertise of the plastic-surgery registrar.'

'Yeah, like he had such a pretty boy face to begin with,' Finn teased.

'Mate, I wasn't the one spending the bucks ordering face cream online,' Harry shot back.

Chloe listened to their nonsense as she carefully shaved a small section around the head gash and cleaned it, before administering local anaesthetic to numb the area. She loved the routine of suturing—the way the curved needle brought the skin edges neatly together, the looping of the silk over the scissors and then the sharp snip to end the stitch. The skin edges joined cleanly and she was applying a dressing when Greg stuck his head through the gap in the curtains.

'Got a minute?'

'Sure.' She stripped off her gloves. 'Back in a minute, fellas.'

She followed Greg, swooshing the curtains closed behind her. 'What's up?'

Greg inclined his head towards the corridor that led to the tearoom.

Luke Stanley stood in the doorway—tall, dark and definitely handsome in his stormy, angst-ridden way.

Delicious shock waves of delight scudded through her, fast followed by dismay. Why couldn't she get a better handle on this crazy reaction to him?

He was holding a little girl whose black curly hair was identical to his own. *His daughter.* She snuggled in close to his broad chest, seeking sanctuary, and she clutched a soft toy tightly as if it would ward off the confusion of the combined sights and sounds of a busy A and E.

Luke's not rostered on.

A thousand questions bombarded her, starting with *Why is he here?* And followed by *Why on earth has he brought his daughter into a place that has the capacity to distress adults, let alone toddlers?*

The child didn't look sick, but then again Chloe's experience with children was so limited that she didn't trust her instincts at all.

Luke, his face a tight mask as usual, raised his free hand and motioned her over.

Mystified and somewhat hesitant, she made her way around the nurses' station and towards him. 'Is there a problem?'

'Yes.' Ragged exhaustion threaded through the words. 'Richard telephoned me half an hour ago. His car's broken down on the way back from Lamington National Park and the roadside service can't get him back here for at least three hours.'

Things started to make sense. 'So you're covering for him?'

He nodded slowly. 'Got it in one. He tells me there's a patient with a laceration close to an eye that needs suturing.'

Chloe glanced at the little girl, who was looking up at her from under half-lidded eyes. For Luke to suture, he was going to have to put the little girl down and someone was going to have to look after her while he did it.

Her mind leapt straight to the logical conclusion and lurched away from it so fast it almost gave her whiplash. 'I wish you'd called first because Mr Jameson's not strictly an emergency. He's on a head-injury chart for the next four hours so Richard should be back in time to suture it. You and your daughter…'

'Amber,' he said quietly.

She swallowed. 'You and Amber are free to get back to enjoying your Saturday afternoon.'

He sighed, the sound weary and resigned. 'The three hours is only a ball park estimate, and seeing as I've woken Amber from her nap to get here, it's best I stitch it now rather than risk being called back later.'

And how are you going to do that? She refused to ask the obvious question and said instead in her best professional voice, 'I'll set up a suture trolley for you.'

'Thanks, but I can manage that on my own.' He smiled—only one of a very few true smiles she'd ever seen on his face—and it raced into those amazing, clear, green eyes of his, which were now fixed firmly on her.

Its effect was like a bomb detonating inside her, but instead of releasing shrapnel and carnage it was spinning out glorious, wondrous need that liquefied everything inside her. Her knees threatened to sag and she pressed her back up against the wall, seeking support.

This couldn't be happening. One smile should *not* do this to her.

You know better than this. He's difficult, unreasonable and a basket of pain.

Her body didn't care about protecting her heart and soul—it was too busy savouring every addictive whoosh of attraction. It wanted nothing more than to slide down the wall and fall panting at his feet. Better yet, have his hands touch her, his long fingers caress the hypersensitive skin under her arm and—

She fought every sensation, struggling to pull herself together and banish the surge of mind-altering lust that had just blindsided her.

'…minding Amber for me?'

The lust vanished the moment her brain decoded his question. *No, I can't do that.* 'But…' *Think!* '…she doesn't know me, and I'm on duty and…' Her voice trailed off as the smile faded from his eyes, replaced by something so stark it actually hurt her to look at it.

His body stiffened and he looked as if he might shatter into a thousand pieces if anything brushed against him. 'I'm sorry to impose on you, Chloe. Please know that if I had any other option, I'd take it.'

The remote and prickly surgeon was firmly back in place. This time, though, she could see the bewildered man underneath the façade—the professional who knew he had a job to do vying with the father who was worried for his daughter. She recognised how much it had cost him to ask for her help.

She tried to say *no* to his request but her mouth refused to form the word. Despite the fact she'd normally wade through shark-infested waters to avoid spending time with children, it would be utterly heartless to refuse him. Instead, she found herself hauling in a fortifying breath.

'Sure,' she said. 'I can mind Amber.'

After all, how hard could it really be to mind a toddler for twenty minutes?

'I'm back,' Luke announced as he walked into the tearoom.

'Oh, good,' Chloe said with heartfelt emphasis.

He had the oddest sensation of things being totally back to front. He'd expected Amber to be the one counting down the minutes until he returned, but his daughter was quietly drawing, her head bent in concentration over a huge piece of paper. Chloe, on the other hand, was walking fast towards the door as if she couldn't get out of the room quickly enough. 'How did it go?'

'Fine.' She smiled but it didn't quite reach her eyes.

'Really? She can be pretty full on and she exhausts me. Sometimes I think a complicated piece of surgery is easier.'

A slow smile of relief crossed Chloe's face. 'Thank goodness. I thought it was just me. She was clinging onto her rabbit for dear life until I found the crayons and then she was a different child.'

He gazed at his beautiful daughter who was dealing with all sorts of experiences she wouldn't have had to had Anna still been alive. All he wanted for Amber was security, so that she'd grow up to trust and not be fearful of change, but it was a big ask, especially when he had to rely on the kindness of strangers.

Chloe Kefes is hardly a stranger.

He rubbed the back of his neck. 'In situations like this my sister would usually mind Amber but she's holidaying in central Australia. Thanks for helping me out, Chloe, I really appreciate it.'

'You're welcome.' She tilted her head quizzically, as if she was pondering something, and her ponytail swung out, the tips of her chestnut hair brushing against the soft skin of her neck. His fingers instantly itched, wanting to reach out and touch her—to dip into the hollow at her neck and then trail a path along her collarbone.

He quickly grabbed a mug off the bench, wanting to stop the feeling from going any further but at the same time not wanting her to leave. He'd been at home with Amber all day and he needed a conversation with an adult. 'Can I make you a tea or a coffee?'

She caught her bottom lip with her teeth. 'I should probably get back to work.'

He understood her prevarication. He'd hardly been easy to work with lately and he was probably the last person she wanted to chat with casually, but she'd helped him out and he wanted to make amends. Besides, sharing a coffee in the hospital tearoom with an almost-two-year-old chaperone was *the* safest place to chat with Chloe.

He rocked back on his heels. 'Greg said to tell you the rush is over for now and to take your time.' He saw her open her mouth to protest and he quickly cut her off with, 'I did the half-hour HIC check on Finn and Harry so you've got time. Besides, I know where they keep the stash of chocolate biscuits.'

'Chocolate?' Her eyes danced. 'Well, in that case, you've convinced me.'

'Biccy?' Amber looked up hopefully from her drawing.

'Yes, blossom, you can have one,' he replied, before looking back at Chloe. 'What's your drink of choice?'

She flicked out her thumb as if she was hitchhiking. 'I'll have a latte if you're able to work that machine.'

He grinned, enjoying the feeling. 'Not only can I work it, I totally dominate it. I did a barista course in Italy.'

Disbelief raced across her high cheeks. 'Seriously?'

'I'm not just a difficult plastic surgeon,' he offered by way of an apology.

'That's great to hear,' she said with a smile. 'I'm looking forward to seeing the different sides of you on the ward.'

No one had ever really taken him to task quite like this. Not his family. Not even Anna. 'Are you always this direct?'

She shrugged almost too easily, as if she was pushing something away. 'If I don't stand up for myself, no one else is going to.'

Her words dragged across his skin and something akin to sadness for her seeped in.

'Draw doggie more?' Amber held out the crayon to Chloe.

Chloe hesitated before moving slowly over to his daughter, almost as if she was forcing herself. Accepting the proffered crayon, she sat down next to Amber and quickly sketched a golden dog with big brown eyes. 'There you go, sweetie.'

'Chester.' Amber clapped.

'Chester?' Luke set down the latte with milk frothed to the perfect temperature in front of Chloe, wondering where Amber had learned the word.

'My new puppy.' Chloe sipped her coffee and her eyes drifted closed for a moment, before popping open again. 'Oh, my, you weren't just bragging, were you? You really can make coffee.'

Her astonishment made him laugh. 'There's no risk of me getting a big head around you, is there?'

'Not a chance.' She winked at him and then took another sip of her coffee, only this time her eyes stayed open. Behind the lenses of her glasses, bliss flared.

It was the bliss of the coffee but it caught him, cementing his gaze to hers and igniting the remnants of the heat he'd convinced himself he'd got under control. Heat that burst into flames of longing that licked parts of him he thought had died along with Anna. Should have died with Anna.

Every cell in his body yearned to touch her and his hand urged him to slide it over Chloe's and let his palm absorb her warmth and her energy. He imagined hearing her laugh again and just the thought streaked through him, making him feel alive—making him feel like a man again instead of a widower, a father and a responsible surgeon.

Hell, forget laughter, he wanted to kiss her—wanted to feel her body softly leaning into him and her curves melding to his. His lips would press against hers and then he'd feel hers yield so he could savour her heat, her essence and her taste. Did she taste like almonds and sunshine, like the scent of her hair? Or did she taste of the same hungry and desperate need that burned hot and vibrant inside him?

She gulped and the movement swooped down her neck and across her breasts. Breasts whose round, sweet curves defied any attempts to be rendered asexual behind her utilitarian uniform. Her body was one of curves, dips and swells, calling out to be cupped and traced and caressed by his hands, his mouth and his tongue.

His blood thundered through him—draining his brain and filling his groin, his heart pumping hard and spreading the intoxicating arousal into every cell of his body. Waking him up. Demanding he take action.

The scream of his need drowned out everything around him. Only Chloe existed, he was immune to everything else.

Chloe tried to haul air into her cramped lungs but the raging desire in Luke's eyes held her in its delicious grip. Tingling and throbbing need rushed her, sweeping through her, gaining volume, gaining intensity and control and crying out to be met. If she hadn't been sitting down her legs would have collapsed from under her as every cell gave in to the heady wonder of ecstasy.

Stop it. This is crazy.

She knew she had sexual needs but she'd learned the safe way to deal with them—on her own. Using a man to help her was so far from safe she refused to go there again. Jason had burned that lesson into her. Even with no emotional baggage, Jason, who had been reliable and easygoing, had proved to be dangerous to her heart and hazardous to her mental health. Getting involved with a rude and difficult traumatised widower with a child would be emotional suicide.

He's not always rude and difficult. You've caught glimpses of the man he was.

And, damn it, she had and that was the problem. This afternoon he'd made a real effort to be pleasant and she'd seen a different side of him. The Luke of previous weeks she could resist, but this Luke, the one who made coffee to die for, the one with the fire in his eyes that matched the burn of her body, left her wide open and without protection.

'Want to see Chester,' Amber announced loudly.

Luke's eyes widened so much that the inky black of

his pupils almost obliterated the intense green. Lust vanished instantly, jolted out by shame and parental responsibilities. He swung his gaze away abruptly and focused on his daughter.

Relief flowed through Chloe, mixed with irrational disappointment. The moment of aberration for them both was over and she should be pleased.

I am pleased, she told herself firmly. Lust didn't belong in her life and, given the horrified expression on Luke's face ten seconds ago when his daughter had broken the moment, he didn't want it either.

'Want see Clo's doggie,' Amber said, as if she sensed neither of them had heard her the first time.

'Blossom, Chloe's puppy isn't here,' Luke said faintly.

'Where doggie?'

'At her house.'

Amber stood up. 'Let's go, Daddy.'

Luke looked as if he'd been hit over the head by a shovel. 'We can't go and see the dog, Amber.'

The little girl responded to the slightly sterner tone in her father's voice like a very normal toddler. She stamped her foot. 'Want to see puppy.'

'No.' Luke moved to pick up Amber but she ducked behind Chloe.

Chloe tried not to laugh at the child's determined antics, deciding that Amber's stubborn streak matched her father's. Right now he was looking utterly bewildered, confused and a just little bit cross. She felt a modicum of responsibility.

'I'm sorry, Luke. I showed her a photo of Chester when she was upset at you leaving. I don't have much experience with children and I didn't think she'd be so set on meeting him.'

He shook his head. 'You don't need to apologise. You're the one that helped out here.'

Chloe felt Amber's warm fingers pressing on the backs of her knees and something softened inside her. 'Will she be really upset if she doesn't meet him?'

Luke sighed. 'She has to learn she can't have everything her own way.'

'Doggie, woof-woof.'

'Yes, they say woof-woof,' Luke said, holding his hand out towards Amber.

Chloe's heart turned over. This little girl had stoically coped with being minded by a stranger in a strange place. And she'd been a tense stranger at that. She'd used the picture of Chester to help herself relax with Amber as much as to try to distract and entertain the child. Now all Amber wanted was to meet the puppy that Chloe had gushed and made so much of a fuss about. It seemed only fair to offer.

Don't do this. Even her father says she can't have everything her own way.

The entreaty in the little girl's eyes and the warmth of her hands on Chloe's legs tugged hard at her protective shell.

Do the right thing.

She pressed her thumbnail against her teeth, knowing how hard doing the right thing could be. 'Luke, emergencies aside, I'm off in about two hours. I'd be happy to show the p-u-p-p-y to A-m-b-e-r then, if that helps.'

Luke heard the offer and immediately felt trapped. Showing Amber the puppy meant spending more time with Chloe, and after that moment of insane electricity that had buzzed between them across the table, he didn't trust himself. God, what the hell was happening to him?

He'd been rock-hard and lusting after a woman in front of his daughter.

A woman who wasn't Anna.

Guilt slugged him and the faint nausea that had been with him on and off for months rolled again in his gut. Amber would inevitably survive the disappointment of not seeing the puppy but did she deserve that just because he'd lost control of himself?

Yes.

No.

Maybe.

He closed his eyes against the stress-induced silver spots that danced into his vision, knowing exactly what he had to do and not wanting to do it.

CHAPTER FIVE

'CHESTER'S WORN HER OUT.' Chloe tilted her head towards Amber, who'd fallen asleep on her father's chest, her inky curls pressed flat against his polo shirt. The child looked serenely cute and adorable, which she was, and Chloe felt the familiar lump build in her throat whenever she thought about her childless life.

Don't go there.

'Really? Chester's worn her out?' Luke said, rolling his eyes before glancing over at the puppy, who was snoring gently, snuggled up on one of Amber's old baby blankets inside a broccoli box that he'd found for him.

He grinned. 'I think it may have been the other way around.'

Chloe laughed. 'Either way, they're both out for the count.'

Amber and the puppy had run non-stop for an hour and then, as the sun had started to set, both had zonked out cold, which was how she'd come to be sitting with her legs tucked up under her on Luke's couch in his cottage. She stifled a yawn and caught Luke smiling at her.

'Sun and surf are a lethal combination,' she justified as she tried not to let his smile do dangerously delicious things to her. 'All those positive ions.'

He laughed. 'More like two thirty-somethings being out of condition and run ragged by a toddler and a puppy.'

'Hey, speak for yourself.'

His jet brows rose. 'Someone's a bit defensive about turning thirty.'

She didn't know his age but she guessed he was four or five years older than her. 'Did you find it hard?'

His eyes darkened and the humour in his face faded. 'Believe me, Chloe, there are much worse things in life than turning thirty.' He rose abruptly—suddenly swaying violently.

Chloe shot to her feet and grabbed his arm to steady him and protect the sleeping child. 'Are you okay? Sit down before you drop Amber.'

He leaned against her for a moment, the weight making her stagger slightly until she widened her stance. 'Luke?'

He stared at her blankly, as if he hadn't heard her.

'Are you dizzy? Is it postural hypotension?' she asked, flipping through the most likely possibilities.

He blinked quickly, as if he was clearing his vision, and shock flared in his eyes. He straightened up fast, keeping Amber pressed close. Everything about him screamed *man protecting motherless child*.

'I'm fine,' he said briskly. 'There's wine in the fridge and some cheese and dips if you want to throw them on a plate while I settle Amber into her cot.'

She watched him walk away, surreptitiously checking his balance, but he was very steady on his feet and his gait devoid of any rolling motion. The dizziness must have been a combination of rising too fast and grief, given he'd probably been thinking about the death of his wife.

A moment before he'd stood up she'd wanted to say, *I*

*know there are worse things than turning thirty. Some of
them have happened to me too.*

Fortunately, that moment had passed and she hadn't
voiced the thoughts. Self-disclosure rarely ended well and
she had to work with Luke so, just like with her other colleagues, she planned to keep her past very much to herself.

His invitation to stay for a drink had been unexpected
and the sensible thing to do would be to make her excuses,
take Chester and drive home to her apartment. Her empty,
rented apartment.

Luke's house—it was really a tiny cottage—was nestled
in a small enclave of rainforest garden. With the beach at
its front and the lush environs of wild, green tropical plants
at its back, it seemed like a step back in time to the old
Gold Coast. The Gold Coast that had existed before the
glitz, glass and steel skyscrapers of today. Being so different and quaint, it should hum with warmth, but the walls
were bare of any artwork or decorations. Her apartment
in comparison suddenly didn't seem as quiet or as empty.

The only photo in the open-plan room was of a strik-
ingly beautiful woman with blue eyes, blonde hair and a
wide smile.

Chloe would stake her life it was a picture of Luke's
wife, Anna. She quickly looked away, feeling like an el-
ephant in comparison to the svelte and designer-dressed
woman. *Comparisons were odious*, she quickly reminded
herself, and there was no need for them anyway. Luke, with
his wedding ring welded firmly on his finger, was obviously still very much in love with his wife.

If there was one thing Chloe knew about herself, it was
that no man could love her. She had a list of examples
starting with her father and ending with Jason. However,
despite knowing all that, there was this *thing* that hov-

ered between her and Luke. She knew she shouldn't stay around and explore it, but today at work, and now over the last hour, he'd made her laugh and smile and she'd enjoyed herself.

Was it so bad to want more of the same?

She pulled open the fridge door, pleased to see a bottle of her favourite *sauvignon blanc*, but as she slid it from the shelf she couldn't see any cheeses or dips. She bent her knees, turned her head and even moved some things around with her left hand but all she could find was a container of black olives and, more surprising, a packet of potato chips.

She took them both out, found some bowls to decant them into and then poured the wine. She was just returning the bottle to the fridge when Luke appeared. She handed him a drink.

'Thanks.' He frowned at the contents of the bowls. 'Couldn't you find the cheese?'

'There isn't any. Maybe you've eaten it already?'

'No, I only bought it this morning.' He put down his glass and opened the fridge door, looked inside and then closed it, confusion clear on his face. 'I don't get it. I was in that new deli down on Palm Avenue and while Amber was busy eating all the samples I bought some Brie, some blue vein and that gorgeous crumbly stuff from Tassie. So where is it?' He sorted through a pile of green shopping bags and then rubbed his temples.

She'd noticed he did that a lot and recalled his dizzy spell. 'Do you have a headache?'

'Hmm?' He looked up distractedly. 'Sorry, what?'

'You were rubbing your temples and I wondered if you had another headache.'

'Not a headache. More like a dull throb from being too hungry.'

'Have some chips.' She passed them over with a smile. He touched one. 'Why are they cold?'

'They were in the fridge.'

This time he dropped his face into his hands before pushing his fingers through his hair with a long sigh. 'I tell you, shopping and unpacking with a toddler is obviously enough to make me lose my mind.'

He looked so weary and woebegone that she reached out and briefly touched his arm. 'Amber's like a rechargeable battery. She's either totally full on and claiming all of your attention or she's fast asleep. A bit like Chester, really.'

She laughed at the comparison despite the fact that being with the puppy was a lot more straightforward than being with Amber and much less fraught with emotions. Spending time with the child was like being on a roller-coaster. There were moments of joy and fun and troughs of abject floundering and sadness.

'Luke, I've been known to come off night duty, buy groceries and leave half of them behind in the supermarket.'

'Now you're just trying to make me feel better,' he said with a slow smile.

The addictive warmth she got every time his eyes crinkled at the edges—taking away the pervading sadness that always circled him—glowed again. 'Is it working?'

'I think it is.' He took a long sip of his wine and studied her intently. 'I'm famished. I'd offer to cook for you but that would probably be an insult to all your great help today. How do you feel about take-out Malaysian satay from Mr Megat's?'

'Don't feel you have to feed me.'

'Well, I need food and you're welcome to join me,' he

said with a shrug, before picking up his mobile phone. 'Are you in or do you have to dash home for a hot date?'

She laughed loudly at the improbability of that.

'I'm surmising from your mirth that your social life is as exciting as mine.' He texted the food order and grabbed the bowl of chips.

She glanced at the photo of Anna, trying to decode if there was anything more to this invitation than to share food. 'Do you want a social life?'

His gaze followed hers and he flinched. 'Anna filled the weekends with events, and after a busy week I wasn't always thrilled to have to go out.'

'But now life seems quiet?'

'Chillingly so.'

She thought about how her life had changed dramatically at sixteen when she'd discovered she was pregnant. How the experience and eventual fall-out had put her in a different realm of understanding from her peers. 'Have the invitations dried up?'

He stared out of the large windows towards the horizon. 'People feel uncomfortable around me.'

'And you don't make it easy for them.'

His head swung around sharply and indignation duelled with admiration on his face. 'You really don't pull any punches, do you?'

Her shoulders rose and fell. 'Am I wrong?'

'I want to say yes but I can't.'

He was standing so close to her that his heat and scent of spicy musk spun through her nostrils. His hypnotic eyes with their mix of grief and pain hooked hers and he slowly reached out his fingers, tucking some stray strands of hair behind her ear.

'What's made you so scarily perceptive, Chloe Kefes?'

His touch shot through her like an electric shock—sparking and zinging bliss into every cell. Raising her hand, she pressed her palm against his cheek, feeling the rough scrape of stubble. She wanted to extend her touch—run her fingers across his silver-streaked temples, bury them in his hair and pull his head down to hers. She wanted the burn of his lips on hers.

The haunted look deep in his eyes stopped her cold.

Her hand fell away. He didn't want her to kiss him. She stepped back, putting distance between them, and swallowed the hurt. Forcing a laugh to break the tension, she said, 'If I told you the secret of my perceptiveness, I'd have to kill you.'

Luke laughed—a real, deep, full-bellied chuckle that wrapped around her with the comforting caress of relief and the scratch of regret.

'Perceptive and dangerous,' Luke quipped as he fought his desire to kiss her. 'Remind me never to cross swords with you.' His body wanted her in his arms so desperately that his muscles ached, but his head and heart told him otherwise. He could feel Anna's gaze on him, radiating from the photo across the room. Added to that, Chloe's abrupt stepping back and her tight expression had clearly said, *Don't kiss me.*

Good. At least they were on the same page.

Neither of them wanted to act on this crazy heat that sizzled between them. Hell, neither of them wanted it to exist. Surely knowing that had to help.

You think?

He shouldn't have invited her for dinner but it had seemed such a natural progression after their pleasant afternoon together.

You like her.

Yes, he'd concede that. He'd certainly enjoyed her company and the hour on the beach with her and the puppy. Watching both of them chase Amber and being chased back had seemed blessedly normal. He didn't have many moments like that any more.

You want more of them.

He rubbed his jaw with his knuckles. 'It's been a lovely afternoon, Chloe.'

'It has.' She laughed, the tinkling, magical sound filling the room. A room that hadn't known much joy since he'd moved in.

He wanted in on the joke. 'What's so funny?'

Her hair fell forward for a moment, masking her cheeks, and then she looked up, embarrassment dancing around her dimples. 'I guess I wasn't expecting us to have a fun time. I mean, who knew, right?'

'Who knew indeed?' His laughter joined hers as he thought about their inauspicious start a few weeks ago, but today they'd got along well and he appreciated her no-nonsense honesty. Unlike so many of his friends and colleagues, she didn't tiptoe around him, wondering what to say and making him feel edgy in the process. Chloe made him laugh and he needed that. He wanted it. He wanted more afternoons like today.

The only thing he didn't want was the rush of heat that came alive between them now and then, but neither did she, so where did that leave them?

Friends.

He saw the allure of that—uncomplicated time spent together. Win-win for both of them. A declaration of friendship would also draw a line in the sand, leaving no room for ambiguity. That alone would douse the fire that burned between them and totally reset things. With friendship on the table, it would give them clear and precise instructions on how to move forward with no misunderstandings. He raised his glass. 'To friendship.'

As she rolled her shoulders back, her hair brushed her jaw, sliding across her tilted chin. Clear eyes met his and, with a faint smile playing on the bow of her top lip, she raised her glass and tapped it gently against his. 'To friendship. Pure and simple.'

Heat licked his blood.

There's nothing simple about it.

He drained his glass in one big gulp.

'And here's the miracle-worker now,' Kate said as Chloe arrived on the ward for her afternoon shift.

Chloe glanced behind her, looking around for the person they were obviously talking to, but she found no one. She immediately checked her watch. 'I'm not late, am I?'

'You're fine,' Keri said, shaking her head indulgently. 'Kate's being silly and celebrating.'

'Oh, why? What's happened?'

Kate exchanged a knowing look with Keri before saying, 'I've just done an entire ward round with Luke Stanley.'

'Poor you.' The automatic response—the one used by every nurse on the ward in relation to Luke Stanley—tripped off her tongue.

That's not strictly fair any more.

She ignored her censuring inner voice as Kate continued.

'He was polite, well mannered, and he only had *one* complaint, and that was perfectly reasonable.'

Chloe smiled. 'That *is* worth celebrating.'

Keri nodded. 'And there's more. While you've been

swanning about on your days off, we've had four...' she held up her left hand with her thumb crossing her palm '...that's *four* days of Luke being easier to work with. Even Richard's smiling again without the aid of chocolate.'

'That's great news,' Chloe said, picking up the roster and starting to assign nurses to patients.

She hadn't seen Luke since Saturday night when she'd thanked him and left his house after eating way too much of the delicious satay beef and chicken and even more of the spicy peanut sauce. Luke, who'd complained of being starving, hadn't ended up eating much at all and she'd noticed he'd taken some ginger for an upset stomach. Soon after that she'd left because he'd been looking exhausted but had been too polite to mention his weariness.

On Monday, she'd messaged him a photo of Amber with Chester on the beach. The puppy's coat had shimmered golden against Amber's inky curls, but it was the smile of delight on the little girl's face that had made Chloe's heart yearn and laugh. His reply text had thanked her for the photo and for helping him out on Saturday. At least, that was what she thought it meant because *Gear photon rhnkas agoa for saris eat* didn't make a lot of sense. It was either auto-correct gone mad or Amber had got to his phone and pressed random buttons.

Chloe was truly pleased that last Saturday seemed to have been a turning point for Luke. Perhaps admitting that he was finding it tough juggling work and home had relaxed him enough so that he wasn't being as difficult or demanding at work.

'And we owe it all to you,' said Kate.

Her head snapped up as a spark of adrenaline zipped around her, putting every part of her on alert. 'I don't understand.'

'No need to be coy with us, Chloe. We know.'

A sinking feeling weighted down her stomach. 'Know what?'

'That you spent time on the beach with your dog, Luke and his little girl.'

How was it that the Gold Coast, with its population of almost half a million, could mimic a small town?

Because you used the beach close to where many of the hospital staff live, stupid.

'I did.' Chloe concentrated on assigning the afternoon staff, matching their skills with the patients' needs and definitely not offering Keri any more information about last Saturday. She'd learned a long time ago that it was best to wait and find out what people actually knew before volunteering more.

'And...?' Keri's tone was full of interest.

'Chester was a big hit with Amber. I guess because he's close to her size,' Chloe said, as she calculated exactly how she was going to juggle things to cover the dinner break.

'I think Chloe was a big hit with Luke.' Kate nudged her gently as she prepared to do the dangerous drug handover count.

'I doubt that very much.' Chloe flinched at the inference that she and Luke were more than just friends. She hated it that she still felt sad whenever she thought about his *let's be friends* declaration because it should have thrilled her. She should have high-fived the man because wasn't she all about keeping her life simple? Not doing the relationship thing with any guy, let alone a grieving widower with a child?

'All I'm saying is that the man's been a different doctor since Monday morning.' Kate's brows rose knowingly. 'You do the maths.'

Chloe decided to play it straight because she didn't want to draw any more attention to herself. 'I just happened to be around when he needed a hand with Amber. Remember, his wife hasn't been dead all that long.'

Kate shrugged. 'It's been over a year and he won't grieve for ever.'

The memory of the baby girl who'd been ripped from her all those years ago dumped over her again. Her jaw tightened, making it hard to speak. 'There's no time limit on grief.'

'He's a man with a child, Clo,' Kate said matter-of-factly, as if her words explained everything.

Chloe frowned as a rising sense of outrage started to simmer. She didn't really understand why she was feeling like this but everything told her to keep it under control.

Her mouth didn't listen. 'Exactly what is *that* supposed to mean?'

'It means he'll eventually want a mother for his child,' Keri said, giving Chloe's shoulder a friendly squeeze. 'I'll let you in on a secret. Often the best relationships are the result of one person being in the right place at the right time.'

A flare of fury burned under her ribs and she shrugged Keri's hand away. 'What are you both saying? That I'm waiting in the wings for him to notice me? Look, I helped him out *once*. End of story. Do *not* read more into this than there is and don't go creating a future that's never going to happen.'

Her heart hammered hard against her ribs with an intensity that stunned her. She told herself to stay calm, but as her hands slapped her hips she knew calmness had fled long ago. 'Just because Luke Stanley has a Y chromosome doesn't mean he's automatically looking for a mother for his child. He's still very much in love with Anna. But all that aside—' her voice rose dangerously high '—when have I ever said I wanted to be a mother?'

Keri's eyes widened and she took a step back with her hands held high. 'Whoa, Chloe.'

She wanted to drop her head in her hands and tear at her hair but that would only make things worse. Oh, God, why had she overreacted? She never did that. She was the epitome of calmness and good cheer—a public persona she'd worked really hard at so she could avoid exposing herself in situations like this.

Shame you couldn't do it today.

She may as well have put a huge flashing sign over her head advertising the fact she was single for more reasons than just not having met the right guy. Oh, why had she even mentioned motherhood to two women who were career mothers?

'Sorry, Chloe,' Kate said, her face stricken. 'We thought you'd be fine with some teasing.'

She racked her brain for a reply—one that could give a reasonable excuse for her outburst and keep these two insightful women far, far away from the truth. Her brain bounced from option to option. The tried and true default excuse of being tired wasn't going to work this time because she'd just had four days off.

For some reason, the memory of the flare of desire in Luke's eyes last Saturday, followed by his horrified expression, rose in her mind.

To friendship. He'd retreated from desire because he still loved his wife, and there was her excuse.

She swallowed and wrung her hands. 'I'm sorry, I overreacted, it's just if you'd seen his face when he talked about Anna...' She mustered a wry smile, letting the silence work for her before saying, 'So shall we do the dangerous drug count?'

Kate and Keri nodded, allowing her deliberate change of topic to go through without hindrance. Only Chloe knew both of them too well to know that this was unlikely to be the end of it. They'd try again, but forewarned was forearmed and next time she'd be ready.

CHAPTER SIX

'CHLOE, HAVE YOU got any ibuprofen?'

Luke stood at the nurses' station, looking like death warmed up. His presence on the ward was unexpected, given he'd completed his rounds earlier with Kate. It was the first time she'd seen him since Saturday and back then he hadn't looked one hundred per cent either.

'Have you got a temperature?' Her hand automatically shot to his forehead, her palm registering the heat of his skin. It wasn't overly warm but it still made her palm tingle and she stifled the delicious shiver that threatened to shoot straight to the apex of her thighs and make her sigh.

His eyes darkened to moss green at the familiarity of her touch and waves of tension beat at her palm.

What are you doing?

She quickly jerked her arm away and embarrassment swept through her, chasing out her craving for him and leaving only excruciating awkwardness. How could she have touched him like that? Like she had the right to be in his personal space when she had no right at all, especially after his explicit statement about being friends.

Friends, Chloe. Friends. Get it right. 'I'm sorry. I shouldn't have done that, I...' The tight look on his face stole her words. *Oh, hell, shoot me now.*

He'd fixed his gaze on the wall behind her and his

lips, which had pressed into a straight line, now softened slightly. 'There's no need to be sorry. You're a nurse and it's an instinctive action.' He moved his head with a jerk, as if he was making himself look at her. 'I don't have a fever. I just have a normal headache, which isn't budging.'

She thought about his upset stomach from a few days ago. 'Headaches and nausea. Sounds like you're prodromal and fighting a virus.'

He rubbed his eyes and shook his head. 'No. It's probably just allergies. I'll swing by the pharmacy and get some nasal spray but meanwhile I'd appreciate some paracetamol or ibuprofen to nuke the headache so I can get through the outpatients' hand clinic.'

'Sounds like you've got a busy afternoon.' She passed him the analgesia and poured a glass of water from the filtered-water dispenser.

'Busy is good.' He quickly tossed back the tablets and chased them down with the chilled water.

'True.' Her eyes strayed to his Adam's apple, which rose and fell as he swallowed—a delectable bulge that delineated the strength of his neck.

Heady need returned, storming through her and making her swallow. She dropped her gaze fast, pulling her chin down and hiding behind a curtain of hair that fell forward, thankfully covering the flush she could feel burning her cheeks. Why, oh, why did he have to be such a perfect specimen of a man? It should be illegal for a man to have such thick, dark lashes—lashes that caressed his cheeks when he blinked and made her think of butterfly kisses.

He threw the disposable cup across the space towards the bin. When it fell short and landed on the floor, he looked baffled. 'Has someone moved the bin?'

She laughed at his incredulity. 'No. Accept that you missed.'

'I never miss,' he said sharply, the word slicing through the air and reviving memories of the oft-intolerant surgeon he'd been up until a few days ago. 'I've been tossing things into that bin for three years.'

Having lived with her brother for many years, she knew the oddest things upset men, and obviously this uncharacteristic lack of co-ordination was an affront to Luke's ego. 'Like I said, perhaps you're fighting a virus and it's putting you off your game. Try and get to bed early tonight.'

Oh, my God, shut up! You are not his mother.

His thunderous expression cleared as his wide and generous mouth pulled up into a grin, sending sexy creases into his jet stubble. He gave her a mock salute. 'Yes, Ms Kefes, I promise to take care of myself.'

She wanted the floor to open up and swallow her. *Friendship pure and simple,* her brain taunted her.

If every meeting was going to be like this one—lurching from lust-fuelled desire to attempting to be a dispassionate work colleague while trying to find the right level of friendship—she was probably going to have to step back completely and return to the surgeon and nurse relationship they'd had before.

Luke spun on his heel, wondering where the camaraderie he and Chloe had finally found on Saturday had gone. She seemed tense and was in full-on nurse mode, except when she'd pressed her hand against his forehead it hadn't felt like a clinical touch at all. He'd wanted to cover her hand with his own, slide it gently down his face to his lips, kiss her palm and then trace her lifeline with his tongue.

Thank God, guilt had slewed through him, whipping him hard and reminding him of *all* the reasons why he couldn't do that—the very least of them being because they were standing in a public ward in their workplace.

Anna would be here today if it wasn't for you. The least you can do is respect her memory.

I am, damn it. Chloe and I are just friends.

The thought reminded him of something and he turned back towards Chloe. 'Ah, Chloe, I've been meaning to thank you for sending me that photo of Amber on the beach. Sorry I didn't get back to you sooner.' He shrugged, aiming for added casualness to mask how very non-casual he really felt. 'You know how it is.'

Her kaleidoscope eyes, with their flecks of green and brown, dazzled him with surprise. 'You already thanked me. You sent me a text.'

He tilted his head, trying to shake free the memory, but he got nothing. The recollection of her text arriving was crystal clear and he could easily picture her name appearing on his phone. The memory gave him the same buzz he'd experienced when it had arrived four days ago. Back then he'd wanted to reply straight away but he'd looked at Anna's photo and had made himself wait.

Unlike lust-fuelled lovers, who replied instantly, desperate for the next rush of a return text, platonic friends waited. They could only be friends. He had *not* sent the text.

'I think, Chloe, I'd have remembered if I'd done that.' Sarcasm he couldn't stop oozed through the words.

Her chestnut brows drew down, setting off a tremor that rolled across her straight, slim shoulders, over and around her generous feminine curves until it reached her sensibly work-shoe-shod feet. Every single part of her screamed, *He's lost the plot.*

Her smile was muted. 'Granted, most of the text was gobbledygook and it didn't make a lot of sense.'

'Amber must have got to my phone,' he said, calling on a lie. Amber was not allowed anywhere near his phone because it was a work tool. No patient or colleague ringing with an urgent request should have to deal with a toddler.

As he heard Chloe's murmured acquiescence, his mind grappled with the continual and unnerving blankness about the text. It wasn't the first time he'd had blanks like this—the missing cheese, the chips in the fridge, his sister gently reminding him that he'd already phoned her earlier in the day to tell her he'd organised a plumber to fix their pool pump that had failed.

Plenty of single parents coped with a gruelling job and raising a child and they did it without losing their marbles. Why was he finding it so hard? Was it all down to grief?

Honestly, Luke, how do you manage complicated surgery when you can't even remember to buy milk on the way home?

Anna's voice, which had started to fade over the months, suddenly boomed loud and clear in his head. He instantly relaxed. All of his blanks were to do with home and family tasks—none of them pertained to work. Anna had run their domestic lives with precision and vigour, and he'd rarely had to do anything in that realm.

When he'd got back from France Steph had supported him but now, with her on holiday, he was doing everything, plus checking on her property and working full time. All of it was a steep learning curve. Everything would get easier—he just needed some practice.

A patient's buzzer rang, jolting him out of his thoughts. 'I'll let you get back to it.'

'Yes.' Her feet didn't move.

He got an intense feeling she wanted to say something to him but instead of opening her mouth her teeth snagged the plumpness of her bottom lip.

His heart kicked up. *Leave now.* 'Have a good afternoon.'

His words came out tighter and harsher than he'd intended and seemed to jerk her out of deep thought.

'You too. Bye.'

She walked away from him, straight towards Room Three to attend to Mr Tran, whom he'd operated on earlier in the day to release a tight hand contracture.

He hauled his gaze from the sweet swing of her hips and strode towards the elevators that would take him to Outpatients and, thankfully, to back-to-back patient appointments that would keep him completely occupied for the next three hours. His mind would be full of his patients' problems and there'd be no time or room to think about anything else.

Not Anna. Not the fact he'd missed an easy shot at the bin, and definitely not about huge, hazel eyes in a smiling, round face that had held concern for him.

Concern that scared the hell out of him.

Chloe was working yet another afternoon shift. Thursdays on Ward Six were always frantic because it was one of two elective surgery operating days. Granted, any day could be busy because emergencies happened randomly, but the pace of the ward always picked up on Wednesday afternoons, starting with the paperwork and history taking connected with admitting a new patient. Twenty-four hours later the ward was in full swing and handovers were done at the end of the bed because no one could be spared off the floor.

Chloe had always thought the most sensible staffing roster would be if Keri and Kate split up the day between them so that the unit manager and her second-in-command covered sixteen of the busiest twenty-four hours between them. But ideas and real life didn't always collide. Keri took her daughter to mini-musicians class on Thursday afternoons and Kate's boys played basketball. It appeared that neither of these events could happen on different days, which meant on most Thursdays, just as the ward reached its zenith of activity, Keri and Kate departed, leaving Chloe in charge. Today was no exception and Chloe had moved puppy school to Fridays.

When she was in charge, she arrived thirty minutes earlier than her allotted start time so she could get a handle on the ward before her staff arrived. Today she was here even earlier, but instead of taking the lift up to Ward Six, she pressed the 'LG' button and got out at the operating theatre suite. Pulling on scrubs, shoe covers and a hair cover, she made her way to the viewing area outside Theatre Three.

The small gallery was almost full of medical students and interns but she spied a seat in the far corner at the front. No one had taken it as it involved eight people standing up to allow access. She had no qualms at all making them stand up because she refused to stand on her tippy-toes at the back. She wanted a front-row seat to watch Luke performing this rather unusual operation.

The theatre was full of staff, including two operating teams along with two scout nurses. Richard, close to graduating as a plastic surgeon, was leading the team that was harvesting the toe and Luke was in charge of the attachment team, bringing tiny nerves and arteries together and repairing tendons so the toe could function as a thumb.

'Why isn't he using the big toe?' one of the medical students wondered out loud.

'Balance,' she replied, and all eyes turned to her, filled with surprise that a nurse had the answer.

They didn't know she'd spent a rapt hour yesterday listening to Luke telling her about how Ethan Popovic had lost a finger in a sheet-metal factory accident and how he was going to transplant one of his toes to his hand.

They also had no clue that she'd had the privilege of hearing him explain the specialised angiograms of the patient's left hand and right foot, which showed the blood and nerve supply to both areas. He'd pointed out how he'd mapped the transplant and he explained the need to structure the bone of the toe to fit its new function as a thumb.

Throughout the explanations he'd been the surgeon, she'd been the nurse and they'd spent a companionable time together. She'd been fascinated and enthralled, but mostly she'd been relaxed because talking about work with Luke was safe. Very safe. And she needed safe with him because anything else was murky, unclear and completely unsettling.

'The patient's only twenty-five,' she explained to the crowd, 'and he's into extreme sports. If he'd lost his big toe it would impact on his ability to return to rock climbing. This way he has a chance, but using the second toe actually makes the surgery more complicated.'

'Cool.' The student was impressed.

A screen in the room allowed for close-up views of the surgery but as this wasn't a specific teaching operation there were no microphones and the volume had been switched off. It was hard to read expressions on theatre staff as their faces were covered by masks, so Chloe used their body language to gauge the tone of the theatre and to see how everyone was faring at the five-hour mark of a possible seven-hour operation.

The scout and scrub nurses—the litmus test of tensions in the operating theatre—were doing their usual visual code and eyes were shining, which was a good sign. Richard had stepped back, his role in the surgery over, and his forehead was clear of any frown marks. Luke's shoulders were square but not overly tense, and his long, tapered fingers moved surely and easily, almost underplaying the difficulty of the delicate and minute work they were doing.

A sense of awe and wonder flowed through her at his talent. His skill was out and out amazing and a flash of something flared inside her. She realised she was proud of him. She wanted to turn around and say to those around her, *Be really impressed. You're seeing something truly special.* She smiled to herself. Maybe she was finally getting a hang of this friendship thing after all.

Luke glanced up from the surgical field for a moment, staring out towards the window, his eyes bright green behind wide, clear protective glasses. Leaving her arm close to her side, she flicked up her hand in a low wave—a private and supportive acknowledgment that she was there. There for him. As a friend.

She waited for the flash of recognition to spark in his eyes so she could imagine his endearing smile hidden behind his mask. Granted, he didn't smile a lot but when he did it lit up his face and she could glimpse the man he'd once been—happy and content.

His stare continued, only it was vacant and unresponsive. She tried not to give in to the chill of disappointment that settled like a lead brick in her belly.

He's concentrating, that's all.

She wanted to believe that but there was something about his gaze that troubled her.

He did this when you were at his house. He swayed.

Oh, God. Her breath froze in her lungs, her hands tensed in her lap and she wanted to dive through the glass that separated them and grab him.

A second later Luke blinked, his eyes frantically flicking left and right, up and down, as if he was confirming where he was and what he was doing. He gave a curt nod to the scrub nurse, who immediately wiped his brow with a gauze swab, and then his fingers started moving again, returning to making minuscule stitches.

Chloe blew out the breath she'd been holding and glanced around. No one else seemed to have noticed the moment when time had stood still. There'd been no ripple of concern from the theatre staff either—no widened eyes, no frowns, and neither of the scout nurses had moved quickly, yet she was certain she hadn't imagined that empty look, as if Luke had vanished for a moment.

You're overthinking it.

You need to talk to him.

Her watch beeped, reminding her it was time to head up to the ward. Most of her didn't want to move but she had to make sure everything was ready for when their patient arrived back from Recovery. Apologising to the others, she sidled out, her legs brushing theirs, and made her way straight up to the ward.

'How's it going down there?' Keri asked the moment she arrived.

'Good, I think. The patient's probably ninety minutes away.'

Keri nodded. 'We've delayed Mrs Luciano's pre-med.'

'Luke's doing another operation today?' Chloe couldn't

believe that he would do that on the back of such challenging surgery.

'He's got another two. They're quick and easy carpal tunnels but even so, you're going to be busy tonight.'

'Always am on Thursdays.' Chloe smiled.

'That's what I want to talk to you about. Kate's pregnant and—'

Pregnant. Chloe's blood seemed to whoosh to her feet as she tried not to let her own regrets and pain swamp her.

Keri laughed at her expression. 'I know. It's a huge surprise, especially as Phil had a vasectomy.'

Not just pregnant but unplanned too.

More than a decade may have passed since she'd been pregnant but loss and regret lingered, waiting to rush back in and remind her that she would never experience pregnancy again—planned or unplanned.

She forced the muscles of her face to pull her mouth into a smile. It was like moving concrete. 'Kate's pregnant? How great is that?'

'Well, it is now she's got her head around it,' Keri said prosaically. 'At first she was pretty cut up about it because they only wanted two and a third means a bigger car and extending the house.'

'I can see that,' Chloe said faintly, not believing her words for a moment. So many people took pregnancy for granted and it was only those who couldn't conceive who realised there was nothing ordinary or everyday about it at all.

'Anyway...' Keri got back on track '...I want you to apply to be second-in-charge when Kate's on maternity leave. You're an asset to the ward and you're doing the job a lot of the time anyway. You deserve to have the formal position, which will look good on your résumé, and I'm imagining that the extra money won't hurt either.'

'That's very true.' Chloe wanted to squeal and high-five, but she kept her excitement in check.

Keri smiled. 'It's an advertised position so you have to apply and jump through the hoops. However, I'll be giving you a glowing reference.'

'Thanks, Keri, I appreciate your faith in me.'

The unit nurse manager checked her watch. 'We'd better start handover or I'll be late for Tahlia's music.' She started walking down the corridor to the patient's room.

'Maddie phoned in sick so I've organised an agency nurse to cover her patients. Mr Morgan's IV needs resiting and as you've got the knack with his dodgy veins, we've waited for you. His dressing is now twice daily and you might need to pacify his wife because she's worried that...'

And we're on. Chloe started writing notes and strategising the shift, all other thoughts pushed firmly out of her mind.

The shift was ticking along nicely. The patients had been fed and many were being entertained by visitors, which gave the nurses a little hiatus from answering buzzers and left them free to get on with other jobs.

'Who's in charge?'

Chloe jumped as she recognised the furious strains of Luke's voice blasting into the air from further down the ward. 'Then go and find her. Please.' Luke's steely tone turned the pleasantry into a lethal weapon.

At the yell, the student nurse Chloe was supervising while she undertook Mr Morgan's dressing dropped the tweezers onto his belly, breaking the sterilization.

'Someone's not happy,' the jovial man said with typical Australian understatement.

'Apparently not.' Chloe wanted to rush out of the room and find out what on earth was going on but first she said, 'Emily, you need to de-glove, get new tweezers and glove up again. You're right to do that without me, aren't you?'

The student nodded, her eyes wide as the sound of Luke's fury slid under doors, boomed around curtains and filled every space.

'Good.' Chloe mustered her best professional voice, given the inexcusable yelling that was raging around them. 'Excuse me, Mr Morgan, I'll be back as soon as I can.'

'Take your time, love,' Mr Morgan said with a wink. 'I thought it was only the neurosurgeons who were the volatile ones.'

She hurried out into the corridor to find the agency nurse, Jean, speed-walking towards her.

'Chloe, the plastic surgery consultant wants to talk to you. I don't know what the problem is but he's seriously cross.' Jean touched her arm. 'Do you want me to come with you?'

'Thanks, but I'll be fine.'

Jean didn't look convinced. 'Are you sure?'

She nodded, despite the thread of anxiety that was building inside her. She found Luke pacing back and forth outside the nurses' station. Anger beamed off him but underneath it all she saw shadows of exhaustion. She bit her lip. She'd never seen him this wound up before. What was going on with him?

'Luke,' she said firmly, 'I believe you wish to speak to me.'

He spun around—an unrecognisable six-foot-four-inch

tower of fury—with eyes blazing and every tendon bulging. 'You bet I do. What the hell sort of a shoddy—?'

She held up her hand like a stop sign. 'Let's go into the treatment room first, shall we?' She walked towards the room, giving him no other choice than to follow.

His long, firm strides quickly overtook her smaller ones. 'Fine,' he ground out of a mouth so taut it must have hurt to speak, 'but telling you in private won't change the fact you've stuffed up royally.'

His fury buffeted her and Chloe closed the door behind them, leaning against it for a brief moment to gather her reserves. She didn't recognise this Luke and she didn't like him. 'What's upset you so much that you've broken protocol by yelling on my ward?'

His arms flew out in front of him, gesticulating widely. 'I've broken protocol? Now, that's rich.'

'The problem, Luke?' she prompted quietly, trying to direct his anger to the cause and bypass the personal attack.

'The problem is…' his voice rose in derision '…that right now I'm supposed to be operating on Mrs Lewinski, but instead of fasting I've just walked into the ward to find her scarfing chocolates.'

Chloe felt herself frown. 'Are you sure?'

His black curls bounced with resentment. 'I'm not blind, Chloe. Of course I'm sure.'

She'd inadvertently confused him. 'Sorry, I meant are you sure Mrs L. is on the list? I don't recall seeing her name.'

His shoulders squared to right angles. 'Are you calling me a liar?'

She swallowed a sigh, wondering where the reasonable man whose company she'd enjoyed so much had gone.

'No,' she said, keeping her voice steady despite her hammering heart. 'I'm dealing with facts.'

She pulled the printed theatre list out of her pocket and scanned it. 'Her name's not here.'

'Let me look at that.' He jerked the paper out of her fingers so fast that a corner ripped.

'A "*please*" would have sufficed,' she muttered, fast losing patience with his rudeness.

Luke didn't respond. He was too busy staring wild-eyed and disbelievingly at the list. 'You've obviously got the wrong version.'

Pointing to the date and time at the bottom, she said, 'This was updated at three. I've taken every phone call since then and there haven't been any calls from you or Theatre, making changes.'

She rested her hand on his arm for a moment, thinking about how he'd stared at her through the glass but hadn't actually seen her. 'You've been so preoccupied with the Popovic case, perhaps you thought you'd told us to add Mrs L. to the list but in actual fact you forgot to make the call.'

He threw her hand off his arm with a jerk. 'Don't patronise me.'

'I'm not.' Her fraying patience snapped. 'I'm trying to find a reason why you're behaving so obnoxiously. You do realise that you are?'

Stormy seas didn't come close to matching the swirl of emotions in his eyes. 'I'm *trying* to do my job.'

'This isn't the way to do it.' She met his gaze and took the hit of his wrath. 'Everyone here tells me how understanding and accommodating you were before...' *Oh, God, why did I just go there?*

His eyes narrowed to taunting slits of green. 'Go on. Say it.'

As every part of him turned rigid, she realised that if she'd thought his body had been tight with tension before, she'd been way off the mark. He was strung so taut he might shatter. Sympathy diluted her infuriation with him. 'Luke, I didn't—'

'Yes, you did.' His gaze—like the sights of a loaded gun—pinned her to the wall. 'You wanted to say, before my wife died. Or, to be more precise, before I killed her.'

'Don't be ridiculous.' Her words shot out of her mouth as every part of her rejected what he'd said. She knew innately he was wrong. Oh, so very wrong. 'You didn't kill Anna.'

He shuddered and dragged his hands through his hair, curls tangling with his fingers like tropical vines. 'Oh, yes, I did. I drove my beautiful wife, the only woman I've ever loved, into the path of an oncoming car.'

His grief and guilt hit her like a tsunami, catching her up in its massive grasp and rolling her over and over before flinging her, winded, onto the shore. She didn't think—she just moved instinctively. Her hands cupped his cheeks and she tilted his head down, angling it so he couldn't look anywhere but at her.

Luke felt the warmth of her fingers on his face and recognised the entreaty in her eyes but none of it was enough to change a damn thing. God, he'd just gone ballistic and been insufferable with Chloe, and accused everyone of doing the wrong thing when he'd been the one firmly at fault. How could he have been so adamant that he'd put Mrs Lewinski on the list when he'd never made the call?

You are seriously losing your mind.

What if you lose your cool with Amber? What if you tear into her like this?

The thought choked him and he dug his thumbs into

his temples, trying to deaden the daily throb that had become a part of him. Anna had been dead for over a year but his life was still spiralling out of control, with grief firmly in the driver's seat. Driving him. He hated it and yet no matter what he tried, he lacked power over it. Six months ago Steph had suggested he see a grief counsellor and, desperate to do something, he'd gone. Once. He'd left angry when she'd told him that time would heal. Over a year had passed and time had done squat.

'Luke.' Chloe's voice implored in the unruffled and reasonable tone he'd come to associate with her. 'Listen to me. Anna's death was an accident. A car accident.'

He shook his head but her hands held him so tightly it barely moved. 'It was an accident I caused. I drifted onto the wrong side of the road and the gendarmes said I must have fallen asleep at the wheel.'

Her hands moved to his shoulders. 'Do you think you did?'

She'd just asked the question that tormented him every single day. 'No. Yes. I don't know. I never had before.'

Intelligent eyes scanned his face. 'Were you exhausted at the time?'

He closed his eyes for a moment and when he opened them she was still waiting for his reply. 'No. That's the thing. I was working at Le Centre Léon-Bérard in Lyon, doing post-cancer reconstructive surgery. We'd been there a couple of months and I always had *mercredi*...' He corrected himself. 'Wednesday afternoons off. We used the time to visit somewhere new in the Lyon district and that day our neighbour had offered to mind Amber and insisted we dine at Le Petit Cochon. The accident happened on the way there.'

'What do you remember about it?'

He squinted, trying yet again to visualise the scene and to conjure up more information, but he saw the same image he always got. 'Anna was laughing at something I'd tried to say in mangled French. She spoke it so much better than I did.'

The dull throb behind his eyes intensified. 'The next thing I can remember is waking up to crushed metal, the scream of sirens and no clue where the hell I was.' He gripped her arms tightly as his throat threatened to close. 'I killed her, Chloe, and I can't remember a damn thing about it.'

He wanted to lean his forehead against hers, seek her comfort and warmth, but he didn't deserve any of it. He spun on his heel, moving fast, away from the touch of her hands and the sympathy in her eyes. The abrupt movement made the floor tilt and silver spots bounce in front of his eyes. Nausea clogged his throat and everything spun.

He grabbed at a metal dressing trolley, trying to steady himself, but it skated away from him. He tried again and heard the jarring clatter of metal hitting linoleum. The contents of his stomach burned his throat and then he gagged. Vomit filled his mouth and he hurled.

'Luke!'

Chloe's voice sounded shrill and faint. Darkness crept across his mind and he threw out his arms, trying to grab her. His knees jerked out from under him. Everything went black.

CHAPTER SEVEN

FOR A SPLIT second Chloe stared, horrified, as Luke writhed on the floor at her feet with his eyes rolled back, vomit and blood pouring from his mouth and his muscles jerking and spasming. He was fitting—a full-blown, tonic-clonic seizure.

Move! She slammed her palm onto the emergency buzzer located on the wall, grabbed a plastic oropharyngeal airway and fell to her knees, knowing she had to wait until the fit finished before she could slide it into his mouth. As his arms and legs flailed, she protected him from hitting any more equipment and injuring himself further.

Time slowed down to nothing, the fit seeming to go on and on for ever when in reality she knew it was less than two minutes.

Jean, the agency nurse, appeared, summoned by the emergency buzzer. 'Can I—? Oh, God.'

'Draw up diazepam, pass me that oxygen mask and then ring a code red.' Chloe tried to sound cool and controlled when every part of her screamed, *I am so scared for him.*

'I'm on it.'

Finally, Luke's jerking slowed and his pale face and blue lips started to flush pink.

'Luke.' She had no idea if he could hear her because,

although he was breathing on his own, she was certain he was unconscious. 'I'm going to roll you onto your side.'

She went through the motions of preparing him for the recovery position. Starting on his right side, she placed his right arm at right angles to his body with the palm of his hand facing up and then she put his left hand onto his chest, palm down. Lifting the knee of his top leg, she bent his leg so his knee pointed at her and then she tugged. His body moved slowly onto his side.

She heard Jean hang up the phone after calling the code red. 'Luke, I'm suctioning your mouth.' She deftly moved the sucker around his mouth, and after checking his throat was clear she finally slid the plastic airway into his mouth. 'Now I'm going to put an oxygen mask on your face, okay?'

His beautiful green eyes fluttered open for a moment, their gaze unfocused and glazed, before closing again. His inky lashes brushed his cheeks.

Chloe bit her lip and stroked his forehead. *What's going on inside that intelligent brain, Luke?*

She didn't want to think about the thousand possibilities—none of them good—so instead she fitted the green elastic of the oxygen mask over the back of his head and tried to make the mask as comfortable as possible. Jean passed her a pillow she'd grabbed off the trolley and Chloe put it under his head.

The doors to the treatment door were flung open with a thud and the emergency response team rushed in. 'What have we got?' the ICU registrar asked.

Still on the floor, Chloe turned to face them. 'Luke Stanley. Postictal.'

The shocked expletive that fell from the registrar's mouth matched the stunned expressions on the rest of the team's faces. A fitting patient was never good, but it was always worse when it was one of Gold Coast City Hospital's own.

'I've given him oxygen and I'm about to put in an IV,' Chloe said, needing to focus on the clinical stuff because her mind didn't want to go anywhere near the fear that was tearing up and down her veins. Fear for Luke. Fear for Amber. Fear for herself. 'Then I'm accompanying him to MRI.'

Not one of them disagreed.

'Chloe?' Luke asked groggily, his eyes struggling to focus.

He knew he was lying down and all he could see were fuzzy silver bars, but his nostrils detected the fresh, fruity scent that was synonymous with Chloe. He tried to raise his head but pain ricocheted through him, making him gasp.

'I'm right here, Luke.' She squeezed his hand. 'Don't try to move. Do you know where you are?'

Banks of bright white lights made his head ache and a stinging sensation burned the back of his left hand. He closed his eyes, trying to make sense of it. The last thing he remembered was being in surgery. 'I'm at work.'

'You're in the radiography department.'

He heard her matter-of-fact tone but the words sounded like jabberwocky and skated across his mind, not sticking. Nothing made sense, especially not this foggy feeling. His free hand touched his leg. *Skin.* Where the hell were his scrubs? What was going on? His fingers found the edges of a hospital gown.

What the—?

Fear ripped through him, halting all the questions with a primal need to protect his child. He struggled to sit up. 'Amber. Where's Amber?' Searing pain dropped his head back to the pillow. 'Amber. Daycare. I need to pick her up.'

'Luke, you're about to have an MRI,' Chloe said softly. 'I've spoken to the daycare centre and if I have your permission, I can collect Amber for you.'

She'll be safe with Chloe. Relief flowed around the edges of confusion about an MRI. 'You have it.'

'I just need you to say that to the director.'

She held a phone to his ear and he heard the director's voice asking him if Amber could be released to Chloe Kefes. His mouth tasted like the bottom of a birdcage and his tongue felt thick and unwieldy but he managed to say, 'Yes.' A moment later the touch of the phone left his ear.

'Luke, it's Ken Mendaz,' a gravelly voice said.

He felt a broad hand touch his ankle as he recognised and decoded the broad accent of Gold Coast City's neurosurgeon. 'Why are you in Theatre with me, Ken?'

'We're in Radiography, Luke. Remember? You're going to have an MRI.'

MRI? Did he remember? Everything seemed to jumble together into a tangled mess he couldn't unravel. God, why did his brain feel like sludge? The only clear thought he had was that Amber was with Chloe. *No, going to be with Chloe.* He didn't know why but it felt right.

Male voices he didn't recognise told him to roll over and then he felt himself being lifted and lowered onto the machine's bed. As it started to move he called out frantically, 'Chloe.'

'Yes, Luke?'

'Amber needs her bunny.'

'It's all going to be fine, Luke. It's all going to be fine.'

Why did Chloe sound like she was going to cry? It was the last clear thought he had before the blackness crept back in.

* * *

'Hey, bro', how's it going? You'll never guess—'

'I'm not Luke. I'm Chloe Kefes. Is this Stephanie Markham?'

Chloe pressed Luke's phone up against her left ear while holding Amber on her hip with her right arm. The little girl had finally fallen asleep after fretting for over an hour and sobbing, 'Daddy, Daddy, Daddy.' Chloe had wanted to sob with her.

'Yes, this is Steph.' The voice was friendly but firm. 'Why are you using Luke's phone?'

'I work with your brother and I'm afraid he's not very well.' Chloe crossed her fingers. 'Are you able to get back to the Gold Coast tonight?'

'Oh, God. What's happened?'

Chloe closed her eyes at the dread in Luke's sister's voice. There was no easy way to break this news. 'Luke's being operated on right now for a...' she grabbed a steadying breath '...brain tumour.'

A cry of despair howled down the line and then she heard a deeper male voice in the background saying, 'Honey, what's wrong?'

That was followed by a fainter, 'It's Luke.'

'Is he going to be all right?' Steph's tremulous question hung in the air.

I don't know. I wish I did. The picture of Luke on the operating table with the back of his head devoid of curls and shaved clean, with a central line in his chest and an endotracheal tube in his mouth, slugged her. The tear on her heart, which had been lengthening all evening, ripped a little bit more.

'We'll know more when he's out of the operating theatre

and after the pathology comes back,' Chloe said, trying to sound professional and together. 'I'm ringing you because you're listed as Luke's next of kin and Amber needs her family. I'm caring for her at the moment but how soon can you arrive?'

Silence vibrated up and down the line.

Slight panic skidded through her. 'Stephanie?'

'Oh, Chloe,' she wailed. 'We're stranded in Arkaroola. It's been raining here and further north for over a week. All the creeks are flooded, the roads are washed away and… ten days…' the line hissed and spat, starting to break up '…more…get out.'

Her head pounded with the enormity of Luke's sister's news and desperation made her say, 'What about a plane? A helicopter?' *Anything*.

'Sorry…ranger…police…text…reception… Amber… love.'

The line went dead.

Chloe stared at the phone. It was the twenty-first century but the tyranny of distance in the outback was still as real today as it had been a hundred years ago. Luke's sister, his only next of kin, wasn't able to get home to care for him. Luke was alone.

Amber stirred against her shoulder—a defenceless little girl already without a mother, and right now her father was fighting for his life.

She dropped her head gently onto Amber's soft curls, breathing in the sweet smell of baby soap, feeling the weight of the child in her arms and the soft thump of her heart against her chest. Chloe's heart quivered. Amber was a child full of life—not a memory of a life not lived—and she needed care and protection. *My protection*.

'Oh, sweetie, life's so not fair,' Chloe murmured into her hair, uncertain if she'd spoken the words for Amber's benefit or her own.

'Chloe. Wake up.'

She felt a hand on her shoulder and her eyes flew open to see black leather. *Where am I?*

It all came flooding back. She was curled up around Amber, both of them sleeping on a couch in the ICU staff room, tucked up under theatre towels. She sat up and immediately made sure Amber was still covered.

Sarah Watson, an ICU nurse, held out a mug of soup towards her. 'Here.'

'Thanks.' She accepted the proffered drink. 'What time is it?'

'Three.'

Three a.m. Nine hours since Luke had fitted in front of her. It seemed like a lifetime.

'Luke's awake but groggy,' Sarah said. 'I'll stay here with Amber while you go see him and then you must take her home. Both of you need a decent sleep.'

'Thanks.' Chloe stood slowly and automatically smoothed down her hair, which had fallen free of its tie hours ago. She was glad there wasn't a mirror about because she didn't even want to think what she looked like after sleeping rough in her uniform.

She made her way to the cubicle where Luke lay, his black hair the only colour about him. The machines of ICU surrounded him, somehow managing to dwarf a tall and vital man.

Pain shot through her. He looked so vulnerable.

She caught his right hand in hers and whispered, 'Luke.'

His eyes fluttered open and he smiled a goofy smile. 'Hey, babe,' he said softly. 'You came back.'

Her heart cramped and she stifled a cry. Something about his tone and expression told her unequivocally that he thought she was someone else. *He thinks you're Anna.*

A twinge twisted in her gut and she didn't know why it bothered her so much. 'I'm Chloe, Luke.'

The light from his eyes faded as his jaw jerked and then he closed his eyes. When he opened them, his focus was clear and penetrating. 'How's Amber?'

'Fast asleep. How are you doing?'

One side of his mouth twitched upwards. 'No so bad for a guy who's just had his head opened like a sardine can.'

She stroked her thumb across the back of his hand. 'You scared the hell out of us.'

He squeezed her hand. 'Sorry.'

'What do you remember?'

'Not that much. Ken told me it was a meningioma.'

She nodded. 'A benign brain tumour, thank God, but how something that causes so much havoc can be called benign is beyond me.'

'Slow growing,' he said succinctly. 'Cancer's faster.'

'So slow growing that the symptoms are insidious and only make sense in hindsight.' She took the moment to explain. 'Like chips in the fridge.'

He rubbed his jaw slowly as a light dawned in his eyes. 'And forgotten text messages.'

'Yes, and blacking out for short moments. Ken said, depending on what the tumour was pushing on at any given time, you could have had symptoms on and off for two years.' She took a leap of faith, needing to say the words and hoping he would truly hear them. 'As a friend, I have to tell you something important.'

He studied her face, his gaze holding steady. 'What's that?'

Say it. 'You didn't fall asleep at the wheel in France, Luke. It would have been a blackout. I'm sorry Anna's dead, but you don't hold any culpability. You had no control over this tumour. No one knew it was there. The car crash was truly an accident.'

She's right. Luke's sluggish mind had a moment of clarity and he closed his eyes, feeling Chloe's fingers tighten on his own. He let her genuine empathy seep into him. For months and months he'd whipped himself for falling asleep at the wheel, aghast at what he'd done and wondering how he'd allowed it to happen. The insoluble puzzle had its answer. He had his answer.

It won't bring my darling Anna back.

He knew that. But at the same time it seemed like a weight had lifted from his soul. 'I want to go home.'

Chloe's laugh held a hint of hysteria. 'Give it a week, Luke. There are things to organise, and your sister's stuck—'

'Two days.' He squeezed her hand and then, feeling the cloying pull of the drugs stealing his concentration, he let himself drift back into a peaceful sleep.

'We're home!' Chloe called out rather unnecessarily, given that Amber and Chester were already running through the house, squealing and barking and looking for Luke.

She dumped the shopping bags on the retro green Laminex table she was certain must have come with the cottage rather than Luke seeking it out at a market. Unzipping the blue cooler bag, she quickly threw all the cold things into the fridge. It was a normal domestic routine that took place in houses all around the country with men and women alike—one parent having taken the child out to give the other adult some breathing space. Only in this household nothing was normal. She wasn't the parent, Luke wasn't the partner and this wasn't even her home.

It has times when it feels like it.

Don't go there. Neither of us wants it and it's never going to happen.

'Hey.' Luke appeared in the kitchen with Amber on his shoulders and Chester bouncing next to him. Amber's hands ran back and forth over Luke's head, fascinated with the touch and feel of his now healed suture line and his hair.

Chloe still got a jolt of surprise whenever she saw his haircut—a number three he'd insisted she give him the day he'd got home from the hospital. Under the onslaught of the fast-moving clippers, his curls had fallen to the floor and she'd worried he'd regret their loss.

She'd been wrong. Instead of the short style making him look like a thug, it made his eyes a more arresting green and the rest of him leaner and more gorgeous than ever.

'Hey, yourself,' she said, her eyes taking her fill of him. *Snap out of it. Be the nurse.* 'Did you sleep?'

He smiled as he lifted a squirming Amber off his shoulders and set her down at her little blue table. 'Yes, Nurse Kefes. I'm a good patient and I've had my afternoon nap, but I didn't sleep as long. I'm taking it as a good sign that I'm improving.'

He opened a tub of playdough for Amber and set her up with a muffin set and a sausage maker, before turning back to Chloe. 'I hear the park was a big success.'

'Ducks, Daddy,' Amber said excitedly. 'Bread. Feed ducks.'

'You did, sweetie.' Chloe laughed, remembering how amazing it had been to watch the little girl go from being tentative and clinging tightly to her legs to enthusiastically flinging bread at the quacking chestnut teals. Every day she felt a tiny bit of her heart leave her, stolen by the antics of Amber, especially when the little girl wrapped her pudgy arms around her neck and snuggled in close.

'I don't think she's hungry, though, because she ate more bread than she gave to the ducks.' A flicker of inadequacy churned her stomach and she frowned. 'I must remember to always take some food with me.'

'Chloe,' Luke said with mild reproof, 'you're doing an amazing job. I've had almost two years to learn all that stuff and you've been thrown in at the deep end. We can't thank you enough.' He leaned in and casually brushed his lips ever so briefly across her cheek before quickly pulling out a kitchen chair.

'Sit, Chloe.' His tone was so matter-of-fact he could have been calling Chester to heel. 'I'll rustle up a Vegemite sandwich for Amber and a coffee for you.'

'Thanks,' she said faintly, almost falling onto the chair. A blast of conflicting emotions rocked through her, stealing the strength from her legs. Again.

The kiss—no, it hadn't been a kiss, she told herself sternly. It had been an appreciative peck, a chaste touch.

It was something she could totally imagine him giving his sister or a maiden aunt and it aptly summed up the surreal situation in which she was currently living. Every moment of every day she was straddling the line between being a caregiver and a platonic friend to a man who made her blood run hot and filled her dreams. Dreams that woke her panting, tingling and tangled up in her sheets.

All of it was utterly, mentally exhausting. All of it was dangerous to her long-fought-for safe and relationship-free life.

Two weeks had passed since Luke's surgery. His skin

staples had been removed from his scalp and the only re-
sidual effects he'd experienced from having a benign tumour cut out of his brain were weariness and some minor
co-ordination issues that were improving every day.

His moments of confusion in the first few days were
now non-existent and recently there'd been times, when
she was so tired from running around after Amber
and caring for Luke, that he'd thought faster and more
cogently than her.

'Steph called while you were out,' Luke said, over the
hissing sound of steam through milk.

Luke's sister tried to phone every day for an update because she and her family were still stuck in the outback because of impassable roads. Although Chloe was yet to meet
Steph, she'd initially spoken to her daily for the first week
and she really liked the practical, no-nonsense woman. Just
recently Luke had taken all the calls.

'How is she?' she asked, glad to have a topic of conversation that shut out the cacophony of thoughts that came
under the banner of *way too complicated*.

'Frustrated.' He set a coffee down in front of her, complete with latte art of a fern, similar to the ones growing
in the shady secret garden.

She adored spending time in Luke's garden and at some
point every day she and Amber would go there and play
with the water play set. Initially, Chloe had thought Amber
would play on her own but she didn't seem keen to do
so. After consulting some normal childhood development
books, Chloe realised her expectations were far too high.
Now she joined in playing tea parties and pouring water
through the water wheel to make the boats sail.

Very occasionally Amber would get so involved in her
play or be so engrossed with Chester that Chloe could

actually take ten minutes of uninterrupted, blissful reading time.

Luke slid into the seat across from her, his expression serious. 'We all assumed Steph would be back by now and I feel that Amber and I are imposing on you.'

'Don't be silly,' she blurted out, rushing to reassure him despite the cautious voice in her head that said, *The longer this goes on the tougher it's going to be to leave.* 'What are friends for if not to help out?'

He frowned. 'Chloe, you've taken precious annual leave to work harder than you do at the hospital. I know how much work toddlers can be.'

She did too and she'd learned fast. 'Yes, but Amber's gorgeous and a joy to mind unless she's overtired. Not unlike someone a bit bigger than her,' she teased with a wink.

'Are you referring to a grumpy plastic surgeon?' His eyes sparkled and he gave her an impish grin.

The familiar swirl of attraction that she both loved and loathed spun through her as it did every single time he smiled at her. She sobered. 'You're hardly grumpy any more. Having a tumour in your head can't have been easy.'

'So it appears.'

He got a far-away look in his eyes and she tried not to panic. He hadn't fitted since before the surgery and this look wasn't a blackout. She'd come to call it his *Anna look.* He did it occasionally when he was thinking about his wife.

He pulled back to the present. 'I feel more like myself than I have in a very long time.'

'I've noticed the difference.'

His gazed fixed on her so intently it was as if they were the only two people in the world. Her mouth dried and she wanted to dive into those pools of liquid green.

'I'm glad,' he said softly. 'I didn't like being that person.'

His words wove around her, charging the air between them and pulling them together. Her head tilted forward as if tugged by an invisible thread, and so did his. She could feel the warmth of his breath on her face, smell a hint of mint, see the flare of his nostrils and the sheen of sweat on his top lip.

Kiss him.

This time she didn't pause to argue. Instead, for the first time in two years she let her body take over. Her forehead tilted until it rested gently on his. Her eyes fluttered closed as her lips opened, ready to touch his lips.

Coolness streaked across her forehead, telling her he'd pulled back. Her eyes shot open and she saw him sitting ramrod straight in his chair with his fingers tightly interlaced and knuckles gleaming white.

'How's the coffee?' he asked, looking everywhere but at her.

Fighting the shock of disappointment that he'd moved away from her, she struggled for equilibrium. She slowly stirred her coffee, watching the beautiful fern pattern bleed away to a mess of brown and white. A mess that perfectly reflected her life.

Stupid, stupid, stupid, Chloe.

Apart from Nick, there wasn't a man out there who cared much about her and she needed to remind herself of that. Right now.

She raised her chin, determined to look at him—to act as if she hadn't almost kissed him. Somehow, against a tight throat, she managed to croak out, 'It's a bit bitter.' *Or is that just me?*

She batted the thought away. 'Is this the new blend you asked me to pick up from the deli?'

'Yes.' He flicked open a magazine until he came to a

page with a picture of a shiny machine that wouldn't look out of place in the space programme. 'I think I need a new coffee machine. What do you think of this one?'

She saw the five-digit figure and choked. 'That's six months' rent.'

Something close to guilt crossed his face. 'Talking of rent, can I pay yours while you're here? It's the least I can do with how much help you've been.'

That would be wonderful, thank you. But accepting his offer would only cause her more grief. She had to hold some part of herself back from Luke to survive. 'That's very kind of you, Luke, but it's all good. I've been taking care of myself for a very long time now and I've got it sorted.'

Deep creases furrowed his brow and he gave her a long enquiring look filled with concern.

A flutter of panic eddied in her gut that he was about to ask her why.

'Story, Daddy?' Amber appeared with her favourite book about a train and climbed up onto her father's knee.

Thank you, sweetie.

Luke pressed a kiss into Amber's hair. 'Sure thing.'

Two dark heads pored over the illustrations in the story, with Amber calling out, *'Toot-toot.'*

And Luke would reply, *'Off we go,'* in his deep, melodious voice. Both of them were so engrossed in the story it was like they were the only people in the room.

Chloe's heart lurched unexpectedly in her chest and she rose quickly, clearing the table and stowing the coffee mugs in the dishwasher. It was a timely reminder that Luke and Amber were a self-contained unit and she couldn't allow herself to think for a single moment that she belonged in that tableau.

CHAPTER EIGHT

CALLIE STARED AT the baby in front of her. He'd just been admitted and she'd finished examining him but was pulling blanks on his diagnosis. She liked to have some clues before ordering rafts of tests but today she was struggling.

'That's a really big frown for a pretty face, Dr Richards.'

A rush of heat stormed through her and she didn't need to look up to know exactly who was standing next to her. The man was sex on a stick and oozed charisma. As much as Callie had tried to tune out the hospital gossip, it was impossible because every second nurse and every third intern, irrespective of his or her gender, was trying to date the man.

Be cool, be calm, be detached, and at all costs be witty. 'Ah, the ever-charming Dr Coleman.' *That's not witty.* 'How are things?'

He smiled his easy smile—the one that lit up his face and lit up Callie. 'Things are good,' he said in his sexy American drawl. 'Better than you, I think.' He inclined his head towards the baby. 'Problems?'

'Yes.' She met his gaze and beyond the ever-present charm she detected professional concern for her little patient and a genuine interest.

Run the symptoms past him. He might be able to help. Talking to Cade about the baby would also help her in her campaign of thinking of him only in terms of a fellow doctor—her current campaign to maintain precious distance. 'Would you mind talking through his history with me, please? I'm missing something.'

'Happy to.' He tilted his head, all professional attention. 'Shoot.'

Years of well-honed skills came to the fore. 'Baby Nicols, born at term and abandoned. Mother unknown. He's been in foster-care for four weeks but is irritable and failing to gain weight.'

'Drug screen results at birth?' Cade asked, as his high forehead creased in concentration.

'Not done.'

His brown brows rose sharply and if he'd wanted to blurt out, *'That would never happen in the States,'* he managed to stifle it.

Callie couldn't get all parochial or take offence at his expression because she'd been horrified herself when she'd found out the tests hadn't been carried out. 'I know it's supposed to be standard procedure when the patient's history isn't known, but the baby was born in the outback and examined in a tiny clinic. He appeared healthy at birth and, given the lack of medical infrastructure, everything stopped at a routine exam, despite the fact that he's not the most attractive baby on the planet—'

'Oh, I don't know.' Cade smiled his hypnotic smile. 'I've seen stranger-looking kids, that's for sure. So how's he ended up here on the glittering Gold Coast?' He stroked his finger along the baby's forehead.

Callie stared at the action, trying to align the inveterate playboy with a man who was so gentle and caring with children.

'Callie?'

She quivered at the way his accent rolled over her name and was immediately horrified that her body had done that, let alone the fact she'd allowed her thoughts to be side-tracked. 'Um, the foster-mother's visiting her sister. She says today he won't feed at all and she's given him saline drops to try and clear his snuffly nose.'

Cade unlooped his stethoscope from around his neck and listened to the baby's heart rate. 'Slightly elevated, but that fits the story of baby with a cold.'

'That's what I thought but that doesn't account for the substantial weight loss. On the chart, he falls firmly into the failure-to-thrive category. His low weight gain isn't due to this cold.'

Callie reached over and undid the baby's nappy. 'This rash could be nappy rash except...' She picked up the baby's feet.

Cade blinked and moved in for a closer look. His cologne floated around Callie and she moved sideways so as not to breathe it in, knowing it would undermine her best intentions of staying detached.

He clicked on his penlight. 'I can see tiny blisters. Are they anywhere else?'

She nodded. 'Yes, on his hands and around his mouth too. With that pattern, the logical thought is *Candida* but it doesn't look anything like it.'

Cade scratched his head. 'So let's recap. Failure to thrive, irritable, the sniffles and a rash. All vague symptoms and could be due to a thousand things. Are you waiting on blood tests?'

'I was about to do them.'

He cupped the baby's cheek and using his torch examined the nose. 'Did the foster-mom say if the nasal discharge had ever been thick mucus?'

She shook her head. 'I asked and she said it was always clear. In fact, she said it was watery and constant, but it never got— Oh, my God.' A wild thought shot into her head, which she was tempted to dismiss instantly, but the shared look of comprehension in Cade's dark brown eyes confirmed exactly what she was thinking. 'Listen to his lungs again, please.'

'You bet.' Cade slowly and carefully moved his stethoscope around the baby's tiny rib cage.

It took everything Callie had not to interrupt and say, 'Can you hear any congestion?'

Finally, he pulled the earpieces out. 'We'll get an X-ray to confirm but, yeah, I think he's got some consolidation there.'

'It can't possibly be what we're thinking, right? I mean, he doesn't have a saddle nose.'

'Neonatal congenital syphilis?' Cade nodded. 'It's rare but it does exist in disadvantaged groups so I'm thinking, yes. I've never seen it but this little guy's mama probably didn't have any prenatal screening or care so it's possible.'

'I'd say definitely no prenatal care.' She wished they knew who the mother was because she needed treatment too. 'I'll order full bloods, LFTs and a lumbar puncture and get him started on IV penicillin.'

'Treating him will be the easy bit,' Cade said, with a twinkle in his eye.

'What do you mean?'

His lips curved into a delicious smile. 'If the paperwork for a notifiable disease in Australia is anything like it is back home, you'll be tied up in red tape for days.'

She laughed, understanding perfectly. 'Sad but true. Thanks for your help, Cade. I'm not sure I would have got to even considering this diagnosis without you.'

'Oh, you would have,' he said, his tone genuine and complimentary, 'but I'm happy to help.' He slid his hands into his pockets to retrieve his buzzing phone and read a text message. 'I have to go. I'll catch you around, Callie.'

'Sure.' She nodded, happy to watch him walk away knowing they'd just worked together professionally and relatively painlessly.

A new beginning.

Hopefully, yes. A new beginning without the crazy attraction that had caused her so much angst.

Callie picked up the phone and called the nurse in charge of infection control. 'Lisa, it's Callie Richards. You're never going to believe this, but we've got a baby here with congenital syphilis and...'

An hour later, with all the barrier nursing in place, Callie stripped off her gloves, having completed the last of Baby Nicols's tests—the lumbar puncture.

Scooping up all the test tubes and vials, she said to the nursing staff, 'I'll drop all these off at the lab and on my way back I'll call by the coffee cart. If you're quick, I'll take your orders and bring coffee back.'

'I can do that,' Sara Hennessey said, pulling a coffee list off the board. 'I always write one up for each shift just in case we get an offer like this.'

Callie laughed. 'That's taking organisation to a whole new level.'

'Hey,' Sara said with a steely look in her eye, 'it's coffee.'

'It's an addiction. You and Luke Stanley should form a club.'

'Oh, don't worry, we've talked about it,' Sara said, full of enthusiasm. 'As soon as he gets back, we'll be drafting members.'

'I'll think about it. Meanwhile, I'll be back in a bit.'

On her way out, Callie paused at fattening-up corner to get her fix of now-healthy babies and to remind herself of why she did her job. Then she trekked to Pathology and ran up the stairs to the coffee cart. After handing in the order for six coffees of various permutations and combinations, she used the brewing time to browse the magazines in the nearby small gift shop. As she flicked through the pages, catching up on all the celebrity news, she reassured herself that even though she knew her pre- and post-divorce life was a mess, it looked almost functional compared with what went on in Hollywood.

'Cade, hi! You got my text?'

A beguiling female voice drifted into the shop. Callie looked up, keen to see who was talking to Cade, but the tall cluster of mobile card stands occluded her view. She couldn't see Cade or the woman with the New Zealand accent but she could hear the conversation so clearly it was as if she was part of it.

'I sure did, Natalie,' Cade replied as smoothly as ever.

Natalie? The paediatric registrar—tall, willowy, blonde and gorgeous—who'd started six months ago at the hospital was a Kiwi, and Callie was certain her name was Natalie. The woman could have modelled for a European fashion house and her arrival had generated almost as much comment from the male staff as Cade's had from the females.

'So?' Natalie almost cooed, clearly flirting. 'What do you think?'

'I think you'll look stunning in black lace,' Cade said, his deep voice caressing the words like velvet.

Black lace? Callie's hand scrunched the magazine she was holding and the shop assistant shot her a killing look.

She mouthed, *'I'll buy it.'* She didn't dare speak and reveal she'd been eavesdropping. That would be far too embarrassing.

'I plan to, Cade.' Natalie's voice dropped to a sexy burr. 'That's if you like black lace. If not, I could always wear white and be the *blanc* to your *noir*. After all, there's something divine about a man in a tux.'

Callie instantly imagined Natalie's forefinger running down Cade's chest.

You don't care, okay? she told herself sternly. It was nothing to her that Natalie was inviting Cade to the Gold Coast's A-list event at the *Palace* and it was equally nothing to her that he'd accept. One thing was certain—they'd make a stunning couple and catch the eye of photographers. She could picture them splashed all over the social pages. Cade Coleman would be in his element surrounded by the rich and the beautiful.

'It was really kind of you to think of me,' Cade said, 'but A-list events aren't really my scene.'

What? Callie wanted to knock herself on the side of the head to adjust her hearing. Was it possible that Cade was turning down both Natalie and *the* social event of the year?

'You told me you loved car racing.' Natalie's cooing voice developed an edge. 'Do you have any idea the favours I had to give out to get these tickets?'

'I'm sorry, Natalie,' Cade said gently, 'but I never asked you to get the tickets. I'm sure your efforts haven't been completely wasted. No doubt there's a long line of guys who'd be more than happy to accompany you.'

'Oh, there is,' Natalie ground out, 'but remember it's your loss.'

Incredulity poured through Callie. The fact that Cade Coleman was turning down a beautiful woman was far more significant than when he'd rejected her slightly drunken invitation at the wedding all those weeks ago.

'Okay,' Cade said. 'It's been good to see you, Natalie. I'll catch you around.'

I'll catch you around. He'd used the exact expression he'd used with her when he'd left the ward. It was his default farewell—friendly yet casually detached.

Detached.

The word slammed into her, illuminating so many things that had confused her about this charming and supposed playboy. Back in the day, his brother, Alex, had told her *he had a problem with women.* She'd taken that to mean he was a player but weeks had gone by since he'd arrived in Australia and, despite all the rumours of women throwing themselves at him, there wasn't one report that he'd actually gone on a date with anyone.

You flirted.

Sure, they had, *once*, but they hadn't dated. She'd run fast from the idea and he'd never offered. Perhaps he was running from the idea too. For the first time since she'd met him, she realised that Cade Coleman's carefree charm was a ruse. A ruse that kept people at arm's length.

It immediately begged the question, *Why?*

Luke came back inside from having put the wheelie bins out on the kerb. It was crazy how something so prosaic and mundane could be so enjoyable. For the first time in months he felt almost normal—not that he'd felt abnormal before but he'd definitely felt not quite right. During his convalescence he'd realised that for well over a year he'd assigned many of the signs of the tumour to his grief for Anna, which had effectively masked the nebulous symptoms.

Now that the bastard clump of cells was no longer in his head, he felt totally different. God, he still missed Anna, he always would, but it was more of a contained sadness than fury at himself and the world. He hadn't realised how exhausting and draining those emotions had been and he was immensely glad they were gone. He gave thanks every day that he'd been diagnosed before he'd inadvertently done any harm to his beloved daughter.

He was desperate to get back to work as soon as possible and make amends to his staff. He was determined to be the most amenable plastic surgeon ever, as well as taking them out for a meal. Nothing said *sorry and thank you* like good food and wine. He just had to clear a few hurdles first.

The fact he hadn't experienced a seizure since the one that had led to the diagnosis of the tumour was an enormous relief and with each passing day he saw the worry lines on the bridge of Chloe's nose fading. Ongoing seizures would have meant a career change, and although his good friend Tom Jordan, the neurosurgeon from Sydney Harbour Hospital, had carved out a new and successful career post-trauma, Luke was thankful he wouldn't have to do the same. He knew how tough it had been on Tom.

Luke's current hope was that at his next doctor's visit Ken Mendaz would give the *all-clear* for him to live alone again. Not that he didn't enjoy Chloe's company and presence in the cottage, he did. In three short weeks she'd managed to give his cottage a totally different feel.

The fragrant, fruity zing of her pomegranate and mango soap lingered in the bathroom, her glasses often rested on the coffee table, precariously balanced over the spine of whichever book she was reading at the time, and he didn't even want to think about the watermelon-pink lace bra and panties he'd seen fluttering on the clothesline.

To cope with his seesawing feelings about Chloe—feelings that confused the hell out of him—he tried to think of her in terms of his nurse and Amber's caregiver. When Chloe was the brisk, caring, no-nonsense woman who, like his sister Steph, verged on being bossy, he could relax. The problems started when Chloe laughed. Smiles immediately followed, wreathing her face, and then her dimples danced and her eyes sparkled with so much energy and life that he wanted to be part of it. He wanted to hold her close and inhale her joy.

Only that would dishonour Anna and complicate his friendship with Chloe, so the sooner she and her damn cute puppy moved back to her apartment, the sooner his life could return to normal.

What's normal? There's been no normal since Anna died. Chloe's real and she's here.

La, la, la, not listening. There's only ever been Anna and I still love her.

He ran his hand over his head but there was no joy to be found tugging at his hair—just the prickly feel of stubble against his palm. He spun his wedding ring on his finger. The gold band had been in position for a decade and was as much a part of him as the silver streaks in his hair. Streaks that had moved into place after Anna had died. The colour had vanished from his hair just like the colour had vanished from his life.

At least today he'd clawed back some normalcy. He'd driven his car for the first time since his surgery and his reflexes and reactions had been perfect. Chloe had suggested they take Amber to SeaWorld to celebrate this milestone and he'd agreed. They'd laughed at the antics of the seals, been awed by the sleek athleticism of the dolphins, eaten ice creams and generally enjoyed the day. It had been fun and easy, which typified most of his experiences with Chloe.

Thankfully, there'd only been one of those unexpected moments when he'd had the overwhelming urge to wrap his arms around her, haul her close and kiss her senseless.

Fortunately, for most of the time Amber, with her boundless energy, was as good an antidote to unwanted lust as cold showers. Still, Chloe moving out of the cottage would remove all temptation. He didn't want to be tempted. Hell, last week he'd almost kissed her and that would have been a disaster.

All he wanted was to live his life in a way that honoured Anna and Amber.

He latched the gate and slipped quietly back into the kitchen. As he eased the screen door closed, he heard voices drifting down the corridor. The old hall boards creaked under his feet as he walked the short distance and paused just outside the open door of his daughter's room.

'Bunny's here, Teddy's here, Clowny's here,' Chloe said.

'Amber's here.' Amber giggled at her own joke.

'She is and now it's nigh'-nigh' time,' Chloe replied with a smile in her voice as she pulled up the quilt.

''Nother story?' Amber asked hopefully.

'Your daddy read you three. Snuggle down.'

Luke grinned. Chloe did bad cop so much better than he did. Despite her protestations that she didn't know much about kids, she had the knack of settling Amber down pat. A week after his surgery they'd fallen into a routine where he bathed Amber, read her stories and kissed her goodnight.

Chloe would then put her to bed and, miracle of miracles, Amber usually settled without fuss—something she'd rarely done for him since Anna's death. Tonight was the first time he'd ever watched Chloe put Amber to bed.

His daughter obeyed Chloe's no-nonsense instructions and did indeed wriggle down until the quilt rested under her chin.

Amber peeked up at Chloe. 'Clo tell story.'

Chloe's sigh held traces of humour, as if she'd anticipated this request and she rested her elbows on the top of the cot. 'Once upon a time there was a little girl called...'

'Amber.'

'Yes...' She laughed. 'A little girl called Amber who has a daddy who loves her very, very much.'

'Daddy hurted head.'

'He did, sweetie, but he's all better now.'

Luke listened to Amber's contributions and his breath caught in his chest at the realisation that this story was a nightly routine. Chloe must have instigated it to reassure Amber during the fraught few days he'd been in hospital.

A rush of thankfulness filled him. Chloe was utterly amazing and he owed her so much. With Steph only just leaving Arkaroola now, he didn't know how he would have managed these last three weeks without her. What did you buy someone who'd stepped into the breach without thought for herself? Neither flowers, chocolates, good wine or even a spa voucher seemed to be anywhere near enough to express his gratitude.

'Clo and Chester here,' his daughter said, clapping her little hands.

'Just for a little while.' Chloe reached out, brushing Amber's curls off her forehead before tucking bunny in close.

'Love Chester.' Amber yawned.

'Me too.'

'Love Clo.'

'Ohh.' The word came out strangled and filled with something akin to pain.

Luke shuddered and every nerve ending went on alert. Without knowing why, he strode into the room with a driving need to protect Chloe. He leaned over the cot and smiled at Amber. 'Has my girl got an extra kiss for her daddy?'

Chloe quickly stepped back and as Amber's pudgy arms wrapped themselves around his neck, he heard Chloe's footsteps leaving the room.

CHAPTER NINE

A COUPLE OF minutes later, after Luke had settled Amber, he found Chloe nestled in the corner of the couch with her feet tucked up under her—sitting the way she always did.

She looked up guiltily, her glasses flashing in the light and a glass of wine in her hand. 'Sorry.'

It was the first time he'd seen her drink any alcohol since she'd moved in. 'Don't apologise. Just because Ken's put me on the wagon for medical reasons it doesn't mean that you have to be teetotal.'

'Good.' She took close to a gulp.

He sat down next to her, worried about her reaction to Amber's childish declaration. Amber cheerfully told everyone she loved him or her, from the childcare workers to Chester. 'Everything okay? Amber not stressing you out?'

'Everything's fine,' she said over-brightly. 'Wasn't today a fabulous day? Amber's expression when the seal balanced the ball on his nose was priceless.'

He recalled that moment vividly. Their eyes had met over the top of his daughter's curly head, sharing her delight, and he'd had to stop himself from kissing Chloe. A week ago he'd brushed her cheek with his lips in an attempt at a friendly, platonic kiss—the type shared by good friends. Lust had detonated deep inside him, releasing a visceral craving for her that was so strong it had terrified him. He'd avoided touching her ever since.

He was sticking to friendship. 'Thanks for making today happen, Chloe. The picnic was delicious and you thought of everything. I think you probably had a kitchen sink in that backpack of yours.'

'I doubt that. Still, Amber's taught me that when Nick and Lucy's twins are a bit older, at least I'll be able to do the auntie thing and take them to the park and survive.'

'Hey, you remembered the nappies and the wipes and in my book that's everything.' He smiled at her, wanting to banish her brittle aura and lighten her unusually blue mood. 'One day you'll make a great mother.'

'Never going to happen.' She drained her glass and quickly refilled it, the action defiant and filled with agony.

He felt himself frown, trying to make sense of her statement. She was wonderful with Amber and she'd been equally good with the little Balinese boy, Made, all those weeks ago when he'd first met her. 'Don't you want children?'

Her top teeth pulled at her bottom lip, worrying it, and then she sighed. 'It isn't just a matter of want.'

He leaned back in the couch, understanding the modern woman's dilemma. 'You're only just thirty, Chloe. There's plenty of time for you to meet the right guy, settle down and have babies.'

A short, sharp pain jabbed him near his solar plexus and he found himself rubbing the spot, wondering what it could be.

'Meeting someone isn't the problem, Luke,' she said sharply, before standing up. 'Anyway, enough of all that. It's been a big day, I'm tired so I'll say goodnight.'

The regret on her face made him sit forward and catch

her hand in his. 'You can't just say something like that and then walk away.'

'I can.' She blinked rapidly as if she was holding back tears.

'I don't want you to.' He continued holding her hand, feeling her pain hurtling into him like storm waves pounding against the uprights of a pier. 'We're friends, Chloe, and you've helped me so much. Let me help you.'

'There's nothing you can do.'

'Try me.'

She stared at him, her eyes luminous and hurting, and then she dropped her gaze to his fingers interlaced with hers. She sat down very slowly as if she really wanted to fight it and then a long silence played out.

He let her take her time.

She finally raised her head and looked at him. 'You know how nothing can ever bring Anna back to you? Not even a miracle?'

Hell, yeah. He nodded, wondering where she was going with this. 'Sure.'

'Well, same.' She was sitting so close to him that her leg lined his and her hipbone brushed his and her heat and distress flowed into him. 'No medical miracle can make me pregnant.'

He thought about her brother, Nick, who had a specialist patient list of infertile couples. Surely she knew that he had successes against all the odds and delivered babies born of women who'd experienced years of infertility. There was always hope.

He wanted to throw her a bone to lessen her pain. Squeezing her hand, he said, 'Don't rule anything out, Chloe. The human body is amazingly resilient.'

She closed her eyes and sagged against him for the

briefest moment before sitting up straight again. 'Resilience won't help a damn, Luke. I had a hysterectomy at sixteen.'

His jaw dropped. Of all the things he'd anticipated she might say, this wasn't one of them.

Chloe registered the flash of shock in Luke's eyes and followed its trajectory across his high cheeks before it buried itself in his dark stubble. Why had she blurted out her secret? Why had she told him? She didn't tell *anyone* and Luke certainly didn't need to know. It wasn't like they had a future together—take one infertile woman and one grieving widow and mix… Nope, not a good combination, no matter which way you looked at it.

But you've told him. It's out there, so deal with it.

She steeled herself for the anticipated questions, for the probable censure and disapproval, and the change in his behaviour towards her. She knew the drill. She'd been there, done that and got the T-shirt. First with her father and more recently with Jason. His horrified expression combined with the way he'd stepped back from her so fast—as if she had leprosy—was burned on her soul.

Luke's eyes darkened to mossy green and then he silently wrapped his arms around her, pulling her in close.

She gave in to the unexpected hug and buried her face in his shoulder, absorbing his empathy and appreciating that he wasn't offering her any platitudes. He probably knew how worthless they really were, having heard them all when his wife had died. The slow, strong, rhythmic beat of his heart thudded against her chest and she wanted to stay there, snuggled into him, for ever. Safe, warm and not judged.

You need to move.

The elapsed time had now passed *normal support* and was fast moving into the *getting-awkward* stage.

She raised her head and noticed the big, damp spot on his shoulder. 'I've made your shirt all wet. Sorry.'

'No problem. Amber's done a lot worse.' He smiled and reached for her wine, passing it to her with his left hand and leaving his right arm loosely slung around her shoulders. The light played off his wedding ring.

He still hadn't asked her why such a tragedy had befallen her and that unnerved her. The unasked question was like the click of a landmine—it was going to go off, but exactly when she had no clue.

Sipping the *sauvignon blanc*, she vacillated on what to do or say next but the weight and wonderful warmth of his arm around her was draining her brain. Staring straight ahead, she decided to explode the landmine herself. 'On the few occasions I've told people, they usually have questions.'

His fingers played with her hair. 'Of course I want to know why you needed such catastrophic surgery at such a young age but I also get it if you don't want to tell me.'

He understands.

Relief flowed into her. He'd met grief head-on, just like she had. He knew the massive chasms that could suck you down, trapping you in darkness whenever you dared revisit places that haunted you.

Maybe it was that understanding, maybe it was the caring warmth of his arm against her or even the relaxing effects of the wine—did it matter? No, but for some inexplicable reason she wanted to tell him.

She moistened her lips. 'It's not a quick story.'

He gently squeezed the top of her arm and his insightful gaze rested on her. 'I've got all the time in the world.'

She took in a deep breath and started. 'My parents are Greek, traditionalists and strict. My mother is scared of my father and my father rules the family with a will of iron…'

Luke kept his arm around Chloe, hearing her soft voice, listening to her story and wishing desperately that she didn't have a story to tell because he knew it was going to be hellishly bad. No gynaecologist would remove a sixteen-year-old's uterus unless he had no other choice. Unless it was to prevent her death.

'Nick, as the first born,' Chloe continued, 'was the golden boy who could do no wrong—and, unlike me, he never did. I love him dearly and sadly my actions cost him a lot. Unlike me, he toed the family line, obeying my father, working hard at school and generally doing what was asked of him.'

He stroked her ear. 'It's my understanding that in Greek families it's often a lot easier to be male.'

The flecks of brown in her eyes shone starkly against the khaki green and she gave a small nod of agreement. 'My father has certain beliefs about how women should be raised and educated. At the end of year ten he refused to re-enrol me at school. I was bereft. I tried pleading, crying, throwing things. You name it, I did it, but it was useless. Nothing Nick, my mother, the principal or I could say or do would change his mind. Legally, I could leave school.'

His utter shock at a child having her education stolen from her must have shone on his face because she gave him a wan smile.

'It's archaic, I know. My father had my life planned out according to what he considered was best for me. As well as helping *Mama* at home, he ordered me to work in my uncle's fish and chip shop. I hated that job almost as much as I hated my father, but there was one positive…'

She shrugged. 'Well, at least, at barely sixteen I thought it was a positive.'

'What was that?'

'I got to walk to and from the shop each day, which gave me fifteen minutes of blessed freedom there and back. My Anglo friends fell into two camps. Those who thought I was incredibly lucky to be out of school and those who couldn't understand. Rick, a good mate, fell into the "*couldn't understand*" camp and he'd meet me in the park to give me books and homework pages so I could try and keep up. Nick helped too.'

He'd always liked Nick Kefes. 'He's a good man, your brother.'

'Beyond good.' She blew her nose and blinked rapidly. 'I got away with doing schoolwork at home for six months until my father found my stash of books and went ballistic, including scaring Rick so much that he was too petrified to help me again. From then on I was escorted to and from the shop but my father couldn't control the people I met while I was working and I met Darren, an apprentice carpenter. I started sneaking out at night to meet him.'

She gave a short, tight laugh. 'He was my knight in shining armour, promising me that he'd save me from my life and we'd move in together. We were just kids but I was so desperate to get away from home I believed him. To cut a long story short, we had sex and I got pregnant.'

Her tone reminded him of when he told people about the car accident. *Anna died.* Emotionless, detached, pragmatic. It was the only way to tell the story without breaking down.

He wanted her to know he understood. 'That must have been terrifying for you.'

'At first it wasn't because I truly believed that Darren would take care of me. It took me a couple of months to even realise I was pregnant so I was twelve weeks before I told him. He promised me everything would be fine and then he disappeared and never contacted me again. I didn't believe that he was gone for good so I waited a few weeks and then panic set in.

'I was seventeen weeks pregnant, I had no money, no friends, and my mother and brother had limited resources to help me. And I knew my father would throw me out of the house if he ever found out. It was the first time in my life I realised I was utterly alone. I visited a clinic and had a late-term abortion.'

She shuddered against him and he immediately pulled her back in close against his shoulder and pressed a kiss into her hair. 'It sounds like you didn't have a choice.'

She sucked in her lips, her jaw tight as if she was readying to get the next bit of the story over and done with as fast as possible. 'I went home after the termination, told my mother I had a heavy period and went to bed. The pain was excruciating and I truly thought I was dying. I didn't realise that I was. When Nick came home from doing my shift at the shop, I was almost unconscious and half my circulating blood volume was in the bed. He called an ambulance and I arrested on the way in.'

Her voice became the one she used at work—brisk, factual and professional. 'For most people a termination of pregnancy is very safe but I was unlucky. My uterine wall was very thin and the procedure perforated it. To save me, they had to sacrifice—'

'Your uterus,' Luke interrupted, wanting to save her from having to say it.

She nodded. 'And things went to hell after that. My father, having had the doctor at the hospital explain to him the reason why his daughter had almost died, kicked me out of the house the day I was discharged home. He met me at the front door with my bag packed. I'd shamed the family.'

Luke thought of Amber and his heart cramped in his chest. How could any father do that to their child? 'Surely Nick helped you?'

Her eyes swam with tears. 'Nick saved me. When our father refused to have me home, Nick left too. We spent a few weeks in emergency housing and then, with both of us working in menial jobs, we managed to get a flat. The fact Nick passed his year twelve that year is testament to his brilliance.

'I was barely functioning on any level, but I feared being homeless more than anything so I kept working. I cleaned houses, I waited on tables and did pretty much anything I could to earn money. I owed Nick so much and I happily worked two jobs to help him get through six years of medical school. Three years after that, when he started his obstetrics specialisation, I enrolled at university and started nursing.

'It was the best thing I ever did and in the last couple of years I've really found my feet.' She shot him a look that said, *Don't disagree with me.* 'I'm happy and content.'

He wasn't convinced. 'You're a great nurse and I'm glad for you that you love your job. But you do know that there's more than one way to have a child. Plenty of couples adopt.'

She stiffened as if he'd hit her. 'I used to think that way too,' she said tartly, 'right up until two years ago when my then fiancé broke off our engagement because I was incapable of giving him his *own* child.'

Luke wanted to hit the unnamed bastard. 'You deserve so much better than that, Chloe.'

She shrugged. 'Yes, well, it's a moot point really, so it doesn't matter.'

'Don't say that.' His words rushed out, hating it that she sounded so resigned. 'You're beautiful, bright and vivacious. Any decent guy would be lucky to have you.'

She turned and lifted her gaze to his, doubt shimmering in her eyes. 'What planet do you live on, Luke? I'm damaged goods.'

He wanted to blast out her doubt and her cynicism, make her realise how truly beautiful and amazing she was and how much she deserved to be loved. Only he knew how inadequate words could be. How little they did to help when life threw up moments of immeasurable cruelty, and how easy it was to dismiss and discard them. No, words were useless here. This needed action.

Without pausing to think, he lowered his head and kissed her.

Luke's lips touched Chloe's so very lightly that for a fleeting moment she thought she must be imagining the connection. Her mind had to be creating the idea of him kissing her and fulfilling a long-held dream, because there was no way it could possibly be real.

Her tongue traced the edges of her bottom lip and she tasted a hint of mint and a *soupçon* of musk—the flavours of Luke. Then the tip of her tongue registered a different feel—his lips. Flavours met fire, her entire body lit up with blinding need and she opened her mouth and took him as hers.

She heard a guttural moan in the back of his throat, and in it she recognised longing, wanting and lust that perfectly matched her own. Her hands reached out, pressing against him, feeling the strong musculature of his chest underneath the soft cotton of his shirt. She spread her fingers, needing the touch to believe this was really happening.

His hands cupped her cheeks, tilting her head, angling her mouth to his, and then he deepened the kiss. His tongue caressed her mouth so gently and so reverently that one tiny part of her wanted to cry. The rest of her was too busy riding the waves of wonder, joy and rising desire to think at all.

His lips and tongue roved over her mouth, finding the special places that directed the spinning rafts of tingles zipping in her veins straight to her core. He captured her moans of sheer delight with his mouth and returned them to her more potent than before. She needed to feel him, all of him, and she wrapped her arms around his neck and in the process knocked her glasses against his head.

'Ouch.' He laughed, rubbing his temple where her frames had dug into him.

'Sorry.' She put her fingers over his.

He stared at her through glazed eyes.

She held her breath, cursing her glasses for breaking the moment and waiting for him to realise they'd been kissing each other like a couple who'd been given two minutes to live. Waiting for sanity to move into his out-of-focus gaze and pull him away from her completely. The way it had every other time they'd shared a sexually charged moment.

You can be the one to stop this right now.

I don't want to.

And she didn't. It had been so long since she'd been made to feel like a desirable woman that she didn't want to let the feelings go. She was no fool. She certainly didn't have stars in her eyes that this meant anything more than the two of them giving in to the lust that had shimmered and spun between them for weeks. It wasn't a future—it was just *now*.

He smiled at her. Her heart sang and then everything went into slow motion. He reached out his hands and slid her glasses off her face, discarding them on the coffee table. Then he gently dragged the hair-tie from her pony-tail and ran his hands through her hair, smoothing it down before carefully bringing it over her shoulders. 'That's better. Now I can see your beautiful eyes.'

Bringing his head down close, he kissed her eyelids with such delicacy that as her head fell back she cried out from the sheer joy of it. As he lowered her on the couch, she slid her hand between the placket of his shirt, the backs of her fingers brushing his skin. Shocks of wonder rocked her and she pulled him down with her.

He trailed kisses from her jaw to her hairline, before burying his face in her hair. 'You smell like a tropical fruit basket.'

She laughed. 'Is that a good thing?'

He rose up on his arms and stared down at her, desire hot and glittering in his eyes. 'Absolutely.'

'You smell like salt and sunshine,' she said, unbuttoning his shirt.

'Is that a bad thing?'

She pushed his shirt off his shoulders and marvelled at the view. 'I'm not complaining.' Rising up, she pressed kisses to his sternum, tracing her tongue along his skin—sucking, licking and tasting—the heady combination making the muscles between her legs twitch. She was desperate to feel him inside her.

He shuddered at the touch of her mouth and she wanted to high-five someone. Anyone. She wanted to call out to the world that she'd made that happen. Luke Stanley wanted her. *Her.*

The muscles on his arms bulged as he pushed up from her and shucked his shirt. Then he leaned back on his haunches and grinned, his face alight with desire and devoid of all the strain and pain she always associated with him. 'Someone's overdressed.'

His long and dextrous fingers whipped her T-shirt over her head and then his gaze shot straight to her aqua and black lace bra. He groaned. 'Do you have any idea how tough it's been, seeing your underwear on my clothesline and imagining what it looks like on you?'

Her nipples puckered in delight that he'd been working as hard as she had to fight the attraction between them, but a niggle of worry made her say, 'Sometimes reality doesn't live up to expectation.'

His fingers traced the black lace that decorated the edge of the bra and brushed the swell of her breast. 'The reality's more than fine, Chloe.' He lowered his mouth and suckled her through the lace.

White light streaked through her and she bucked against him, feeling his erection through his jeans.

'If you like that, then you might like this.' He focused his attention on her other breast until she was writhing under him and desperate to get rid of the bra so she could fully enjoy the hot and wet ministrations of his mouth against her tight and begging skin.

She pushed at his chest. 'Take it off. Now. Please.'

'Anything you say.' He reached one hand around and fumbled with the clasps.

The bra didn't move and the thought that he was out of practice flitted across her mind. She batted it away—fast—not wanting to think about the reason why he was out of practice. Real life didn't belong here. This was just a moment in time between two people who needed to lose themselves in each other.

The bra finally fell away. She dropped it on the floor next to his shirt and immediately wrapped her fingers around his belt. 'Let's get rid of everything, then, shall we?'

'I like the way you think.'

He kissed her hot, hard and fast as she pushed his pants off his hips and down his legs so he could kick them off.

Neither of them had factored in shoes and one moment he was kissing her and the next he was on the floor. Half laughing and half concerned, she managed to splutter out, 'Are you okay?'

He rubbed his hip and gave a wry smile. Grabbing her hand, he said, 'I'm too old for couch sex and you deserve better. Come on.'

'Just a sec.' She reached for her shirt, suddenly embarrassed she had to run to his bedroom half-naked.

'Oh, no,' he said, his fingers flicking the shirt out of her grasp. 'No one is getting dressed.' The next moment she found herself hefted over his shoulder, held in place by one of his hands deliciously splayed over her bikini-clad bottom. Lucky for her, the thin silk did nothing to shield her from the heat of his palm and the gentle and delicious kneading of his fingers.

As he strode down the hall and entered his bedroom, she trailed her hands down his naked back until she slid them underneath the elastic of his boxer shorts, cupping his buttocks.

He stopped with a jerk. 'Do you want me to drop you?' he asked, his voice gravelly with desire.

'Only if you fall with me.'

He lowered her carefully and then, like a jet-black panther, he crawled slowly up the bed, his moss-green eyes fixed on her face. As he moved, he trailed the forefinger of his right hand up the arch of her foot, along her shin, across her inner thigh. Just as he got close to the apex of her thighs and she was breathing out, *'Oh, yes, please,'* he skirted the sensitive area and traced his finger around her hip. From there he skated it across her belly until it came to rest between her breasts. Her skin burned for more of the addictive and erotic touch.

Now he was straddling her, his lean body all corded muscle, taut tendons and thick, blue veins. Powerful and strong, he hovered over her, trembling with leashed tension ready to be cut loose on her, but she had no fear. He was beautiful. She wanted him so much but well-honed survival skills kicked in despite the risk that it would bring his past flooding back and ruin everything.

She raised her hand and cupped his cheek. 'Condoms?'

A muscle tensed in his jaw. 'I don't have any.'

She held his gaze. 'It's not a problem unless you have something.'

'I'm fine,' he said abruptly.

The next moment his lips pressed hard against hers and she lost her breath to him, as if he needed it more than she did. His tongue lashed her mouth—taking and giving, searching and finding. His desperate need for her overpowered everything, as hers did for him.

Her body sought his, pressing against him, feeling his length mould to hers and yet wanting to be even closer. Her hands roved all over his back, caressing, exploring, finding the dips and the crevices and committing them to memory. Wanting this to last for ever but knowing it was just one moment in time.

His mouth dropped down her belly, his tongue swirling around her belly button stud as his fingers found her aching, throbbing clitoris. She gasped, thrashing underneath him.

'Am I hurting you?' Concern stopped his fingers.

'God, no, it's amazing.' She moistened her lips at the touch she'd never known from a man before, and was amazed at how much her body begged for it. 'Keep going.'

His deep and melodic laugh rained over her as his fingers worked their magic. Whirls of sensation built on each other, each strand intensifying the delight until she lost touch with the sights and sounds of the room and with the feel of the mattress against her back. The only thing that existed were his fingers on her and the agonising ecstasy that surged through her, demanding she ride it to the peak and be willingly thrown wherever it took her.

Lights danced across her vision as her head whipped from side to side. Control slipped utterly and she screamed his name. As she shattered into a river of bliss, his mouth covered hers, sharing the moment.

She broke the kiss and gripped his shoulders. 'Thank you.'

He smiled gently. 'You're welcome.'

She pushed his shoulder, rolling him over and going with him. 'I think that deserves a return favour.'

His fingers drew circles on her buttocks. A muscle twitched in his cheek. 'Can I choose the favour?'

A shiver shot through her at what he might suggest. 'Maybe.'

He whispered in her ear and she relaxed. 'No problem.'

After all, he'd just given her the best orgasm of her life and she trusted him implicitly.

She rose up on all fours and his hands massaged her

back and her breasts, making her body sing before he gently entered her, the length of him filling her completely. She sighed at how good it felt. His lips touched the middle of her back as he started to move slowly and she met each thrust with her own.

I can't see his face.

The thought skittered across her mind before vanishing quickly as her body took over. Their rhythm gained momentum and their bodies became one, driving each other forward until, with a cry, they spun out on a stream of fulfilment and then collapsed, utterly sated.

CHAPTER TEN

LUKE LAY ON his back, panting and staring at the ceiling.

What have I just done?

Guilt burrowed in. He'd just had sex with a woman who wasn't his wife. What had started as a quick kiss to show Chloe that she was very much a desirable woman had ended in mind-blowing sex.

He rubbed his palms across his face, feeling the edge of his wedding ring drag against his cheek. *I'm sorry, Anna.*

Twice he could have called a halt, apologised to Chloe and walked away. He'd been given two perfect opportunities—his for the taking—and he'd ignored them, letting his body drive the agenda, deaf to reason. Sex with Chloe was the last thing either of them needed in their messed-up lives, so why had he done it?

Because it's been a damn long time, his body chimed in, stirring again as Chloe's legs tangled with his. *You're a healthy, red-blooded male.*

God, he'd forgotten how amazing sex could be—the rush of euphoria followed by the feeling of contentment that now swam in his veins.

Chloe rolled against him, her hair tickling his nostrils with that intoxicating, fresh scent, which invigorated him every time he inhaled it. 'I'm guessing maybe you haven't had sex in a while.'

He gazed down at her, into a face filled with concern for him, and his heart both ached and squeezed. It unnerved him and he didn't want to think about it. 'Did you think I was out of practice?' he joked, trying to keep the conversation light.

She trailed her fingers across his chest. 'Your clothing removal's a little rusty so you lost points there.'

'Is that so?' He captured her hand in his. 'And for overall performance?'

'Let me see...' She cocked her head as if she was giving it serious thought. 'The judges gave you nine point nine.'

He grinned at her, ridiculously pleased. 'Not so rusty after all.'

'Not where it counts, no.'

She rested her head on his shoulder and he automatically pressed a kiss into her hair. It felt companionable and uncomplicated. Nice.

'This is the first time you've had sex since Anna died, isn't it?'

The words slammed into him, making him flinch, and his throat tightened.

She raised her head, her gaze demanding an answer. 'Luke?'

He closed his eyes and the blurry image of his beloved wife appeared, so he opened them again. Fast. 'Yes.'

'It was just sex, Luke,' she said matter-of-factly.

He felt himself frowning. 'What do you mean, just sex?'

She chewed her lip. 'Exactly that. Two adults taking a moment because they both needed it. Sex can be simple, you know. Casual. It doesn't have to have strings attached.'

The weight of age and time bore down on him. 'I never did that.'

Chloe sat up fast—shock and surprise making her feel

dizzy. As she pulled the sheet up under her arms, her mind roved over what he'd just said. She'd been leading the conversation, trying to check out if Luke was okay because although she'd never experienced the death of a partner, she was certain that the first time he had sex with someone other than his wife might trigger some tough emotions. She hadn't counted on his lack of experience before he'd committed to Anna. 'You've never had casual sex before?'

His expression mixed sadness with an element of being offended. He pushed up and rested his back against the headboard, his broad and beautiful chest on full view. 'I met Anna in my final year of high school and we started dating. We lost our virginity to each other after our exams.

'I imagine our families thought the relationship would flounder soon enough but we'd applied to the same university college so being separated by geography wasn't an issue. When she finished her economics degree, we moved in together. Four years after that, during my residency, we got married. I loved being married,' he said with a sad smile, 'so, yeah, I'm a one-woman guy.'

She tried not to let his probably unintentional barb pierce her as she wrapped her mind around the sort of relationship he and Anna had shared. 'That's a big love,' she said faintly, hating the way her voice sounded. She'd never experienced anything like it.

'Yeah.'

He stared out into the distance with his *Anna look* and her entire body ached. Why had she asked if she was the first woman since Anna? She could have just enjoyed the sex, said *thank you* and returned to her own room. But, no, she'd gone and brought his late wife into bed with them.

Great going, Chloe. You suck at everything to do with men. Make an excuse and leave now.

She opened her mouth to speak but Luke spoke first. 'So this sex with no strings attached...' his green eyes sparkled, partially obscuring the permanent sadness that lingered there '...is it something you might be interested in?'

Keep safe and say no.

His gaze implored and every good intention inside her started to crumble, one resolution at a time. She sought to find a way it might work for both of them, knowing what they'd both experienced at the hands of life. A way to keep her heart contained and intact. 'I'm not looking for a relationship, Luke.'

He nodded. 'Exactly. Neither am I.'

'So no commitment, no regrets?'

'Are you up for that?'

Yes. 'Maybe.'

'Maybe?' He grinned, reaching for her. 'Seeing you refined and defined my offer, I'm taking that as a *yes*.'

She raised a brow. 'And that's your seduction technique?'

He pulled her into his arms and ran his tongue along her collarbone before dipping into the hollow at her throat.

Her head fell back and her breasts rubbed deliciously against his chest, pebbling into tingling nubs.

He nuzzled her décolletage. 'How am I doing?'

Her breath sped up, pulling in and out, hard and fast as her body liquefied. 'Keep...practising.'

He laughed—a wicked, deep, sensual sound—and then he did exactly what she'd told him.

Amber was sitting at Luke's feet, stacking plastic containers from the big kitchen drawer. He marvelled at how something so simple and easy could give such enjoyment and he wondered why she had a boxful of expensive toys when all it took was this. He'd noticed that Chloe often pulled the drawer out when Amber was weary and fractious, and it was always a hit.

He wasn't immune to the irony that a childless woman had taught him more about his daughter than he'd been able to teach her.

As Amber played, Luke and Chloe cooked dinner. Or, to be more precise, Chloe was cooking and he was cheerfully being a kitchen hand, following instructions and dicing all the vegetables for the stir-fry. A week had passed since the night a consoling kiss had catapulted them into bed together and although Chloe always returned to her bed around midnight, they started every evening in his. He wondered why he'd been so fearful that sex would cause complications. This *no commitment, no regrets* idea of hers was an unexpected gift and it had gone a long way towards lessening his guilt about Anna.

This wasn't love. It was sex—pure and simple. It might have taken him seventeen years to discover casual sex but he was now making up for lost time.

It's not really casual when it's just with one person.

He turned the volume down on his conscience and poured Chloe a glass of wine. 'I was thinking—'

'Sounds dangerous,' Chloe quipped with a smile as she set the wok on the gas burner. She loved this time of day, with both of them in the kitchen, working together, Amber close by and Chester in his basket.

He grinned at her. 'Very funny. I've been thinking that it's time to start the ball rolling towards me returning to work, and that starts with me doing a full day at home alone.'

Her hand tightened on the spatula as her heart cramped.

This is it. The real world is bursting your bubble of denial.
'So you need me to move out?'

'God, no.' He wrapped his arm around her waist and kissed her swiftly.

She hated the relief that trickled through her on the coat-tails of desire. 'What then?'

'Well, I was thinking if you go back to work and Amber goes back to daycare, I can run the house and meet you at the end of the day with a glass of wine and a basic meal.'

'The wine idea is tempting,' she teased.

'If you're horrified at the thought of my cooking, feel free to take over,' he said without heat.

She ran the logistics through her head. 'What about when I'm rostered on lates? Can you cope with dinner and the bewitching hour with Amber?'

His face sobered. 'That's the real test. I need to be able to cope with that before I can even think about dealing with patients and surgery.'

'True.'

'So, what do you think?'

Post-surgery, with his sister away, he'd needed Chloe's help. Now, with every passing day he needed it less and less, but he wasn't pushing her to leave and he was asking her opinion of his plans. Did it mean something?

Don't overthink this.

'I think it sounds like a plan. I'll call Keri.'

He kissed her again—long and slow—as if sealing the deal.

'Daddy.' Amber tugged on both their legs. 'Up. Me cuddle.'

Abruptly, he pulled away from Chloe and scooped his daughter into his arms. 'Who's my best girl?' He kissed her curls.

Chloe's heart did a ridiculous lurch.

No commitment and no regrets, remember?

Catching the glint of Luke's wedding ring, it was impossible to forget.

'How's Luke?'

Keri rushed up to Chloe the moment her feet hit the shiny linoleum floor of the ward.

'When's he coming back?' Kate asked, now visibly pregnant and wearing a voluminous maternity uniform.

The pang Chloe normally experienced on seeing a pregnant woman didn't sting nearly as much as it usually did, but as Keri and Kate started firing questions at her, she didn't have a moment to reflect on it.

'He's doing really well,' she said with a smile. 'If everything goes according to plan, he'll be back here in less than two months.'

'Wow, that's amazing. People usually take at least three months to recover from brain surgery,' Kate said.

'Yes, but they don't have me looking after them,' Chloe quipped, ready to steer the conversation around to ward work. She was doing a nine a.m. to three p.m. shift today to cover the busiest hours.

'You did an amazing thing, taking on looking after Luke and his little girl,' Keri said. 'Especially with how you feel about children. I bet you're glad to be back at work.'

Am I? Dropping Amber off at daycare had been fraught. She could still feel the little girl's arms clinging to her and her sobs ringing in her ears. The childcare worker had extricated Amber and mouthed, *'Just go.'*

Chloe, blinking back tears, had done just that but part of her heart had stayed behind. The moment she'd parked the car in the hospital car park, she'd telephoned to check on Amber. The carer had reassured her that Amber had settled quickly and was busy talking about Chester.

Chester was spending the day with Luke and she wondered how Luke was faring with the grocery shopping and the installation of the new dishwasher he'd bought. Chester was probably stealing the grey hoses and Luke would be yelling at him and cuddling him at the same time. She stifled a smile, thinking about how he let her dog get away with just about everything. She really needed to get Chester back into his training regime or he'd end up being a huge dog with no manners.

After a month of the three of them living side by side and sharing everything, today she felt as if she was missing a limb. Although she hadn't even started her shift, she couldn't wait to get home and share her day and hear all about his.

The cottage isn't home. Your dusty apartment is home.

But it was getting harder and harder to remind herself of that.

Chloe mustered up a bright smile for Keri and Kate, deciding to take the easy option and not disabuse them of their thoughts about her and children. 'You're right. After four weeks of chasing around after a toddler, coming back to work will be a relief and a rest.'

Liar, liar, pants on fire.

Keri's smile wavered slightly. 'We're just glad our career nurse is back.'

Is that what I am? For the first time in a long time her beloved job didn't hold quite the same allure.

As Chloe slid her key into the lock on the cottage door, the shrill chirping of the cicadas stopped and she could hear the gentle wash of the waves against the beach. It was a dark, windless night and she'd just worked her first late shift since returning to work five days ago. Tiptoeing quietly into the sleeping house, she slipped off her shoes and went directly to the shower to wash off the ward. Experience with Luke's hot-water service had taught her to run the shower for a full minute before she got in, rather than doing a freezing St Vitus dance in the cubicle.

She turned on the taps and then stripped off her clothes. She was just dumping everything into the laundry hamper when arms went around her waist. She jumped in surprise and then a very familiar body pressed against her back. Luke's skin touched her spine and silk boxers caressed her behind.

His lips nuzzled her neck. 'I missed you.'

Joy poured through her and she put her hand up behind her and touched his head. 'I'm here now and I'm all yours as soon as I've had a shower.'

'I thought I might join you.'

A thrill of anticipation shot through her and she turned in his arms to face him. 'That sounds perfect.'

He grinned, shucked his boxers and joined her in the shower. It wasn't a large shower, and it was impossible to turn around without their bodies touching, but she wasn't complaining one little bit.

Grabbing her shower mitt, he squirted coconut-scented gel on it. Starting at her shoulders, he used the mitt in circular motions across her back before he tossed it aside and pressed his thumbs into the tight muscles of her shoulders.

'Busy shift?'

She sighed at the delicious, relaxing touch that was making coherent thought difficult. 'Tough shift. Burn victims. The youngest is eight.'

'Hell.'

She heard his concern and his frustration that he hadn't been there. 'In another month you'll be back at work, dealing with it all.'

'It can't go fast enough.'

His hands moved down her back and those talented fingers, which could stitch the tiniest vessels together, pressed firmly against each vertebra of her spine and massaged the connected muscles and tendons. It was all she could do to stay standing.

'I had no idea you had this talent.'

He kissed her shoulder. 'I have hidden depths.'

She laughed. 'You just want to get lucky.'

'Is it working?'

She imagined the twinkle in his eyes and the grin on his face and her heart swelled. 'Keep on going and I'll let you know.'

The warm water cascaded over them and his hands reached her buttocks. She pressed against his hands, wanting their touch and hoping they would slide between her legs, because she knew he was particularly good at that, but after a brief but wonderful massage his hands fell away.

She opened her eyes to see him reaching for her shampoo and the next moment his hands were in her hair, washing it and caressing her scalp. Then he reached around her and washed her breasts and her belly. Half of her wanted to turn around, wrap her arms around his neck and her legs around his waist and feel him deep inside her, but his touch was so tender and thoughtful that she didn't want it to stop.

A sob rose in her throat.

This touch wasn't sexual—it was full of caring and reverence. Her parents had abandoned her and Jason hadn't loved her enough. Nick was wonderful and cared for her but it hadn't been like this. This was something in an utterly different sphere.

This is love.

I love him.

The thought exploded in her head, freezing her breath in her lungs and cramping her heart.

No. How did I let this happen?

Despite everything she'd told herself about holding back and keeping her heart safe, she'd fallen in love with Luke. Deeply and irrevocably in love.

Unaware that her life had just turned upside down, he turned off the shower, guided her out onto the waiting mat, towelled her dry and then wrapped her in an enormous, fluffy bath sheet.

Falling in love with him might not be a disaster, her endorphin-infused brain told her as her body whimpered, limp with need and with the wondrous emotions of feeling treasured. She kissed him. 'Thank you. That has to be the best coming-home-from-work welcome I've ever had in my life.'

Dark green eyes gazed down at her and he took her hand. 'I haven't finished yet.'

He led her to his room, lowered her onto the bed and using the combination of his mouth and hands selflessly took her to the dizzying heights of bliss. As she floated back down his hands started to turn her over but she stopped him. Cupping his cheeks, she said, 'I'd like to try something different.'

His face took on a guarded look. 'O...kay.'

She rolled him over and straddled him, wanting to see the face of the man she loved shatter in ecstasy when she took him to that amazing place. Wanting him to watch her taking him there.

Gently lowering herself over him, she sighed as he filled her, his shaft rubbing that sensitive place where she craved to be touched. She moved her hips, creating the friction she knew he'd love and anticipated his thrusts meeting hers.

He didn't move.

Her hands touched his chest. 'Luke?'

His lust-glazed gaze collided with her shoulder. 'Hmm?'

'Is this working for you?'

He didn't reply.

She leaned down and kissed him—long and deep, using her tongue against his mouth just how he liked it.

He groaned and thrust into her, slowly at first but quickly gaining both length and speed.

She tore her mouth away from his and matched him thrust for thrust, riding him and taking him higher and higher and closer to release.

His breathing quickened and she recognised from the sounds that he was close. As her body screamed for her mind to let go, she fought it, wanting him to orgasm first. She gazed down at his face. He shattered with his eyes closed and his face turned away from her.

Her heart ripped and bled.

CHAPTER ELEVEN

'OH, MY GOD, look at your hair!'

Luke's sister Steph had just jumped out of her family's four-wheel drive and was staring at him in his driveway. She threw her arms around him, squeezing him so tightly that he could barely breathe. 'We've been so worried.'

He patted her back appreciatively. 'No need for that. I told you I was fine.'

She sniffed against his shoulder. 'I know, but I never believed you.' She drew back and recovered herself, wiping her tears away with the back of her hand. 'Marty, girls,' she called into the vehicle. 'Come and give Luke a great, big hug.'

Squeals of delight were quickly followed by arms being wrapped around his knees, hips and waist. He hugged and kissed his nieces, thanking each of them for the drawings they'd sent him.

Marty slapped him on the back and pumped his hand. 'You're looking good, mate.'

'I feel good.' And he did. Really good. Better than he'd felt since— He stalled the thought, not prepared to go there.

'That tumour really did a number on you,' Steph said thoughtfully. 'You've looked so grey and drawn for so long and now look at you.' She smiled broadly. 'You're glowing and happy.' Glancing around, she said, 'Where's my gorgeous niece?'

'Napping.'

'Whoa, bro'. Amber's having an afternoon nap? You really *are* on top of things.'

He was about to mention Chloe when Elspeth squealed.

'Mummy, look!'

'Aw, he's so cute,' Lexie said, breaking into a run.

'Can I hold him? Please?' Jess, the youngest of the three girls, pleaded.

His nieces had spied Chester, who'd somehow managed to escape into the garden.

'You've got a dog?' The rising inflection of Steph's voice matched the incredulity on her face.

He shook his head. 'He's Chloe's dog, but Amber's convinced Chester is her own personal property.'

'Oh, is Chloe still here?' Steph asked, interest clear in her gaze.

As if on cue, the screen door swung open and Chloe stepped out. Her chestnut hair swung around her face, some curls catching on the arms of her glasses, and she looked beautiful, tanned and relaxed, wearing a pink silk top and green shorts.

Steph punched him in the arm. 'No wonder you're looking so happy.'

Guilt and pleasure pummelled him, the mixture leaving an odd taste in his mouth. 'We're just friends, Steph.'

That would be friends with benefits.

No way in hell was he elaborating on *that* to his sister.

Steph raised her brows. 'Maybe you should be more.'

'Don't go there, okay?' he ground out tersely. 'If you promise to behave, I'll introduce you.'

Steph laughed and, completely ignoring him, walked straight up to Chloe.

Chloe, who'd been on tenterhooks inside, agonising over whether she should wait until Luke brought his family in to meet her or whether she should take the bull by the horns and introduce herself, had her dilemma solved for her when Chester escaped.

Butterflies batted her stomach and she hated how nervous she felt about meeting the Markham family. Now Luke's sister was making a beeline for her. Chloe sucked in a deep breath and extended her hand. 'You must be Steph. It's lovely to finally meet you.'

'None of that handshaking stuff,' Steph said, moving straight in for a hug. 'We can't thank you enough for what you've done for Luke and Amber.'

The warmth and affection in Steph's hug made Chloe's throat tight. This family who barely knew her, valued her. 'No problem. I was happy to help out.'

Luke appeared and inserted himself between them. He casually slung one arm over his sister's shoulder and the other around Chloe's waist in a familiar affectionate gesture that he often used with her.

'Time for coffee,' he said.

Resisting the urge to drop her head on his shoulder, she said, 'Steph might want tea.'

'Nah,' he said, 'she wants coffee.'

Chloe rolled her eyes. 'You just want to show off that new machine of yours.'

'She's got you pegged, bro'.' Steph elbowed Luke in the ribs in a sisterly way. 'Marty can't wait to show you his new diff lock.' She shot Chloe a conspiratorial look. 'Boys and their toys."

'Enough of that sexist talk, thank you very much,' Luke

said, with a twinkle in his eye, 'or you can make your own coffee.'

'That's far too serious a threat to ignore, Steph,' Chloe said, teasingly. She pulled open the screen door. 'The sad thing is that not only is he full of himself about his coffee prowess, he does actually make fabulous coffee.'

'I'm the perfect man.' Luke winked at her and gave her hand a quick squeeze before walking into the kitchen.

Her heart cramped. *I know you are, and that's my biggest problem.*

An hour later, after everyone had eaten their fill of fruit, cake and coffee, Luke met Chloe in the hall as she was coming out of the bathroom. Trapping her between himself and the wall, he leaned, closed his eyes and kissed her.

The thrill that shot through her every time he did that hadn't diminished over time. If anything, it had intensified despite the warning voice in the back of her mind that loving him was dangerous because he couldn't love her back.

'The kids are desperate to go to the beach so we thought we'd head down now. Will you come too?'

'Sure, but you guys go now and I'll come down when I've cleared up the food and stacked the dishwasher.'

He tucked some strands of hair behind her ear. 'That can wait.'

'Picture sandy, wet and tired kids needing baths and dinner in two hours' time. Life will be much easier with a tidy kitchen.'

'Beautiful and practical.' He smiled down at her. 'Thanks.'

'Daddy!' The sound of Amber's running feet and the click-clack of Chester's claws on the wooden floor got louder.

'You're up, Dad,' she said, giving him a gentle push.

'See you soon.' He dropped an affectionate kiss onto her forehead before turning and catching Amber in his arms.

'Plane, Daddy.' Amber stretched out her arms.

Luke zoomed his squealing daughter up the hall and Chloe watched, smiling, as the two people she loved with all her heart shared so much fun.

She walked into the kitchen and stopped in surprise. Steph was pulling clear wrap over the remains of the moist chocolate beetroot cake Chloe had baked. 'I thought you were going to the beach?'

'I am. We are,' Steph said with a smile, 'but it's not fair to leave you with this mess. Two of us attacking it will halve the job and the time. Besides, with that lot out of the house, I can finally get some time to really thank you.'

Chloe ran some hot water into the sink, feeling embarrassed. 'You already did that when you arrived.'

Steph shook her head. 'Then I was thanking you for the nursing care. Now I'm thanking you for bringing my brother back into the world. He's a totally different man now, thank God.'

Chloe squirted detergent into the water. 'Most of that's because he no longer has a tumour in his brain.'

'I'm sure that's a part of it, but I haven't seen him this happy and content in a very long time.'

Using everything she had to stay strong, Chloe said, 'I'm glad, but I doubt it's me. I think it's helped that he no longer blames himself for Anna's death.'

'I can't help noticing how affectionate he is towards you,' Step said matter-of-factly.

'He's like that with everyone.' Chloe hoped the heat in her cheeks would be attributed to the steam rising from the sink.

'No, he's not.' Steph's questioning gaze zeroed in. 'Medically speaking, Luke's able to live alone now, isn't he?'

'Yes.' The moment the tiny yet loaded word escaped her lips Chloe wanted to suck it back.

'And your stuff's still in the bathroom.'

It's not a question. She's looked and seen. Stunned at the directness of the conversation, Chloe stared at Luke's sister, unable to form a coherent sentence.

'I know how ridiculously independent my brother can be, and if he didn't want you in his house, he'd have asked you to leave. I imagine if you didn't want to be here either, you would have left too.'

'Do you put all of Luke's friends in the witness box?'

Steph gave her shoulder a squeeze. 'Sorry. It's just I haven't seen him this at ease since before Anna died, and I know the reason is you.'

Chloe's hands jerked on the plastic bowl she was washing, sending suds spraying everywhere. The image of Luke always closing his eyes when he touched her burned her brain and she didn't want Steph to get the wrong idea. 'Luke doesn't love me, if that's what you're getting at.'

'I know my brother and I recognise when he's in love.'

Her heart did a ridiculous lurch and she turned to look at Steph. 'Really?'

She nodded. 'You love him too, don't you?'

There was no point denying it. 'I do but…'

'There don't have to be buts.'

She chewed her lip. 'There do,' she said, remembering Jason. 'I had a hysterectomy. I can't give him a child.'

Steph silently passed her a towel. 'This conversation suddenly needs wine.' She opened a bottle and poured two generous glasses. Taking a seat at the table, she said, 'Luke has a child. His need to be a father has already been fulfilled, so don't spend a moment worrying that will be a problem. Do you love Amber?'

'Of course I do,' Chloe said with surprising heat.

'Good.' Steph nodded, her face filling with empathy. 'I never had any problems having the kids and I can't imagine how it must feel knowing you can't have a child of your own. I wish I could help.'

Chloe found herself trying to make Steph feel less guilt about her own fertility. 'That's very kind of you but, short of surrogacy, there's nothing you or anyone can do.'

Steph stared at her as if she'd just been hit and winded. 'Are you okay?'

Steph nodded vaguely, as if she'd been distracted and had lost the thread of the conversation. 'I'm fine. So you've enjoyed spending time with Amber?'

Chloe sucked in her lips and blinked. 'I used to avoid children because it was all too painful. But Amber's such a joy in my life.'

'She's a sweetie, that's for sure. And she'd make the cutest flower girl at a wedding.' Steph winked.

Luke's still wearing a wedding ring. Chloe shook her head as reality dumped over her like cold water. 'You're jumping the gun, Steph. Luke and I haven't even discussed beyond next week, let alone the future.'

'Well, from what I've seen today and the way you two are playing house with Amber, the future's looking pretty damn rosy.' Steph raised her glass and grinned at her. 'I'm never wrong, you know. Talk to him.'

I know my brother and I recognise when he's in love.

The words gave her permission to let her mind wander back to the night in the shower. *I missed you.* The memory of his tender touch on her body sent a shiver through her and she started cataloguing all his little affectionate touches—the way he slung his arm over her shoulder, tucked her hair behind her ear, and moments like just a short while ago when he'd checked she was included in his family's trip to the beach.

All of it said he cared. Really cared. Was Steph right? Did Luke love her? Had she been so busy being fearful that, like her father and like Jason, he didn't love her that she'd purposely focused on all the wrong things in self-defence? Like a wedding ring that had been part of him for a decade so that he might not even notice he still wore it? Or that closing his eyes when he touched her and when they made love was really just to savour her taste and her feel?

Had concentrating on those things blinded her to the many and oh-so-very right signals?

You'll never know if you don't ask.

And therein lay the problem. The idea of asking him both excited and terrified her in equal measure.

'If I can survive my sister's family ripping through the cottage like a tornado, then going back to work will be a breeze,' Luke said, his voice filled with laughter. He sat down next to Chloe on the two-person swing chair out on the deck.

Chloe leaned into his open arms, loving the feel of snuggling in against his chest and the steady beat of his heart. The sounds of the waves lulled her, along with the gentle movement of the seat. She sighed, enjoying the peace now that the Markham family had left and Amber was fast asleep.

'Your nieces are totally full on but gorgeous. How can Marty and Steph look so relaxed after spending two months confined with those three powerhouses in a four-wheel drive and a tent?'

Luke laughed. 'Steph loves it. If she had things her way, she'd have another baby at the drop of a hat and...'

Chloe glanced up at him, wondering why he'd stopped talking, and she met green eyes filled with apprehension. 'What?'

'Sorry.' He pressed a kiss into her hair. 'I didn't mean to upset you by talking about people who can make choices about whether or not to have children.'

Tears burned in her eyes at yet another example of his solicitousness, and her heart swelled. Steph's words, *I know when my brother's in love,* which had been playing across her mind for the last five hours, gained even more volume.

She ran her fingers down his arm. 'It's kind of you to worry about me but, really, I'm fine. I didn't even get a twinge when I saw Kate in her maternity uniform.'

He smiled down at her. 'Good for you.'

'I think looking after Amber's really helped me get things into perspective about children.'

He wound some strands of her hair around his fingers. 'I'm glad. You're amazing with her.'

'She's easy to love.' And she was. Endearingly easy.

'Most kids are.' He kissed the top of her ear and followed it by tracing the edge with his tongue.

Her body liquefied at the erotic touch but her brain screamed, *This is it. Your opportunity to tell him how you feel.*

'Now you're close to going back to work, I guess I'm wondering where this is going.'

He blinked at her—his gaze slightly out of focus. 'Where what's going?'

'This. Us.' She stretched out her arm to encompass the deck and the cottage. 'Sharing the care of Amber, sharing a house.'

He stilled. 'Aren't you happy?'

She smiled, her heart so full it was overflowing. 'I'm deliciously happy.'

'So am I.'

He cupped her cheeks with his hands, gently caressing the skin with his thumbs, and then he kissed her—deep, long and hard.

Her body slackened, craving him and preparing for him. *Focus. Tell him first. Celebrate second.*

Somehow she forced strength into her wobbly limbs and sat up, planting her feet firmly on the ground.

His eyes sparkled with anticipation. 'Inside? Good idea. Sex on this swing will land both of us on the deck.'

'I don't want to go in just yet. Luke…' Her mouth stalled at the words she needed to say.

He smiled expectantly at her, waiting for her to continue.

Just tell him. He's shown you a hundred different ways that he loves you. Heck, his sister even noticed. It's going to be fine.

'Luke, I've changed since we met.'

He picked up her hand. 'I know, you said. You're at peace with your infertility and that's great.'

She shook her head. 'I don't mean that. Well, I sort of mean that.'

Bemusement crossed his face. 'You're not making a lot of sense.'

'Sorry.' She met his gaze. 'I love you.'

He stared at her, surprise clear on his handsome face. 'No.' Incredulity clung to the tiny word.

She smiled at him, understanding his disbelief and urging him to believe her. 'I know I said I'd never allow myself to fall in love again but I was wrong. I've realised that up until I met you I was never in love. This thing between us is nothing like I've ever known. I love you and Amber with all my heart.'

He stood up so fast that the momentum sent the swing careening wildly. Crossing the deck, he reached the railing and gripped it tightly, his knuckles gleaming white in the moonlight. 'We're friends, Chloe, remember? No commitments, casual, easy, that was the deal.'

He hurled the words she'd spoken a few weeks ago right back at her, the tone both accusatory and horrified. Her heart stung with the slap of them.

Make him understand. 'I know that's what I said, what we agreed to, and I meant it at the time. I had no plans to ever love again, but it's happened.'

She thought about all the tiny, thoughtful things he'd done for her over the weeks, adding them together where they added up to one big thing—love. Walking over to him, she rested her hand on his shoulder. 'I don't think I'm the only person here who's changed.'

He shrugged her hand away and faced her. 'What are you talking about?'

'I think you love me too.'

Raw horror streaked across his face, dominating every other emotion. It reached out like the bony hand of the grim reaper and grasped her tightly around the throat, crushing her larynx. Crushing her soul. She anticipated what was coming next and she wanted to cover her ears so she didn't have to hear his words.

'I love my wife, Chloe. I've only ever loved Anna.'

The softly spoken words shattered her heart into a thousand damaged and jagged pieces. She bit into her fist to stop herself from crying out. What had possessed her to listen to his sister? Why had she gone against her better judgement and ignored what she knew to be true and instead dared to dream?

Foolish, stupid, idiotic Chloe.

His green eyes—racked with a tight tangle of indecipherable emotions—sought her gaze and she let him pull her into his arms.

'You're incredibly special to me.' He stroked her hair. 'I'm extremely fond of you, and Amber and I want you here with us. Nothing has to change.'

Feeling battered and bruised, her head fell against his shoulder as if she could no longer hold it up on her own. Resting there, in her favourite place, she breathed in his scent of salt, sand and musk and again felt the thud of his heart beating against her breasts—solid, rhythmic, life affirming.

Nothing has to change.

She could so easily continue living here with the two people she loved in just the same way as she had for the last few weeks. A picture of it formed in her mind.

Something deep inside her snapped.

A king wave of long-contained, life-damaged emotions dating back to her childhood washed through her with a deafening roar, strewing and spewing debris until it filled her to overflowing.

Noooooooooooooo.

Everything has to change.

Value yourself.

Her very first memory was a look of disappointment on her father's face. No matter what she'd done or said, it had never been enough to earn her father's love, and then he'd shunned her in her darkest hour. Her love hadn't been enough for Jason and now it wasn't enough for Luke.

Luke's betrayal hurt the most. He was the *one* man she'd

thought was different. The one man, with the exception of her brother, who had treated her with honour and respect. His many and varied considerate actions—like remembering exactly how she liked her coffee and noticing when she was feeling strung out and insisting she take a break—had combined with a heap of other tiny but thoughtful things to show her that he truly cared for her. Loved her.

How wrong she'd been.

She might have got that wrong but one thing she did know was that she didn't deserve to be treated like this—like a second-class citizen begging for affection. She deserved so much more.

You've never asked for more from anyone.

It's time to start.

Her shattered heart started cobbling itself together—ragged and bleeding—readying itself to put on the fight of its life.

Luke patted Chloe consolingly on her back in a similar way he did with Amber when she was upset. His mind strained and creaked, feeling as dazed and as confused as it had just after his surgery. He had no idea where Chloe's unexpected declaration of love had come from, but he was desperately hoping it was an aberration and she'd let it go. She'd told him emphatically that she didn't commit, that she didn't want a relationship, which was the only reason he'd had sex with her.

The only reason?

He refused to answer his own question.

Chloe raised her head and stepped out of his embrace. 'You're *fond* of me?'

'Of course I am.' He smiled encouragingly. 'Like I said, you're incredibly special to me.'

If her eyes had been lasers, he'd have been burned to a

crisp. 'You're fond of Mr Megat's satay, Luke. You're fond of Chester. I am neither one of those things.'

He trod carefully, knowing there were unexploded mines everywhere. 'I never said you were.'

'No, you didn't,' she said flatly.

Her grim expression didn't offer him any hope that the fact he hadn't said the words was a good thing. He ran his hand over his head and sighed. 'I don't understand where all this is coming from. I thought we were happy with the way things are.'

'*You're* happy with the way things are.' Her voice rose, edged with steel, and it carried out into the night air. 'And why wouldn't you be? After all, I cook, I clean and I look after Amber. Hell, I'm the housekeeper you get to have sex with.'

A flame of rage licked at the edges of his control. He hated the way she'd just reduced what they'd shared into something mean and squalid. 'Hey, who's been doing the cooking and the cleaning and the bulk of the childcare recently while you've been at work?'

'You want a medal or a chest to pin it on?'

'Now you're being juvenile.'

She threw her arms out. 'Am I? I don't think so. The thing is, Luke, I don't exist to make your life easier. That is not my sole purpose in life.'

'I know that.' He hardly recognised the woman in front of him and he reached for her, wanting to convince her she was very wrong, but she dodged him.

'Never for one moment have I ever thought that. In fact, I've worked hard at making it clear to you how much I appreciate everything you do for us.'

A flicker of something close to sorrow flashed across

her face. 'Yes, you've done that extremely well. I've felt very appreciated, which is part of the problem.'

'I don't understand.'

She gave him a pitying look. 'I'm a woman with feelings, Luke, and a huge capacity to love.'

Guilt clawed at him like the talons of a bird of prey. 'I've never hidden from you that I love Anna.'

Her chin shot up and he saw regret shining brightly in her eyes. 'You're right, you haven't. I just thought you loved me, too.'

Her pain barrelled into him. 'I'm sorry, Chloe. I never meant for you to get the wrong impression about us. Anna and I...' He fought to find the words to describe the love they'd shared. 'It only happens once.'

She closed her eyes and swayed.

He shot out his hand, closing his fingers around her upper arm to steady her, worried she was going to faint.

She opened her eyes and pulled away from his grasp so fast it was as if his touch had burned her.

'Chloe, please.'

She shook her head and wrapped her arms around herself. 'You've made things very clear, Luke. You don't love me so I have to go.'

Panic exploded. 'I'm not asking you to leave. Those two things aren't mutually exclusive, Chloe.'

Her eyes widened beyond what he'd thought possible. 'Yes, they are.'

'Yesterday they weren't.' He threw out his hands in frustration at her behaviour. 'Chloe, you can't just change the rules without notice.'

'Goodbye, Luke.'

The thought of her leaving gutted him but rising fury took hold. She was being illogical and irrational. She'd just turned their agreement upside down by expecting more. She was the one being totally unreasonable. He lashed himself to his anger—the safest of all his roiling and chaotic emotions—and he fought back. 'So you're leaving, just like that? At ten o'clock at night? What about Amber? You said you loved her.'

Pain slashed her face. 'I do.'

'Well, you've got a funny way of showing it. She's not going to understand why you're suddenly not here any more. Why you've abandoned her. She lost her mother and now—'

'Don't you *dare* lay a guilt trip on me,' she said, her voice deathly quiet. 'I'll explain it to her.'

Incredulity poured through him at the thought. 'And exactly how are you going to do that?' he yelled, giving up all pretence at trying to be the calm and logical one. 'She's barely two.'

For a moment Chloe looked torn and defeated but then she squared her shoulders. 'Chester and I will take her for walks on the beach so she can still spend time with us. I'll ease out gently.'

He didn't want to think about Chloe and Chester on the beach, playing with Amber, without him. Or about her easing out of his life. 'And if I don't allow you to do that?'

Shock and devastation filled her eyes. 'As her father you could do that but I hope you'll be adult enough to set aside how you feel about me and do what's in her best interests.'

He hated the way she was looking at him as if she loathed him. Damn it, this wasn't his fault. Did she think she could just turn their lives upside down with no warning and have everything her own way? 'You do realise this has to go both ways? You know Amber sleeps better at night when Chester sleeps at the end of her bed.'

Chloe bit her lip. 'I guess there can be access arrangements with Chester. He can sleep over occasionally.'

This is what getting divorced must be like.

The thought skidded across his mind before being buried by his resentment that she was ruining something that had worked so well for both of them. For Amber. For all of them.

She wants my love.

His heart threw off a crazy beat. Could he say it? Could he tell her that he loved her? 'So all of this angst could have been avoided if I said I loved you?'

Her eyes narrowed. 'And meant it.'

He thought of Anna—the love of his life since he'd been seventeen—and the words died on his lips. 'I can't lie to you, Chloe.'

A tremble whipped across her body. 'I know. I've always known.' She walked briskly to the French doors. 'Box up my stuff, text me a time when you're not here and I'll come over and collect it, and then I'll leave my key.'

The deck felt like it was tilting under his feet. 'There has to be another way, Chloe.'

'There isn't.'

She stepped inside, picked up her bag and her dog and without a backward glance walked out the front door into the night.

The ensuing silence suffocated him.

CHAPTER TWELVE

'I'M CHASING PEOPLE for extra hours, Chloe, and as you're our most flexible staff member I'm starting with you first,' Keri said, her expression hopeful.

'Sure.' *The more hours the merrier.*

No, scrub that. Nothing was merrier, but more hours at work meant less time to think about how her life had imploded so dramatically forty-eight hours ago. She was happy to stockpile hours and money because she had less than a month to find a new position. A new job far, far away from the plastics ward.

She'd been up all hours, tweaking her résumé, and had applied for a job in Paediatrics as well as one in the cardiac surgery unit. She really didn't want to leave Gold Coast City but just in case those two jobs didn't work out, she'd also applied to the only private hospital where Luke didn't have admitting rights.

The job of her heart was the paediatric job—her way of being with children—but in the short term she'd take any-thing on offer because there was no way she was working on the plastics ward when Luke returned from sick leave. She just hadn't told Keri that yet.

'Great,' Keri said, writing on the roster. 'I'll slot you in for Friday between five and seven p.m.'

Chloe frowned. 'Actually, Friday's the hospital barbecue.'

Keri nodded. 'And the family carnival, which is why I'm asking you.'

Because I don't have a family. Her heart, so badly battered and bruised, barely had the energy to react. 'Actually, I'm taking Chester...'

Keri laughed. 'It's designed for children, not dogs, Chloe. He'd run amok in the petting zoo and he won't be allowed to use the bouncy castle.'

'No, but Amber will.'

Interest flared in Keri's eyes. 'You're taking Amber?'

'I am.' It would be her first visit with the little girl since she'd left the cottage and she couldn't wait to see her. She bit her lip, not wanting to think about how she and Luke had organised the arrangements via text. Short, sharp, brief, impersonal texts from Luke with the subtext of bitter acrimony.

'But I spoke to Luke yesterday when I was running through the plastics department's RSVPs,' Keri said, her forehead creasing. 'He told me he isn't coming.'

'That's right.' *Because I am.* She bit her lip to stop the threat of tears that permanently threatened to spill and she picked up the fluid balance charts to shut out the bewildered look he'd worn on his face when she'd left him.

You caught him unawares. He'd believed you when you'd said you'd never love again.

She stomped on the temptation to feel guilty. She couldn't afford guilt if she was to stay standing.

'I guess he has another appointment.' Keri sounded disappointed.

'I guess so. I offered to take Amber because she likes bouncy castles.' She wanted the conversation over. 'I can fill in on the roster for any other days in the next two weeks. Email me the dates and times.'

It was bad enough that Luke couldn't love her. She wasn't adding to her pain by disclosing to anyone at the hospital how much of a fool she'd made of herself. No, she was keeping the whole sordid episode to herself.

It wasn't sordid. They were the best weeks of your life. Right up to the moment he told you he couldn't ever love you.

The ache that had become part of her burned again.

She swallowed against it, reminding herself that the alternative to staying with Luke while knowing that he didn't love her would be worse than this.

How is that possible?

She didn't know the answer to that. All she knew was that she had to value herself, because if she didn't, no one else would. If Luke couldn't love her then they couldn't be together. She just had to get through these first dark days. She was a survivor and she'd keep doing what she needed to do by taking one step at a time. She'd get through one hour, one shift, one day and one entire night—one long, lonely and excruciatingly empty night at a time.

She'd already got through two. Just.

Thank goodness for her beloved dog. Only he too was sad, desperately missing Luke and Amber and whimpering at night while she silently cried. He'd stare at her with a puzzled look in his big, brown eyes and then lick her tears. She'd broken all the rules, and Chester now slept on her bed as she stared at the ceiling and told herself she'd done the right thing. Was doing the right thing.

Giving herself a shake, she made a decision. Tomorrow she'd ring Nick and Lucy and offer to mind the twins so they could have a date. The babies would keep her so busy she'd have no time to think about Luke, Amber and everything she'd lost.

It was worth a shot.

* * *

'Night-night, Amber,' said Luke, tucking his daughter in.

'Where Clo? Want Clo.'

Luke sighed. This conversation had become his nightly routine since Chloe had left. 'You'll see her tomorrow.'

'Chester?' Amber asked hopefully.

'And Chester.'

The house was so quiet without the antics of the puppy that Luke had actually gone online earlier and typed *'Child-friendly dog'* into a browser after he'd heard himself call Chester to come for a walk. Hell, he'd even asked Chloe for an opinion on an issue concerning the foundation before realising she was no longer in the cottage.

If he hadn't seen a recent MRI of his brain, he'd be convinced he was losing his mind.

He kissed Amber. 'Sleep tight, blossom.'

For the first time in two nights Amber snuggled down without further delays.

As he quietly closed her door, relief trickled through him that things might be finally getting back to normal.

What's normal? Things haven't been normal since Anna died.

But they'd been normal with Chloe.

He struggled with the thought. How could that be? He still missed Anna. Granted, it wasn't the same desperate loneliness it had been at the start when half of him felt like he'd died too, but he still felt her absence.

He walked into the laundry and smoothed out some clothes for Amber to wear tomorrow, justifying that within the hour they'd be crushed, so there was no point in ironing them. The truth was he didn't have the energy. All the domestic tasks he'd got such a sense of satisfaction from doing these last few weeks were suddenly chores.

That's because you did them with Chloe.

Now she'd gone and the house was dismal. Why the hell had she fallen in love with him and ruined something that was working so well? He'd been asking himself *that* question over and over since she'd left.

Because you told her you didn't love her.

He hated the answer and a fizz of anger stirred.

There's no crime in loving my wife.

He did a desultory toy tidy-round as much to shut out his unwanted thoughts as to avoid an injury to his feet. He picked up a board book and as he rose he came face to face with Anna's photo. He picked it up and her blue eyes stared out at him as if she knew everything about him.

She did.

They'd grown into adults together. Made two five-year plans together, dreamed of having four children and enjoying a long and happy future, only to experience a vastly shortened version of it. 'It should have been longer, Anna.'

She didn't reply. She never did, and now the memory of her voice in his head was muffled and barely discernible. In all their years of being a couple, they'd never had a conversation about one of them dying young, or what either of them thought the remaining partner should do in that event. Why would they? They'd expected a lifetime together, and he'd never pictured his life with anyone else.

He returned the photo to the side table where it sat next to a specimen vase containing a single strand of pink and white Singapore orchids.

Chloe.

It was a typical, caring, Chloe gesture. She was truly amazing and it wasn't that he didn't value her or care for her deeply—he did—but he couldn't switch love on and off and it was unfair of her to expect him to do that.

He dumped the toys into the basket and noticed the three spherical sand spinifex grass heads Amber had collected on the beach the day Steph had visited. He would have made Amber leave them at the back door but Chloe had brought them inside and placed them on the bookshelf. It was a simple decorating touch—connecting the indoors to the outdoors—and their golden colour contrasted perfectly with the dark, polished wood, adding warmth to the cottage.

He moved into the kitchen and was greeted by the newly framed and hung painting that Amber had made at daycare. She'd insisted the bright yellow splotch of paint was Chester and the blue blob was herself. Chloe had printed the date on the bottom right-hand corner and had written in her neat handwriting, *'Chester and Amber at the beach.'* He smiled at the bright, primary colours that dominated the otherwise empty wall, giving the kitchen heart.

A breath-sucking jolt thudded through him. This was the only painting in the house. When he'd moved in, he hadn't cared about decorating. He frantically glanced around him, suddenly seeing the cottage with new eyes. His coffee was in labelled containers and the tea towels matched. He backtracked into the main room. A vase of cheery daisies sat on the coffee table, and a bowl filled with assorted shells and coral surrounded a scented candle that he remembered Chloe lighting one night after Amber had gone to bed. Through the window, out on the deck, he could see the shadows of the hardy, salt-resistant yucca plants in their funky containers. Chloe had suggested he buy them from the farmers' market and use them to soften the utilitarian space.

Somewhere along the line, in the last few weeks, the cottage had gone from being a house to a home.

Chloe had changed it.

When he'd moved in, it had been just a place to live that didn't hold haunting memories of Anna. He'd existed in it rather than lived in it. Chloe had made the cottage a space he felt comfortable in, somewhere he wanted to be—a place he belonged.

Not in the last forty-eight hours.

His gut lurched. He missed her so much.

I'm the housekeeper you get to have sex with.

No. Acid burned his stomach as his entire body rejected her statement. Chloe was so much more to him than that. The domestic help she'd given him anyone could have done. It was everything else about her he valued. She'd made him laugh, she'd challenged him, and at times she'd infuriated the hell out of him. She'd shared the highs and lows of raising Amber with him, which he'd treasured. And when she hadn't been around, he'd thought of her constantly.

That's love.

No, it isn't.

He thought about Anna. How they'd loved and laughed, bickered over trivial things and had cried together when Amber was born. How he'd looked forward to coming home at the end of each working day to share his day with her and hear about hers. How he'd loved being married and having a life partner and a friend.

Chloe's been that to you, too. You love her.

I can't love her. I love Anna.

You love them both.

His breath stalled. There it was. Starkly simple. He'd been blessed with two amazing women in his life and he loved them both.

He'd never thought he was capable of loving another

woman, he'd never thought he'd want to love someone else, but it had happened. Chloe had quietly moved into his cottage and into his heart, and in her calm and happy way had brought him back to life.

The guilt that had been plaguing him about her now made sense. For weeks he'd felt like he was having an affair, cheating on Anna and their life together. Now he could finally see that it hadn't been anything like that.

The twinge he always got when he thought about Anna came, but it felt different. Once a throbbing pain, it was now a mellow and mild ache. His love for her would always be a part of him—she'd been his first love and the mother of his child. Death didn't change that.

Peace settled over him, and for the first time since the car accident he no longer wanted to fight the change that had been foisted on his and Amber's lives. He wanted to embrace it. He tugged off his wedding ring. Chloe was part of that change.

It only happens once.

Nausea rolled in his stomach. He'd told the woman he loved that he could never love her.

Urgency spun through him. He had to tell her he'd been stupid and wrong and he had to do it now. He grabbed his phone and punched in Steph's number.

His sister answered promptly. 'Hey, Luke, what's up?'

'I seriously need your help.'

'What's wrong? Is it Amber?' Panic threaded through her voice.

'No, she's fine.' He rubbed the stubble on his head. 'No one's physically hurt.'

'You're not reassuring me here,' she said, sounding like she was sensing his desperation. 'You never ask for help.'

'It's Chloe. I love her.'

She laughed. 'That's not a secret, Luke.'

He rubbed his jaw. 'It was to me until five minutes ago.'

A short silence wavered on the line before a sigh broke it. 'Oh, Luke…'

The gravity of what he'd done to Chloe forced his eyes closed for a moment. 'Yeah. I need to talk to her. Can you come over and stay with Amber? Right now?'

'See you in fifteen.' The line went dead.

Chloe was flicking through a magazine. She'd tried reading a book but she couldn't concentrate, so she'd gone for something lighter. Celebrity gossip wasn't working either. She glanced at the clock. Nine p.m. She was on duty at seven in the morning so she should probably go to bed but really there was no point because sleep would elude her.

Chester suddenly sat up, his ears pricking up, and then he shot out of his basket, raced to the door and barked at it.

He never barked at the door. 'Quiet, Chester,' Chloe said, dropping the magazine onto the couch. 'Back to your bed.'

Chester ignored her, his barking becoming louder and more frantic. Over the noise, Chloe heard knocking.

She peered through the peephole.

Luke.

She blinked and peered again, not believing the image her eye was seeing.

Luke paced back and forth outside her door.

Slipping her hand around her now frantic dog's collar, she opened the door. Chester lunged forward, all slobbering tongue and love-me-Luke Labrador adoration, desperate for a pat from the man who'd broken her heart.

You're a traitor, Chester.

'This is an unexpected visit,' she said, noticing that the

dark shadows under his eyes, which had vanished in recent weeks, had returned.

Luke nodded. 'May I come in?'

No. Yes. 'Why?'

'I need to talk to you,' he said, keeping his gaze fixed on her face as he reached down and patted Chester. 'And neither of us wants your neighbours to hear our conversation.'

Her bleeding heart dripped some more. 'I don't want to hear our conversation. You made yourself perfectly clear the other night.'

He flinched. 'Chloe, please. May I come in?'

Oh, God, what if he wants to cancel my time with Amber? The thought terrified her, but as much as she didn't want him in her apartment, because it was her Luke-free zone, she also knew she wasn't prepared to risk losing access to Amber. Sighing, she turned away from the door. Leaving Chester with Luke, she walked back into her apartment and stood by the balcony doors.

Luke gave Chester a super-fast cuddle in the hope it would calm the dog down and then he dumped him in his basket and said, 'Stay.'

The puppy looked up at him, all woebegone and filled with disappointment, but thankfully he obeyed the sternness in Luke's voice.

Chloe, on the other hand, looked remote and detached. Everything about her lovely, lush body was sharp and angular, as if she was surrounded by protective steel pickets—pickets he'd put there.

'How are you?'

Great start, Luke. Nothing like inane social chitchat after you've broken someone's heart.

'Fine.'

Her face was drawn and exhaustion clung to her. 'You don't look fine.'

She pressed her hands against the back of the couch. 'Why are you here, Luke?'

'Can we sit down?'

She shook her head.

He rubbed the back of his neck as her animosity rolled into him. He'd planned his speech out in his head and it started with both of them sitting down and him holding her hand.

Not going to happen, pal.

'I love you, Chloe.'

She blinked at him and then she laughed—a bitter, twisted sound that plunged deep into his heart. 'This *is* very unexpected, given you told me you're a one-woman man.'

'I was. I am.' He implored her to understand.

'Oh, and that really clears things up.'

Her sarcasm whipped him. Hell, none of this was coming out how he'd rehearsed it.

'I've missed you, Chloe. The house is so empty without you.'

The shards of brown in her eyes sparked like flint. 'I think you're confusing missing me with missing my domestic and child-rearing help.'

'That's ridiculous and you know it.' But as his defensive tone hit the air, he acknowledged his culpability.

'Do I?' Her hands hit her hips. 'I feel used, Luke. Like I was convenient to you for a time right up until I asked for something, and then I was discarded.'

He shook his head and a wry smile tugged at his lips. 'You're a lot of things, Chloe, but convenient was never one of them.'

Her head jerked up. 'That's supposed to make me feel better?'

Discarding every idea he'd come up with on the drive over, he crossed the room and kneeled on the couch so he was facing her. 'From the moment I saw you that first day at the hospital when I was organising a nurse for Made, you've turned my life upside down. You've made me feel things I hadn't felt in months and months. You brought me out of my fog of grief and back into my life, but as amazing and wonderful as it was, as it is, it scared the hell out of me.'

Chloe stared down into his face, matching up his words with the heartfelt feelings on his face. He was speaking the truth. 'Why did it scare you?'

'Because it felt like I was cheating on Anna.'

'Oh.' She didn't know what else to say as she tried to absorb the unexpected information.

'You told me the other day that you felt very appreciated by me and that was part of the problem. I didn't understand what you meant then, but I do now. I realise I've been in love with you for weeks. You noticed it, Steph noticed it and probably the entire neighbourhood noticed it,' he said drily. 'I was too busy running from it to recognise it as love.'

She thought about how much she loved him and if that was even a tenth of how he'd felt about Anna, she now understood. 'Because you felt like you were betraying Anna by loving me.'

Relief flooded his face. 'Yes. That's it exactly, but I now see that's so very wrong. Crazy even.'

She didn't resent Anna Stanley, but she wouldn't be a normal woman if she didn't have some concerns about his love for herself, given what he'd just told her. 'You said that love could only happen once for you.'

'I was stupid.' He pressed his hand over hers. 'I now see and understand how untrue that statement is. I've loved Anna and I love you. I've been blessed to know the love of two good women.'

She bit her lip. 'I'm not Anna, Luke. I can't be her. I can only be me.'

He nodded frantically. 'I only ever want you to be you because that's who I've fallen in love with. I loved Anna and my love for her is in our memories and the legacy of her that lives in Amber.' He put his hand against her cheek. 'My love for you is a living, breathing thing.

'I know without a moment's doubt or hesitation that I love you. Truly love you. I love waking up in the morning with your fragrance on my pillow, I love how you sing off-key in the shower, how you dance around the house with Amber and how you've brought so such wonder and delight to my life.'

He really does love me for me.

Her heart fired happiness into every part of her. 'I love you, too.'

'Thank God.' He smiled up at her and still on his knees said, 'Please marry me and share my and Amber's lives?'

Joy flooded her. 'Yes.'

His arms wrapped around her and he lifted her up and over the back of the couch until she was sitting on his lap. He kissed her—a kiss of love and commitment and filled with desire.

She sighed and snuggled in against him, feeling like she was home. 'Luke, are you sure you're okay with not having more children?'

Green eyes hooked hers. 'I'm okay if you're okay.'

'Amber's a joy,' she said, thinking of her little girl.

He stroked her hair. 'She is, and I have everything I need with the two of you in my life, but this isn't all about me. Would you like her to have a brother or a sister?'

'An overseas adopted brother or sister?'

'Yes, or a biological one.'

A flicker of unease ran through her. 'You know that can't happen.'

He kissed her. 'Please hear me out.'

Putting his hands on her hips, he adjusted her slightly so she was looking directly at him. His eyes shone brightly with his love for her and she knew intrinsically he'd never hurt her despite the fact she knew she couldn't possibly have their child. 'I'm listening.'

'It could happen if we think outside the box. We could use IVF to have a child.'

Why was he saying this? 'Luke, I don't have a uterus to grow a baby in, and there's only been one or two uterine transplants that I know of and the recipients are yet to give birth.'

He rubbed her back. 'You don't have a uterus but Steph does. She's spoken to me and offered to be a surrogate.'

Short of being a surrogate... She gasped, remembering the conversation she and Steph had shared in Luke's kitchen. 'Your sister would do that for us?'

'Yes, if we wanted to try for a child of our own, she would.'

The rush of emotion hit her so hard she burst into tears.

'Hey, hey, it's okay,' Luke said, kissing her tears. 'We don't have to try if you don't want to. I'll support you in any decision you make. It's all going to be fine, no matter what.'

For years Nick had been her only family and suddenly

she had a partner, a daughter, a sister and the possibility of another child. 'I'm…not…upset…' she sobbed out, as even more tears flowed. 'I'm…happy.'

Luke looked utterly bewildered. 'Really?'

'Really.' She sucked in a noisy breath and nodded. 'It's just a lot to take in.'

'Take your time. There's no rush to make any decisions.' He kissed her on the nose. 'Actually, there is one rush thing.'

'What's that?'

'Getting you and Chester packed up and back to the cottage with Amber and me, where you both belong.'

She smiled at him, every part of her tingling with happiness. 'Home.'

'That's right. Our home.'

She wrapped her arms around him and kissed him, pledging her love and her hopes for their future and receiving his in return.

Callie swallowed a sigh and squared her shoulders. The Gold Coast City Hospital's annual staff picnic was in full swing and blessed by perfect Queensland sunshine. The golden sand of the beach was warm and some families were enthusiastically entering the sand-sculpture competition, buoyed by the prize of a trip to Port Douglas. The sea rolled in light but perfect waves for those taking advantage of the learn-to-surf lessons, and the lifeguards watched carefully as people played in the shallows and further out in the sea kayaks.

Up on the grassed area above the sand line—under the towering Norfolk pines—the barbeque and kids' carnival was in full swing. With the aroma of onions and sausages on the air, little children squealed on the bouncy castle while adults and teens alike screamed on the rotor as the floor dropped away from their feet.

'Chloe, hi!' Callie called out rather too loudly, waving to catch the nurse's attention. She was frantically looking for some fellow single colleagues to do an activity with. So far, the only people she'd met were busy with their children.

Chloe returned the wave and made her way over. 'Hey, Callie. Isn't this great?' She positively bubbled with happiness.

'I guess. To tell you the truth, I always find it a bit daunting with so many couples and families en masse. Us single girls have to stick together, right?' She heard the tightness in her laugh and tried to smooth it out. 'Do you want to try a surfing lesson with me?'

Chloe smiled apologetically. 'Sorry, Callie, I—'

'Clo, look me.'

Both of them turned to see Luke striding towards them with his daughter high on his shoulders. She was waving at Chloe with one hand and holding out her other arm, which had a pink helium balloon tied to it.

When Luke drew level with them, he leaned in and kissed Chloe firmly on the lips. When he broke away, he grinned and said, 'Hey, Callie. Have you heard? Chloe's agreed to marry me.'

The news broke over Callie with a combination of delight and dismay. The world was full of couples, and today they surrounded her. 'That's great news,' she said brightly. 'Congratulations to both of you.'

'Thanks.'

Chloe and Luke grinned goofily at each other until Amber lurched sideways, reaching for Chloe.

'I guess with the rug-rat you're not up for a surfing lesson.'

'Sorry,' Chloe said, not looking the least bit sorry at all as she swung Amber into her arms. 'We're off to the petting zoo, but after that Amber's going to her aunt's so perhaps we can catch up with you in the bar tent?'

'Sounds like a plan,' Callie said, knowing that from her point of view it wasn't a plan at all. New love and the all-encompassing happiness that went with it was particularly hard for her to cope with because it reminded her of how wonderful she'd felt when she'd married Joe and, by contrast, how it had all ended so bitterly.

Chloe's mention of the bar tent drove the idea of surfing lessons out of her head. Suddenly she could do with a drink.

She struck a course in the direction of the refreshment tent and a couple of minutes later she walked into the large marquee. Half of it was open to the air and the other half was enclosed. As she entered the roofed section, it took her eyes a moment to adjust to the gloom after being out in the bright light.

'Callie.'

She instantly recognised that slow and sexy American drawl, which seemed to give her name a third syllable. Cade was sitting at the bar.

He raised his glass to her. 'Let me buy you a drink.' She hadn't seen him since he'd helped her with her diagnosis of the abandoned baby—the day they'd worked together so easily and companionably. Part of her wanted some more of that simple, easy camaraderie. 'That would be *shout* you a drink,' she said with a smile as she slid onto the bar stool next to his. 'We'll get you talking like an Aussie yet.'

He grinned. 'You wanna beer?'

She shook her head. 'I'm more of a champagne girl.'

'That doesn't sound very much like an Aussie sheila,' he said, using the old-fashioned slang word for woman.

She laughed. 'Have you been taking language advice from an eighty-year-old?'

He tilted his head. 'So you're not a sheila?'

'I may have been if I'd been born in 1933.'

'I think the barman's been yanking my chain.' He tapped his glass on the bar. 'Stuart, a glass of champagne for Callie and I'll have another beer.'

'No worries, Doc.' The barman immediately dispensed the drinks.

She noticed Cade's dark brown hair was damp. 'Been swimming?'

'I tried the sea kayaking. What about you?'

'I...' She toyed with lying that she'd built a sandcastle.

'What?' His eyes dared her to speak.

Oh, what the hell. She didn't care what he thought of her. 'I pretty much came straight to the bar.'

He laughed. 'Been that good a day, has it?'

'Actually, it was a great work day. I discharged home three babies. It's the bouncy castle chaos out there that I don't cope with so well.'

'So being here at the bar is more about being in an adults-only zone than the need for alcohol.'

She smiled at him, welcoming his understanding. 'Pretty much.'

'Yeah.' He took a slug of his beer. 'Working with sick babies is totally different from the mayhem out there. Kids kept running into my ankles.'

She raised her glass to him. 'To the kid-free zone.'

He clicked her glass and winked at her. 'To the adults-only zone.'

A shiver of lust rocked through her and she crossed her

legs, trying to stop the tingling that burned at the apex of her thighs.

His gaze rolled over her body, admiration in his eyes.

She soaked it up, loving the way it made her feel like a vibrant, sexy woman.

'So, Callie, what are your plans for the evening?'

'I don't make plans, Cade. I just let things roll out and see where they take me.'

His eyes danced. 'I like the sound of that. Do you care for company?'

She gave him a wide smile.

EPILOGUE

'YOU'RE BREAKING MY hand,' Luke said quietly.

'Sorry,' Chloe said.

She crushed it even harder when she heard Nick say to Steph, 'One or two more pushes and our niece or nephew will be born.'

The labour ward was full to overflowing with her family and she could hardly believe that her baby—her and Luke's baby—was about to be born.

'That's good to hear,' Marty said with feeling, rubbing his hand. 'I'm not sure my fingers can take much more of this.'

'You and me both,' Luke said with a grin.

'Both wimps,' Steph muttered.

Marty wiped her brow. 'Quite right, sweetheart. You're the amazing one here.'

And she was. Chloe was in awe and filled with gratitude at the gift Steph was giving them. Together she and Steph had endured hormone injections and ultrasounds. Chloe had experienced the egg harvests and Steph the implantations. It had taken four attempts before they'd finally succeeded in creating a pregnancy.

Throughout it all Steph had been amazing. She'd taken to being a surrogate with the same gusto with which she approached life, and each day she'd shared the pregnancy with Chloe. When the baby had kicked for the first time, she'd called Chloe at two-thirty-nine a.m. to tell her. Chloe had attended every prenatal appointment and Steph had always told the staff, 'I'm just the incubator. Chloe's the mummy and I'm the doting auntie.'

Steph had shared everything, and Chloe couldn't have felt more involved or more grateful. Now this precious nine months was about to end. And everything was about to start.

Steph grunted and then the contraction hit. She leaned forward, gripping her knees, and pushed.

Chloe edged closer, peering over Nick's shoulder.

'You're doing great, Steph. Keep it going.'

'Arrggh.'

A flash of black, a gush of fluid and Nick said, 'The head's born and no cord around the neck.'

Chloe held her breath and glanced up silently at Luke. He squeezed her hand.

The baby rotated, its face pink and squished, and then Steph pushed again. The shoulders slithered out and the body followed with the thick, pulsating cord across its legs.

Our baby. Her heart stuttered as she willed it to be healthy.

'Is it a niece or a nephew?' Steph asked, falling back onto a bank of pillows.

Nick grinned. 'Come on, Chloe and Luke. Come and learn the secret I've been keeping for twenty weeks.'

Luke nudged Chloe forward. 'You do it.'

She glanced at the baby's legs and her throat threatened to close as love poured through her. 'A little boy. Amber's got a brother.'

'Luke, cut the cord.' Nick held out the scissors.

Luke, his eyes shining bright with tears, accepted the scissors and severed the cord between the two clamps.

The baby gazed up at them both with huge, dark eyes as if he'd been here before and was remaking an acquaintance.

With trembling hands, Chloe wrapped their son in a bunny rug and picked him up, hardly able to believe this was their baby. Their own flesh and blood, given life by his aunt. 'Oh, Steph, I can't begin to thank you.' She kissed her sister-in-law as tears poured down her cheeks. 'He's beautiful.'

Steph grinned, despite her exhaustion. 'Of course he is. He's yours and Luke's child, not to mention my nephew.'

Luke put his arm around his beautiful wife's waist and gazed down at her and his son. 'He's got the Kefes's Greek nose.'

Chloe laughed. 'Poor little guy.' She placed her finger across the baby's palm and his fingers automatically gripped it. 'He's got your long fingers.'

'We should take him to meet Amber.'

His words tumbled out over Chloe's, matching them exactly.

'You go and do that while I get cleaned up,' Steph instructed. 'The girls will all be champing at the bit to meet... What are you going to name him?'

Luke met Chloe's eyes, confirming the name they'd discussed. She nodded, smiling at him. He looked at Steph. 'He's Steven, after you.'

'Oh.' His usually practical sister blinked rapidly. 'You didn't have to do that.'

He kissed her forehead. 'We wanted to. We can't thank you enough.'

She nodded. 'It's what family does. Now, go be the parents and do all the hard work.' She picked up her husband's hand. 'Marty and I are looking forward to being his aunt and uncle, spoiling him rotten and then handing him back for you to sort out.'

Luke kissed his sister and then ushered Chloe out of the ward to a waiting room where Nick's wife, Lucy, was minding all the children, along with her twins.

Amber, now four, jumped up the moment they walked into the room and raced up to them. 'Is it a girl?'

Chloe sat down on the couch and Luke picked up Amber, hugging her hard. 'You have a baby brother.'

Amber wrinkled her nose. 'Can I still cuddle him?'

'Of course you can,' Chloe said.

Luke sat down next to Chloe and popped Amber between them. Chloe carefully placed Steven in his sister's arms, supporting the baby's head. Luke supported his body.

'What do you think, Amber?'

'He's heavier than my doll.'

Chloe laughed and rested her head on Luke's shoulder. 'I can't believe this has really happened. That we could be this blessed.'

Luke stroked his son's head and ruffled his daughter's curls, knowing exactly what Chloe meant. Four years ago he'd never imagined he could ever be this happy again.

'I love you so much, Chloe Stanley.'

'I know you do, and I love you right back.'

She smiled at him in her serene way and he knew that everything was right in his world.

* * * * *

GOLD COAST ANGELS: HOW TO RESIST TEMPTATION

BY
AMY ANDREWS

MILLS & BOON

First published in Great Britain 2013
by Mills & Boon, an imprint of Harlequin (UK) Limited.
Harlequin (UK) Limited, Eton House, 18-24 Paradise Road,
Richmond, Surrey TW9 1SR

© Harlequin Books S.A. 2013

Special thanks and acknowledgement are given to Amy Andrews
for her contribution to the *Gold Coast Angels* series

ISBN: 978 0 263 89921 4

Harlequin (UK) policy is to use papers that are natural, renewable
and recyclable products and made from wood grown in sustainable
forests. The logging and manufacturing process conform to the
legal environmental regulations of the country of origin.

Printed and bound in Spain
by Blackprint CPI, Barcelona

Dear Reader

I hope you have been enjoying the *Gold Coast Angels* series. Having been a part of a few continuities now, I can tell you without hesitation how very much I enjoy them. It's nice not to write in isolation for a change, to live in a world that you build together with your fellow writers, brick by brick, and where everyone knows you!

I hope you are buckled up for Cade and Callie's story. Cade was one of the secondary characters in the hugely successful *New York City Angels* series, and I know readers have been clamouring for his HEA.

The problem is both Cade and Callie have baggage—relationships that have broken them and made them determined to hold themselves back. Their careers have taken priority in their lives and they like it that way!

But fate has different ideas for these two, and I hope you enjoy their dance as they realise that career is just one aspect of a whole life. And that sometimes you need to give in to temptation and surrender to a higher power—love.

Happy reading!

Amy Andrews

Amy Andrews has always loved writing, and still can't quite believe that she gets to do it for a living. Creating wonderful heroines and gorgeous heroes and telling their stories is an amazing way to pass the day. Sometimes they don't always act as she'd like them to—but then neither do her kids, so she's kind of used to it. Amy lives in the very beautiful Samford Valley, with her husband and aforementioned children, along with six brown chooks and two black dogs.

She loves to hear from her readers. Drop her a line at www.amyandrews.com.au

Recent titles by the same author:

HOW TO MEND A BROKEN HEART
SYDNEY HARBOUR HOSPITAL: LUCA'S BAD GIRL*
WAKING UP WITH DR OFF-LIMITS
JUST ONE LAST NIGHT…
RESCUED BY THE DREAMY DOC
VALENTINO'S PREGNANCY BOMBSHELL
ALESSANDRO AND THE CHEERY NANNY

**Sydney Harbour Hospital*

DEDICATION

To three awesome writers—
Marion Lennox, Fiona McArthur and Fiona Lowe.
I am honoured to be in your number.

CHAPTER ONE

IT HAD BEEN a long time since Cade Coleman had felt so objectified. But standing in front of a ballroom full of appreciative women with their chequebooks out took him right back to the 'bad old days'.

Back then he'd been pool and garden guy to a bunch of bored Beverly Hills housewives. But now? At thirty-five he was *Dr* Cade Coleman, neonatal specialist, one of the shining stars in the crown of the Gold Coast City Hospital. His reputation was impeccable and his passion for the little lives in his care had driven him to blaze his way into the relatively new arena of prenatal surgery.

He'd come far since losing his way—and his virginity—to a string of gorgeous cougars, and even though he was here tonight, on the opposite side of the world and in the name of charity, the irony was not lost on him.

'What will you bid?' the emcee, a well-known celebrity and another gorgeous cougar who looked like she might just buy him herself, called to the crowd. 'Remember, Dollars for Dates raises an extraordinary amount of money every year for the neonatal unit and this year...' she paused and gave Cade the once-over, much to the crowd's delight '...we've saved the best for last.'

Cade smiled good-naturedly. When he'd been asked to participate in the annual fundraiser, he hadn't hesitated. He didn't mind squiring around any of the aging Gold Coast charity queens populating the crowd for a night—not if it meant he could expand his prenatal surgery options.

'Do I have two hundred dollars?'

An excited murmur ran through the crowd as people considered their options. Then, from towards the back a very hesitant, 'Fifty,' could be heard.

Cade clutched his chest and feigned his very best insulted look. 'Ma'am, you wound me,' he said, his voice easily projecting to the rear of the room.

The crowd laughed as the emcee cooed, 'Oh, and he's an *American*, ladies. How very exotic.'

'Two hundred,' a voice called from the left.

Callie Richards, admiring the spectacle from her table, glanced over at the bidder, smiling at the total lack of hesitancy this time. Seemed the accent was a real clincher! And then the bidding was off.

Not that she could blame any of them. Cade Coleman had been setting hearts aflutter ever since his arrival at the hospital a couple of months ago. Being tall, tanned, lean, ripped *and* foreign would do that.

So would looking dashing and debonair and just a little bit Rhett Butler in his tuxedo.

God knew, she wasn't immune to those broad shoulders and all that brash American confidence despite what she knew about him from Alex, his stepbrother—and probably the closest thing she had to a friend in the entire world, even if he did live on the other side of the planet.

According to Alex, Cade had fled the US over a problem with a woman. *The apple didn't fall too far from the tree.* Which only meant that Cade had baggage. And explained why, to the best of her knowledge, he'd been resolutely single since his arrival.

Not that it had stopped her making a fool of herself

with the man. Getting tipsy and flirty with him at a wedding, not long after their rather rocky first acquaintance, and being subsequently rejected had been a particularly humiliating incident. Sure, he'd been nice about it, but it had been a *long* time since Callie had been turned down by a man and it had stung.

Having to work closely with him in the intervening time had been fraught despite the professional detachment she practised so well. But given that they both specialised in neonatology, he was hard to avoid.

It had only been recently that she'd felt they'd moved beyond that dreaded night and slipped into an easier relationship.

The bidding stalled at eighteen hundred dollars. 'Come now, ladies,' the emcee implored. 'Surely a handsome doctor who spends all his days saving tiny little babies' lives is worth a little more?'

'Two thousand five hundred.'

A ripple of excitement ran around the room and Callie craned her neck to see the woman who had made the clear, determined bid that had come from the left. She followed the direction everyone else was looking to find the bidder had risen to her feet—Natalie Alberts.

Tall, willowy, blonde and gorgeous, the New Zealand paediatric registrar, who'd been pursuing Cade from the moment he'd set foot in the hospital, looked like she was about to get her man.

Callie glanced at Cade as the emcee enthused, 'That's more like it!'

His toothpaste smile was still firmly in place but Callie, having been at the other end of one of his rejections, had intimate knowledge of that *get-me-out-of-here* look in his eyes.

Cade sighed inwardly as he forced his smile to widen

and his body language to exude a *but-of-course* veneer. Who wouldn't want to pay *more than a lot of people earned in a month* for the pleasure of his company?

Holy crap.

A few hours' wining and dining a nice woman with a charitable heart was one thing. Spending those hours with someone who'd made no secret she wanted to marry him and have his babies? That had stalker nightmare written all over it.

He'd come to Australia to reinvent himself. To move away from the man he'd been in the past and the secret shame of it all. This was his second chance and he wasn't going to blow it by falling into his old womanising ways. He was here for his career—not female companionship!

'Do I have an advance on two and half thousand, ladies?'

Callie felt distinctly sorry for him. He'd gone from basking in the attention to a forced smile and a guarded look in his eyes that she doubted many could read. But as someone who avoided dates at all costs, Callie could easily interpret it.

He'd rather swallow the contents of a poisoned chalice than go on a date with the gorgeous Kiwi.

Or maybe that was just a date with *any* woman in possession of such robust predatory intent. It could certainly threaten his stringently single status.

'I have two and half,' the emcee called. 'Going once.'

Callie watched as Cade ran a finger along the inside of his collar and stretched his neck from side to side—his smile still firmly plastered in place.

'Going twice.' The muscle at the angle of his jaw tightened.

'Two thousand six.'

It was only when all eyes swivelled to Callie that she

realised she'd even uttered a word. But apparently she'd done more than that. Not only was she also on her feet but she'd actually *upped* the ante.

Natalie's gaze narrowed and speared right through Callie's chest. 'Three thousand,' she said, glaring with particular vehemence before turning to look triumphantly at the emcee.

'Ah, that's more like it.' The emcee clapped as she looked expectantly at Callie.

Oh, bloody hell. Callie glanced at Cade, expecting to see an even bigger look of dread in his gaze, but to say his relief was palpable was an understatement. He smiled at her—a genuinely huge grin—and everything inside her turned to water.

'Any further advance?' the emcee asked, looking directly at Callie.

Cade kicked up an eyebrow and the smile warming his brown eyes caused her pulse to do a strange jitterbug inside her chest. That damned eyebrow told her *the ball was in her court.*

Callie sighed, resigning herself to keep going. But he sure as hell owed her big-time!

'Three thousand and one.' Callie nodded.

'Two,' Natalie immediately shot back.

'Three.'

'Five hundred,' the determined blonde countered.

'Six.'

Callie didn't take her eyes off Cade the entire time. He'd relaxed now, his head bobbing back and forth between his two bidders as if he were sitting at centre court during the Australian Open.

'Seven.'

Callie gritted her teeth. 'Eight.'

Natalie's strong, clear 'Four thousand' caused a few little gasps around the room.

'Four and a half,' Callie returned.

'Five!'

More gasps as the emcee said to Cade, 'Well, now, Dr Coleman, this *is* getting interesting.'

Cade grinned and drawled, 'Yes, ma'am.' And Callie swore she could hear the sound of cells sighing as every female in the room leaned in a little closer.

Callie all but rolled her eyes. Cade was enjoying himself, getting a little too smug now for his own good, and a part of her just wanted to drop him right in it and leave him in the clutches of Natalie. After all, had he helped her out when she'd needed someone to scratch an itch not so long ago?

Nope.

He'd politely rejected her. And that itch was still there. If anything, Cade and his bloody tuxedo had intensified it. So quite why she was helping him out she had no idea.

A modicum of humility might not go astray.

'Do we have an advance on five thousand?'

Aware of the expectancy pushing in around her, Callie's gaze flicked to the excitable emcee, who was looking directly at her as she bounced on her toes and shuffled from foot to foot like a toddler with an urgent toilet problem. She glanced sideways at a very hostile Natalie before returning to Dr Full-Of-Himself.

She didn't say anything, just met his gaze and let the seconds tick by. 'Very well,' the emcee said. 'If there are no more bids…'

Callie folded her arms. The room fell silent, as if holding its breath.

'Going once at five thousand dollars.'

Cade's pulse spiked on a surge of adrenaline as Callie ignored the emcee's call for further bids. He knew that the striking redhead didn't owe him anything. Certainly, after he'd rejected her advances—which had been damn hard when she'd fit *just right* against his body—she didn't owe him salvation.

Then why bid in the first place?

She couldn't let him glimpse a way out and not follow through, surely?

'Going twice.'

He narrowed his eyes as he looked at her. She quirked a sexy arched eyebrow at him.

She wouldn't, would she?

Cade swallowed and reached for his collar, the stage lights suddenly hot again on his skin. *Please*, he implored with his eyes.

Please.

He wished he could speak. Tell her he'd pay her back— every cent. It would be worth the ridiculous amount of cash to keep Natalie's particular brand of desperation out of his life. She was a nice woman and a competent doctor but she just wasn't for him—no woman was—and encouraging her in any way, shape or form was asking for trouble.

Callie saw the moment his bravado faltered and uncertainty once again ruled his gaze. Humility. *Atta boy.*

'Five one,' she said, as the emcee opened her mouth again and raised her gavel.

The crowd was too busy gasping and murmuring to notice Cade's ever-so-slight shoulder sag and the relaxing of his jaw, but Callie did. Their gazes met and the *I owe you* in his eyes was clear.

So, she hoped, was the *damn right* in hers.

'Miss?'

The emcee was addressing Natalie, and Callie, along with the rest of the ballroom, looked at the willowy blonde with bated breath. A cold blast of hostility lobbed her way as Natalie's mouth tightened. She shook her head at the emcee, conceding defeat, and Callie admired her restraint. Someone who set a limit and stuck to it had ironclad impulse control.

It wasn't something she'd ever been known for—her rash propositioning of Cade being one good case in point. Tonight was an even better one! She hadn't even planned to bid and now she was out of pocket five grand.

Cade Coleman owed her for sure!

With no other bidders the auction wrapped up quickly and the entire ballroom stood and clapped as Cade sauntered off the stage and headed for Callie. When he got to her table he reached for her hand and kissed it in a very European manner.

Callie couldn't deny, as his lips brushed her knuckles, how very Prince Charming it was.

'Thank you,' he said over the noise of their applauding audience, a camera flash or two adding to a Hollywood feel. 'I am in your debt.'

Callie gave him a half smile but kept her tone brisk. 'You have no idea.'

He grinned as the band struck up a number and the clapping eased. 'How about we discuss that a little further on the dance floor?'

Their hands still clasped, Callie glanced over at the rapidly filling space. There wouldn't be a lot of room to move out there. She wasn't keen to revisit the memories of the last time she'd suggested they dance *or whatever*, in particular the rather humiliating way it had ended. 'Do you think that's such a good idea after last time?'

'I think we're a little past that now, aren't we?'

Were they? Callie could easily recall the embarrassment even if he couldn't. Maybe he was so used to women coming on to him they all just melded into one. But he was right. They'd worked together since then and had slowly moved into friendlier territory. Hell, they lived on the same floor of the same apartment complex.

Clearly, he wasn't holding that night against her so why should she?

Plus, they *were* both adults. No matter how persistent that itch had become beneath the touch of his lips and the nearness of his broad male frame.

She inclined her head, conscious of their audience. '*One* dance,' she murmured.

Cade put his hand on her back as he ushered her past tables and through the milling crowd onto the dance floor. He resolutely ignored the way her clingy, emerald-green dress dipped low at the back and how her rich Titian hair, piled high in a curly mass on her head, exposed her nape and the fascinating indentations of her spine.

They took up position towards the outside and, as the song was slow, he slid one hand onto her waist and the other captured hers. They didn't speak and she stared resolutely over his shoulder at some point behind him, but he was conscious of the curve of her hip, the shift of her body beneath his palm and the heady aroma of frangipani as they moved together.

Someone jostled them from behind and his hand automatically slid to the small of her back as their bodies moved a little closer to accommodate the restricted space. Her hair brushed his cheek, as soft as a petal and, as something primal stirred in the vicinity of his groin, Cade was suddenly conscious of just how long it had been since he'd been with a woman.

Of how much he missed it.

The Sophie debacle had sent him packing both physically and emotionally as he'd fled first to the opposite side of the USA and then the opposite side of the world. And he'd convinced himself that he was done with women and dating.

That his career came first.

Yet one dance with Callie Richards was making a mockery of all that.

'I'll write you a cheque first thing in the morning,' he said, suddenly uncomfortable about owing her anything.

Callie's eyes fluttered closed as his breath stirred the hair at her temple and his accent slithered down her spine and tingled where his palm held her fast. She pulled back slightly until she was looking into his eyes. Light brown with tawny flecks. Like amber. Like whisky.

'You think I can't afford five grand?' she challenged.

Cade's gaze was drawn briefly to the way the subdued light from the magnificent overhead chandeliers glowed in the rich emerald of her eyes before being distracted by her mouth. Her lipstick was a deep scarlet and seemed to beckon with a simmering but subdued sexuality. 'I didn't say that.'

Callie shrugged. 'It's a damn good cause. I'd be a lousy representative of the hospital I work at and the unit I love if I didn't show my support in some way.'

'Five thousand bucks is a little extreme,' Cade said dryly.

'Oh, I don't know,' Callie said, settling back to peer over his shoulder again as his raw masculine scent found its way past her usually impenetrable veneer. 'I'll consider it my public service for the year. Plus, I'm thinking it might be good to have you in my debt.'

Cade grimaced as her hair brushed his cheek again. 'That's what I'm afraid of.'

Callie laughed at the dread in his voice. She didn't like to give anyone control over her life, either. A disastrous teenage marriage had taught her that. 'Don't worry,' she said as the occasional brush of Cade's thighs caused her pulse to flutter, 'I'll wield my power wisely.'

Cade snorted—*screw that*. He'd avoided dating since his arrival in Australia, but *obligation* was to be avoided even more. 'How about we just get it over and done with?' he suggested. 'You paid five thousand dollars to go out on a date with me so...let's do it.'

Callie shut her eyes, trying to tune in to the music rather than the slow thick pounding of her pulse at his *'let's do it'*. He didn't mean *it*, and she had no desire to go out on a date with him. Mind-blowing, head-banging sex, sure, but he'd already made it perfectly clear that any horizontal recreation was off the table. And she just didn't do the whole dating thing.

'I don't date,' she said.

Cade frowned. 'What do you mean, you don't date?' Wasn't that what women wanted?

'I don't date,' Callie repeated, as she once again pulled back to look at him. 'Haven't since my teens. I refuse to. Like you, it would seem.'

Cade wasn't sure what to make of that. He'd spent his entire adult life dating women as a way into their beds. And then done a complete about-turn and spent the last couple of months deflecting those who wanted nothing more than to score a date with him. Her lipstick glistened in the subtle light from above and he couldn't believe a woman in possession of such a fine mouth didn't enjoy many a date.

'I've never met a woman who didn't date. Or who didn't want to, anyway.'

'Oh, is that only a male prerogative in the good old US of A?' Callie enquired sweetly. 'I think you're meeting entirely the wrong type of woman,' she continued. 'I'm honoured to be your first.'

She smiled at him and Cade's loins heated at the deliberately provocative language coming from that sexy painted mouth. 'Is there a particular reason why you don't like to indulge in pleasant social discourse with the opposite sex?'

'Is there a particular reason why *you* don't?' she countered. Her reasons were her own and not up for discussion. As she suspected his were.

Cade gave a half smile. He'd never been told so politely to mind his own business. 'Touché,' he murmured, and they swayed in silence for a moment or two before he said, 'So you paid five grand for nothing?' he clarified.

Callie shrugged. 'Not necessarily. You never know when the need for a male escort might just pop up.'

'Great,' Cade grumbled, feigning his best insulted look. 'Now I feel like a gigolo.'

'Well, at least you're the expensive kind.'

He blinked at her bald inference and then laughed. To his surprise she joined him and the light, throaty noise enveloped him in its sexy resonance. He'd heard her laugh before, of course—at work. She was always kidding around, when appropriate, with the staff on the NICU or the wards—particularly the male staff.

Oh, yes, she had great rapport with her male colleagues and she was resoundingly liked by them all. It was obvious she enjoyed being 'one of the boys'. The blokey, slightly off-colour language and good-natured ribbing came easily to her.

She felt pretty easy in his arms, too, and her laughter reminded him again that it had been a long time since he'd allowed a woman inside his head.

'It's the accent, isn't it?' he said suddenly, a little miffed that the woman in his arms seemed to have no interest in him whatsoever. It might be all his conceited American arrogance, but women were *always* interested. 'It's too brash, right?'

Callie smiled. 'Nope.'

'But you don't think it's exotic and charming?' he pressed.

Callie shrugged. 'I prefer the British accent.'

'Damn,' Cade murmured. 'That Hugh Grant has a lot to answer for.' She laughed and it curled straight into his ear and brushed down the side of his neck. He thought a little more. 'It's that we work together?'

Callie sighed at his persistence. 'Look…it's not you. It's not your accent or that we work together. I just prefer to…cut to the chase…with men.'

She looked at him, their gazes meshing. 'I'm not looking for a husband or to cede control of my life to someone. I like sex,' she said, figuring from what she knew of him that Cade would appreciate the direct approach. 'I don't need a candlelight dinner before or to snuggle afterwards. I'm busy with a career that pretty much takes over my *whole* life so I know what I want and how to ask for it. But you've already made it clear that you aren't interested so…there's no need to pretend.'

Suddenly Cade understood where Callie's hesitancy to cash in her chips was coming from. 'Ah, I get it. This is about me rejecting your advances that time.'

Callie frowned. 'No. It's not.'

'Okay,' he said, not believing her for a moment. But she had given him the perfect opportunity to clear the air over that. 'About that…'

Callie shook her head. 'No. Let's not go there, please. It was a major error of judgement on my behalf and, as you're probably aware, I don't make errors of judgement.

It was a weird night.... Weddings kind of do that to me. And I was a little tipsy.'

'It's okay,' Cade said.

'No. It's really not,' she insisted. 'I embarrassed myself. And you. I still feel embarrassed about it. So if we could not talk about it now, or ever, preferably...' Callie could feel her cheeks growing warmer by the second as she squirmed through her speech. *Hell—was this song never going to end?* '...that would be good.'

Cade ignored her. 'It wasn't that I didn't find you attractive. I hope you don't think that.'

Of course she'd thought that. She'd been tipsy and essentially alone in a sea of colleagues at a wedding—it had pushed *all* her buttons. His it's-not-you-it's-me had pretty much fallen on deaf ears.

She'd been mortified.

And rejected *again* by a man. A position she'd worked hard to avoid over the years. It had taken a long time to regain her sexual confidence after Joe but she had, and she'd wielded it ruthlessly. *She* took control sexually. *She* was in the driver's seat. *She* said who, where, when and how often.

She knew a sure thing when she saw it—even through wine goggles. And every ounce of her female intuition had told her Cade Coleman had been a sure thing.

Right up until the second he'd politely declined.

'Of course not,' she lied.

'It wasn't,' Cade repeated. Hell, Callie was put together just the way he liked. In fact, it was taking all his willpower not to lean in and taste that scarlet mouth. His hand tightened against the fabric over her lower back as things south of his navel stirred at the mere thought.

'I've messed a lot of things up...back home,' he conceded, even though he wasn't quite sure why he was telling her or why it was important that she know his rejection of her come-on hadn't been about her.

Callie nodded. 'Alex said you'd had woman trouble.'

Cade paused. He kept forgetting that his stepbrother and Callie went way back. It was through their association he'd landed the job at Gold Coast City Hospital in the first place. He waited for her to say something else but she just swayed, waiting for him to continue.

He smiled and shook his head at her lack of curiosity—most women he knew would be digging in earnest to find out more about his 'woman trouble'. The fact that she wasn't only ramped up her appeal even further.

'Yes,' he said, dragging his head back into the conversation. Woman trouble was decidedly correct. 'And so I'm here to start over. Concentrate on my career. Avoid the casual sex scene and romantic entanglements. To be honest, they were never very satisfying anyway, not in any *real* sense. Not the way my career...my patients are.'

Callie smiled at him realising for the first time what kindred spirits they were—like she and Alex. She was conscious of the fabric of his tux beneath her palm and she smoothed it, absently signalling her approval.

Cade grimaced. 'That probably doesn't make a whole lot of sense.'

'Not at all,' Callie murmured, her palm still smoothing along the line of his shoulder. 'I think you and I speak the same language.'

'We do?'

'Sure. We live to work. And everything else is superfluous. That's a good thing.'

He gave her a puzzled look. 'Women don't usually see it that way.'

Callie smiled. 'I am not your *usual* woman.'

Cade was about to mutter 'Damn right' when the music

faded to a close. Couples were parting and clapping and they followed suit.

She leaned in close and put her mouth to his ear as they left the dance floor. 'But I'm still going to call in my debt one day.'

The brush of her lips and her warm breath arrowed straight to his groin and the stirring bloomed to full-blown arousal.

CHAPTER TWO

CADE WAS STILL THINKING about her parting shot on Monday morning in his office when he received a page from the woman herself. He'd thought of little else over the course of the weekend and even now as he reached for his phone he found himself smiling.

He couldn't remember anticipating anything this much in a long time. Certainly not a date!

He dialled the extension appearing on his pager screen, a zing in his veins. 'I knew it wouldn't take you long to crack,' he said when she answered on the second ring. 'I knew the accent would get you sooner rather than later.'

He could hear the smile in her voice as she said, 'Sorry, still on team Hugh.'

Cade grunted. 'I could grow a floppy fringe?'

'I thought you didn't date, either?'

'I don't. But we have an outstanding transaction. It's a pride thing.'

'Ah…so it's your *ego* talking. Poor Cade,' she cooed.

Cade laughed. 'I'm sure my ego will survive.'

'I'm sure it will, too,' she quipped.

'Was there a reason you paged me or is it your sole purpose in life to be disagreeable?'

Callie laughed in his ear and his body remembered vividly the havoc her laugh had wreaked on Saturday night.

'I need a consult,' she said. 'I'm looking at a twin-to-twin transfusion syndrome and I want to give the parents all their options, including that new-fangled fetoscopy thing you do.'

Cade grinned at the faux reverence in her voice. 'On my way.'

Five minutes later there was a knock on her door and Callie took a moment to mentally prepare herself before she said, 'Come in.'

She was glad she did. Cade in a tux was a sight to behold. But Cade in a business shirt, stethoscope casually slung around his neck and his tie askew—utterly befitting the image of the dashing, maverick, prenatal surgeon—was tempting on a whole other level. He appealed to the *doctor* in her and, for Callie, that was way more dangerous than looking sexy in a suit.

'Hey,' he said.

His smile was open and friendly and his gaze was full of familiarity, and the sense of emotional danger she felt when he was around increased. 'Thanks for coming,' she said. 'Have a seat.'

And then she launched straight into her spiel because she suddenly realised that with Cade, everything she'd practised over the years was in peril. That smile could make her do something crazy, like throw every ounce of caution and control she'd ever exercised to the wind.

It could make her put her heart on the line for him. A man who was as reluctant to get involved and as burned by life as she was. Hadn't her heart already suffered enough at the hands of a man who wasn't capable of love?

No. She'd dodged a bullet when Cade had rejected her advances. Putting herself in front of the gun again was just plain stupid.

'Kathy Street is a twenty-six-year-old multipara. She

has three children under five and is now twenty-two weeks with her fourth pregnancy, identical twin boys.'

'With a monochorionic placenta?'

'Yes.' Callie nodded. 'She had a scan at twelve weeks, which diagnosed the twin pregnancy, and was supposed to have her standard nineteen-week ultrasound but missed it due to personal circumstances.'

Cade frowned. 'Which were?'

'The recent floods prevented her from making the nineteen-week scan. They live three hours west in a small farming community that was flooded in for two weeks and the last week they've been cleaning up and trying to get back on their feet. Yesterday was the first chance she had to get to the medical centre for the ultrasound, which is, by the way, an hour's drive.

'The GP was concerned she was large for dates, which Kathy had put down to carrying twins and the breathlessness and exhaustion she was feeling down to the stress and hard work of mopping up. But the ultrasound...'

Callie handed over the images that Kathy had brought with her.

'It shows a larger twin with evidence of polyhydramnios and enlarged bladder and the smaller twin with next to no amniotic fluid or discernible bladder.'

Cade looked at the dramatic images. The larger twin, or the recipient twin as it was medically known, was sitting pretty in its over-filled sac while his brother, the donor twin, was practically shrink-wrapped inside his.

'They were referred here immediately and travelled up last night.' Callie turned to her computer and retrieved the data she was looking for. She swivelled the monitor round for Cade to see. 'These are the images I took just now,' she said.

Cade shifted forward but the angle and the light in the

room made it difficult to see properly so he perched on the edge of her desk, letting his leg swing a little as he leaned in towards the screen.

As he watched he was thankful he worked in, and had had exposure to, the more advanced technology of a large modern hospital. Still images were fine but to be able to see the babies in action, so to speak, was much more helpful. Callie had been thorough with all her measurements and the colour Doppler flow study was particularly helpful.

Callie looked up at him. 'I think she's a good candidate for FPLT.'

'Well, they're obviously too young to deliver. Certainly fetoscopic placental laser therapy is an option but reduction amniocentesis would be a more conservative approach.'

Callie smiled. Cade Coleman was not known for his conservative approach to medicine or else he wouldn't be blazing a trail in prenatal surgery, but it was good to know he wasn't a cowboy, either.

'Yes. But I think Kathy and Ray's personal circumstances lend themselves much better to a one-off therapy like FPLT. You and I both know that removing the excess amniotic fluid from the recipient twin is a procedure that often needs to be done multiple times with associated risk of premature birth each time. Not to mention the need for stringent follow-up.

'They don't live close to a treatment centre, which would cause a lot of undue stress both physically and, I suspect, financially for them. And she'd need to be on bed rest for the remaining pregnancy. Kathy is not a bed rest kind of woman—she has three little kids and a farm that she helps run. We'd have to admit her for the rest of her pregnancy to ensure that.'

'She'll still need to rest after laser therapy.'

'I know,' Callie agreed, tapping her pen absently against the wooden desktop. 'But if she's non-compliant or poorly compliant, at least the basic cause has been dealt with.'

Callie had grown up around women like Kathy—they worked hard from sun-up to sundown. Rest was something people in the city did.

'I think she'd be much happier having weekly follow-up ultrasounds locally than stuck in a city hospital, worrying about how her hubby is coping with the kids and the farm.'

She put down her pen and stared at him for a moment. She didn't think she'd have to work this hard to convince Cade Coleman, of all people!

'It has the best outcomes for both twins over any other treatment,' she said. 'Prior to your arrival, Kathy and Ray would have to have travelled to Sydney for this.'

He grinned. 'You know you're preaching to the converted, right?'

Callie shot him an exasperated glare. 'Well, what are we waiting for?' she said, standing up. 'Let's go and talk to them.'

He followed her through an interconnecting door to the next room, where a couple sat quietly holding hands. After the introductions were over, Callie gave them a reassuring smile.

'You've both had a lot to take in this morning,' she said. 'Before I get on to treatment options, have you got any questions about the actual condition?'

Kathy's husband, Ray, nodded. 'Yes. I'm sorry, it's all a little overwhelming. Did you say that the twins are sharing the same blood supply through the placenta?'

Callie smiled again encouragingly. 'Kind of,' she said. It was often hard for laypeople to understand complex medical conditions and part of Callie's job was helping them to understand. If that meant she had to go over and over the information again, that's what she did.

'Your twins share the same placenta—that's common for identical twins. Usually in this scenario each twin has its own separate connection to the placenta via its umbilical cord, but in TTTS the placenta contains abnormal blood vessels, which connect the umbilical cords and circulations of the twins.'

Callie paused to check that Kathy and Ray were following. She glanced at Cade, indicating for him to jump in. 'So essentially,' Cade said, 'blood from one twin is transfused into the other twin.'

'That's the donor twin, right?' Kathy said. 'The recipient is the twin who gets the transfusion?'

Callie nodded. 'That's right. The recipient twin has a lot of extra stress put on its heart because of the extra fluid. Also the kidneys produce a lot of urine to try and remove some of the excess fluid, which leads to a build-up of amniotic fluid. That's what I showed you on the scan earlier.'

'That's why I'm so big,' Kathy stated.

'Yes,' Cade confirmed. 'It's called polyhydramnios. But the donor baby has hardly any amniotic fluid because it's donating all its blood to its sibling and therefore producing hardly any urine. The donor twin also becomes quite anaemic.'

Cade paused, too, for a moment, glancing at Callie. Ray and Kathy seemed to have grasped the basics. They looked shaken but, from what he'd gleaned already about people from 'the bush', as they called it here, also stoic. Something that was confirmed a moment later when Ray cut straight to the chase.

'Okay. So how do we fix it?'

Callie ran down the rather short list of options from

doing nothing, which would almost certainly lead to the death of one if not both twins, to bed rest and nutrition to treating the symptoms with serial reduction amniocentesis and stringent monitoring.

'There is one more option,' she said. 'I've asked Dr Coleman here because he offers a one-off treatment that is curative.'

Ray frowned. 'So let's do that.'

Cade looked at Callie and she nodded for him to continue. 'Well, it is a little out there for a lot of people. It's called fetoscopic placental laser therapy and involves me operating on the placenta while your twins are still in utero.'

Ray looked shocked. Kathy said, 'You can do that?'

'Can and have,' Cade confirmed. 'You are the first TTTS case I've seen since coming to Australia a couple of months ago but I have performed this procedure over a dozen times in the States.'

Cade went on to explain what exactly the operation entailed. He talked about the high operative and twin survival success rates and ran through the benefits as well as the potential complications—from having to repeat the procedure on rare occasions because all the aberrant vessels hadn't been destroyed to inducing labour and the subsequent complications to do with premature babies.

He was thorough, answering their questions as he went along, and Callie couldn't help being both pleased and impressed. Invading the safe, sterile world of the uterus was cutting-edge stuff but it should never be taken lightly or dived into willy-nilly.

'You'll probably want some time to discuss it,' Callie said when Cade's spiel had come to an end and the questions seemed to have been exhausted. 'Why don't you guys go down to the coffee shop and figure out which option you want to go with?'

Ray nodded. 'If we decided to go ahead with the laser thing,' he said, addressing Cade, 'how soon can you do it?'

'Tomorrow,' Cade said. Prenatal surgery was rare so there wasn't exactly a waiting list. 'We'll admit Kathy straight away, run some more tests and I'll get a team together. Not sure if it'll be in the morning or the afternoon yet.'

'Okay, thanks,' Ray said. He stood, helping Kathy to her feet, then reached out and offered his hand to Cade. 'Thanks, Doc.' He nodded at Callie. 'You'll hear from us shortly.'

Callie reached into her trouser pocket and handed them a card. 'Page me on this number whenever you want.'

Callie watched as Ray opened the door and ushered Kathy through it. 'You reckon they'll go for it?' she asked Cade as the door shut behind the Streets.

'They seem like really practical people, so I think they will.' He looked at Callie. Her gorgeous red hair was constrained in a high ponytail today and in the daylight her green eyes dazzled. 'You wanna assist tomorrow if they do? I'm going to need another set of hands in case I have to deliver twins.'

Callie grinned. Standing next to Cade while he saved two little tiny lives had danger to her peace of mind written all over it, but it wasn't something she wanted to miss, either.

'Wild horses couldn't keep me away.'

Which was why the next morning she was standing in her scrubs and theatre clogs, her hair contained in a blue cap, a mask covering her nose and mouth, eagerly watching the monitor as Cade advanced the fetoscope through the amniotic sac of the recipient twin—Joshua—towards the connecting vessels on the surface of the placenta. It was a strange and beautiful underwater world, like in footage she'd once seen of a sunken galleon, and she held her breath as a little hand was illuminated by the beam of light shining from the end of the scope.

'Beautiful, isn't it?' Cade murmured.

Callie, standing opposite with her arms folded, her body turned to face the monitor, glanced at him and recognised the same sense of awe that was bubbling inside her. 'Amazing,' she agreed, her gaze straying immediately back to the screen.

Cade watched her for a moment longer. With the mask firmly in situ, hiding the classic features of her face, he had no idea what colour lipstick she was wearing or if, indeed, she was wearing any. Instead, he'd found something equally captivating: her eyes.

The mask isolated and emphasised the flecks of turquoise amidst the green of her irises. He hadn't noticed them before and he couldn't think why. He guessed his determination to concentrate on his career was paying off if he'd missed the fascinating hue of Callie's eyes.

He was obviously getting good at it.

So, why, suddenly, was that such a depressing thought?

He turned back to concentrate on the job at hand—on Kathy, anesthetised and depending on him, on her babies, on locating the problem vessels.

'Laser, please.'

The scrub nurse handed him the fibre and he threaded it down through the same sheath the scope was using, without taking his eyes off the visual on the screen. Once the laser was in place he set about coagulating the aberrant blood supply, running the beam along the length of the vessels and obliterating them for good.

It didn't take long and he was satisfied when he was finished that the procedure had been curative. 'That ought to do it,' he announced, as he withdrew the fibre.

Callie glanced at him and her eyes shone with excitement—like they needed any extra enhancement! 'Well done! You going to take some of that amniotic fluid while you're in there?'

He nodded. 'Yep. Looks like I've got a good couple of litres I can relieve Joshua *and* his mother of.'

In the end Cade withdrew one and a half litres before declaring himself satisfied. Kathy would feel an immediate difference in the tightness of her belly and her breathlessness, and Joshua's heart and kidneys would not have to work as hard. Andrew, his twin, also now had a chance to develop normally.

And as the cherry on top, Callie was looking at him like he hung the moon.

And all-round great result.

Kathy and Ray thought so, too, when four days down the track she was ready for discharge. The twins were doing well, no complications had developed and they were thrilled to be heading home with weekly follow-up from their local medical centre.

'Thank you so much,' Kathy said to Callie as Ray zipped up her bag. 'You saved our boys' lives.'

Callie laughed. 'I think Dr Coleman deserves those accolades.' She'd only seen Cade on and off briefly over the intervening days, which was just as well because she was fast developing a crush on his medical prowess.

As if his body wasn't bad enough!

'We both do,' a deep voice rocking a sexy accent said from behind her.

Kathy laughed as Callie turned. 'See, Cade agrees with me.'

Callie's stomach went into free fall at the sight of Cade lounging in the doorway. His business shirt was rolled up at the elbows, his tie knot loosened, somehow making him look more wicked frat boy than a skilled prenatal surgeon. '*Cade*,' Callie said, turning back to face Kathy for the sake of her sanity, 'is being too kind.'

'Nonsense,' he said, and Callie didn't need to look around to know he was closing in—she could sense it. 'You put the twins' interests first and sought the most cutting-edge treatment option available. That's gutsy. Trust me, a lot of doctors out there rank voodoo higher than what I do.'

His sleeve brushed hers as he drew level and Callie's stomach looped the loop.

Ray stuck out his hand and Cade shook it as he said, 'Voodoo or not, we owe both of you.'

'Just remember,' Callie said. 'Weekly ultrasounds are vital. *Vital*. A good diet and rest, too. You're at a higher risk of premature birth so you really do need to take it a little easy.'

'I will,' Kathy promised.

'Ray?' Callie said, addressing him. 'You and I both know that Kathy wouldn't know how to take it easy if it came up and bit her on the backside so I'm relying on you to police it, okay? It's *very* important.'

'Hey,' Kathy objected good-naturedly.

Ray nodded, ignoring his wife. 'No worries, Doc.'

'Is she always like this?' Kathy grumbled to Cade.

Cade looked at Callie speculatively. *Who knew?* He knew she was a consummate professional. He knew she was an excellent neonatal specialist. He knew she wasn't afraid to take a risk.

But he hadn't stuck around long enough in any of his dealings with her in the past to know what her bedside manner was like. To know that she fussed over her patients—and not just the babies.

Who'd have thought that beneath her busy, professional exterior she was a bit of a softie?

'Only with those who don't obey my rules,' Callie jumped in, not wanting to hear whatever answer Cade was cooking up in his brain. Talking about her like she wasn't here was just too intimate somehow and she'd already been forced into enough intimacy with him this week, thanks to this case.

Sure, they'd worked on cases before—the occasional consult—but this one felt more personal. Was it timing, landing so soon in her lap after the fundraiser and her five-thousand-dollar bid? Or the excitement and professional milestones involved? Or was it the rapport they'd both built with Kathy and Ray as they'd worked together in the fight for their twins' lives?

'You must be ready to knock off,' Kathy said, changing the subject. 'Please tell me you guys swan off to glamorous city nightclubs on the weekend, dancing and drinking fancy cocktails until the sun comes up.'

'Don't answer her.' Ray smiled. 'She's just trying to live vicariously.'

Kathy stuck her tongue out at her husband. 'Spoilsport. Do you know how long it's been since I had a cocktail or danced till dawn?'

Callie laughed at the note of longing in Kathy's voice but couldn't help but notice the protective way she cradled her belly. 'I hate to break it to you but a glass of red wine and an early night is about as exciting as it gets.'

'Yep,' Cade confirmed, 'hitting the beach is about it for me.'

Although he did have a sudden hankering for Shiraz.

When Callie's foot hit the still-warm sand a couple of hours later she told herself it was about getting some fresh air. Just because she didn't often come to the beach it didn't mean she couldn't. She had felt restless after work and when the ocean was a stone's throw away it had seemed stupid not to take advantage of it.

Not that she wanted to swim. But a walk was a healthy outlet for her restlessness and if she should happen to bump into Cade in his boardies—all wet and clingy—well, that wouldn't exactly be a tragedy.

With a good hour before the sun would even begin to fade from the sky, Callie slogged through the thick, softer sand, heading straight for the shoreline where it was easier to navigate. The patrolled area of the beachfront was relatively busy and she dodged groups of teenagers whooping it up in *thank-god-it's-friday* jubilation and holidaying families taking advantage of the damaging Australian sun finally losing its sting.

The tide was on its way back in as Callie set out, walking away from the impressive Surfers Paradise skyline behind her. A brisk wind picked up her hair and she was pleased she'd pulled it into a loose, low ponytail. The way strands had already tugged free and whipped across her face didn't bode well for the state it would be in when she got back to her apartment.

She kept her eyes fixed on the choppy ocean as the crowds thinned out. An occasional jogger passed her but other than that it was just her footprints in the sand before the ocean quickly erased them. Water occasionally licked at her ankles and splashed up her legs and she pulled the skirt of her strapless black sundress up a little, anchoring it into the elastic sides of her underwear to try and keep the hem dry.

The number of people swimming lessened as she moved farther away from the flagged area and Callie couldn't help but feel concern for those who were swimming outside the boundaries of what the professionals considered safe. The Gold Coast was known for its fabulous beaches and magnificent surf, which was one of the advantages of working at the GCCH—killer views from every floor. But it was also notorious for its dangerous rips and all-too-frequent drownings.

The last thing she wanted to do on her *relaxing* walk was to have to pull someone out of the ocean half-dead.

Realising she was thinking like a doctor rather than enjoying the ambience, Callie, reined in her thoughts.

Beach. Zen. Bliss.

Relaxing.

No NICU. No sick twins. No work for two whole days. No on-call, either.

Breathe in. Breathe out.

Breathe in. Breathe out.

That worked well for a few seconds until the form of the jogger heading in her direction became clearer and she realised it was a shirtless Cade. That's when she forgot the breathing-in bit for a moment or two until the words 'Oh, hell' fell from her lips of their own volition and things returned to their normal function.

Sort of.

What a fool she'd been to think he looked better in his scrubs than a tux. *Clearly*, his birthday suit was going to win hands down when it came to things Cade looked good in. Certainly if the top half was anything to go by!

He recognised her at about the same time she recognised him and he gave a surprised smile and a half wave as he continued to pound towards her. She slowed her pace as his tanned, nicely muscled chest swayed closer into her line of sight with every movement of his body.

Her gaze dropped lower, following the fascinating trail of hair that arrowed down, bisecting the ridges of his abdomen before disappearing beneath the band of shorts that rode *very* low on his hips.

She stopped as Cade pulled up in front of her and said, 'Hey.'

Sweat beaded on his forehead but he didn't even have the decency to be too out of breath or smell sweaty. In fact, her nostrils flared as salt and sand and sea mixed with Cade's earthy male fragrance. A wave swamped her ankles and she didn't even notice until he grabbed her elbow and pulled her higher up the beach.

'You jog,' she said, dragging her gaze to his face, where a slight shadow darkened his jaw. 'I thought Americans preferred the gym.'

Cade laughed at the stereotyping. 'I used a gym in New York because it's a bit far to the beach. But in L.A. I used to jog on the beach all the time.' He stuck out a leg and bent at the waist, performing a stretch now that he'd stopped running so abruptly.

'I have to say, though, I'm a little disappointed. I thought Australians were supposed to have kangaroos on their beaches. I haven't seen one yet.'

Callie frowned for a moment before realising he was calling her on her gym quip. 'Funny,' she said.

He stood and grinned. 'So, are you swimming?' he asked.

'Oh, no.' Callie shook her head. 'I don't swim in the ocean.'

Cade raised an eyebrow. 'Why not?'

'I like to be able to see what's swimming around with me.'

'Ah, you're scared of being taken by a shark.'

Given that sharks were just one of the hazards in Australian oceans, her fears were more varied than that, but it would do for the purposes of this explanation.

'Pretty much.'

'You know that's really rare, right? Sharks are much more frightened of us. Statistically very few people worldwide die from shark attacks.'

Callie gave him a bald look. 'I come from a small country town. It's a four-hour drive to the nearest beach. Statistically *no one's* ever died from a shark attack where I'm from. I'd like to keep it that way.'

Cade laughed. 'Okay. But you don't know what you're missing.'

'Thanks, but I think I'll stick to the sand, if you don't mind.'

Callie's mobile rang and she fished it out from where she'd stashed it in the cleavage of her strapless bra. Cade lifted an eyebrow at the action. 'Didn't want to bring a bag with me,' she said, as she looked at the display. 'Hell. It's my mother. Hold on for a moment—it won't take me long.'

Cade watched her as she walked away slightly and talked. The wind blew her skirt against her legs, outlining their athletic length, the elastic waist emphasising the curve where his hand had rested the other night as they'd danced, and the strapless top showed off the beautiful curves of her shoulders and collarbones and outlined the thrust of her breasts. Hair had escaped from her ponytail and was blowing across her face, which was free of make-up.

So this was casual Callie. He'd seen her around the apartment building, but only either coming home from or going to work. Other than that he'd seen her in a stunning green dress.

He had to wonder how she'd fill out a pair of blue jeans.

Or his sheets, for that matter.

Callie ended the phone call quickly and he watched as she stuffed the phone back where she'd pulled it from and felt about fifteen years old when his belly clenched at the glimpse of cleavage.

'What are you doing on Sunday night?' she asked, as she walked towards him.

Cade blinked at the unexpected question. She looked harried and he had a feeling he knew where this was going. 'Going on that date with you?'

She nodded grimly. 'Good answer.'

'Your mum?'

'My parents. They're passing through on their way to visit my uncle up on the cape.'

It wasn't exactly how Cade had pictured she'd call in her debt, and dinner with *the parents* had been something he'd spent a lifetime avoiding. But this was purely a business transaction. 'Where are we going? What should I wear and who do you want me to be?'

Callie stared at him blankly. She loved her parents but they'd never understood why she'd moved away from home or why she hadn't tried harder to make her marriage work. An evening of recriminations wasn't her idea of fun. Cade would be a good buffer. And something else for them to talk about other than her and Joe.

'Don't know. Don't care. And just…be yourself. I'll let you know the details on Sunday.'

Cade nodded. 'I can do that.'

'Right, well, I'm going to head home,' she said. God knew, she could do with that drink now.

'Sure I can't tempt you to come in?' Cade said, nodding at the surf.

Callie was sure he could tempt her to do almost anything but she knew how she dealt with uncertainty and the feeling that her life was spinning out of control.

Sex. And she couldn't take another rejection right now.

'Nope. I'm fine.'

'Suit yourself,' he said, saluting her as he headed for the water.

'Wait,' Callie said. 'You're not supposed to swim here,' she said. 'You're supposed to swim between the flags.'

Cade grinned. 'You're not much of a rule-breaker, are you?' he said, before running the rest of the way into the sea and disappearing into a wave.

Callie waited for his head to bob up before she moved on in case her non-rule-breaking self needed to pull him out of the ocean when a rip chewed him up and spat him out.

She still needed that date on Sunday night, after all.

His head bobbed up and she relaxed. 'You don't know what you're missing,' he called out.

She glanced at his chest. Oh, she knew all right.

CHAPTER THREE

CADE GOT HIS WISH on Sunday night when he knocked on Callie's door and she stepped out in a pair of faded denim jeans that hugged her butt, legs and hips to perfection. She wore a dark purple blouse that was firm around her breasts and rode low on her cleavage but was loose around her torso, the hem fluttering to her waist. Her hair was down, framing her face and falling lightly on her shoulders.

Dark kohl and mascara highlighted those amazing eyes and a touch of gloss on her mouth made sure he'd be looking nowhere else.

He gave a low whistle and she laughed but it sounded strained and didn't reach her eyes. 'And to think you passed this up,' she quipped, as she pulled her door closed and brushed past him.

'Can I renege?' he teased as he followed her. The swing of her denim-covered buttocks was a thing of beauty.

'Nope. You blew it,' she said. 'And now you'll always wonder.'

Cade grinned. Well, she was definitely right about that. Although, to be fair, he'd spent a lot of time wondering before tonight, as well.

They travelled down in the lift to the underground car park in companionable silence and it wasn't until they were on the road that either of them spoke again.

'Getting used to driving on the left?' Callie asked.

When he'd offered to drive to the restaurant she'd agreed. Tonight was probably going to require a degree of alcoholic fortification just to get through it, so having a designated driver was one less thing to worry about.

Cade nodded. 'Yep. Only driven down the wrong side a few times.'

Callie blanched. 'A *few* times?'

He shrugged. 'It was back at the beginning.'

'Well, your car seems to have escaped unscathed.'

'Yep.' He smiled, stroking the sports steering wheel of the sleek RX8. 'No harm done.'

She looked appreciatively around the interior of his car, which still had that new smell. 'Just as well,' she murmured.

'You like?'

Callie looked at him. She liked everything she saw. *Everything.* Cade was looking whistle-worthy tonight in his blue jeans and trendy T-shirt. 'Very nice. The RX8 is a great vehicle. Great torque.'

'Ah, a woman who knows cars *and* looks good in jeans,' he teased. 'I may just have hit the jackpot.'

Callie smiled, ignoring his flirty tone. Cade obviously felt safe with her, knowing there was no romantic intent behind their date. His wolf-whistle and his flirty lines were probably just backed up from months out of the dating scene. She wasn't about to let any of it go to her head.

'I prefer retro myself,' she said. 'I have a shiny red Alpha Spider. It's twenty years old but still looks amazing and runs like a dream.'

'Well, now, I'm gonna *have* to go for a spin in that some time.'

'I'm sure it can be arranged,' Callie said.

There was another minute's silence as Cade negotiated some traffic. When he'd turned onto the main road he flicked her a glance. 'So, anything I need to know?'

Callie startled at the question, her pulse speeding up as she thought about all the things no one knew. *And never would.*

She understood he didn't want to put his foot in it on their 'date' but there were some things that were best left in the past. And that included her disastrous marriage. Her mother, who was still deeply mortified by the divorce all these years later, certainly wouldn't be bringing it up.

'No.'

Cade kept his eyes on the road. 'Well, how about the basics? Like where you're from? At the beach you said you were from a small country town.'

Callie nodded, her heart rate settling. The basics she could cope with. 'Yes. Broken Hill. It's in far western New South Wales, about a ten-hour drive from Sydney.'

'That's a mining town, isn't it? That's where BHP originated?'

Callie nodded, impressed by his knowledge. Although Cade looked like someone who knew the stock market and BHP shares were as blue ribbon as they came. 'Yes. That's right.'

'So your dad… He's a miner?'

'Yep. As was his dad before him and his before him. As are my three older brothers.'

Three brothers? That certainly explained why she got on so well with her male colleagues—but Cade would have bet that Callie was an only child. There was a distance she put around herself that he understood. Alex had always had it. 'And your mother?'

Callie thought about all the things she wanted to say about her mother but wouldn't. She looked out the window. 'She's a housewife.'

Cade thought he heard disapproval. He approached his next query gently. 'If you don't mind an observation,' he said, pausing as he searched for the right way to say what he needed to say. 'I get the impression that you and your mother don't really...get on? Is there something I should know there?'

Callie almost laughed at the understatement but she felt too brittle. Like she might just snap in two if she let even the smallest laugh pass her lips.

'No. It's fine,' she said, turning her head to look at him. 'We get on. I love her. I love them both.'

'Okay...'

Callie knew from Alex that Cade's childhood hadn't exactly been a picnic, so she felt she was being trivial even talking about the topic. She'd had a family who loved her, a roof over her head, food in her stomach and a small-town network that looked after their own.

Much more than Cade and Alex had ever known.

'They just weren't very encouraging or supportive of my...choices, that's all. They never said to me, "Girl, you've got a brain in your head, you need to go to university". They wanted me to stay in Broken Hill. Get married. Have children.'

All the things she'd wanted, too. Wanted with all the zeal and passion of a silly seventeen-year-old desperately in love with her high-school sweetheart.

But nothing had ever prepared her for what had happened after the big white wedding. She'd never known her coveted white picket fence could become a lonely prison, trapping her inside, too confused and inexperienced to know how to fix it.

'So...you left to do medicine and that caused a rift?'

Callie almost laughed out loud at the abbreviated version of the worst couple years of her life. 'Yes,' she said, as she turned her head to look out the window again.

Her brevity spoke volumes and Cade didn't have to be psychic to know that Callie didn't want to talk about it. Something he understood intimately. But he also understood family breakdown and estrangement, and from what little she'd told him she didn't have a lot to complain about.

'They must be proud of you, though,' he probed. What he'd have given to have heard his father say, *I'm proud of you*.

'They are, I guess, in their own way. They just…don't understand me.'

Irritation spiked in Cade's bloodstream. Having grown up in a *completely* dysfunctional household himself, he didn't think Callie realised how lucky she was to have not just two parents who loved her but the support of an entire community. And if this had been a *real* date he'd have shut his mouth and thought of the pay-off at the end of the night.

But as this night wasn't going to end up between the sheets maybe it wouldn't hurt for Callie to have a reality check. 'Some people would say you've had it pretty good.'

Callie looked back at the terse note in his voice, which made his accent clipped. His profile was hostile, his jaw set into a rigid line. 'I'm sorry, Cade,' she said, reaching her hand out and placing it on his forearm. Even it felt tense beneath her fingers. 'I know things were…rough for you growing up. I *do* know how good I had it.' She gave him a rueful smile. 'Just ignore my whiny little princess act.'

Cade looked briefly down at her hand, warm on his arm. *She knew things were rough?* What exactly had Alex told her? Alex, who was even more tight-lipped about their past than he was.

Just how close had his brother been to Callie?

'There it is,' she said, yanking him back from the hiss

and bubble of troubling questions that swirled in his brain. She removed her hand and pointed to the beachside restaurant and Cade flicked on the indicator and turned into the car park.

Callie was nervous as she walked into the restaurant. Apart from semi-regular phone calls, it had been three years since she'd seen her parents. She'd gone back to Broken Hill for Christmas and had stuck out like a sore thumb next to her blissfully married brothers with their perfect wives and multiple children.

It had driven her nuts that she was a highly successful neonatal specialist, at the top of her field, but somehow she'd felt like the family failure. *The black sheep.* And the 'when are you going to get married and have some kids of your own?' questions just hadn't stopped. Seriously—was it *that* wrong not to want to be a baby machine?

Her parents hadn't arrived yet and a waiter showed them to a table set against the massive floor-to-ceiling windows. A waiter who'd smiled very appreciatively at Callie after giving her a rather thorough once-over. Callie smiled back. She'd deliberately worn clothes that said 'I'm a sexually confident woman' because it was important for her to project that. God knew, a few hours in the company of her parents would certainly suck her back to a time when she hadn't been.

A dark, painful time.

So she needed that. She needed the waiter flirting with her. And the two guys at the bar checking out her butt. Cade sure as hell wasn't interested and tonight she needed to know she was attractive to men, that she was desired.

Because her parents were about to remind her of a time when she hadn't been, and that *always* messed with her carefully constructed control.

Callie ordered a glass of red wine and Cade a light

beer, which were promptly delivered by another waiter who looked at her with invitation in his eyes. Aware that Cade was watching, she let her gaze linger on the twenty-something for a moment before she turned to stare out the window. She took her first fortifying sip. Between the alcohol and sufficient male adoration she figured she could get through the evening.

The sun was setting but it was still light enough to see the whitecaps of the choppy ocean and the surf rolling in.

'Great view,' Cade said.

Callie dragged her gaze back inside. 'Yes,' she said, fiddling with the stem of her wineglass and then her cutlery. The waiting was killing her. She looked at Cade, desperate for a distraction. 'You don't look much like Alex,' she said.

Cade felt the usual tension creep along his shoulders and crawl up his neck whenever talk turned too close to home. 'That would be because we're stepbrothers. Not blood relations. My father married his mother.'

'Oh. Sorry. For some reason I always thought you were half-brothers.'

The less he said the better. 'No.'

Callie nodded. 'So it was your father who…?' She trailed off, not knowing how to put it. Not knowing how Cade felt about it.

'Used Alex as a punching bag?' he supplied, the memories leaving a bitter taste in his mouth.

Callie refused to flinch at the harshness of his tone. 'Yes.'

Cade's reply was clipped. 'Yes.'

'I'm sorry,' she said. 'That couldn't have been easy. Growing up like that.'

Cade snorted. That was an understatement. After Alex had been pushed to his limits and left, violence had given way to neglect as his father had drunk himself into a stupor. That's when Cade had found solace and financial security in the bored, pampered women of Beverly Hills.

'I'm curious about your relationship with Alex. Did you and he…?'

Callie kicked up an eyebrow. Did Cade seriously think she would kiss and tell? 'We're friends,' she said firmly. Yes, they'd had a crazy one-night stand, but they'd realised fairly quickly it had been a mistake and that they were better friends than lovers.

And that was none of Cade's damn business.

'And that's it?' Cade frowned. 'It's just that…Alex is a *very* private person. I can't begin to imagine him confiding in anybody about what happened to him…to us. He nearly lost Layla because he couldn't open up to her.'

Callie shrugged. She and Alex had just clicked. Maybe it had been their turbulent pasts and their insistence on absolute privacy that had drawn them together and cemented their friendship. Maybe it had been their feisty, outspoken personalities. Maybe it had been their utter respect for each other's professional abilities.

Or a combination of all of them.

But to this day she still spoke to him more than she did to her own family. And she missed him and his pragmatism more than she ever would have thought possible. She was happy that he'd found love with Layla. Genuinely happy.

'He never said very much,' she clarified. Neither had she. They just weren't spleen-venting kind of people. But they'd opened up more to each other than they'd ever done with anyone else. 'I learned more from what he didn't say.'

'He told you he was a victim of domestic violence,' Cade said. 'That's big for him.' He'd barely even spoken to Cade about it, even though Cade had witnessed it on too many occasions to count.

Callie shrugged. 'I think he felt a certain sense of distance and...freedom on the other side of the world.'

Cade was about to push some more but he could see an older couple coming through the doors and hailing a passing waiter. The man had a shock of red hair and a big ginger-going-to-grey fuzzy beard. 'I think they're here,' he said.

Callie turned, her pulse quickening. She waved at her parents and felt a familiar mix of emotions churning inside her. Love, affection, fondness, attachment.

Disappointment. Anger. Regret.

She turned to Cade. 'Good to go?' he asked. She nodded and he stood as Callie's parents made their way over. Callie followed suit and then her mother hugged her followed by her father and she performed the introductions. Cade offered his chair to Callie's mother so she and her husband could sit side by side, and then he joined Callie around her side of the table.

'Well, that's not a sight we see much back home,' Duncan Richards said as he sat, nodding to the view out the window.

'No, it's quite something, isn't it?' Cade said.

'So, you're not from around these parts, then?' Duncan asked, as the waiter handed out menus and another smile for Callie. Not that she noticed. She could feel her mother's gaze on her, assessing her, trying to figure out where she'd gone wrong in the rearing of her daughter.

Callie kept her eyes firmly fixed on the menu and let the men fill up the gaps about where Cade was from and the differences between the two countries. But she knew soon enough the conversation would get around to her and her life, and as soon as the waiter had taken their orders her mother dived in.

'So how have you been, darling? It's been such a long

time since we've seen you. All your nieces and nephews are getting so big. You're missing out on *so* much. And Anne-Marie is almost ready to pop with their fourth.'

Margaret Richards sent a strained smile Cade's way before returning her gaze to Callie. 'You're obviously enjoying yourself in the big smoke. Tell me all about your fabulous career. How many babies have you delivered now?'

Cade would have had to be deaf not to hear the brittle emphasis on 'fabulous' and even though he had rebuked Callie earlier for her trivial complaints, he suddenly felt very sorry for her. Maybe it *was* worse to have someone who pretended they cared than someone who didn't give a damn at all.

Beneath the table he slid his hand onto Callie's thigh and gave it a squeeze. As a show of support, of solidarity.

It was warm and soft beneath his hand and he hadn't counted on how very much he didn't want to withdraw it.

He had to force himself—one finger at a time.

Callie felt heat jolt from his palm and streak all the way up her inner thigh to settle between her legs. And it didn't matter that his hand was gone almost as soon as it had landed, that place between her legs was humming away like an electric current.

She chose to concentrate on that rather than her mother's persistent belief that she was an obstetrician.

'I don't deliver a lot of babies, Mum. That's not really my job. That's why there are midwives and obstetricians.'

'So you don't deliver babies at all?' She looked at her husband with a confused frown before looking back at her daughter. 'But I thought you were a baby doctor?'

Callie took a moment to bite back a sharp retort. Every time they got together she had to explain what she did.

'I deliver a few. But my main job is to work with sick

newborns, usually ones that are admitted to NICU. I work with a lot of premmie babies usually. I also deal with pre-natal issues, conditions that can affect babies in utero, before they're born. So does Cade.'

She turned to Cade and smiled at him with what she hoped were her most desperate eyes. *Please help me.* 'In fact, Cade operates on babies while they're still inside the uterus.'

Margaret gasped. 'You can do that?'

Cade got the message in those amazing blue-green eyes loud and clear. He chuckled. 'Yes. We can now. Sometimes. In the right circumstances.'

Callie was relieved, sort of, when they talked about what Cade did all through the first course. When the waiter cleared the plates Callie was left in no doubt her mother was in total awe of Cade's medical skills. And she tried not to let that hurt because she knew, had always known, that her mother was old school. She didn't think that medicine was something a woman should be doing. Hell, she had been horrified when the first female GP had set up practice in Broken Hill.

The day Callie had told her she was leaving to study medicine, her mother had gone straight to church and said a prayer for her. In fact, Callie was pretty sure she was still on the regular prayer list at the local church.

Callie couldn't bear it any longer. 'How's work, Dad?' she asked, changing the subject.

They talked about the mine for a while as the coffees were served, which segued into her mother catching Callie up on all the home-town gossip she couldn't care less about. People Callie had known what seemed like a hundred years ago, who she'd gone to school with or her brothers had played footy with. Who was married to whom and how many kids they had. Who was getting married. And who weren't married but *living in sin. And* having children.

Callie, who had declined coffee in preference for a fourth glass of wine, was just about at screaming point. If nothing else, it was rude to talk about people Cade knew nothing about—not that he appeared bothered. And he was much too polite to interrupt. Callie, however, was not, and she was getting ready to tell her mother enough already when the most startling piece of gossip was revealed.

'Joe is having a baby.'

Callie really wished her mother had chosen a time when she wasn't in mid-swallow to drop that little piece of information. She practically inhaled the wine she'd been drinking and plonked the glass on the table as she coughed and spluttered.

Cade frowned at Callie's reaction as he automatically rubbed her between her shoulder blades. *Joe?* Who the hell was Joe?

Callie caught her breath and looked at her mother, amazed that she was even mentioning his name in front of someone who might ask about him and she might have to relive the whole embarrassing chapter again. But maybe she'd assumed that Cade already knew about Joe?

'He's not married, of course. Who is these days?' she tutted. 'But he moved to Noosa a couple of years ago and now he's with this girl... What's her name?' she asked, turning to Duncan.

'Raylene.'

'Ah, yes, that's it. Raylene.'

Callie's head was spinning so much she forgot that Cade was even there. 'Joe *left* Broken Hill?'

Her ex-husband was a born and bred Broken Hill local. For three generations his family had run a massive cattle property just out of town and he had been a huge part of that, eagerly awaiting the day it would all be his.

And now he lived just a two-hour drive north?

Margaret shrugged. 'Well, she's a city girl so...what was he to do?'

Callie blinked at her mother's casual attitude. So it was okay for wonderful *ex*-son-in-law Joe to leave but not her? When Callie had left it had been a *betrayal* and she had been giving up on her dead-as-a-doornail marriage and her family and her roots, but it was perfectly fine for Joe to leave?

Anger, thick and hot, like mercury, bubbled through her veins but was smothered by even heavier emotions. Joe, *her* Joe, had left the only life he had ever known to settle far away with another woman? *And* they were having a baby together?

Joe, who hadn't touched her in the whole year they had been married. Joe, who hadn't wanted her. Joe, who had blamed her for not being sexy enough, alluring enough, beautiful enough to arouse him.

No matter what she'd done.

No matter how hard she'd tried. No matter what sexy lingerie she'd bought or what aphrodisiac she'd cooked or what humiliating movies she'd hired.

The shocking reality that their issues *had* been her fault after all clawed like talons at her gut. She'd driven herself crazy over the years thinking just that, and had worked hard to convince herself that it had been him and his intimacy issues that had caused their sexless marriage—not her.

Hell, she'd even at one stage during their brief marriage entertained the notion that her husband might be gay. Which was the most absurd, bizarre thing to have thought, honed in the pit of absolute despair from her confusion and naivety. He was the blokiest bloke she knew, for crying out loud. It was why she'd fallen for him—he'd been so incredibly manly.

Footy, cricket, fishing. Swilling beers with the boys at the pub on Friday night.

Riding, shooting, fencing.

He could rope a calf and castrate a cow in his sleep. All the girls at school had wanted him. All the guys had wanted to *be* him.

She was sure Joe was as straight as they came. Which had only made it all the more confusing.

She'd spent the last decade of her life getting out from under his taunts about her inadequacy as a woman. Sleeping with man after man. Seizing control of her sex life, making men want her, making them beg and need.

Proving Joe wrong.

But, faced with Raylene and *the baby*, she couldn't do it any more. It was time to face facts. It had been her. Joe hadn't found her sexually attractive.

Cade squeezed her thigh as Callie's silence stretched. 'Are you okay?' he murmured.

No. Callie was decidedly not okay. She was reeling. She wanted to get out of there. She wanted to walk. She wanted to run. She wanted to find a man.

She *needed* to be with a man really freaking badly.

A man who could prove with his actions, *with his body,* that it wasn't her. That *he* was into her. She needed a little worship. Some goddamn sexual adoration.

And she needed it badly.

'Callie?'

She looked up into Cade's concerned face. *Cade.* She needed Cade. The only man who had turned her down since Joe. If she could get Cade, she'd be able to prove it hadn't been her.

That she *was* desirable.

'Callie?' This time it was her mother, her voice slightly shrill. 'Are you okay?' she demanded.

Callie pulled herself together with a monumental effort. The last thing she needed was for her mother to read too much into her reaction. 'I'm fine.'

'I told you this would happen,' Margaret said. 'He was always going to find someone else. Someone who would stick by him.'

It took all of Callie's willpower to nod and say, 'I know. And I'm really pleased for him. That he found someone. That he's happy.'

Because, God knew, they'd been miserable.

'So, Duncan, tell me about your trip,' Cade said after a few more awkward moments had passed. 'Callie tells me you're heading up to the cape.'

Callie could have kissed him as the topic shifted. In fact, she planned on doing just that. And a lot more. She just had to get him alone. Get away from her parents and this train wreck of an evening and seduce his brains out.

Thankfully, being from the country worked in her favour for once and her mother was calling it a night twenty minutes later. Callie hugged them and wished them a safe trip, but she knew in her heart of hearts she wasn't sorry to see them go. She always felt like a failed nineteen-year-old in her mother's eyes, disgracing the good Richards name with a divorce after only one year of marriage.

Regardless of what she'd made of her life since then.

And she really didn't need that. Especially not tonight, after the news of Joe, when she already felt completely inadequate as a woman.

Her parents left in a cab five minutes later and Cade turned to her. 'Are you okay?' he asked.

He wasn't sure quite what had gone on or who Joe was

but he was pretty sure Callie had been involved with him at one stage and clearly still wasn't over him.

'Sure,' Callie lied.

The lights in the alcove outside the restaurant shone on his dark brown hair and she itched to run her fingers through it. To strip off his shirt and run her hands all over a chest that she'd already seen on full display. To unzip his fly and know the essence of him. To feel him hard and moving inside her. To get lost in the ecstasy. To watch him as he got lost, too.

And she didn't care that they had to work together. Tonight she needed this.

She needed him.

Cade frowned down at her, unconvinced. 'Come on, let's get you home.'

Callie shook her head. She didn't want to go home. She wanted to stay right here in this moment and let the churn of emotions she was feeling dictate what happened next.

She didn't want him returning her to their reality. Not before she'd altered *his* reality forever.

She looked up at him in the half light. 'I feel too restless to go home. You wanna go for a walk on the beach?'

CHAPTER FOUR

CADE WALKED A PACE or two behind Callie as she trod bare-foot across the sand, making a direct line for the water's edge. They'd taken their shoes off as soon as their feet had hit the deserted beach and left them where they fell.

When she reached the line where waves met shore, she crouched and rolled up her jeans to her knees. She stood, her gaze fixed on the horizon as water rushed around her ankles, her hair flying behind her in the stiff ocean breeze.

Cade couldn't help but wonder what kind of power this Joe held to turn Callie from nervous but resigned earlier in the evening to tense and all but mute now.

Cade drew even with her and also rolled up the cuffs of his jeans. He stood silently bedside her for a while, also admiring the view to the horizon. Clouds scudded across the heavens, obliterating any moonlight, but stars peeked through in patches. He found it hard to believe that on the other side of this vast ocean was everything he'd ever known and loved and a whole bunch of other things he didn't want to think about.

Cade sucked in a deep, salty breath. 'You wanna talk about what happened just now?' he asked.

Callie shook her head, her hair whipping across her face as she looked up at him. 'Oh, God, no.' She didn't want to talk about it. She didn't want to think about it. She didn't want to remember it had ever happened.

In fact, she wanted to forget. And she knew the perfect way to do so.

'You don't want to talk about this Joe person?'

Callie snorted, tucking strands of her flyaway hair behind her ear. 'I paid five thousand dollars for this date. You think I want to talk about some ancient history from Broken Hill?'

Cade wasn't fooled by the casual dismissal. The wind whipped her brittle tone straight into his ear and he recognised her effort at self-defence all too well.

'Okay, sure...' He stuffed his hands into his pockets. 'It's your date.'

'Good,' she said, hoping he'd be as compliant later. 'Let's walk.'

Callie was pretty sure they were alone on the beach and given it was nine on a Sunday night were likely to stay that way, but she didn't want to seduce Cade in full view of the restaurant and a popular park complete with public boardwalk.

They walked in silence, for which she was grateful. The lights from restaurant and the boardwalk faded as they left them behind, the beach growing darker as trees loomed to the right, affording the beach more privacy. Better night vision and occasional glimpses of the moon were enough to guide their way.

After about ten minutes of nothing but the sound of the breeze and waves Cade said, 'So how'd you get into medicine if it wasn't something your folks encouraged you to do?'

Callie startled at the sudden sound. Her brain had been considering more pressing matters, like how invasive sand could be in certain areas. His voice slithering between them had been unexpected.

It certainly made her think she could probably cope with a little sand in places that had never seen it before.

'Long, boring story,' she said dismissively. And one that took her back to a place and time she was desperately trying to escape.

'Are we in a hurry?' he asked.

Callie stopped walking. He'd heard more than enough about her tonight. Even if he didn't understand any of it. She turned to face the ocean. 'You wanna go for a swim?'

Cade looked around. She was staring out at the horizon again. Like she might just like to swim and keep swimming far away from whatever was eating at her. But he knew, better than anyone, that some things just couldn't be escaped.

Wasn't that what Alex had said to him as he'd left the US? *The only way to get past your problems is to confront them.*

'But there are no flags.' He feigned shock as he walked towards her.

Callie shot him a sarcastic smile. Tonight she didn't care about flags or sharks or whatever the hell else might be in the water. Tonight her past had come back to haunt her and, frankly, was making her a little crazy.

Driving her, nagging her, needling her.

You're not sexy enough.

You're not good enough.

You're not woman enough.

It ran like a chant through her head to the pounding of the waves. Each crash reinforcing it like a mantra in her head.

Goading her into recklessness, into irrationality, into insanity.

And one look at Cade's strong profile shadowed by the night told her he was her craziness of choice.

'Well, I guess,' she said, reaching for the hem of her top and hauling it over her head, the wind instantly sweeping cool fingers over her torso, 'tonight is my night for living dangerously.'

Cade blinked as Callie stood before him in her jeans and bra. A better man, a *gentleman*, might not have looked but it had been a long time since he'd been up close and personal with a half-naked woman and his gaze dropped without a moment's hesitation, taking in every gorgeous millimetre. From the tips of lovely shoulders to the creamy rise of breasts to the depths of wicked cleavage.

His throat felt as dry as the powdery white sand up closer to the tree line and he swallowed. 'Er...Callie, I don't think you should do that.'

Callie ignored him, wondering just how naked she was going to need to get to goad him into action. She'd hoped this might be enough but it looked as though Cade was employing that bloody willpower he'd already used to devastating effect.

Well...failure wasn't an option tonight.

'Oh, I think I should,' she said, unzipping her fly and wriggling out of her jeans, careful not to take her knickers with them. 'I think tonight is the perfect night.'

Then she kicked out of her jeans and was standing before him in nothing but her underwear. And his gaze dropped again, taking in the curve of her waist and the length of her legs.

'Are you coming?' she asked.

Cade dragged his gaze back up her body with difficulty. She was standing there with her hands on her hips and he knew he should say no. That getting in the water with a half-naked, wet, slippery Callie was playing a very dangerous game. He should tell her how statistically you were more likely to be the victim of a shark attack at night—that ought to do it.

But she was standing there in her underwear, looking at him expectantly, and he could hardly let her go in by herself, could he? And not just because of potential predators, but in case she did do something completely foolhardy, like make a break for the horizon.

After two hours with her mother and four glasses of wine someone was going to need to chaperon her.

He sighed then reached for the hem of his shirt and stripped it off. 'You do know it's going to be freezing, right?' he said as he threw his shirt on top of her clothes then picked the pile up and tossed them higher up the beach away from the reach of the waves. The tide was going out but Cade wasn't risking it.

Callie nodded absently, her skin already breaking out in goose-bumps. But what she had planned for them would warm them up pretty quickly. Even the striptease he was performing as he shucked off his jeans was causing a thermal reaction deep inside her belly.

Cade turned back from throwing his jeans on the pile to find her inspecting the fit of his clingy boxers. Fire streaked to his groin and something pulled tight in his gut.

'Ladies first,' he said, sweeping his hand towards the water to indicate she should precede him and breathing a sigh of relief when she did.

Big mistake.

She was wearing a thong. He groaned inwardly as two white naked cheeks greeted him. He followed the lush curve of them up to where two flimsy strips of fabric adorned the tops of her buttocks and followed the line of them all the way along her hips where they connected the front of the thong to the back.

More heat, more fire, more tension in his belly.

He shut his eyes briefly before running straight past her into the inky water, praying it was freezing. And embracing the water when it was, sucking in a breath as it soothed the fire in his loins.

Callie got to the edge and gave a little squeal as the first wave splashed right up her bare thighs. 'Crap, it's freezing,' she said to him.

'I do recall mentioning that,' Cade said, thankful it was dark enough not to see if the water was making her underwear transparent.

Callie inched in a little further, sucking in her breath as the water reached the tops of her thighs. 'Bloody hell,' she complained.

'Only one way to do it,' Cade said. 'Just dive right in.'

Callie jumped as another wave rolled towards her, trying to keep as much off her body as possible. 'Let me guess, you're a "ripping the plaster off quickly" kind of guy, huh?'

Cade stood. 'I have no problem at all with forgetting it and getting back into my clothes.'

He was less than a metre away and water sluiced off him in the most fascinating way, clinging to pecs and abs and chest hair like a long slow lick. He was hip deep and his entire torso was exposed.

Getting back into his clothes?

What on earth for, when he looked so damn fine out of them?

A wave headed her way and Callie took a deep breath and dived in. The shock of cold against her skin took her breath away and she emerged from the water spluttering, goose bumps pricking her skin, her nipples erect.

'Now swim,' Cade said, whose head and shoulders

she could just make out through the salt water stinging her eyes.

Callie didn't need to be told twice. She'd entered the water intent on seduction but if she didn't warm up first she wasn't going to be very successful. He struck out and she followed, swimming out not very much deeper before travelling parallel to the beach. He'd stop every now and then, ensuring she had caught up, but he always remained tantalisingly out of reach.

When she had finally warmed up she stopped in chest-deep water and watched him as he swam. His big strong arms windmilled through the waves and seawater flowed off his back as sleekly as off a seal's skin. The moon chose that moment to peek from behind a cloud and she caught the delineation of the muscles of his back.

The water moved against her bare skin like liquid silk now, the ebb and flow of it caressing her belly and thighs, washing against the fabric of her bra and the scrap between her legs. Heat bloomed where everything had been cold not that long ago and she was grateful now for the frigid water. It soothed the buzz in her body that pulsed with the ancient pull of the tide and the primal power of his muscles.

Would he make love with the same kind of unhurried strength?

Cade looked behind him. Callie had stopped. It was too dark to see the expression on her face but he got the impression she was watching him.

Which didn't help the prickle in his blood he'd been trying to swim into submission. He lazily stroked back towards her, pulling up a good two arms' lengths away. 'Warmer now?'

Callie nodded, glad he was close enough to see the water beading on his lips. 'Very.'

She had a sudden vision of licking along his mouth.

Tasting the salt and feeling the coolness of his lips. Pushing her tongue inside to the warmth and the flavour of him. But there was a wariness about him and frankly she couldn't bear rejection tonight.

How the hell was she going to bridge the gap between them without just jumping him?

And then something scraped against her leg and she practically leapt the distance between them in a single bound with a tiny little squeal.

By the time he'd said, 'It's just seaweed,' in her ear she was clinging to him, her face planted into his neck, her legs wrapped around his waist, like an oyster on a rock.

But his arms were around her waist and his body heat was wrapping her in its seductive embrace and his breath was husky in her ear. She could feel the crash of his heart against his ribs as no doubt he could feel hers.

'Sorry,' she murmured into his neck, her mouth brushing the thick thud of his carotid pulse, water droplets tickling her lips.

Cade wasn't sure he was sorry at all. It had been a while since a woman's legs had been wrapped around him and he'd been thinking a little too much about Callie's legs for his own sanity. The aching tip of his erection was so close to the juncture of her spread thighs he knew it would only take the slightest movement, a tiny shift, a well-timed wave to be flush against her.

And then he would be just two bits of fabric and one mental surrender away from being inside her. He shut his eyes and willed his body to behave, pulling himself back from the edge with that supreme willpower he'd perfected.

'Okay, crisis over,' he said, trying to inject some lightness into the thickening atmosphere. 'You going to be okay if I let you go?' he asked.

Callie's hands tightened around his neck for a moment,

wanting to stay exactly where she was—wanting to cling, wanting to rub herself against him. But her overreaction to a piece of harmless seaweed seemed foolish.

And she'd still be close enough to make her move.

'Sure,' she said, the water droplets on his skin, so close to her mouth, taunting her.

Cade let go of her waist, letting the current float his arms out to his side, as far from her waist, *her body*, as possible. Yet still she clung to him, arms around his neck, legs firmly locked in place.

The proximity of her body to his felt so good—too damn good—and Cade's erection surged in the confines of his underwear. He shut his eyes and reached for his fast-evaporating willpower. His hands slid onto her thighs, pausing momentarily at the distraction of their silky smoothness before pushing down on them slightly, signalling her to unlock.

They tightened around him and Cade swallowed hard against the urge to push up into her. *For the love of God.* 'Callie.'

Callie held tightly to his neck as she reluctantly unwrapped her legs. Had she known, though, it was going to bring the apex of her thighs into close and intimate contact with his erection, she would have done it earlier. His harsh intake of breath streaked straight to their point of contact and she ground herself hard against him. She barely registered his groaned expletive or the way his hands grabbed her hips as those damn droplets got too much for her and she licked a hot trail from the hollow at the base of his throat all the way to his jaw.

Cade's intention had been to hold her still or maybe push her away but as her hot tongue lapped at his skin, he shut his eyes, his hands sliding from her hips to the cold bare flesh of her buttocks, urging her back where she'd been, her legs locking around him again. Only this time she sat lower, her hips flush with his, her sex rubbing up and down the length of his.

The sound of the ocean around them faded as her lips trekked a path along his jaw. It was just her and him bobbing in the ocean current and only the harsh saw of their breath between them. 'We really shouldn't do this,' he muttered.

'What?' Callie asked, her tongue tasting the salt behind his ear. 'This?' And she ground herself against him a little more.

'*Yes,*' he muttered, as he held her buttocks fast and did a bit of grinding of his own.

Callie gasped as everything south of her bellybutton clamped down tight. 'I think I should get a little heavy petting for my five thousand bucks, don't you?'

A part of Cade's brain—a small, cold part that had curled up next to his willpower in a shrivelled hypothermic stupor—protested at being treated like a gigolo. But he wasn't thinking with *any* part north of his bellybutton right now.

'I think five thousand dollars buys you whatever you want.'

Callie stopped her exploration of his earlobe, pulling her head back slightly to look into his eyes. They were hooded in shadow but she could feel their intensity boring into hers. She drew in a shaky breath.

'I want you hard and deep inside me.'

Cade's heart boomed like a thunderclap in his chest as her direct request reached inside his underpants and tugged hard at its contents.

'Yes ma'am,' he muttered, as his lips swooped down to claim her mouth in a crushing kiss.

A kiss that he'd been dying to take since the night she'd

got tipsy and come on to him. A kiss he'd been depriving himself of for too long now. A kiss that could make him rethink his aversion to dating.

And it did not disappoint.

Her lips were cold and he sucked the salty droplets of water from them like he'd been wandering in the desert for days. But then she opened to him and inside her mouth was hot. Hot and sweet. Like Shiraz and sin. Inviting him to transgress. Taking him to the dark side. And he plundered with indelicate urgency, his hands kneading her bottom, spurred on by the deep satisfaction in her moan and the dance of her tongue against his.

When he pulled back they were both breathing hard. Callie mewed a protest but he shushed her and whispered, 'Hold on,' against her mouth as he grasped her buttocks tight and headed for the beach. His mouth joined hers again as his quads ploughed through the current and Callie clung to him like some water nymph to her Adonis rising from the ocean.

The waves buffeted the backs of his thighs and calves as he strode out of the sea. He barely registered it above the hum in his blood and the buzz in his loins and the blinding imperative to get her naked, to get her under him, to get inside her.

From nowhere a rogue wave crashed into Cade's knees, knocking him sideways, and he lost his footing. They tumbled into the churn of water in the shallows but didn't lose a beat. The wet sand made a soft landing and their mouths clung and held as Cade finally had her horizontal.

He stretched out along her side, his torso trapping hers against the sand, one knee jammed high and hard between her legs. It was only water rushing in around their heads that caused them to break apart. 'Hold on tight,' he said again.

Her arms anchored fast around his neck and, aided by the buoyancy of the water, he half crawled, half dragged her a little higher up the wet sand where the water just lapped at their feet and legs.

Satisfied, Cade collapsed on top of her, his mouth automatically seeking the heat of hers, his body craving her softness against his hardness as he ground his throbbing erection into the scrap of fabric between her legs.

But it wasn't enough. He needed more. He needed to be closer. He needed all of her. He broke away, easing back onto his haunches between her legs then reaching for the spaghetti straps of her underwear and pulling them down. She lifted her hips to aid him and then arched her back and unclipped her bra. He watched as her breasts spilled free and she tossed the bra aside. Her nipples were taut peaks atop firm, creamy flesh, and his mouth watered.

Cade quickly grabbed for his own underwear, fumbling it off in his haste, kicking it off his feet as he settled between her legs, her hips cradling his, his erection snug against her belly. And this time he didn't kiss her. Instead, he lowered his head to one freezing engorged nipple and sucked it deep into the heat of his mouth. The wind snatched her guttural cry away but not before he heard it, not before its potency had streaked heat to where her belly met the hard, aching length of him.

Callie arched her back and cried out again as he switched sides and treated the other nipple to some instant central heating. She was oblivious to the water rushing up their legs to their thighs and draining away again. Oblivious to the *From Here to Eternity* moment. Oblivious to everything as he pleasured her breasts with his mouth and hands—sucking, licking, stroking.

Oblivious to all but the driving need to make this man want her.

He rocked his pelvis against her and Callie gasped, 'Cade.' His erection taunted the sensitive flesh between her legs and she locked her legs around his waist again.

She was more than ready for him. 'Please, Cade.' She lifted her hips in invitation. 'Now... I need you now.'

Cade's head was spinning. He wanted to grind into her. He wanted to thrust and slam and pound.

He wanted to make her cry out and rake her nails down his back.

'Yes,' he said, kissing her hard, swallowing her desperate little whimper, letting it fill his head like the roar of a crowd.

And he was poised to do just that. To plunge inside her, to hear that gasp of satisfaction. But years of practising safe sex, of fixing up patients who hadn't, gave him pause.

Condom.

Callie felt him still. 'What?'

'Condom,' he said, levering himself away from her slightly.

'Oh, hell.' Callie shook her head. She'd been so far gone, so desperate for his possession, she hadn't even thought of it.

Damn Joe and her mother to hell!

Callie felt ten different kinds of frustration at being so damn close. 'Don't you have one in your wallet?' she hissed.

'No,' he hissed back. 'I don't have a condom in my wallet.'

Callie dropped her arms from around his neck. Trust her to choose a guy who'd taken willpower to a whole new level. 'Removing temptation, huh?'

'Yup,' Cade sighed, dropping his forehead to her chest, wishing he hadn't been so hell-bent on putting the possbility of casual sex as beyond his reach as possible.

They lay like that for a moment or two, both struggling to get their breathing under control.

'Okay, right,' Cade said, rolling off her and springing to his feet. Briskly ignoring how utterly doable she was, lying naked in the sand at his feet, he held his hand out to her. 'Come on, let's go. We can be at my place in fifteen minutes.'

Callie looked at his hand then let her gaze wander to the evidence of his arousal jutting out proud and perfect. 'Make it ten.'

Twelve minutes after they'd got back into the car in hastily thrown-on clothes, they arrived at the underground car park. Callie winced when she saw her reflection in the mirrored wall of the lift beneath the harsh fluorescent light. Her hair hung in bedraggled strips around her head, sand clinging like glitter to the strands and decorating her forehead. Her arms were purple from the cold, her mascara had run a little and her shirt was inside out.

But it didn't stop Cade from pushing her hard against the opposite wall and kissing her long and slow, his hands reaching for her buttocks, pulling her in tight and flush to his hips. Her drowned-rat reflection had planted a seed of doubt inside her but the feel of his erection, still thick and potent, demonstrated her doubts were baseless.

His ardour hadn't cooled one iota.

The doors opened and he grabbed her hand and they hurried down the corridor to his apartment so fast Callie could barely catch her breath. Then he was sliding his key into the lock and the door fell open and he was dragging her inside and pushing her against the wall, kissing her as he kicked the door shut with his foot, and Callie couldn't breathe for the weight of wanting him.

'You're freezing,' he said, pulling away and taking her

hand again, whisking her through the open plan of his living quarters and into his bedroom.

He planted another hard kiss on her mouth. 'Warm shower,' he said, pushing her towards the ensuite. 'Go and get naked. I'm right behind you.'

Callie didn't need to be told twice. She felt cold right down to her bones and her clothes were damp and scratchy from when she'd climbed into them still wet and sandy. She stripped off her shirt and jeans, leaving her totally naked. Their underwear had been God knew where—out at sea probably—and neither of them had wanted to waste any time looking.

She stepped into the shower, leaving the door open, and turned on the hot tap, grateful when the water took only seconds to get up to temperature. She sighed as she dunked her head underneath and warm water sluiced over her freezing shoulders and achingly stiff nipples. She pressed her palms against them to relieve the ache, wishing the ache between her legs could be satisfied as easily.

But then the door clicked shut behind her and a foil packet landed on the soap dish in front of her and two big hands were gliding up her belly, pushing hers aside to claim her breasts, his thumbs stroking across her nipples. His mouth was at her neck and Callie shut her eyes and let her head fall back on his shoulder for a moment as his erection pressed into her back and sensation rippled *everywhere* in delicious hot waves.

'You're so sexy,' he muttered against her neck.

It was exactly what she needed to hear. To know. Callie turned in his arms, her hands sliding up his neck, their bodies pressed together from chest to thighs, his erection steely against the softness of her belly.

Callie stroked her index fingers along his mouth. 'I need you now,' she said, and raised herself up on tiptoe and kissed him long and deep and slow as warm water rained down around them.

Cade didn't need any more encouragement. He hauled her up his body and pushed her back against the tiles in one smooth movement. Her legs locked around his waist as they had in the ocean, except she was warm everywhere now, and he feasted on her breasts, rolling her nipples round and round his mouth until she was crying out his name and begging him for release.

'Goddamn it, Cade,' Callie swore as she blindly groped for the condom she knew was somewhere behind and to the left of him.

Her fingers finally found the hard edge and grabbed it. Dragging in ragged breaths, she tried to undo it with her fingers but she could barely co-ordinate them with his mouth creating such havoc so she tore at it with her teeth, gasping as his mouth pulled and tugged at her nipple.

Finally she liberated it. 'Cade,' she said, pushing at his shoulders. He ignored her to switch sides and her eyes rolled back in her head as she allowed herself to be distracted by the sharp spike of pleasure.

But just for a moment.

'Cade.' She hissed it this time, pushing more firmly at his shoulders.

'Wha—?' he asked, pulling away, and he looked as dazed and lust-drunk as she felt.

She kissed him for long sloppy moments, water from the shower lubricating the kiss to sweet slippery perfection. She pulled back when his erection kicked against her. 'This,' she said, holding up the condom. 'On. Now.'

She was incapable of stringing too many words together. Certainly incapable of putting it on herself. But Cade nodded and she bit her lip as he fumbled, holding her and wrestling it on, but finally, finally managing it all, and then she said, 'Now,' kissing him again and again. 'Now, now, hurry.'

And then he was inside her in one easy movement and she cried out, her head falling forward onto his shoulder, her fingers gripping his biceps at the heat and the burn and the stretch.

Cade stilled as Callie's nails dug into his arms. 'You okay?' he asked, biting back a deep guttural groan.

Callie lifted her head, dazed. She frowned as the delicious fullness inside her sat high and hard. 'Of course,' she gasped. 'Don't stop.'

Cade let out a ragged breath but did exactly as he was told, claiming her mouth in a rough kiss as he set the rhythm between them, cranking it up, kiss by kiss, thrust by thrust. Every thrust took them a little higher, her cries driving him on, the bite of her nails edging him closer.

It didn't take long for the simmer in his loins to get to full boil and as the edges of his world started to fray he slipped his hand between them where they were joined and found exactly what he was looking for.

Callie gasped, her eyes springing open as the direct stimulus threw her build-up into warp speed. Part of her wanted to push it away, to make it last, but the woman who had fought hard for her sexual liberation wanted it now. Wanted the pleasure and release *right now*.

So she relaxed into it, let herself go. And then everything clenched tight and she threw her head back and called his name as she bucked hard in his arms. Wave after wave swamped her, stoked by Cade as he rocked and rocked and rocked into her, finding his own release, calling her name, too.

Callie didn't know how long pleasure rained down on her, she just rode it to the end. Till the last ripple had died off and he'd stopped moving. She opened her eyes and looked down to find his forehead resting on her chest right above the unsteady pounding of her heart. His shoulders heaved as if breathing wasn't easy and she shifted against him, her legs still twined round him, his hardness still inside her.

'Thank you,' she said, lifting her hand to push his hair off his forehead. 'You have *no* idea how much I needed that.'

Cade lifted his head off her chest, pleased to see that sexual satisfaction had melded the blue and green of her eyes into one. He smiled then reached behind him and flicked off the taps.

'Oh, I'm not finished with you yet.'

CHAPTER FIVE

CADE WAS HUMMING when he entered the empty hospital lift on Monday morning. He shook his head and smiled as the doors slid shut. Humming? He couldn't remember the last time he'd felt this...light.

He'd forgotten what fun sex was. For too long he'd associated it with the screw-up with Sophie and had tried hard to ignore how much he needed it, how much he'd missed it, setting himself the punishing task of forgoing it in preference to his career.

Yes, it had been a one-off, but man, oh, man, he felt like a million bucks.

The lift stopped and the door opened to admit Natalie Alberts. And not even that could put a damper on his mood.

'Oh, hi, Cade,' she said, giving him a big smile.

'Morning, Natalie.' He smiled back as the doors whispered shut again, his normal wariness around her lost in his happy haze. 'You off to Outpatients, as well?'

She nodded. 'Baby clinic this morning. My favourite part of the week.'

Cade laughed. 'It's nice seeing healthy babies for a change, isn't it?'

They made general conversation to the eighth floor and

as they made their way along the corridors to the rooms they'd been allocated for their outpatient days.

'Well, have a good clinic,' Cade said as they reached his room.

Natalie smiled again. 'Look, Cade…I heard you're on a panel at the symposium on Friday night and I was wondering… Would you like to get a drink and a bite to eat afterwards? My shout.'

Cade felt his smile slip and his mood deflate a little. *Hell.* Natalie Alberts was nothing if not persistent. And, really, prior to Sophie, he would have been totally up for a little dating and some hot sex. Natalie was, after all, very beautiful. But there was a fragility to her that set Cade's Spidey-sense into hyperdrive. Natalie was Sophie mark two and that was to be avoided at all costs.

Now, if she was Callie… Women like Callie knew the score.

Or at least he hoped she did.

Cade searched around for a suitable reply. He knew he should just come out and say, *I'm sorry, I'm not interested.* But that hadn't worked out so well with Sophie and he didn't need any more guilt on his conscience.

But then Callie appeared in his vision, striding down the corridor towards them and looking a lot like salvation to him.

'I'm really sorry, Natalie,' he said, 'but you know the date that Callie bought at the fundraiser? Well, she's calling it in that night,' he lied. A part of him felt bad but he hadn't had a good experience with telling women the truth. 'She's on the panel, too, so we're heading out after the symposium.'

He was pleased to see that Callie was almost level with them now and he smiled at the woman he'd been nude on a beach with not even twenty-four hours ago and said, 'Isn't that right, Callie?'

Callie pulled up beside them feeling completely naked as Cade looked at her with eyes that said, *I know just how to make you come*. 'Isn't what right?'

'You're calling in that date you bought. Friday night. After the symposium.'

Now his eyes were saying, *Back me up*.

Callie read the situation loud and clear and was just too damn happy to tease him. 'Yep, that's right. He'd better be paying, too, for five thousand bucks,' she joked to Natalie. 'I want my money's worth.'

She glanced at Cade and caught the slight eyebrow rise. A sudden tingle between her legs reminded her that she'd most definitely got her pound of flesh. And then some.

'Oh, right,' Natalie said, looking like she wanted the floor to swallow her whole. 'Well, I hope you have a good night. I'm really looking forward to the panel.' She looked at her watch. 'Better fly, first patient in ten minutes.'

They watched her depart for a moment before Callie turned and batted her eyelashes at Cade. 'I'm really looking forward to the panel, Dr Coleman,' she said breathily.

Cade rolled his eyes. 'Shut up.'

Callie grinned. It seemed nothing could wipe the smile off her face this morning. She felt alive, invigorated, rejuvenated. There was just something about a spot of energetic sex with a skilled lover that ironed out all the kinks.

And dinner with her parents had kinked her up a lot.

Yes, she shouldn't have done it with him. And maybe she should be all remorseful this morning and awkward about facing him, especially after she'd upped and left in the middle of the night. But what was done was done and Callie had learned a long time ago to not apologise for her choices.

Sleeping with a colleague wasn't recommended but, then, it had worked out well for her and Alex. Maybe she and Cade were destined to be best friends, as well?

Her smile faltered at the unwelcome thought, although she wasn't entirely sure why. 'For crying out loud,' she said, the teasing note gone from her voice. 'Why don't you just put her out of her misery and tell the poor woman you're not interested?'

Cade shuddered at the thought of having *that* conversation with a woman again. He'd avoided romantic entanglements just so he didn't have to have those types of conversations. 'No, thanks.' He opened his door. 'But thanks for covering for me. I owe you, yet again.'

A rush of memories from last night assailed her and Callie stood in his doorway, blushing. 'Oh, I think you've more than paid your debt.'

Cade grinned as he sat at his desk. When he'd woken up alone that morning he hadn't been sure if he'd been relieved or not. But he *had* determined that he and Callie needed to have a chat to ensure they were both on the same page.

It was a conversation he didn't mind having with Callie because he knew that Callie wasn't a Natalie. Or a Sophie. Callie was a woman who knew how things were. She'd already told him she didn't date because she preferred to cut to the chase with men. So she wasn't likely to make a voodoo doll in his image.

Or take a handful of pills and wind up in hospital.

'About that… Last night…' he said, swinging his chair a little. 'Should we talk about it?'

Callie rolled her eyes as she crossed her arms over her chest. 'You Americans are such talkers.'

He grinned. 'What can I say? We're comfortable with therapy.'

'Well, you've no need to worry,' she said. 'Last night was great—'

'Just great?' he interrupted, with a wounded look.

Callie rolled her eyes. '*Amazingly* great,' she amended, and then grinned when he nodded his approval. 'But I don't want to marry you and have your babies, Cade. I don't even want to date you. I just wanted to have sex with you. Hell, after a meal with my mother, I *needed* to have sex with you. But that's done now.'

Callie faltered at the slightly depressing thought. Cade's brand of sex *had* been spectacular. Not knowing it ever again would be a real shame.

She gave herself a mental shake at the lament. For crying out loud, it was just sex. She could get *that* anywhere. 'So,' she said, picking up the thread of conversation, 'let's just move on.'

Callie remembered telling Alex something very similar. *Let's move on.* Except for some reason saying it to Cade had been a lot harder.

'Okay.' He nodded. 'So…we're good?'

Cade sought the clarification absently. She was wearing a pencil skirt that came to just above her knee and a blouse that buttoned all the way down the front, and the way her arms were crossed enhanced her cleavage nicely. One part of him was relieved that Callie wanted nothing other than sex from him but faced with the reality of 'moving on', of not getting into that blouse again, he wasn't so sure.

'Absolutely,' she agreed, her gaze falling to the way he wore his tie all pulled loose. She had a vision of walking over and fixing it for him, walking between his legs right into his personal space as she leaned over and lowly slid the knot into place.

And then another vision took over. Her stripping it off him altogether, tying him to the chair with it, climbing onto his lap, straddling him… She jumped when the phone on his desk rang, and blinked rapidly to dispel the inappropriate sexual fantasy.

'I'll see you later,' she said briskly, giving a little wave at him before hightailing it away from the temptation of Cade and his tie.

Friday rolled around quickly. Callie only caught glimpses of Cade for the rest of the week, for which her sanity was entirely grateful. She didn't usually fantasise about men she'd slept with—she just *moved on*—but Cade was in her head a lot.

And then, with only a few hours to go until she was due to sit on the panel, he appeared by her side. She was on the NICU re-intubating a thirty-weeker who had failed extubation. He'd struggled for the first two hours after coming off support and had continued to struggle with four hours of non-invasive CPAP. A chest X-ray had revealed a left-sided collapse.

Callie was aware of Cade the second he neared her but she was focused on the view of the vocal cords down the laryngoscope and wasn't taking her eyes off them for a second. 'Tube, please,' she said, tuning out the noise of shrieking alarms and the palpable tension all around her.

A nurse beside her handed the endotracheal tube and within seconds Callie had it in place. 'I'm in,' she said, withdrawing the blade and the introducer from inside the tube. She held the tube in place while another nurse connected the re-breather bag to the end of the tube and puffed in some gentle breaths.

With her free hand, Callie placed the earpieces of her stethoscope into her ears and placed the bell on the baby's chest, listening all over for equal air entry.

'Okay, let's get it secured and get an X-ray,' she said.

Only then did she turn her head to look at Cade. The first thing she noticed was that damn crooked tie. 'You bored, Dr Coleman?' she asked, her fingers still firmly holding the unsecured tube while a nurse stuck tape to the baby's face, preparing to anchor the tube. Their sleeves touched and Callie's arm tingled in response. 'Needed a little excitement?'

Cade chuckled. 'No, thanks, I can do without that kind of excitement.' The unconscious baby was looking nice and pink now that oxygen was being adequately exchanged but hadn't looked so good a few moments ago.

'All in a day's work,' Callie said, as she shifted her fingers slightly to avoid getting them taped to the tube.

'I have a case I want to talk to you about,' he said.

'Okay, I'll probably be half an hour.'

Cade nodded. 'Page me when you're done.'

It was actually an hour before she and Cade got together in his office. She'd had to pull the tube back half a centimetre and retape it, put in another IV then talk to the parents.

And he hadn't even managed to straighten his damn tie.

'What have you got?' she asked, determined to be all business and not think about his tie or straddling him in his chair.

'Twenty-three-week spina bifida,' he said, pointing to the monitor on his desk.

Callie was careful to keep to her side as she inspected the image on the screen. 'Myelomeningocele?'

Cade nodded. 'A large one.'

'Yes,' she said, as she looked at the large sac-like lesion protruding out of the baby's back from where the neural tube had failed to close during earlier foetal development. Inside it was the spinal cord and nerves, which were getting progressively more damaged.

'Trudy, the mother, is young and healthy—it's her first baby. She and Elliot, the baby's father, have been researching their options since diagnosis on the nineteen-week scan. They've rung several doctors in the US and finally spoke with Alex, who passed on my name. I think, if everything else plays out, she's a good candidate for foetal repair.'

Callie looked at him, the enormity of what he was asking finally making her forget his tie. All babies with spina bifida who required surgical correction were operated on immediately *after* birth to repair their spinal defect, but by then the damage was already done, affecting muscle, organs and bodily function below the level of the lesion.

But it was possible now to operate prenatally, to correct the lesion while the baby was still in the womb to try and prevent the ongoing damage that occurred due to exposure of nerve tissue in utero. They couldn't correct the damage that had already been done, but they could prevent further damage.

It had been performed countless times and for many years in the US. It would be a first at the Gold Coast City Hospital.

'Right.'

'Are you freaking out?' he asked.

Callie shook her head. 'No.' In fact she could feel a tiny little trill of anticipation. 'That's why you're part of our team. That's why I recommended you to the board.'

'Oh, I thought it was because Alex asked you,' he teased.

She glanced up from the screen. 'It was. But you being a prenatal surgeon made my decision a lot easier.'

Callie straightened, her mind racing ahead to what was involved. 'What do we do first?'

'We need to get a whole raft of diagnostic tests done.

A detailed ultrasound, for a start. We'll need to know the exact size of the lesion, the segments of the spine that are involved, degree of hydrocephalus and any evidence of paralysis. I'll need a foetal MRI and a foetal echocardiogram.'

Callie nodded. 'We'll get Sam Webster involved.' Sam was the chief paediatric cardiologist. 'And Diane Coulter can handle the lesion.' She was the top paediatric neurosurgeon at the hospital and had performed countless myelomeningocele repairs on newborns in her stellar career.

'What have you told the mother... It's Trudy, right?'

He nodded. 'Trudy and Elliot are both here. Mainly we've talked about what the condition is and the pros and cons of foetal surgery. They're very keen to go ahead with it but they know a whole stack of tests need to be done first before they're deemed to be good candidates for prenatal surgical intervention. I've arranged for them to come in on Monday and have all the imaging done.'

'You stressed we won't know for sure until we have those results?'

Cade nodded. 'Don't worry. I'm not going to give them any false hope, Callie.'

'And from there, if the imaging is supportive of operating in utero, where do you want to go?'

'I'll get all my ducks in a row with the different specialist teams and we'll set up a multi-disciplinary meeting with Trudy and Elliot Monday afternoon. If they still want to go ahead, we'll do it.'

'How soon could it all be set up, do you think?'

'We'll need to move quickly on this. Hopefully by the end of next week,' he said. 'The baby will be twenty-four weeks by then and viable if delivery becomes necessary.'

Callie sat on the nearby chair. 'Wow,' she said, looking at him swivelling calmly in his chair and exuding absolute confidence.

Cade grinned. 'Something for us to discuss on the panel tonight, I think.'

Callie nodded. 'I think it will fit quite nicely into the topic.'

Which was a massive understatement if ever there was one. The panel, called *Twenty-First Century Foetal Medicine*, seemed purpose-built for the proposed surgery. Certainly the audience of specialists was fascinated by the idea, and the panel ran over time by twenty minutes as Cade answered question after question.

Callie thanked her lucky stars there was a table to hide behind as she squirmed in her seat. Cade's accent and his breadth of knowledge plucked at her body like she was a guitar and he was strumming her strings.

She was a doctor, for crying out loud! She was surrounded by intelligent people. *Every day.* Three of them, in fact, were sitting right beside her on this very panel. But every time Cade opened his mouth and said something in his confident American drawl, her belly heated a little bit more and she shifted restlessly to ease the ache that had taken up permanent residence between her legs.

It was a relief when it was over and she was able to put some distance between them. She'd had a long day and was obviously sleep deprived. Having come straight from work to the five-star Surfers Paradise hotel where the symposium was being held, all she wanted was a shower and her bed. She was on call over the weekend, too, and that was always full-on.

She was gathering her stuff when Cade excused himself from the crowd of people milling around him. He made a beeline for her and asked, 'You want a ride home?'

Callie looked up at him as she hauled her bag off the floor. He was tall and sure and sexy with his tie askew and his hair all ruffled, and she thought, *Hell, yeah, but not the way you mean*.

Cade had always been up front about not wanting to be in a relationship. As had she. They were a one-off deal. No matter how much she wanted to take him home and tie him to her bedposts.

'Cade…Callie.'

Callie turned towards the voice to find Natalie Alberts approaching. She was looking pretty and feminine in a floaty dress. She herself felt decidedly *not*, in a pair of tailored trousers and a plain button-up blouse.

'That was so fascinating,' Natalie enthused. 'The potential outcomes you spoke about are incredible.'

Cade smiled politely. 'Yes. I've seen amazing results.'

'I'd love to be able to watch the surgery,' she said.

'You should be able to watch it from the gallery,' he said. 'I think it'll be kind of full but I'm sure you could squeeze in.'

Callie almost rolled her eyes as Natalie beamed, obviously taking it as some personal compliment.

'So where are you two off to now for your date?'

Callie blinked at the question. She'd forgotten about that. From the stunned look on Cade's face he had, too.

'Oh…we're just going to…go down to the bar,' Callie said, looking at Cade for confirmation.

'Yes,' he agreed. 'We're just going to grab something to eat there. Nothing formal.'

'Oh, excellent,' Natalie said. 'I'm meeting some colleagues down there now.'

Callie kept her smile in place. *Of course she was.*

'I have to say, Cade…' Natalie smiled, her long blond hair falling in a curtain to her shoulders '…I think it's so sweet that you're going through with this thing. You've been such a good sport about it.'

Callie frowned at Natalie. So the frail blonde had some teeth. 'I coughed up five thousand dollars for him,' she butted in, folding her arms. 'There's nothing sweet about it. He owes me.'

Cade smiled at Callie's irritation. 'It's no hardship,' he assured Natalie, his tongue firmly in his cheek.

'Oh, yes, but we all know that these things are just formalities,' Natalie dismissed with a laugh. 'It's all about the donation, really.'

'Not for me it's not,' Callie said, gritting her teeth. 'I fully intend to get my five thousand out of him.'

Natalie looked put out and Callie felt a moment's triumph. How dared the other woman suggest that Cade was just being a *good sport* and humouring her with a date! She had a good mind to rip his shirt off and show her the scratch marks on Cade's back.

Show her she'd already got more than her money's worth.

'Anyway...' Cade said to Natalie as he grabbed hold of Callie's elbow, 'I guess we'll be seeing you down there.'

'Yes,' she said. 'I'll catch you later.'

Callie watched her walk away. 'Cow,' she muttered under her breath.

Cade chuckled. 'She sure pushed your buttons.'

Callie wanted to say, *No, you're doing that*, but refrained. 'Yeah, well, that's because I'm dog-tired. I need a shower. I need my bed.'

Cade shook his head, mainly for something to do other than offering to help her wash her back. God knew, he hadn't managed to have a shower in his own place yet without thinking about how he'd taken her against the tiles.

'Too bad,' he said. 'We have a date to go on.'

'No,' she protested.

'Oh, yes,' he said, as he ushered her towards the lift. 'Just an hour then I'll take you home. Just for appearances' sake.'

Callie was too tired to fight him *and* her bodily urges. It might just be easier to give in to them and let them have a bit longer in his company.

Bloody demanding things, urges.

The bar wasn't too crowded when they arrived. Cade secured them a low round table just big enough to place drinks on with trendy tub chairs near one of the huge windows that overlooked the ocean. He ordered a selection of tapas at the bar and bought her a red wine and a beer for himself.

'Thank you,' she said, as he sat and she took a fortifying sip as the minimal distance between them closed even further with the bulk of his presence.

She could easily slide her hand onto his thigh, should she be so inclined.

Callie took another sip and looked around, reminding herself why she was there. 'Natalie and her pals are at three o'clock,' she said to him. 'Ringside seats.'

Cade glanced over. Natalie smiled and waved and he raised his glass to her and her group. 'She *is* persistent, isn't she?'

'Uh-huh,' Callie said, taking another sip.

'Okay, then,' he said, resigning himself to his fate. 'So, let's do this thing.'

Callie frowned. 'What thing?'

'The date.'

'Well, I'm going to have to be guided by you,' she said. 'Because, seriously, I haven't dated in a *lo-o-ng* time.'

Since high school, to be exact.

Cade unknotted his tie even more and undid his top two buttons. Callie shook her head as she watched him. 'What?' he asked.

Her fingers itched to strip his shirt off him altogether so she gripped her glass harder. 'Why do you even wear one?' she demanded. 'It's always half-off anyway.'

'It's a nod to the dress code but it's kind of my own personal protest. I hate the damn things.'

'Well, take it off, then,' she said, and this time she couldn't resist. She put her glass on the table, reached across the narrow space separating them and made short work of it. The satisfying zip as she pulled it out of his collar went straight to her belly.

'I am perfectly capable of taking my own tie off.' He laughed as she stuffed it in his shirt pocket.

'I know that,' she said, putting her hands firmly back on her glass lest they decide his buttons could do with some undoing, too. 'I know you're perfectly capable of taking *all* your clothes off,' she said, trying to say it with a nonchalance she didn't feel.

'But we have an audience and a woman touching a man's tie hints at intimacy. Which will probably send a louder message to a...certain someone than this stupid fake date.'

Cade laughed. 'That's taking it a bit far, isn't it?'

Callie shook her head and deliberately leaned towards him, hoping to convey intimacy. Which was surprisingly easy. Too easy. But pretending to him that she was *faking* that intimacy was harder.

'Go ahead and laugh,' she murmured, smiling at him like a lover. Which she was. *Or had been.* 'While Natalie thinks that you're just humouring me, you're still going to be number one on her hot-docs-to-marry list. It pays to be convincing.'

Cade was taken aback not just by the sense of her words but also by the look on her face. The Mona Lisa smile, her lowered lashes, her parted lips.

'Is that so?' he asked, as his gazed dropped to her mouth.

'Uh-huh,' she said, her smile flirty now, reaching all the way to her eyes.

Suddenly he couldn't have agreed more. He leaned forward, covering the short space separating them, and kissed her.

She was right—it did pay to be convincing.

CHAPTER SIX

FOR LONG, DIZZYING SECONDS Callie leaned into the kiss. The bar noise around them faded and it was just her and him and a truly breathtaking assault on her senses. Long and slow and wicked, it erased all thought from her head. All she knew was the smell and the taste of him. They filled her up until she was drunk with the power of them.

She was so intoxicated she didn't even notice when he eased up and pulled back. 'Convincing enough, do you think?' he murmured, his mouth still close, his lips almost brushing hers with every movement.

Callie slowly opened her eyes. Her peripheral vision kicked in and the bar noise started to filter back. With a concerted effort she yanked her hormones into line and forced her head back into the game. She smiled at him, keeping her mouth exactly where it was. 'I think that'll do it.'

Then, fighting the urge to clear her throat of its sudden affliction of huskiness, she casually sat back into the cushioned embrace of the chair.

Far away from the temptation of his mouth.

She deliberately took her time crossing her legs ensuring that her foot, clad in a cute kitten heel, angled towards his outstretched leg, lightly brushing against his calf.

Cade felt a bolt of heat travel from his calf straight up

his inside leg right into his underpants. It joined the other one that had arrowed down from his mouth during that hot little kiss.

He raised an eyebrow. 'You do that well. You *should* date. You're a natural.'

Callie shrugged. 'As long as Natalie's convinced.'

Cade looked around him at the speculative glances being thrown their way. 'I should think everyone in this bar is convinced. I think you and I are going to be hot gossip come Monday.'

'Oh, joy,' she muttered, leaning forward to pick up her glass of wine for another swallow.

A sinking feeling settled low in Callie's gut. She'd been the focus of town gossip after her marriage had broken up and it hadn't been pleasant. Since then she'd gone to great pains to be very discreet with her liaisons. And her no-dating policy had certainly helped. No one, for example, had ever known the true extent of her relationship with Alex.

So, why was it she seemed to lose her head around his brother?

'Oh, come on, it's not that bad,' Cade cajoled. Gossip wasn't his favourite thing in the world and he'd been grateful that none had got out about him and Sophie, especially after she'd been admitted to hospital.

But there *were* worse things in life.

That was easy for people to forget in a world that focused on trivialities. But Cade never forgot it. He and Alex had come from a place that had been the very definition of worse.

'Oh, yeah? Just you wait. They'll have us dating next.'

Cade chuckled. 'Wasn't that the object of this?'

'No, the object was for *Natalie* to think we're an item. Not the entire bloody hospital.'

'Is that so bad?'

Callie shot him an exasperated look. 'Are you crazy? They'll have us married off within a couple of months.'

A waiter arrived with their tapas and Cade was glad for the interruption even if it did mean that she withdrew her foot from where it had been lazily circling his calf. It gave the plan forming in his head time to percolate. He waited until they'd both tucked into the goat's cheese and caramelised onion tartlets before saying any more.

'It might be good cover for both of us, you know,' he said. 'Pretending to be a couple.'

Callie almost choked on her mouthful of cheese and onion. She stared at him nonplussed but he just looked back at her calmly, like this conversation hadn't just sunk into the ninth circle of hell.

'Good for you maybe,' she snorted. 'You don't want be involved with anyone at all so it's kind of perfect cover for you. But I, on the other hand, both want, like and *need* to be with a man every now and then. *Dating* you is really going to cramp my style.'

'That's fine.' He shrugged. 'I'm sure I could be persuaded to put out every now and then.'

Callie blinked at the casual statement. Regular sex with Cade. Her belly clenched at the possibilities. But that smacked of a relationship to her—even if it was a fake one. The last time she'd been in a relationship it had ended in a divorce. 'Gee…thanks. Don't do me any favours.'

Cade took a sip of his beer. 'Come on, Callie, think about it. It would probably only take a few dates in the beginning to get the rumour mill churning then there'd probably be minimal upkeep.'

She shook her head. 'No.'

'Would I be so bad to date?' he asked, feigning a wounded look.

Callie glared at him. 'I don't want to date you, or anyone else, for that matter. We've been over this already—I just don't see the point in it.'

Cade frowned. 'The point?'

Callie nodded. 'I'm not going to date anyone I don't want to sleep with. So if we both know how the date's going to end, why not just cut to the chase?'

After that rather emasculating statement Cade was pleased he knew that Callie didn't carry over her cutting-to-the-chase theories in bed. 'I don't know,' he said. 'How about the anticipation? The dance? The slow, delicious build-up?'

Callie picked up her wineglass. 'That's what foreplay's for.'

Cade blinked. 'Wow.' He shook his head. 'You really should have been born a man.'

Callie quirked an eyebrow at him. 'I'm not going to apologise for knowing what I want and going after it. Men, as you so aptly point out, do it all the time. Isn't that what you were like before your sudden celibacy?'

'No,' Cade said, offended. 'I dated. A lot, actually. I'm a damn good date if you must know. Sure, it may have been a means to an end but I enjoyed the anticipation. The dance. And sometimes it didn't go my way. And that was fine, too.'

Cade's formative sexual experiences with his Beverly Hills cougars had been a good training ground for him. Older women liked to tutor and he had absorbed every last pointer from where women liked to be touched to how they liked to be treated.

She raised her glass to him. 'Well, good for you,' Callie said. 'It's just not for me.'

'I bet you it could be,' Cade said as he picked up a stuffed mushroom. 'I bet you and I could fake-date very impressively.'

Callie looked at him. A smear of buttery sauce deco-rated one corner of his mouth and the urge to lean right over and lick it off shook her to the core. To paste it all over his body and lick that off, too. In fact, she wanted to drag him and the tapas plate up to the nearest unoccupied hotel room and do it right now.

She'd *never* had problems walking away from a hook-up before, but for some reason Cade was different.

Which only solidified her convictions. It was time to lay her cards on the table.

But first, that sauce had to go.

She picked up a napkin, reached over and wiped at it. Not a sexy little dab that lovers employed—that would fool Natalie—more like a motherly swipe. But at least it was gone. *And she hadn't used her tongue.*

She scrunched the napkin in her hand. 'I'm not going on a date with you. I'm not going to even *pretend* to go on a date with you,' she said. 'Because I know where it'll end up. Back in your bed. Or my bed. Or the bloody shower again. I don't know why but my body doesn't seem to be satisfied with just one night where you're concerned. And that's just not the way I roll.'

Cade felt her very matter-of-fact admission right down to his marrow. It simmered in his cells and tingled in the scratch marks that were now only faint pink lines down his back.

She wanted him again.

That would be bad if it wasn't so horny.

Bad because it would be straying into fling territory and the last time he'd had a fling it hadn't ended so well.

Horny because having a woman be so up front about her desires, so honest about her attraction, was flat-out arousing.

It was also vaguely insulting that Callie thought he'd

be such a pushover. She was so damn sure of herself sitting opposite him, cradling her wineglass, confident in her body and her sexuality.

Which also happened to be very horny.

'Well, now,' he said, easing himself back into his chair, 'just because *you* have no self-control, it doesn't mean I don't.' He smiled. 'I do believe I've turned you down before. I'm pretty sure I can do it again.'

Callie couldn't believe what she was hearing. That someone so experienced with life's pitfalls could be this naive. Whatever else they had between them, they had chemistry to burn. That was *always* hard to turn down.

She leaned forward a little, her elbows on her knees, her wineglass dangling from one hand. The movement squeezed her breasts together nicely and gave him a good view down her top. Her blouse may have been plain but her cleavage was spectacular.

'So,' she murmured, running a fingertip around the rim of her wineglass, 'you think we can go on a date and just talk about everyday getting-to-know-you type things after a dirty ocean swim, a quickie against the wall of your shower and two hours in your bed and *not* end up back in it at the end of the night?'

Cade swallowed at the deliberately provocative language and the come-on in her actions. But he was hardly some youth still wet behind the ears. He'd spent the last few months shoring up his defences against women and he'd got pretty damn good at it.

He was more than a match for Callie.

'I do. I absolutely do. I promise you I can get through a date without laying a finger on you.'

She smiled at him sweetly. 'But what if I *want* you to lay a finger on me?'

He smiled back. 'Then I'll be strong enough for both of us.'

Callie raised an eyebrow. *This ought to be good.* She didn't like to boast, but she was pretty damn hard to resist when she went into seduction mode. She may have failed miserably at seducing her husband but she hadn't failed since and she wasn't about to start!

The whole stupid premise would be worth it, just to take *Mr Willpower* down a peg or two.

'Fine,' she said. 'When and where?'

'No time like the present. We're on a date already, right?'

Callie wasn't exactly dressed for seduction but one thing she'd learned about every man, bar one: they weren't that fussy. She smiled and sat back. 'Okay,' she said as she did a slow lazy cross of her legs, her foot nudging close to his leg again, and was satisfied to see Cade's gaze stray to the way her trousers pulled across her thighs.

'You go first,' she prompted. 'You're the date aficionado. Impress me.'

'Okay. How about a quick word association as an icebreaker?'

Callie lifted a shoulder. 'As long as I get to turn the tables.'

'Sure,' he murmured. 'Turn around's fair play.'

He reached forward and popped another stuffed mushroom into his mouth, watching her thoughtfully as he ate. She seemed very sure of herself. How much would it take to rattle her?

'Doctor,' he said. An easy one to open with.

She smiled. 'Who.'

Cade laughed. Okay, that he hadn't expected. 'Hospital.'

'Patients.'

'NICU,' he shot back.

'Babies.'

'Emergency.'

'Airway.'

'Alex,' he said.

Callie didn't falter. 'Friend. Best friend.'

'Broken Hill,' Cade continued, inordinately pleased at her quick-fire response to his brother's name.

'Home.'

Callie blinked at the answer that had fallen from her lips. Broken Hill hadn't been *home* for over a decade. She didn't think of it like that. It hadn't felt like home since before her divorce.

Cade raised an eyebrow. 'Ooh, Freudian or what?'

She rolled her eyes. 'Have you finished yet?'

He shook his head. 'Joe.'

Callie sought through a hundred different responses. Teenage sweetheart. Farmer. Best footy player in town. Good friend. Family man. Husband. Provider.

Distant. Messed up. Sexually dysfunctional.

'Ex.'

Cade nodded. She'd taken a while to find that word and there'd been a hell of a lot going on behind her eyes as she'd looked for it.

'My turn,' Callie said, jumping into the sudden quiet. There'd been too much navel-gazing for her.

'Should I be afraid?' he asked.

Callie leaned forward again, aware of the slight gape of her buttons at her cleavage. Aware he was aware of it, too. 'Very.'

'Be gentle,' he joked.

Not on your life. 'Beach,' she said with a smile.

Cade chuckled as she laid down her first ace. 'Shark.'

Callie raised an eyebrow. So, he was determined not to play? 'Shower.'

He shook his head at her persistence. 'Hot.'

'Tiles.'

His gaze locked with hers. 'Very hot.'

'Scratches.'

Cade didn't look away. 'Really freaking hot.'

'Underwear.'

He gave a half laugh as he broke eye contact. 'Beach.'

Callie smiled. *On a beach probably somewhere on the other side of the Pacific by now.* 'Alex,' she said.

Like Callie, Cade didn't hesitate. 'Brother.' Although he'd almost said stepbrother from habit. But they'd got past that. They'd certainly been through more than a lot of brothers had.

'Childhood.'

Cade glanced at her as the softer note of her voice called to him. He hesitated, trying to find the right adjective. 'Tumultuous.'

Callie nodded. Yes. From what she'd gleaned from Alex, he and Cade had been through some very rough times. 'You give in or you want me to go on?' she asked.

He narrowed his eyes at her. 'That depends. What's your next shot?'

'Seaweed.'

Cade laughed, holding his hands up in surrender. 'Enough.' He took a sip of his beer, looking at her over the frosty rim. 'See, that wasn't so hard, was it?'

'Oh, no,' she agreed innocently. 'I can *totally* see why women dig this…icebreaker. Is that what you called it?'

Cade regarded her smart, sassy mouth. She really was a damn near irresistible package. He could see why Alex spoke so highly of her. 'Yes. We have a bit of a laugh and everyone relaxes.'

Callie lifted her glass. 'You know wine works just as well, right?'

He shook his head. 'You Aussies. No finesse.'

He said 'Aussies' in that soft American way, pronouncing the 'A' with a whole lot of breath behind it instead of with a harsh almost 'O' as Australians usually did. It sounded foreign to her ears but also deliciously exotic. 'So what's your next move?' she enquired sweetly.

'We move on to the usual stuff. Movies, books, television.'

'Work?'

He shook his head. 'Not usually. If she's not in the field and wants to talk about hers then sure.'

Callie frowned. 'But you don't talk about yours?' She didn't know what she'd talk to men about seventy-five per cent of the time if it wasn't for work. And the other twenty-five per cent? That required not very many words at all.

'Not really.'

'Why not? You're a prenatal surgeon, for crying out loud. Chicks must dig that.'

He shrugged. 'I'd rather not spend a date talking about myself.'

There was more—Callie could tell. Why was he reluctant to talk about a job that was seriously cool? He did something very few doctors on the planet did. He was like an astronaut, for crying out loud—exploring unchartered territory.

In fact, it was downright heroic. Why wouldn't you sell that to someone you were trying to get between the sheets?

'And?'

Cade drained his beer, looking into the bottom of his empty glass. 'My job varies. There are days that aren't exactly sunbeams and glitter, as you would know.' He looked at her. 'I'd rather not get into any of that with someone who doesn't really understand how that feels.'

Callie was taken aback by his heartfelt honesty. She

knew those days. When things didn't work out. When no bit of machinery or hotshot prenatal surgeon in the world could prevent the tragic inevitability of a baby's death. When life support failed. When hope and optimism and prayers all failed.

When you had to look into a mother's eyes and tell her that her baby was gone.

And he was right. Only people who knew what it was like to have that talk could truly understand how it took a tiny piece out of you every time.

How it left you just a little bit the poorer.

She nodded. 'Of course.'

The waiter came and cleared away their food, giving them a break from the sombre mood. They ordered another round of drinks and when the waiter left Cade looked at Callie and asked her the question she'd avoided answering the other night.

'So how *did* you become a doctor without any support or encouragement from your family?'

Callie regarded him steadily. She didn't normally talk about this stuff with anyone but his admission just now had touched her. She found herself wanting to tell him.

'When I was at school I had a part-time job at the local chemist's. John Barry Pharmacy.' She smiled at the memory of it. 'Mr Barry was a really great old guy. One of those the-sky's-the-limit kind of people, you know?'

Cade nodded. He knew. Not that there'd been any Mr Barrys in his life.

'I did really well at school and he kept saying I should go to university and study medicine because I was smart and really good with the patients. But...'

Callie stalled. But all she'd wanted to do was marry Joe and live on his farm and have a family. And her mother had wanted it, too. So two months after leaving school, and two weeks after turning eighteen, she had done just that. With everybody's blessing.

And she'd been the happiest eighteen-year-old on the planet.

The waiter arrived and put their drinks down. Callie took a long, grateful swallow of her wine.

'But?' Cade prompted as Callie stared into her glass.

Callie lifted her eyes. No doubt Cade had always been driven.... Would he understand? 'I wasn't particularly ambitious back then. I...wasn't ready to do anything about it. So I worked there full time after I finished school and he slowly chipped away at me until...'

My marriage fell apart and my husband left me.

Callie swallowed. 'One day I was ready. And I took the plunge and he helped me apply to unis and for scholarships and...I got in. On a full scholarship because I was a rural student. And I grabbed the opportunity with both hands and have never looked back.'

Cade nodded. He wasn't fooled by her abridged version but it was a start. 'You were lucky to have had a Mr Barry,' he said.

Callie nodded. God alone knew where she'd have been now without him. Still living in Broken Hill in the shadow of her failed marriage probably. 'I owe him a lot,' she agreed. One of the few times she'd been home in thirteen years had been for his funeral.

Cade smiled at her and Callie smiled back, aware that he hadn't been as lucky as her. 'What about you?' she asked. 'How'd a kid from a troubled background get to become a hotshot prenatal surgeon?'

'Ah,' Cade said, taking a pull of his beer, 'again, I try

to keep the dates about the woman. Chicks love talking about themselves.'

Callie snorted. This *chick* didn't. 'Oh, no,' she said. 'I told you mine. And turn around's fair play, remember.'

Cade smiled at her using his words against him. He regarded her for a moment or two, trying to figure out where to start.

'I think I always had this…hankering to help kids. They're so vulnerable…. I wanted to give them a voice and a chance of beating the odds. But it wasn't until after I got out of home and…' *started making some serious money from some very appreciative women, all old enough to be my mother* '…came into some money…that I realised I wanted to be a doctor. That I wanted to start at the beginning. *From* the beginning. Giving vulnerable babies the best chance at life.'

Callie frowned. 'Alex didn't mention you came into money.'

Cade gave a half laugh. 'I didn't. Not like that. I… earned it. Sort of.'

Rich, bored women paid their hot pool boys a lot of money. More than he'd ever seen in his life.

And he'd been very good at his job.

'It's…kind of complicated.'

Callie smiled and raised her glass. 'Now, *that* I understand.'

She took a sip of her wine and then promptly yawned.

'Is this date boring you?' He smiled.

Callie laughed. 'I'm beat. I'm sorry. I'm on call this weekend, too.' She placed her barely touched glass of wine on the table. 'I think I need to call it a night.'

Cade grinned triumphantly. 'See, there you go. You got through a whole date without jumping me.'

Callie shot him a direct look. 'Don't count your chickens. Didn't you say you were giving me a lift home?'

Cade's smiled faded. 'Sure.'

Callie flicked an appreciative glance over his body. 'Oh, the possibilities.'

Callie kept herself in check during the car trip and the ride up in the lift. Cade had eyed her warily, even more so since she'd come out of the hotel bathroom with two buttons popped on her blouse and her hair pulled out of its ponytail. Having him on guard made it harder for her but she wasn't one to give up easily.

When they got to her door he stopped as she unlocked it and pushed it open. 'Wanna come in for a nightcap?' she suggested cheekily.

Cade smiled. 'No, thanks.'

'Are you sure?' she asked as she backed into her apartment, pulling her blouse out of her trousers and starting to undo the remaining buttons.

Cade laughed this time. 'Nice try, but no.'

Not to be deterred, Callie popped the last button and parted the blouse to reveal a gauzy bra with purple satin trim and a diamanté twinkling from the cleavage. Her nipples were clearly visible—it left nothing to the imagination.

'Really?' she murmured.

All the moisture in Cade's mouth evaporated as he remembered how her nipples had tasted. How good they'd felt against his tongue. His loins stirred and he held on to the doorframe just in case. 'I thought you were beat,' he said, his eyes roaming over every millimetre of exposed skin.

Callie loved how he looked at her breasts like he wanted to devour them. Her belly heated and the now familiar ache between her legs started up again. 'There's nothing like the bone-deep satisfaction of a good orgasm to help you get a good night's sleep, I always say.'

Cade dropped his head from side to side, his fingers tightening on the architrave. *Truer words had never been spoken.* 'You are evil,' he muttered.

Callie smiled triumphantly. 'I can be. I can be whatever you want me to be.'

Cade growled under his breath as the stirring became something much more. 'Goodnight, Callie,' he said.

And then with supreme willpower he pushed away from the door and headed for his apartment.

And a cold shower.

Callie stared at the empty space in her doorway where Cade had been only seconds before, looking at her like he'd sell his soul for a night with a little bit of evil. And now there was just dead air and the horrible fluorescent lights of the hallway.

The buzz in her blood became a hum of disappointment. She squeezed her thighs together as the tingle between her legs burned with no regard for how its chance at satisfaction had just walked away.

Again.

Cade Coleman, she decided as she pushed the door shut, was hard on her ego. Had she not already known him carnally—extremely carnally—his *second* rejection of her might have been a devastating blow to someone who *needed* male appreciation more than most.

But she did.

So her ego was going to have to be satisfied with the frank desire she'd seen heating his whisky gaze.

Something she'd never seen in Joe's eyes.

Callie wandered over to the huge sliding doors that

opened onto a small, aged balcony. One of the few advantages of living in a positively ancient apartment block, built way back before the skyscrapers of the strip could ever have been imagined, was its prime position with a one-eighty-degree ocean view.

The breeze blew the loose edges of her blouse open as she stepped out and she welcomed the cooling effect on her heated skin. But the heat still simmered in her blood and there was only one thing that was going to satisfy it.

She tapped her nails against the railing in frustration. Cade wanted her. She knew it. He was just in denial.

And if that wasn't a challenge, she didn't know what was.

CHAPTER SEVEN

CALLIE JAMMED HER HAND between the closing lift doors just as they were about to shut altogether and deprive her of the very fine sight of Cade all alone inside.

They jerked open and Cade quirked an eyebrow at her. 'In a hurry?' he asked.

'No.' She smiled. 'Just wanted to get you all alone.'

They'd spent the last hour in a multi-disciplinary meeting with Trudy and Elliot, talking about the options for their baby. It had been an invigorating discussion and the decision had been made to go ahead and do the lesion repair as soon as possible.

But Callie had found it hard to concentrate. Not even a hellish weekend on call had managed to cool the simmer in her blood and one look at Cade in the meeting, being all hotshot surgeon, had set it boiling.

'I want another date,' Callie said after the doors had slid shut. 'How about tonight?'

Cade grinned. 'You *do* like to cut to the chase, don't you?'

'You get what you see with me. You want pretence, you're looking at the wrong woman.'

Cade had to admit it was one of her most attractive features. Sophie hadn't been straight with him. Not about her plans for him or about her contraceptive cover.

Of course, the fact that Callie also looked hot in her ponytail and black sleeveless dress added to her allure. The dress had a utilitarian look to it with pockets and press studs everywhere his eyes skimmed—breast pockets, hip pockets, pockets over her very delectable backside.

'I thought you didn't date?' he said, keeping his hands wrapped firmly around the railing behind him.

Callie shrugged. 'Would you rather I said, "I want to have another round of sex with you—how about tonight?"'

Cade laughed. 'I think I could read the subtext.'

'So what do you say?'

Cade regarded her for a moment. Callie was great. Hot and sexy and funny. But she was also seriously screwed up. Which was fine—he wasn't exactly emotionally healthy, either. But she was too nice a person to be hiding behind this façade of hers. He wasn't sure what had happened to turn her life into a series of brief, meaningless hook-ups but she was missing out on some of the best times life could offer.

And for some reason he couldn't bear the thought of that.

Not to mention having Callie as a fake romantic interest was a potential win-win for him.

The lift dinged. 'Well?' she said as the doors opened.

Cade let go of the railing. 'Yes, to the date. Maybe, to the sex,' he said as he exited and headed for his office.

Callie blinked at his back. *Damn the man.* 'What exactly does that mean?' she called after him as she scurried to catch up.

Cade was aware of her at his elbow but he kept his gaze fixed firmly ahead. Given that he hadn't been able to get her semi-striptease out of his head all weekend he figured he didn't need to look at a dress that had *access* written all over it.

'You want to use my body for your sexual pleasure, then I demand to be wooed first,' Cade clarified, a smile playing on his lips at his genius plan.

Callie stumbled. *'Wooed?'*

'Yes,' he said.

'What do you mean, *wooed*? Can you...elaborate?'

Cade reached his door and pulled up in front of it. She was frowning up at him and she looked so damn cute he nearly kissed her right then and there. 'I propose we go on...a dozen dates,' he said. 'No kissing. No sex.'

He pressed a finger to her mouth when she went to protest. They were soft and full and a flash of how they'd looked in the shadows last night as she'd exposed herself to him hit him right in the gut. He let his hand drop to his side.

'As I said last night—I'm not going to lay a finger on you. Then, after the twelfth date, and only then will I have sex with you.'

Callie's mouth was still tingling from the press of his finger. 'But...why?'

Cade laughed at her confusion. 'Because it could be fun? And maybe we both learn something about ourselves?' She still looked nonplussed. 'It's my best offer.'

Callie glared at Cade. Damn him for making this so complicated. It was only sex, for crying out loud. Something they'd both already proved they were exceptionally good at.

Especially together.

If she hadn't wanted him so much she could barely see straight, she'd have told him to go and do something quite anatomically impossible with himself. Instead, she did a quick calculation in her head. If she played hardball she could probably have him in four dates—five at the outside.

And if she tried to get through *them* as quickly as possible...

Callie folded her arms. 'Five,' she said.

Cade shook his head. 'Ten.'

'Seven,' she countered.

'Nine.'

She smiled. 'Eight.'

Cade had figured she'd try to beat him down and eight was a number he could live with. Hopefully after eight dates she might change her mind about the institution. Hook-ups and one-night stands weren't exactly a safe way to live your life. That's what dating was for—to weed out the crazies.

Not that it was foolproof!

After eight dates he'd probably be ready to burst anyway. He was pretty sure she was going to play it dirty and there was only so much provocation a healthy male could stand.

Her dress today was a good case in point.

Cade held out his hand. 'You've got a deal.'

Callie shook. 'Tonight?' Might as well get this farce started.

He nodded as he released her hand. 'Bowling. I'll pick you up at seven.'

'Bowling it is,' she murmured, then turned to leave.

He watched as she pivoted. The pockets on her ass pulled nicely and the funky cork heels of her pumps did incredible things for her calves. 'Nice of you to wear that dress, by the way,' he called to her retreating back.

Callie grinned to herself. 'I thought you might like it,' she threw over her shoulder, without looking around.

Cade sighed; had she just exaggerated the swing of her hips?

She was so going to play dirty.

* * *

A fact that was confirmed when he knocked on her door at seven and she came out in skin-tight jeans, a sleeveless shirt that *zipped* up the front, pulling tight across her breasts, and shiny burgundy gloss on her mouth.

'This okay?' she asked innocently.

Cade ran his gaze over the ensemble as a cloud of frangipani enveloped him. 'I approve of your ballet flats,' he said.

'Oh, you don't like the top.' She pouted. 'I bought it at a little boutique this afternoon especially for our first date. It's daring, don't you think?'

Cade looked down at the article of clothing in question. It was daring, all right. He stared at the zipper that had been pulled to mid-cleavage. There was a lot he couldn't see. But what he could see wasn't going to be good for his bowling average. He picked up the big round tab that taunted him and slowly drew the teeth up a couple of centimetres.

'Now it's sensible.'

Callie grinned. 'Spoilsport.'

He grinned back. 'Get used to it.'

Despite the rather annoying sceptre of the zipper and its large tab that swung enticingly every time she moved or jiggled—which was a lot—bowling was fun. They played two games and Callie gave him a run for his money, which was exactly what he expected. Callie had never struck him as a girly girl—regardless of what was beneath that zip or the tantalising glimpses of her back and abdomen as she either bent to bowl or leapt up in excitement when she scored a strike.

Which she did just a little too much for his sanity.

She seemed much more at home on a bowling lane than

in the nail salon next door, which she'd tsked about as they'd passed, talking about a study she'd read on the toxicity of the chemicals they used in such places.

He'd glanced at her nails—they were short, neat and unadorned. Completely unfussy. Not like they'd spent any time in a beauty salon.

Long enough to leave marks on his back for days, though.

Afterwards they sat at the cheap and cheerful café attached to the alley and ate ice cream from cones and debated their favourite movies. It was no surprise that Callie liked action movies. For a woman who oozed sexuality from every pore she spent a lot of time being one of the guys.

Except when she was eating ice cream like it was a spectator sport. The way she savoured each mouthful. Licked the excess off her mouth. Crunched into the cone...

Cade wouldn't have thought watching a woman eat ice cream could be so damn sexy. But he had a very embarrassing hard-on and an image in his head of unzipping her shirt and upending the contents of the cone all over her breasts.

Callie's tongue swiped at the excess ice cream on her mouth as she waited for Cade to finish the sentence he'd started, but he was now frowning instead. 'What?' she asked.

'Must you eat it like that?'

Callie blinked, unaware she'd been eating it *like that*. However the hell *that* was. But she realised pretty quickly as she raised the cone to her mouth and his gaze dropped to where lips met food. And she took a long, slow, deliberate swipe.

The double scoop was chocolate and raspberry ripple and she knew her lips would be coated with it after her porn-queen lick. So, as she swallowed, she darted her tongue out to gather all the sticky excess into her mouth.

'Callie.'

His voice sounded strained and Callie liked that she'd caused him some consternation. 'What?' she asked innocently, going in for another lick.

Cade was barely holding on to his libido. 'We have serviettes for that,' he said, sliding one her way.

Callie was reminded of the night she'd wiped the corner of his mouth with a good-quality linen napkin and how very much she'd wanted to use her tongue instead. Cade looked like he wouldn't mind using his, either.

Maybe this would only take one date.

'Where's the fun in that?' she asked.

Cade shook his head as he resumed eating. 'You are incorrigible.'

Callie noticed he had a little excess ice cream problem going on himself. 'Not at all,' she said. 'Here, I'll show you how much fun it can be.' And she leaned across the short distance between them and put her lips to the corner of his mouth.

Cade withdrew slightly before she got the chance to dart her tongue out. She smelled sweet and tart like chocolate and raspberries and he wondered how sticky she'd be if he stole a taste.

'No kissing,' he murmured huskily, bringing his impulses into check.

Callie shut her eyes at the warmth of his breath on her mouth and the sweet rush that zipped through her system.

'Not kissing,' she murmured, moving in closer again. 'Just getting…' she inched closer '…this bit…' his stubble grazed her top lip as she angled her head for better access 'here…'

And she darted her tongue out, tentatively at first to

the corner of his mouth, where a pocket of sweet caramel taunted her, dipping it in and out quickly, primed for him to pull back. Growing bolder when he didn't, she flattened her tongue into the angle and swiped further afield, along the closed seam of his lips a little and above his mouth where prickly, sticky heaven awaited.

She sighed as it melted against her tongue like fairy floss. Wisely she withdrew, refusing to listen to the dictates of her body and explore further. They had probably four dates to get through before he cracked and it would be foolish to put him on high alert on date number one.

'See,' she murmured, pulling away slowly, loving that his eyes had closed and when they fluttered open the whisky depths looked all smoky. 'I can follow the rules.'

It took Cade a moment to come back from the deceptively simple move laced with sex and sin. She'd barely touched him but somehow left him wanting more.

His hard-on wanted more. A lot more.

He grunted. 'I think that's what's called *bending* the rules.'

'You're right.' She faked a contrite expression. 'I've been naughty. I think I should be punished.'

Cade shook his head. 'Just eat your damn cone.'

On the way home in the car Cade was determined to keep things on track. Nothing like talking about work to achieve that. 'I'm scheduling the surgery for next Wednesday,' he announced.

Callie glanced at him. 'Trudy's?'

He nodded. 'I spent the best part of today getting everyone lined up.'

Callie felt a thrill of excitement at the prospect. Being in the operating theatre with Cade while they performed surgery that wouldn't have even been conceivable not that long ago ticked all her boxes. 'They'll be pleased,' she said. 'I think they're keen to get going now they've committed to it.'

Cade nodded. 'Most people are. The sooner it can be done the better the outcome.'

They talked more about the procedure, which took them all the way up the lift and to her front door. She sensed him growing tenser the closer they drew to her apartment. 'Don't worry,' she teased as she slid her key into the lock. 'I'm not going to flash you again tonight. I'll behave.'

Cade shot her a stiff smile as his gaze dropped to her zip. Part of him had been kind of hoping that she would. He'd been thinking about how her breasts might be revealed as the teeth slowly opened—kind of like peeling a banana, to reveal the ripe, tasty fruit beneath.

Callie noted his interest. It grabbed at her abdominal muscles and sent heat blooming through her pelvis. 'Unless,' she said, stepping into the darkened alcove of her apartment away from prying eyes, 'you'd rather I did?'

Cade didn't say anything as his shoulder fell against the doorframe—he wasn't capable. He was supposed to be the controlled one here but he hadn't been able to get the ice-cream fantasy out of his head and a large part of him—that part occupying his underwear, anyway—really wanted to watch the unpeeling of her breasts.

Callie's heart was beating fifteen to the dozen as Cade's gaze strayed only momentarily to her face before drifting again to her zipper. For a moment she wasn't sure but the heat in her belly, the simmer in her blood drove her and slowly, very slowly, she raised her hand to the round metallic tab of her zip.

She pulled it down slightly. Just a tooth or two, not sure if this was what he wanted. Then his nostrils flared and she knew. Knew in the way a woman who was in touch with her sexuality *did* know. So she kept going, pulling the circular tab all the way to the bottom, feeling the cool air hit her heated cleavage and the skin of her belly as the two sides of her shirt gaped slightly.

It didn't glide open like yesterday to reveal all and she didn't aid it, either, as she had done yesterday. She just looked at him and waited, conscious that his gaze was feasting on her as intensely as his mouth had done that night on the beach. And in his shower. And on his bed.

'Is this what you want?' she asked, her voice sounding odd to her ears, like she'd eaten a cone full of gravel.

Cade was drawn to the delicious swell of her breast as the garish light from the hallway behind him fell across its plump curves in softer relief. The edge of a lacy red-and-black bra sitting halfway across her breasts could just be made out while a marvellous design technique pushed the inner curves of the two lush globes up and together.

A buzz filled his head and Cade swallowed against it. He wanted her to shrug the edges of her blouse farther apart. Hell, he wanted to bridge the safety zone between them and separate the two sides himself. But he reached for the ironclad will that had seen him through med school, homelessness and a drunken, neglectful father.

Through months of denial and celibacy that had been his salvation.

'Not yet,' he said, and turned away before he made a total liar of himself.

Cade decided a few days of distance between dates wouldn't go amiss and resolutely kept to himself as much as possible in a work situation where he seemed to run into Callie at least every other hour of the day.

On the fourth day he entered the NICU staffroom after another meeting about Trudy's surgery, to find Callie the only occupant. She was making herself a cup of coffee and he faltered for a moment in the doorway.

Callie raised an eyebrow at his hesitation. 'Alone at last,' she said, taking a fortifying sip of hot caffeine. The last two cups had gone cold while she'd attended to an accidental extubation and a new admission via Theatres of a twenty-eight-weeker.

Cade gave her a self-deprecating smile. 'I was just going to grab a coffee before going to Theatre,' he said.

'Help yourself,' Callie said, moving out of the way so he could reach the hospital-supplied beverage range, which was hardly extensive.

Cade nodded, stepping into the space she'd just relinquished and busying himself with preparation as he waited for the jug to boil.

'So,' Callie said, 'I'm not sure of the protocol now. Am I supposed to ask you on the second date?'

Cade ripped the top off the sugar packet and dumped in into the mug. 'What's your rush?' he asked.

Callie looked behind her. She had her back to the doorway so she wasn't sure if anyone was nearby and she sure as hell didn't want anyone overhearing their conversation.

'Well, I'm on a timeline here and as you're already making me wait *eight*—' she lowered her voice another notch '—dates before we get to the good stuff, I don't think it's fair that you should drag your feet in between.'

Water in the jug bubbled up the spout and Cade was pleased for the distraction. He took his time pouring it into the mug, adding milk and stirring.

'How about you just concede?' Callie suggested. 'I won't think any less of you.'

Cade gave a half smile as he tapped his teaspoon on the rim of the mug. Truth be told he wasn't sure he could last eight dates and conceding was mighty tempting. But it had become a bit of a battle of wills between the two of them and he'd never backed down from a challenge.

Callie took a step towards him. They weren't indecently close but her body hummed with awareness and she swore she could hear his do the same. 'I'll make it worth your while.'

Cade's smiled broadened. He just bet she would. Was it wrong to be so turned on by her cockiness? 'Do you fancy going to see the new James Bond movie tonight?'

Callie regarded him for a moment. So he was determined to stick to his guns. 'Sure... Okay. Can we sit right up at the back and neck a little?'

He laughed this time. 'No kissing, remember? That's one of the rules.'

Cade noticed some movement in the corridor behind Callie and caught Natalie, phone to ear, approaching in his peripheral vision. *Oh, hell.* She'd already hinted to him yesterday that she'd be more than willing to slip into Callie's place should things not work out between them.

So he did the first thing that came into his head—he closed the short distance between them and dropped a kiss straight onto Callie's startled mouth. He could tell it was startled at first because it just stayed there frozen beneath the gentle pressure of his. But he knew the moment that startlement gave way to compliance. Her lips softened and a sigh parted them as she shifted into the kiss, and for long seconds, as their lips moved in a slow dance, he totally forgot everything around him.

Until Natalie entered the room, talking on her phone, and pulled up short. Callie broke away at the intrusion.

'Oh...s-sorry...' Natalie stuttered, her cheeks flaming.

Callie blinked, trying to get her head back from the cloud it had been stuck in. His scent still filled her nostrils and swirled like fairy dust in the air around her, and she leaned her hip against the nearby counter.

'I'll...just...take this outside,' Natalie said, and departed as quickly as she'd arrived.

Callie narrowed her gaze at him as Natalie virtually disappeared before their eyes. Her lips buzzed. 'I thought you said no kissing.'

Cade was more rattled than he liked to admit by the kiss. It had been meant to be a quick, possessive peck with a not-so-subtle message. Instead, he'd lost his head there for a moment.

He shrugged. 'That wasn't a kiss. It wasn't real. It was just...pretence.'

Callie snorted. It had felt real. It had tasted real.

'Trust me,' he said. 'You'll know when I kiss you for real.'

'Promises, promises,' Callie murmured, injecting a lightness into her tone she didn't feel.

He picked up his coffee with a smile that went all the way to his eyes. 'I'll text you the movie start time later, after I've checked it out.'

And then he walked out of the room, leaving Callie yearning for another kiss.

Real, pretend or otherwise.

Cade survived the movie night. 007 could have died in a fiery inferno and he wouldn't have noticed, but he survived. Callie's arm kept brushing up against him as she hogged the popcorn she'd told him she didn't want when he'd bought it. Also the continual crossing and uncrossing of her legs had been very distracting. The flickering light from the screen illuminated her knees and kept drawing his gaze.

At her insistence they were sitting right up in the back

row in the corner and with the cinema only half-full they were a long way from their nearest neighbour. And those knees and the skirt just above them had been seriously tempting.

He also survived their Sunday drive up into the Gold Coast hinterland. Her tiny shorts and tank top were perfect for the gorgeous sunny day, if not for his sanity, but he managed to limp through their third date without succumbing to Callie's considerable wiles.

The same couldn't be said for coming across her in the special-care nursery the day before the big surgery. He'd ducked in to check on a couple of his babies, pausing by the nurses' station when he spotted her.

She was in a part of the unit known as the fat farm. It was the step-down area for those babies who had graduated from the NICU and special care levels and just needed to fatten up a bit before being discharged. She was standing near an empty cot, cradling what he presumed to be the occupant of said cot, while she chatted with Lucy Palmer, who, as a midwife, was also out of her usual territory.

The bundle squirmed and a little angry fist punched the air. Callie smiled down at the baby, her lips pursing in a shushing motion as she rocked a little. Her hand came up to cover the little fist, her thumb gently stroking over tiny knuckles.

A hand seemed to clamp around Cade's intestines and squeeze hard. It was swift and unexpected. He'd seen her in tiny shorts, in a zippered top and in nothing but sand on the beach that night, but somehow this view of her was the most breathtaking of all.

She looked down at the bundle in her arms with an expression on her face he saw every day here at work both on men and women. The pure wonder of a baby. The miracle of it all. Had she ever wanted a baby? And what would a baby of Callie's look like—a cute little carrot top with attitude to burn, wrapping every male in her vicinity around her little finger?

Cade smiled to himself but it faded quickly as he thought about his own baby with the usual dose of mixed emotions.

Anger and loathing and guilt.

Regret. Relief. Remorse.

When Sophie had told him he was going to be a father he'd been so angry with her over lying to him about being on the Pill, for trapping him *and* for freely admitting it. And he'd been angry at himself. Castigating himself over and over for that one lapse of judgement when they'd been caught out without a condom and thrown caution to the wind. Yes, he'd thought they'd had a safety blanket with her other contraception, but that was no excuse.

And through everything that happened afterwards—her overdose, the miscarriage—he'd carried the anger and the guilt, but there'd been part of him that had been…devastated. He hadn't wanted a relationship, he hadn't wanted a baby, he certainly hadn't had a clue how to love one or be a proper father with no role model worth a damn. Hell, he hadn't even known how to love himself.

Still, a part of him had yearned for that opportunity. And looking at Callie holding the baby he allowed himself to wonder for the first time—what would *his* baby have looked like?

Callie looked down into the sweet face of little Benjii, who had been born at twenty-nine weeks with foetal alcohol syndrome. He was now almost term and his road had been rocky but he was finally over the hump and putting on weight—and already in the care system, with his mother signing over her parental rights two days after he was born.

Every now and then Callie liked to come and visit the babies who had graduated to the fat farm. She'd been involved in all their journeys and it was the pay-off to a job that didn't always end so well.

And she'd wanted this once. So very badly. If things had worked out between her and Joe, she'd have probably had several by now.

'Don't look,' Lucy murmured, her gaze flicking to a point behind Callie's head 'but the lovely Dr Coleman is staring at you.' Lucy had delivered Benjii all those weeks ago and, like some babies inevitably did, he'd wormed under her skin.

Callie froze, the gentle rocking she hadn't even realised she'd been doing screeching to an abrupt halt.

'I hear on the grapevine you and Cade are…seeing each other.'

Callie glanced up, undecided about how to answer. Trying to fool Natalie was one thing but she didn't want this thing she and Cade were doing—whatever the hell it was—to become the stuff of hospital legend. She wanted some wriggle room when they both inevitably went their own ways. Because people would take sides and that's when it got messy.

'It's not really serious,' she said dismissively. 'It's more convenience.'

Lucy frowned. 'That's not what I heard.'

'Really,' Callie said noncommittally, as she took up her rocking again when Benjii protested the loss of movement.

'Well, he's heading this way,' Lucy said. 'And I've got to say he's looking at your butt pretty damn seriously. Kind of like he owns it, if you ask me.'

Callie felt a tiny thrill in her chest as said butt cheeks practically burnt up.

'Lucy,' Cade said, nodding in her direction as he drew even with the women. 'Callie.'

'Cade,' Lucy acknowledged. 'All ready for tomorrow?'

'Ready as we'll ever be.' He turned his gaze to Callie. 'You're a natural,' he murmured.

She was wearing that damn black dress again with all the pockets. It made him want to put his hands in them. Given how many there were, that could lead to something way more.

Callie shrugged, her stupid heart tap dancing in her chest for no good reason. 'I know my way around a baby.'

Cade ignored the terseness in the deceptively soft reply. 'Are *you* ready for tomorrow?' he asked.

Callie kept her gaze firmly on Benjii's cute button nose. 'I'm ready,' she murmured.

Cade frowned. She didn't sound very pumped. 'You need to bring your A game.'

Callie did look up then, insulted by his suggestion. She could feel Lucy's curious gaze darting from one to the other. She held Benjii a little tighter. 'I *always* bring my A game.'

His gaze dropped to one of her breast pockets. 'That you do.'

Cade decided it was best to leave before he did something outrageous in front of a member of staff and an impressionable infant. He nodded at Lucy and said, 'See you tomorrow,' to Callie, his voice gruff.

She knew she should just nod and let him go but after his A-game crack Callie couldn't help herself. 'I might drop by tonight,' she said.

She had absolutely no intention of doing so but seeing the jump of the muscle at the angle of his jaw restored some of her tattered female pride.

Cade felt the sexy threat streak a molten pathway to

his groin. He always felt a little edgy before a big op—the last thing he needed was Callie offering him a way to burn some of it off. He was like a prizefighter before a match—he needed that edge.

His gaze dropped to her mouth. 'I'm having an early night.'

Callie refused to glance away, not even with the added complication of their spectator. 'Okay?'

Cade knew what that question in her voice was. And it was most definitely *not* okay. '*Tomorrow,*' he said, before taking his leave.

Lucy and Callie watched him stride away. 'Wow,' Lucy said, 'Somebody get me some water.' She turned to look at Callie. 'He is *so* hot for you.'

Callie had never been so grateful to have her pager go off. 'Here,' she said, dodging the statement entirely by handing over her bundle. 'Take Benjii—I've got to answer this.'

It had been a long time since Callie had felt comfortable with girly conversations—probably high school. And all the ones after high school had pretty much always turned to sex and she'd been terrified her inexperience and ineptness would show. It had become easier to avoid them altogether.

So it was no hardship to turn tail and run.

CHAPTER EIGHT

WEDNESDAY MORNING DAWNED and Callie had never felt so alive. She practically skipped into the hospital. She saw Cade as they all gathered for an early morning briefing session but everyone was too busy for conversation that didn't revolve around the momentous thing they were about to do. He looked pumped and utterly commanding in his scrubs, standing in front of the extra-large theatre's imaging boards going over the films he had with Diane Coulter, the neurosurgeon.

Most of the procedure would be done under ultrasonic guidance but if Callie had learned anything about Cade while working with him on this case in particular, it was that the man was a perfectionist.

And that made him even more appealing.

Then, before she knew it, Trudy was in the anaesthetic room having her epidural and it was all hands on deck. The spinal anaesthetic would ensure the baby would be asleep during the operation. Trudy would also have a general anaesthetic.

Within twenty minutes Trudy was out of it and everything was ready to go. Cade prepped her abdomen with Betadine and draped it with sterile drapes. Then he was making his first incision and everyone seemed to hold their collective breaths.

Callie stood at the ready slightly to the back and one side in case she was needed to help with an emergency delivery and resus. At twenty-four weeks Trudy's baby was considered viable if anything went wrong.

Caroline and her registrar stood scrubbed beside her, all set to perform the myelomeningocele repair once Cade had exposed the baby's back.

There were others, as well. Two anaesthetists—one for the baby, one for Trudy. Sam Webster was there, monitoring the baby's heart condition via ultrasound throughout. Cade's registrar helped with the procedure. Not to mention the scrub and scout nurses, two orderlies and the crowded gallery above them.

Cade talked through the procedure as he went for the benefit of the staff watching from the gallery. Soon enough he'd done his part, exposing the baby's back, and he was stepping away, hands clasped together in front of him to prevent de-sterilising them.

It was now Caroline's turn to do her bit and repair the large defect protruding from the baby's spine. A defect that would have a very different outcome if the traditional treatment had been the only thing on offer.

Cade was beside Callie now and had he not been sterile and had they not had an audience she might just have moved in closer and rubbed her pinkie along his leg in silent admiration. Then he turned and looked at her and their gazes locked and they shared a moment of pure connection that took her breath away.

It didn't last long, a second or two before he looked away, engrossing himself in the operation again, but Callie had felt it right down to her bones.

Barely a sound could be heard in the theatre as everyone there was aware of the ground-breaking work they were doing. Callie craned her neck to see the delicate neurosurgery Caroline was performing with such skilled fluidity. She, too, talked through the procedure and Callie watched every single move she made with rapt attention.

Almost two hours later the defect had been repaired and the spine closed. All that could be seen were a neat row of soluble stitches along a section of the spine where there had previously been a large mass containing delicate and vital neural tissue.

Callie blinked back tears as the entire gallery clapped. *It was a miracle.*

Then Caroline stepped back and Cade stepped forward, stripping off his gloves and asking the scrub nurse for a new pair. She handed them over and he and his registrar got to work on the next step: closure.

An hour later Callie was in the theatre staffroom, celebrating with the rest of the team. It was an exhilarating feeling, being a part of something so momentous, and to say they all felt a little giddy was an understatement. Of course there were many things that could still go wrong—preventing Trudy from going into premature labour would now be the focus for Nikolai Kefes and his obstetric team—but in this blip in time right now they were going to wallow in a job well done.

Cade was there for a short while on the opposite side of the room, chatting to colleagues, but his gaze kept meeting hers like it had for that moment during the op and she was aware of him like she'd never been before.

And that was saying something!

It was obvious he was feeling high, too. Pride and accomplishment oozed from his scrubs as easily as his sex appeal, and part of her just wanted to pull him into the privacy of the change rooms and do what they both wanted to do.

But then a toast was proposed by Sam Webster and everyone joined in, clinking their coffee mugs. 'We should have organised a cake,' the scrub nurse who Callie clinked with said, and Callie agreed that if ever there was a time for cake this would be it.

But when she looked up from that conversation Cade had disappeared—to check on Trudy, Callie supposed—and soon the impromptu party broke up as everyone returned to their normal jobs.

Which was rather more difficult than Callie had imagined. The highly technical, highly challenging, highly dynamic world of the NICU seemed positively Stone Age after what she'd just witnessed and all day she couldn't shake the feeling of being like a kid on Christmas Eve. Every time she thought about what they'd accomplished she got a little-kid spring to her step.

By the time she'd headed home after checking in on Trudy and Elliott she still hadn't clapped eyes on Cade. But she knew one thing for sure as she kicked off her shoes: she *needed* to clap eyes on him. She *needed* to see him. To talk to him. To debrief. To just ramble about the amazing, incredible experience she'd been part of.

'Cake,' she said out loud.

She'd been thinking about it all day and suddenly it seemed like the perfect entrée into his apartment. She doubted he'd be keen to let her in if she just knocked. The awareness between them in the theatre, in the staffroom this morning, the eye contact that spoke of far more than successful operations, had been a living, breathing entity and it was just the kind of thing to signal an already determined Cade to pull up his drawbridge.

But if she came bearing cake?

Wasn't the way to a man's heart through his stomach? It was, according to her mother, even if Callie had never managed to prove it herself. It wasn't his heart she wanted to get into anyway, but if there was one thing Callie had been schooled in more than any other, it was how to cook.

She had a quick shower, threw on her robe so she didn't get her clothes covered in flour and sundry other cooking ingredients, pulled her hair up on top of her head into a messy knot, poured herself a glass of wine and hit the kitchen.

Chocolate cake. What man didn't like chocolate cake? And her mother had won awards for her chocolate cakes every year that Callie could remember. She probably still did.

Callie could make her mother's chocolate cake in her sleep!

And she set about doing just that.

The fact that she had all the ingredients probably said a lot more about her psyche than she was comfortable with. Over ten years away from home, away from the overwhelming domestic influence of it, away from the feminist black hole of it, yet still she shopped like she was living in the country and the CWA committee was coming around for afternoon tea.

She shook off the ties that threatened to yank her back in time and set the butter and sugar to cream in the industrial-strength electric mixer she'd been given as a wedding present from her mother. It was the only thing she'd taken out of the marriage.

While she waited for that to go a rich shade of white she wandered over to her stereo system, wineglass in hand, and popped on some music. Then she wandered over to her balcony and opened the doors. The noise of the ocean joined the sound of seventies rock and the mechanical beating and the breeze flowed in, parting her gown slightly below the tie at the waist, blowing against her naked thighs and swirling around where they met at the top.

She breathed the salt air into her lungs as she took a sip of her wine. Who'd have thought she'd ever be here? Thousands of kilometres from Broken Hill, a beachfront apartment block, a competent, well-respected neonatal specialist who'd just experienced one of her most pivotal career moments?

Callie grinned as she turned back to check on the creaming progress. Satisfied, she stopped the mixer and cracked the eggs into the bowl. The music drifted around her, louder now it wasn't competing with the beaters. She unscrewed the cap of the vanilla-essence bottle. The aroma infused the air around her with its heady, milky-sweet essence and before she was consciously aware of what she was doing, Callie had dabbed some of it on her neck and behind her ears, exactly as her mother had done to her when she'd been little and had loved spending hours baking cakes in the kitchen.

'Who needs that posh city stuff?' her mother had said as she'd dabbed vanilla essence behind her own ears. 'Best perfume in the world.'

Callie smiled at the memory and got on with making the cake.

Cade heard the music bleeding out from Callie's apartment as he passed by about ten minutes later. It wasn't loud but it was as distracting as hell. He'd planned to walk straight past but he hesitated. Her eyes had sparkled—literally sparkled—that morning during that moment they'd shared and he'd been thinking about them all day. About how aware he'd been of her during the procedure.

The excitement and belief in him she'd radiated had been heady stuff. And he was wired. Really wired. From the success of the day. And from the adrenaline that had flowed like lava through his veins and was still smouldering away.

A dangerous combination, really.

He should just go. But he knew Callie would love an update on Trudy's condition and given he'd just come from Trudy's room, surely...

Cade knocked before he had a chance to talk himself out of it. He'd just stand at the door, relay the info and go.

Except she opened the door in her robe—one that gaped more than was good for him—and sucking on a finger. Not a good sign for a reserve already significantly eroded by her attempts to bed him and the sharp edge of adrenaline.

'Oh, hi.' She smiled, taking her finger out of her mouth. 'I was going to come and see you in an hour or so. I'm baking you a cake.'

Cade wasn't quite sure what to say to that as he followed the path of her moist finger into the knot of hair atop her head. His gaze drifted back down. '*You* bake?'

Callie was in too good a mood to let him dampen it. 'I do indeed.' She grinned. 'And I'm damn good, too.' She stood aside and gestured him inside. 'Come on in. I've just popped it into the oven.'

Cade hesitated, reaching for the self-control he had once been so good at. 'I just came to give you an update on Trudy,' he said, shaking his head and keeping his feet firmly fixed to the floor.

Callie's eyes lit up again. 'Is everything okay?'

Cade gave a half laugh. 'Yes. According to Nikolai, everything is going smoothly.'

'Well, come on, then, you have to come in now. Eat cake and drink wine. We didn't have a cake today—there should have been cake.'

'O...kay,' he said, a little taken back by her frivolity.

Callie wasn't really given to frivolity. Sure, she could

joke around with the best of them but seriousness was more her basic nature. It was funny to see her so...high.

'Just for a while,' he said, and made the fatal mistake of stepping inside. Fatal because something sure as hell smelled good in her apartment and it had better be the cake or he was totally screwed.

He followed her down the short hallway into the open-plan living area, almost identical to his. 'Throw your bag on the lounge,' she said. 'I'll pour you a wine and you can fill me in.'

Cade was determined not to look as Callie reached into the cupboard above the sink for a glass. But he was fairly certain she was naked under her robe and not even a case of rapid-onset blindness would have stopped him looking.

'*That* was amazing today,' Callie said as she placed the empty glass on the cluttered central bench between them. 'You know, I can see why surgeons have giant egos now.' She filled his glass and handed it over to him.

'Thank you. I think,' Cade said, as he took the offering and sat on the nearest stool.

Things shifted interestingly beneath her gown. It was a deep moss green, the perfect foil for her blue-green eyes and her lush Titian hair, and his gaze was drawn to the way the satiny fabric fell across her breasts, clinging like a lover. The way the subdued downlights added sheen and lustre.

Things also shifted inside his trousers.

He took a steadying breath but the pervasive smell of vanilla infused his senses, intoxicating him more surely than any amount of wine. How could her kitchen smell like a bakery—all soothing and homey—and she look the complete opposite?

Wild and sexy.

A gypsy sent to completely bewitch him.

The shifting in his trousers got serious.

Callie stilled as she became aware that his gaze had drifted to where the two edges of her gown crossed over at her breasts. 'You're welcome,' she murmured, as heat pooled in her belly and between her legs.

Meatloaf singing his usual mix of sex and sin seemed like a perfect accompaniment as her nipples hardened beneath his gaze. His nostrils flared and a surge of sexual power flowed through her veins. Part of her wanted to shrug off her gown right there and then and get down to it, but another part wanted to savour the moment.

Who would have known that anticipation could be such an aphrodisiac?

'Have you eaten?' she asked. 'I can throw something together. Or in forty-five minutes we can just…' she shrugged and followed his gaze as it dropped to her cleavage again '…eat cake warm from the oven.' *Possibly plaster it all over your body.* 'I have ice cream.'

Cade was pretty sure he'd be dead from lack of blood to his brain in forty-five minutes. He'd be wise to get the hell out now but the vanilla and her gown was keeping him in thrall. He put his glass down on the counter. 'Are you… wearing anything under that gown?' he asked.

Callie looked down at herself then back at him. 'Nope.'

'Do you think maybe…you could go and put something else on?'

Callie feigned ignorance. 'Like underwear, you mean?'

Cade shook his head. 'Like layers.' *Lots of layers.*

Callie grinned. 'You don't like the gown?' she asked, turning around a couple of time to give him the full three-sixty, her legs flashing a little.

'Callie,' he growled.

She came to a standstill and shoved her hands on her

hips. 'I'm not changing.' She hadn't planned on wearing her gown to his place but *he'd* knocked on *her* door.

Cade took a gulp of wine then stood. 'I think I'm going to go.'

'Oh, no, you're not.' She laughed and reached across the bench, yanking on his skew tie. 'Sit. I promise I won't jump you.' *Yet.* 'Tell me about Trudy and the baby while I clean up.'

Cade acquiesced, falling back onto the stool. It had been why he'd knocked on her door in the first place, after all.

'The first ultrasound looks good. Sam's happy from a cardiology point of view and Nikolai's pleased that the drugs are keeping any pre-term labour in check.'

Callie asked a few more questions as she clattered around, rinsing things in the sink and putting them in the dishwasher. She could feel his eyes on her, watching her every movement, and she set out to make it worth his while. She added an extra swing to her hips, she deliberately dropped a spoon so she had to bend over and pick it up, and when the gown slipped off her shoulder a little she didn't bother to fix it.

And all the time she talked, kept up the chatter to distract him from the fact that while he was sitting in her kitchen, talking shop, she was steadily seducing him.

'You want to lick the bowl?' she asked him innocently, interrupting something he was saying about something she hadn't really heard because the anticipation had become an actual buzz in her head over which she could hear nothing.

Cade looked at the bowl she was offering him, which was coated in a generous amount of leftover cake mixture. Then back at her and her bare shoulder. *He sure as hell wanted to lick something.*

'No. Thanks.'

Callie shrugged. 'Suit yourself.'

She'd deliberately kept the bowl till last and the triumph she felt at his dilated pupils when she stuck her finger in and swiped it around the rim of the bowl bordered on sexual. She scooped up a dollop of gooey chocolate cake mix then popped the finger into her mouth.

She sighed and shut her eyes for a moment, mostly because it tasted pretty damn good but also because she hoped it would turn him on. 'Mmm, so-o-o-o good!' she said, opening her eyes again.

Cade's gaze fell on the moist stickiness of her mouth. He should leave. He really should leave. But her mouth, that gown and the heady aroma of vanilla undulated its way past his defences. And he had a hard-on that refused to budge. 'Smells good,' he said as he tried to convince himself that denial was good for the soul.

They had an eight-date agreement. His erection would work just as well then. *Probably better.*

She dipped her finger in again. 'Are you sure?' she asked.

He gave a terse nod. 'Positive.'

Callie shrugged and scooped another dollop into her mouth, savouring the glorious sweetness on her tongue. 'Mmm,' she sighed again. 'Some things are just worth the temptation, don't you think?'

Cade shot her a look that said he knew what she was up to. 'Nope.'

Callie grinned. She put the bowl in the sink, gave it a quick rinse and loaded it in the dishwasher. Then she picked up the dishcloth and wiped down the cleared bench. She knew that as she bent forward to reach his side that her gown would gape a little and Cade would have a bird's-eye view.

She looked at him from under her lashes as she wiped and his long, slow appreciation of the gape sizzled along her nerve endings. And suddenly she didn't want to play any more. Or wait for the cake to paint all over his body.

She wanted to act.

She grabbed a teatowel and dried the bench off. When that was done she hoisted herself up onto it and in one smooth movement swung her legs round. The satin of the gown was slippery on the marble top and she slithered over until she was directly in front of him. The material had ruched up her bare thighs and she bunched the excess between her legs for a modicum of decency as she placed a foot on either side of him on the arms of the stool.

'So,' she said, watching him closely for his reaction as she leaned forward, her elbows on her partially bent knees, her thighs parted, her gown exposing a decent amount of cleavage. 'What are we going to *do* while we wait for the cake to bake?'

It was risky. She knew he had willpower to burn and she was already pushing it. Sure, his gaze had roamed over her like hot, sticky rain but he was a grown man—he could easily just get up and leave. God knew, Joe would have been off the stool before she could blink.

Cade eyed the length of bare thigh, followed it all the way down to where it disappeared beneath the satin fabric that pooled on the bench between her open legs, hiding what was at the apex from view. His palm itched to follow the path of his gaze, to feel the smooth warmth beneath it, to push the fabric farther down, to pull at the belt at her waist, to open the gown, to look at her in all her glory, to drink her in.

Just thinking about it cranked his edginess up another notch.

'Poker?' he suggested, his voice sounding alien, his throat parched.

Callie raised an eyebrow. 'Strip poker?'

Cade gave a half smile, admiring her persistence. Other parts of his body weren't so laid back and he took a deep, steadying breath to stay focused.

Big mistake.

A strong waft of pure vanilla hit him straight between the eyes. His nostrils flared as the milky sweetness oozed through the cracks in his defences. 'Oh, my God,' he groaned, inching a little closer to her. 'It's *you* that smells amazing.'

Callie was lost for a moment and then she remembered. 'Oh, yes, it's vanilla. I dabbed some on my neck and behind my ears like my mum used to do to me when I was a kid and we baked cakes together.' Her gaze drifted to the flare of his nostrils. She leaned in a little closer. 'You like?'

Cade shut his eyes against the temptation but even so the aroma was dizzying and he didn't know which he wanted more: to kiss her or lick her. His body swayed and when he opened his eyes again he was alarmingly close to her neck, the frantic flutter of her carotid just there, the crossover of her lapels just below, the intoxicating fragrance of vanilla and Callie surrounding him like smoke from a genie's lamp.

Luring him.

Sitting on the bench, Callie had a slight height advantage. She looked down at him through heavy lids as his warm breath coated her skin in need. 'Cade,' she whispered. 'Please.'

'No.' He shook his head against the raw appeal in her voice and the urgent call in his blood. 'No kissing. No sex,' he muttered. 'I'm not supposed to be laying a finger on you.'

'So don't,' she whispered. 'Why don't you just lean in and sniff me instead? You don't need your fingers for that.'

Cade flicked his gaze up to meet her. 'I don't think that's the spirit of the arrangement.'

Callie shrugged and her gown slipped off her shoulder a little. 'I bet a smart guy like you can work around it.' She shuffled a little closer.

Cade almost heard the twang in his head when his resolve snapped. *Damn it.* He wanted to bury his face in her neck and lick there so badly he could barely see straight.

But she was right—he was an intelligent, resourceful guy. He'd stick to his plan if it killed him.

He placed his palms flat on the bench on either side of her, determined to keep them there as he pushed his nose against the pulse and inhaled her intoxicating goodness on a deep guttural sigh. It was soft and sweet and he gripped the bench harder as his head spun. His tongue darted out, tracing the buzz of her pulse, and the sweetness on her skin melted against his tongue, rushing through his system like a sugar high.

Sniffing wasn't kissing. Licking wasn't kissing. And his fingers were pressed hard into the cold marble.

Cade's pulse roared through his head as his sense of smell took over, leading the exploration, following the sweet, sticky scent up the hard ridge of her throat, along the line of her jaw and lingering at the point where hard met soft behind her ear. A lock of hair had escaped her upswept hair to brush her ear and he rubbed his nose against it, too.

'God,' he muttered. 'I just want to eat you.'

Callie's stomach clenched at the husky admission. Her nipples were hard and she squirmed to ease the ache between her legs. His stubble rasped deliciously, beading her nipples even further as his nose travelled to the other side of her face and then explored lower, down the other side of her neck.

She dropped her head back a little so he had full access and she shut her eyes as his nose moved lower and his tongue dipped into the hollow at the base of her throat and along the bared ridges of her collarbones.

The occasional brush of his lips on her skin felt forbidden and decadent.

Cade was operating in pure sensory overdrive now. He was completely enslaved by his olfactory system. When his lips touched cool satin at the point where her shoulder met the outer edge of her gown he turned his face and rubbed his cheek against it. He smelled sunshine with his vanilla.

And he liked it.

It was only when his nose met the V of her gown that he pulled back, and sense started to return. Her eyes fluttered open, a small protest falling from her mouth. 'Sorry...' he murmured. 'I got a little carried away.'

Callie shook her head. 'Don't be.' Then she reached down and loosened the tie of the robe, knowing he wouldn't. She parted it, pulling the wad between her legs away, letting it ooze off her thighs and slip to the bench on either side. The only place it held on was to the tips of her shoulders and that was pretty damn precarious.

Otherwise she was totally bare to him.

She noticed his knuckles turning white as his gaze drifted from her breasts down her belly to the juncture of her thighs. The ache between her legs intensified. He slowly swept his gaze back up her body until their gazes locked.

The simmer in his whisky gaze dried her throat in an instant. 'I think I may have spilled some a bit lower,' she lied.

Cade didn't move for a moment as the aromas of Callie—vanilla, chocolate cake and woman—mingled in his nostrils and swelled like a symphony in his head. And then he was feasting on her, keeping his palms flat and wide on the bench top as he claimed a ripe strawberry nipple.

When she moaned he almost brought his hands to her, lifting them off the bench but remembering at the last moment to stick to his word.

Even if he was making a total mockery of it.

'God, you taste amazing,' he muttered against the soft swell of her as he released one tortured peak to pay some attention to the other.

Callie ran a hand into his hair and held him fast as he sucked hard. There were no rules that she couldn't touch him and she had no intention of not doing so.

'Don't stop,' she gasped, arching her back, pressing as much of herself as she could into the heat of his mouth. Her breasts were incredibly sensitive, revelling in his attention, and, God knew, after the merry dance they'd been on, she was primed to go off at the slightest provocation.

Cade licked in great sweeping strokes from one to the other, paying equal homage, tasting and licking every delicious millimetre of her skin. Her nipples were tight and hard and scraped erotically against his palate.

And her response?

Every little moan, gasp and whimper cranked up the fire in his loins and his erection was just about ready to burst out of its skin. He wanted to push her back against the cold, hard top of the bench, free his erection and plunge straight into her. See her spread out before him, her breasts rock beneath the kitchen downlights, watch her face as she came.

The image filled his head until he was on fire with it.

'Cade.' Callie called his name absently, her eyes shut, her face turned to the ceiling as she cradled his head to her chest and floated in a rainbow bubble. 'More,' she whimpered. 'More.'

Cade lifted his head and looked at her. Her nipples were wet and engorged from his ministrations and he wanted to remember this image forever. Her eyes slowly fluttered open and he suppressed the overwhelming urge to kiss her deep and hard.

No kissing.

'Cade?' she whispered, and it was gratifying to hear her voice was thready, too. Better still to see the blending of the blue and green in her eyes to one mass of want.

'Lie back,' he whispered, his heart racing.

Callie's pulse tripped as his gaze drifted down her body. The ache between her legs pulsed painfully and it was all she could do not to grab his head and push it down there.

But she was going to last about two seconds if he did that. 'If you go there…' she said, licking her lips, her throat dry '…I'm not going to last.'

Cade almost groaned out loud as her tongue did the job he wanted to do—swiped across her lips. 'Lie back,' he repeated with a half smile.

Callie could feel herself weakening by the second. 'But don't you want to…?'

Cade gripped the edges of the bench, the urge to slide his hands onto her shoulders and push riding him hard. 'Lie. Back.'

Callie lay back. Falling first onto her elbows and then, as Cade's head descended and his tongue swirled around her belly button, onto her back, the cool satin of the gown spread out around her like a swathe of emerald grass.

Cade didn't mess around once she was horizontal—he desperately wanted to hear her come apart. His mouth was at the patch of darker red hair between her legs in seconds, drawn by another aroma: the hot, salty tang of woman. He pressed his nose against the soft hair, as he had her neck, but her shakily indrawn breath spurred him lower.

Cade held tight to the bench as Callie bucked, her torso bowing at the first tentative touch of his tongue.

'Cade!' she gasped, and he knew exactly how she felt.

Halfway between stop-I-can't-stand-how-good-it-is and keep-going.

Then the time for being tentative passed and he let loose, sucking and licking—hard. Swirling his tongue around the tight little bead that had her crying out his name, raking her fingers into his hair, begging for more. He wasn't used to doing it no-handed. Normally he used his fingers to pretty devastating effect, too, while his head was between a woman's legs but, regardless, he could feel Callie building quickly. Her hips lifting, her cries ratcheting up.

He glanced all the way up her body as it bucked and bowed. Up over the slight rise of her belly, up her ribcage and over her breasts. Her arms were flung above her head, her hands gripping the edge of bench behind her. It emphasised the roundness of her breasts and his erection surged at the sight before he returned his full attention to her fast-approaching orgasm.

Callie rocked her head from side to side. The ripples had started and she was about to go. She looked down, the sight of her bent knees bracketing his shoulders and his head between her legs as he sat on the stool and feasted on her like she was his own private smorgasbord was all she needed.

'Cade!' she cried out, as sensation slammed into her and her back arched off the bench for long seconds as everything tightened and coalesced. Then her body bucked once, twice, three times, her back practically curling up off the bench as a wave of high-octane pleasure blasted her equilibrium to pieces.

She wasn't sure she was even going to make it through. And he hadn't laid a finger on her.

CHAPTER NINE

CADE DIDN'T STOP until Callie was spent and begging him to stop, her feet drumming on the arms of the stool. 'No more....' she gasped. 'I...can't stand it.'

But he didn't want to stop. He wanted to give her more. To take her to those heights again. He wanted to join her there. He stood, one hand seeking his back pocket and the other reaching for the button on his trousers.

But the sight of her rendered him useless.

Callie was all stretched out before him, eyes shut, arms flung high, loose tendrils of hair floating around her head, her chest rising and falling rapidly, her nipples engorged with blood, several shades darker than the strawberry pink of earlier. A slight flush tattooed her abdomen. Her legs were parted in wanton abandon.

And all this amidst a sea of green fabric. It was a visually stunning sight and for a moment, caught up in the blatant sexuality of it all, he looked his fill.

She looked like Titian himself could have painted her—all wild red hair and unashamed nudity. He could have called it *Sated*, framed it in heavy gilt and hung it in a museum next to any of his other nudes. Of course, Callie was too athletically shaped to be one of his models but her unselfconscious pose could definitely inspire great art.

'Cade?' she murmured huskily, opening her eyes, lifting her arms up, holding them wide open in silent invitation.

Her voice yanked him back to the aching hard-on in his trousers. 'Hang on,' he said, his accent laced with desire, burred around the edges, softer, not as pronounced.

He yanked down his zip and retrieved his wallet, kicking the stool back at the same time as it hampered his movement. Callie's legs collapsed as it toppled and banged to the floor.

'Sorry,' he muttered, as her thighs hit the bench and her legs, bent at the knee, swung freely over the side.

She shook her head and looked up at him. 'Just hurry,' she gasped. 'I want to feel you inside me.'

Cade didn't need any more encouragement as he found the condom in his wallet—the one he'd started carrying again when Callie had made her intentions clear. He reached into his underwear and freed his raging erection. It felt good to be out, surging against his hand as he swiftly donned the protection that felt ten times too small around his taut girth.

And then he was reaching for the edges of the gown beneath her. 'This,' he said as he yanked and she slid closer, her butt aligning with the edge of the bench, 'is going to screw with the no-sex clause.'

Callie's breasts jiggled enticingly and he leaned over on a groan and sucked one into his mouth as her ankles locked firmly around his waist. 'Aren't we done with that?' she gasped.

Cade removed his mouth, guiding himself to her entrance, careful not to *lay a finger on her*. The bench was just the right height and he pushed in just a little, satisfied to hear the harsh suck of her breath. 'Not yet,' he murmured. 'Matter of principle.'

Then he leaned over her again on bent elbows, their

torsos aligning, his forearms flat on the bench on either side of her ribs.

'Oh, well, two out of...' Cade thrust, cutting her off, and all that could be heard was his groan and her gasp. Her hands grabbed his shoulders, her nails digging in. '...three isn't bad,' she finished.

Cade dropped his forehead to her shoulder, his eyes closing as he savoured the feel of her clamped around him—hot and tight. The press of her breasts, the sting of her nails. But soon enough a primal beat pulsed through his head, urging him to move again. To rock. To thrust. To pound.

And it would not be ignored.

He eased almost all the way out before sliding back in again, feeling her squeeze him tight all over again. She grabbed his back, lower, her moan stoking the fire threading through his veins, urging him on.

She was so wet and hot and he'd done that to her. *Him.* He pulled out then thrust again. And again.

'More,' she gasped. It was right near his ear and he gave her exactly what she wanted.

He went harder, faster. Deeper. She cried out. Her legs unlocked, her knees bending to bracket his hips, each foot coming to rest on a buttock, her heels pressing in, holding him tight and close, urging him deeper.

So he went deeper, pushing in till he was seated high and hard inside her—right to the hilt for both of them. Gliding into the same spot over and over as she cried out in pleasure.

His own pleasure rushed at him fast. Building slowly and gently to begin with then, as the keening noises at the back of her throat turned into full-fledged whimpers, suddenly hitting fever pitch as her feet started to drum urgently against his buttocks.

He tried to hold it back as long as he could. To ignore the drag and the claw of it. But it rode him hard and he gasped into her neck as it kicked into hyperdrive.

Callie wasn't sure if it was the way he was angled over her, putting just the right amount of pressure and thrust over just the right spot, but she built again quickly. By the time he was coming apart in her arms, groaning his release into her neck, muttering, 'Callie, Callie, Callie,' over and over with each frantic thrust, she was there, too.

It was somehow richer this time, deeper, more satisfying. Travelling to *every* part of her body as she bucked against him. Immersing her in light and heat and a glow that held her suspended in its thrall.

Neither of them moved for the longest time. They just lay together, joined, struggling to settle the rapid beat of their hearts, to get their breath back. *Their minds back.* One hand had entwined in his hair, holding his head against her shoulder, while the other held on hard halfway down his back and they lay there, spent—replete—until the world righted itself.

Cade moved first, lifting his head off her shoulder to stare down into her flushed face. She looked just like she had the first time: utterly sexually paralysed.

'Look, Mom,' he murmured. 'No hands.'

Callie laughed. 'Yes, very clever. *But* you still caved in. You still had sex with me. And,' she said, looking down his body, 'with all your clothes on.'

Cade smiled. 'What can I say? You make me lose my mind.' He kissed her then, long and slow, savouring the taste of her.

'Oh, so you're kissing me now,' she said, her heart squeezing at the tenderness as he pulled away.

'Yup. Kissing and...' he brought his hands to her face

and traced both sides of her jaw with his index finger '…laying on fingers. *Everywhere*. I have nothing more to prove.'

Callie's eyes drifted shut. 'It was always doomed to fail.'

He smiled as he dropped his face to her neck to nuzzle it. 'That cake's smelling good,' he murmured as his nose followed the lingering scent of vanilla to her ear. His lips caressed the soft place behind it. 'How much longer?'

Callie opened her eyes and raised her arm to look at her watch. 'Fifteen minutes,' she said, her arm gliding onto his shoulder as she enjoyed his lazy afterplay.

'Good, that'll do,' he said. 'Hold on.'

And then, still joined, he was pulling her upwards, gathering her close, sliding his hands beneath her bottom and lifting her off the bench.

Callie laughed as she locked her legs around his waist. 'Where are we going?'

'Your bed,' he said. 'I hope you have a good supply of condoms in this place.'

Callie licked his neck. 'I never run out of anything. It's the country girl in me.'

'Yee-haw,' Cade said as he strode in the direction of her bedroom.

Half an hour later, cake completely forgotten, they were lying in the dark, gasping for breath again. Cade had disposed of the condom and they were staring at the ceiling, their heads still spinning. With her door shut and the night shadows playing on the walls, the rest of the world felt very far away.

'Man,' Callie said, 'you are *good* at that.'

It was surprising how many men weren't. And it was most definitely surprising which ones turned out to be duds. Just because a man looked good didn't necessarily mean a damn thing. Callie had learned early to never judge a book by its cover.

Cade laughed. He felt ten feet tall and bulletproof at the frank appreciation in her voice. 'I had some good teachers.'

Callie turned her head. Their night vision had been given a good workout already and she could see every plane and angle of him in the greyscale of the night. 'Teachers? Plural? Oh, do tell.'

Cade realised he'd let something slip that he'd never told anyone. Not even Alex. But there was just something about Callie that encouraged confidences. Maybe it was their alikeness, maybe it was because he knew she guarded her privacy as much as he guarded his, maybe it was because he already felt she knew so much about him because of her friendship with Alex.

Or maybe it was just the rush of endorphins. But he found himself telling her anyway. 'When I was sixteen I just couldn't live at home any more. My father...'

Cade stopped. He didn't want this to become a tale of woe about his awful home life. Because this chapter was really where his life had turned a corner.

'Let's say it was completely untenable to live at home by then.... Anyway, I was in the right place at the right time and landed this job at a posh house in Beverly Hills. Cleaning the pool, maintaining the gardens... Stuff like that.'

'You still went to school, though?'

Cade nodded. 'Yeah. I'd go straight from school to Sharon's.'

Callie raised an eyebrow. 'Sharon, huh?' She smiled, scooting over to prop her head on his shoulder. He sounded so American, talking about Beverly Hills and pool boys, and she wanted to touch him some more.

'Sharon was divorced, loaded and with no kids and no

need to work there was nothing much to fill her days. Or her nights.'

Callie raised her head slightly to look at him. 'She was your first?' He nodded. 'How old was she?'

'Forty-three. A *very* well put-together forty-three.'

Callie blinked. 'She was old enough to be your—'

'Mother,' Cade finished for her. 'Yes, I guess she was. But she was nice and I really hadn't had a lot of niceness.'

Callie nodded and lay back on his shoulder. It was easy to forget that Cade had come from a broken home. The man oozed success and confidence like pheromones. However messed up her brief marriage had been, however much it had damaged her, at least she'd grown up in a secure and loving household.

Cade stroked his fingers down her bare arm, lost back in time. It had been the first time he'd felt cared for. He didn't need a psychiatrist to tell him that was all kinds of messed up. But he'd never known his mother, had only known Alex's mom for a few brief years before her death, and the only other person he'd connected to—Alex—had walked away from his father's brutality the first chance he'd got.

Cade had blamed him for a long time for that—not any more. But when there'd been just him and his father, who could have won gold had neglect been an Olympic sport, home hadn't been an option.

'She took care of herself, you know?' he said. 'Took pride in herself and her home. She looked great, smelled even better. They all did.'

Callie quirked an eyebrow, turning on her side so she could see his face. 'All?'

Cade nodded. 'Sharon had a lot of friends.'

'Let me guess,' Callie murmured. 'They were *nice,* as well.'

Cade grinned. 'Very accommodating. They tutored me

in the fine art of what women want and after a few years of cleaning their pools and mowing their lawns I also had enough money to go to medical school. I wouldn't have had that start without Sharon. I sure as hell wouldn't have got it from my father.'

Callie absently stroked her finger in a lazy circle down the meaty pillow of his pec, around his nipple and back again. 'So that amazing sexual prowess of yours is compliments of a bunch of cougars?'

Cade chuckled. 'I guess you could say that.'

'Well, I bet you had natural talent even back then,' she said, brushing her fingers lightly over his nipple.

This time Cade's laugh was closer to a hoot. 'Oh, I was fairly green.' He shut his eyes as Callie's lazy caress fanned the coals of his desire. 'The first time wasn't pretty. But...' he quickly displaced Callie from his shoulder, rolling on top of her and pinning her to the bed '...I was a very quick study.'

Callie's breath caught as Cade's mouth found the hollow of her throat. 'Something vital for every prenatal surgeon,' she said as she shut her eyes and extended her neck so Cade could ravage it to his heart's content.

Cade loved that he could still smell the heady aroma of vanilla despite his very best attempts at licking every lingering trace from her skin. 'What about you?' he murmured, as he nuzzled along a collarbone. 'Was Joe your first?'

Callie's eyes blinked open in the night. The fizz bubbling through her veins evaporated.

Cade felt her stillness instantly. He pulled his head away from the fascinating contours of her shoulders to look down into her face. 'Come on, Callie, I told you mine.'

Callie shook her head. 'This is not truth or dare,' she said, avoiding his suddenly intense gaze.

'True,' he murmured, going back for her neck again, 'but that could be fun. You do truth and I'll do dare. Trust me,' he said, grinding his revived erection against the heat between her legs as his lips brushed farther south. 'I'll make it worth your while.'

Callie shut her eyes again as her belly clenched and her hormones betrayed her. 'You like to play dirty.'

'Oh, we haven't even skimmed the surface of how dirty I can be.'

And to make his point he swiped his tongue across her rapidly hardening nipple and then sucked it into his mouth, grazing the tip with his teeth, nipping the sensitive flesh until her nails dug into his shoulders and her back arched off the mattress.

'So,' he said, lifting his head and blowing on the mauled tip. 'Joe?'

Callie opened her eyes as the warm air rapidly cooling her raw flesh was its own kind of torture. He was looking at her so intensely and she thought, *I could love this man.* It was a bizarre thought at the wrong time with an inappropriate man but locked in this embrace with him she felt she *could* tell him anything.

'Joe never wanted me like that.'

It was the first time she'd admitted it to another person. She'd been torturing herself with the knowledge for years—deep inside her head where it had bounced and echoed and grown into a monster that had driven her to seek solace wherever she could find it.

Cade frowned, supporting himself on his elbows, his hands framing her face, brushing hair off her forehead, circling his thumbs against the soft points of her temples. 'Oh. I'm sorry. I got the impression that you were in love with Joe.'

'I was,' Callie said. 'I even married him.'

It was Cade's turn to become still. '*You* were married?' He thought about it for a second. 'Hang on, you're not still married, are you?'

Callie shook her head. 'No. It only lasted a year.'

'How old were you?'

'Eighteen.'

Cade gaped. 'You got married at *eighteen*?'

He couldn't believe what he was hearing. Callie had once been *married*—at *eighteen*. He shifted off her, knowing he couldn't have this conversation with the distraction of his erection. He tucked a hand under his head as he rolled up onto his bent elbow, his other hand sliding onto her belly.

Now some of the reasons behind Callie's relationship with her mother were making sense. Who got *married* at eighteen any more?

He tried to put the pieces together in his head. 'What did you mean when you said that Joe never wanted you like that? Do you mean…the marriage wasn't…consummated?'

Callie had the absurd urge to laugh at the very old-fashioned English word coming out of Cade's very American mouth. 'That's right,' she said. 'Went into it a virgin, came out of it a virgin.'

The bitterness and derision in her voice could have sharpened knives. 'So…what happened?'

Callie wished she knew. It had been thirteen years and she still didn't have a clue. 'He just didn't want me…. He was never interested.'

'You obviously didn't try before you bought.'

Callie shook her head. 'He wanted to wait. For it to be *special*.' She shrugged. 'I'd loved Joe forever. I was thrilled that he'd put me on this pedestal where I was precious and virtuous. He'd had so many girlfriends. But he chose me. All I'd ever wanted to do was marry him and have his babies.'

Cade couldn't reconcile the ambitious woman he knew with the starry-eyed girl she was talking about. 'What happened on the wedding night?'

'He said he was tired, it had been a long day and a crazy few weeks. And he was right, it had been, and I was so happy...I let it go. Then the next night there was another excuse and the next until every night there was a reason not to make love to his wife. I didn't know what to do. I tried everything that my inexperienced little mind could think of. I bought lingerie, I cooked dishes famed for their aphrodisiac powers, I...'

Callie stopped. Some of the things she'd done to get her husband to want her were still humiliating. She joined her hand with Cade's, traced the network of veins there as she continued.

'I hired some truly awful dirty movies. He was nice about it those first couple of months, apologetic, telling me it'd get better. But when it didn't we started to argue. I wanted us to see someone about it. He refused, saying there was nothing wrong with him, that it was me. That *I* wasn't sexy enough. That *I* didn't do it for him.'

Cade could hear Callie's voice thickening with emotion as she spoke and not even the night could cloak her troubled gaze as he absently rubbed his palms against her belly in a soothing gesture. That certainly explained why Callie had *needed* to have sex with him after dinner with her parents when Joe's name had come up.

'You have to know now that it's not true, right?' he murmured.

Callie nodded. 'Oh, I've got a lot of years on me now that says Joe was wrong.' But a part of her would never recover from his taunts.

'Is he gay?' Cade figured he'd might as well just come out and say it. 'Because I don't understand how any straight guy could have you willing and able in his bed and not take full advantage.'

'You know, after I left I did wonder from time to time but, honestly, I can't see it. He'd been with a lot of girls before me. Hell, you heard Mum—he's currently got one knocked up, moved away from Broken Hill with her. You've got to understand—if you're from the land you don't just leave. He has to be utterly besotted.'

'Was he…dysfunctional? Did he have problems getting an erection?'

'Oh, no, he seemed to have plenty of five a.m. specials.'

'But what about at other times?'

Callie remembered a particularly mortifying incident. 'I caught him masturbating once. It looked in fully functioning order to me.'

Cade dropped a kiss on her shoulder. 'That can't have been easy.'

'Nope. I was pretty pissed off about it.'

'What did he say?'

'He said I should be happy he wasn't going outside our marriage to find satisfaction.'

Cade winced. 'Ouch.' He dropped another couple of kisses. His own home life may have been a wreck but his sexual experiences had always been positive. They'd given him a good sense of himself. 'So you left?'

'No. He called it off. It caused a bit of a scandal. I was devastated, humiliated that I couldn't make my marriage work and at having to move back home again. My mother was horrified. How was she going to hold her head up around town again? And then when word got out that Joe had gone for an annulment instead of a divorce, the speculation and gossip were rife. Thank God for Mr Barry. Getting out of Broken Hill was the best thing I did.'

'Amen,' Cade agreed. He didn't say anything for a while and then something occurred to him. 'So who *did* you lose it to?'

Callie looked at the ceiling. Another story she'd never told anyone. It must have been something about the darkness encouraging confidences because she found herself spilling this one, as well.

'Some bar hook-up when I first went to Sydney. I don't even know what his name was but he told me I was sexy and he looked at me in a way Joe never had. It was pretty sordid, really—in the back of his car parked out the front of the uni. But I was sick of feeling so gauche, pretending I knew what my friends were talking about when the conversation turned to sex, which it inevitably did.'

Cade propped his chin on her shoulder. 'I'm sorry,' he murmured. 'Everyone's first should be special.'

'I didn't want special. I wanted it *gone* and he was more than happy to oblige.'

Cade watched the determined set of her jaw. He knew now why she liked to set the sexual agenda. He lifted a hand and brushed a stray strand of hair back off her forehead. Then he stroked a couple more times because he liked touching her.

'What can I do to make it up to you?'

Callie pulled her eyes off the ceiling as his finger swirled around her belly button. Just looking at her like that, with sex and lust and desire in his eyes, made it up to her. Bolstered her sexual ego.

She palmed his cheek, smiling. 'Just how dirty is dirty?' she asked.

Cade grinned, his fingers trekking lower. 'Open your legs and I'll demonstrate.'

* * *

An hour later the urgent trilling of an alarm pierced their deep sexual exhaustion. Cade sat bolt upright in bed, displacing Callie who was disorientated for a second.

'The bloody cake!' he swore, leaping out of bed.

Callie was right behind him when he opened the bedroom door to the acrid smell of something burning. They hurried to the kitchen to find black smoke bleeding out from around the door.

'Hell!' Callie said, dashing to the oven door and yanking it open. A cloud of smoke billowed out, stinging her eyes and pushing her back.

Cade grabbed a cloth from the nearby bench as the smoke escaped. He reached into the oven and pulled out the cake, keeping his head averted as he rushed the burnt offering to the sink and threw it in then turned the tap on. Callie turned the oven off, coughing as her lungs protested. While Cade doused the cake she scurried to the sliding doors, opening them wider then flicking the nearby fan switch to high to dissipate the smoke.

When the alarm finally stopped ringing Cade turned away from the sink and looked at her surveying her apartment, hand on hip. They were both breathing hard. 'I hope no one called a fire truck,' he said. 'We're not exactly dressed for company.'

Callie looked down at her nudity then at his and laughed. The crisis had been averted and they did look kind of absurd.

'Shall we go back to bed?' he asked.

Callie paused. Anyone else she'd have asked to leave. She made a habit of never spending the night with anyone. But this felt different somehow. She'd opened up to him— they'd opened up to each other. She'd been as emotionally naked to him earlier as she was now physically naked. And she didn't want him to go. She nodded. 'Right behind you.'

Callie woke the next morning to her alarm clock at 6:00 a.m. Back home in Broken Hill she'd never needed an alarm clock. But she'd quickly embraced the city habit when partying and shift work had taken over her life.

She was disappointed to find she was alone.

A first.

The fact that she hadn't suggested Cade leave after their rude awakening was also a first. Having been so scarred from her relationship with Joe, she'd spent a long time running from any romantic entanglements. She'd learned early that relationships often didn't live up to their expectations and she'd doubted she could ever survive another disaster.

But she felt a connection with Cade. The same kind of kindred-spirit connection she felt with Alex—only more. She loved Alex as a friend but she already knew that Cade was never going to be friend material.

Maybe if they took their time through the remaining dates, if they took it slowly between the two of them, it could become something more?

Callie rolled out of bed with a smile on her face.

She tracked Cade down in his office an hour later. 'Here you are,' she said. 'I bought you something.'

Cade looked up from his computer screen. Callie was holding a bakery box. He gave her a ghost of a smile. 'You shouldn't have.'

Cade had come into work early to check on Trudy. Satisfied all was okay he'd come back to his office to catch up on some paperwork. An email from Alex had been waiting in his inbox and he'd opened it eagerly. There had been the usual stuff about Layla and work, but a mention that an L.A. real estate agent had let Alex know their old house was up for sale had been unexpected and taken the shine off yesterday and his night with Callie.

It had reminded him of a time when he hadn't been a successful prenatal surgeon. When he'd been trapped in an inner suburban shoebox with a drunken, neglectful father. It had reminded him of a past he'd been running away from ever since. And that coming to Australia had been another escape. An escape from the mess with Sophie.

And that was what he was *supposed* to be doing.

His brother's cheery *Say hello to Callie* sign-off had also grated.

It had been a general downer.

'It was the least I could do,' Callie said, sitting on the chair opposite him, 'after promising you cake and not delivering.'

She waited for him to make some quip about just how well she'd delivered but it didn't arrive. 'You left early.'

'Yes. I wanted to check on Trudy.'

Callie nodded. 'I'm on my way there now.' She asked some questions about Trudy's progress but Callie got the impression that Cade's mind wasn't on the job. Was he regretting not having stuck to his eight-date edict last night?

When they'd exhausted the subject of Trudy, Callie tentatively stepped into the breach. 'Cade...I just want you to know that I had a really great night last night.' She smiled. 'You sure know how to show a girl a good time. And the stuff I told you... I've never told anyone about Joe...about being married. Not even Alex knows.'

Cade's breath seized in his lungs. *You sure know how to show a girl a good time.* The sentence reverberated around his head—they were the exact words that Sophie had used. And Callie had the same expression on her face and in her gaze—the one Sophie had got when she'd looked at him. Dewy-eyed.

And right in that moment Cade realised he'd made a terrible mistake. A massive error in judgement. That was exactly why he'd been keeping away from women and the dating scene in the first place. Things were getting into dangerous territory. Hadn't he, too, told her stuff he'd never confessed to another living soul before?

This thing with Callie was now a fling, bordering on something else—the next thing, whatever that was. And he remembered way too vividly what had happened the one and only other time he'd had a fling. Sophie had wound up pregnant and then, when he'd been shocked and angry and unable to cope, she'd taken a handful of pills and a bottle of vodka, winding up in Emergency then miscarrying the baby.

A baby he hadn't wanted. A baby he felt guilty about every day.

Of course Callie wasn't likely to turn into a bunny boiler but he still felt the wild gallop of his heart as the walls started to close in on him. They were going too quickly and he couldn't breathe. He couldn't be responsible for Callie's baggage. Her emotional or psychological wellbeing. Not when he wasn't coping with his own.

Cade raked his hand through his hair. 'I think we need to talk....'

CHAPTER TEN

IT DIDN'T TAKE Callie long to figure out she'd got things horribly wrong. *Way to go, Callie. Way to read a situation!*

And that was before he'd even said a word.

He had that look. The same look she'd always employed when she was about to tell some hapless guy who hadn't known the score or had thought he was going to be the one to change her that she really had meant only one night.

The whole *it's-not-you-it's-me* routine.

'I don't think we should keep dating,' Cade said, starting out tentatively. 'The only reason I said eight was to keep you away from my body as long as possible.' He shot her a smile. 'But I think after last night that's kind of moot.'

Callie nodded automatically. 'Of course.'

'It's just that neither of us do this kind of thing as a rule,' Cade added. 'In fact, we studiously avoid doing it, so we may as well just…quit while we're ahead.' *Before something dire happened.*

'Of course,' Callie repeated. 'Absolutely.'

'I came here to concentrate on my career and that's what I really need to do.'

'Yes…of course…. Couldn't agree more,' Callie said, hoping for the convenience of a hole to swallow her. She stood. 'As you know, I don't date at all so this was always an aberration for me.'

'Callie.' Cade stood, too. Callie was taking it as he'd expect from someone as relationship-phobic as himself. But he knew more about her soft underbelly now.

The insecurities beneath her tough exterior.

'This isn't about me not finding you attractive enough.'

Callie swatted her hand through the air at him. 'I know that.' She did. She really did. 'I think you've more than proved that to me,' she said, injecting light and bounce into her voice.

'Yeah, but something tells me there's part of you that will always see certain actions from men as a comment on your desirability.'

Callie shrugged. 'Years ago maybe, but not today. I'm past that.'

Cade's eyebrow kicked up. 'And that night on the beach was…?'

Callie grinned, despite the situation. That night on the beach had been amazing. 'Those were extenuating circumstances.'

Cade grinned back at her, the initial discomfort at the awkward conversation evaporating as he remembered Callie on the beach wearing nothing but sand.

'So…' He paused. 'Friends?'

Callie nodded, still smiling. Looks like he was going to *have* to be friend material. Okay. That was fine. She could do friends. She could intubate/cannulate/resuscitate a twenty-four-weeker—*she could do friends.* 'I'd like that. Just like me and Alex. Keeping it in the family,' she joked.

Cade nodded also but he didn't find it very funny. His and Alex's relationship had been rocky but it had mended—grown and matured—and they were as close now as they had been as kids. But part of him didn't want Callie to be *friends* with Alex.

And he wasn't even going to think about how screwed up that was.

For the next few days Callie refused to let her mind wander into what-ifs. Cade had made his position clear and she respected that. *She really did.* Admired it, even. So few people said what they meant these days, particularly in the relationship part of their lives. If Cade wanted to be friends, then she'd make it work.

She was grateful to him, really, for getting her back on track. She'd made it to thirty-three as a respected, successful neonatal specialist. She led a rich, full life without the hassles and disappointments of romantic entanglements. She was exactly where she wanted to be.

And now she had a friend to share her accomplishments with. She'd missed Alex on the other side of the world and while they emailed and chatted on Skype, it wasn't the same thing as having that easy camaraderie surrounding you on a daily basis.

And now she could have that with Cade.

Sure, it was bound to be a little awkward at first. More awkward than it had been with Alex because she and Cade had been more emotionally intimate right from the start. She and Alex had shared a one-time physical thing and their emotional closeness had happened gradually over the months that had followed. With Cade the emotional and physical had been heavily intertwined from the get-go.

But the awkwardness would wear away in time and their mutual respect and professional admiration would be a solid basis for friendship.

In the meantime, she was grateful to be too busy to

think about it too much. The unit was full and they had some complex premmies who required very intensive care. She got home each night after fourteen hours on her feet and was just too exhausted to think about anything else other than her bed.

Of course, she couldn't control what went on behind closed eyelids, which was frustrating, but her dreams were bound to lessen in time, surely?

On Monday morning, after no complications, Trudy was discharged from hospital. Callie hoped that they could get the pregnancy along as far as possible to give the baby the best start in life but, like her dreams, that wasn't something she could control, either. Still, she'd be keeping a close eye on Trudy's progress via Nikolai.

She went back to her office after popping in to say her goodbyes to Trudy and Elliot. She had a smile on her face, knowing that she'd been a part of an amazing journey in the couple's lives. Thanks to Cade.

Thankfully her phone chose that moment to ring and derail the direction of her thoughts. She almost kissed it as she picked it up.

'Dr Richards,' she said. There was silence for a few moments on the other end. 'Hello?'

'Callie...it's Joe.'

Callie blinked. *Joe? Her* Joe? Ex-husband Joe? *Yep, that ought to distract her from thoughts of Cade.*

'Callie?'

She wanted to deny it. To call the person on the other end a liar. To yell and say, *How dare you impersonate my ex-husband?* But it was him. It may have been thirteen years since she'd heard his voice but it was still the same— deep and sexy in that broad-country-accent kind of way.

'I'm here,' she said.

'I'm sorry to ring out of the blue like this.'

Callie didn't know what to say. Several responses crossed her mind. *Why the hell did you, then? Is that all you're sorry for?* And the forerunner: *Go to hell, you misogynistic bastard.*

But Broken Hill manners came to the fore. 'What do you want, Joe?'

'How have you been?'

Callie almost laughed. Bizarre had turned into surreal. 'Joe, you didn't ring me to ask me how I was and I think we're way beyond pleasantries. I'm really very busy. Was there something that you wanted?'

There was a pause on the end of the line then she heard him laugh. 'Wow,' he said. 'You grew some balls.'

'Yeah. Thanks to you.'

Another pause. 'It's Raylene. She's my...'

'Your pregnant partner,' Callie finished. 'Yes, Mum told me.'

'Right... Well, there's been some problems with the baby. He was diagnosed on his nineteen-week ultrasound with an enlarged bladder. They told us that this often resolves spontaneously but we've had two ultrasounds since and it's been worse on each one. They've diagnosed him with something called LUTO. That's lower urinary—'

'Tract obstruction,' Callie interrupted. 'I know what it stands for.'

'Of course...sorry... Anyway, they're referring us to Brisbane. But I know you're a neonatal specialist, Callie, and I trust you... According to your mum, you're the best, and I want the best for my little boy, Callie. I want you.'

Callie didn't even begin to know where to start with this conversation. She couldn't decide which was more bizarre. Her ex-husband contacting her after over a decade of silence. Or the news that her *mother* had said she was the best.

She must have been more stunned than she knew because Joe said, 'Callie? Are you still there?'

Callie gave herself a mental shake and got her head back into the game. Which was a tiny unborn baby suffering from LUTO, a potentially lethal condition—and she could help. The history she and Joe shared was secondary. Callie looked at her watch. Midday. 'How soon can you get here?'

Joe's sigh was audible. 'Two hours, depending on traffic.'

'I'll be waiting. Page me when you get here.' She gave him her number.

'Callie… Thanks…'

The gratitude in Joe's voice was clear but Callie wasn't about to give him a free pass. He'd made her miserable and while eighteen-year-old Callie would have been polite and forgiving, the thirty-three-year-old version wouldn't.

'Drive carefully,' she said, then rang off.

Callie didn't realise her hands were shaking until she replaced the phone in the cradle. Hell, she was about to see Joe again after all these years. *And Raylene.* Who was pregnant with his baby.

She wasn't sure how she was supposed to feel. She wasn't sure how she *actually* felt. A jumble of emotions tumbled around inside her like a giant clothes dryer—apprehension, nervousness, dread.

It was surreal, bizarre and it was happening.

So she did the only thing she could. She started making some phone calls.

A few hours later, Cade stood waiting for the lift to arrive. He was expecting a page from Callie any time now to let him know when her newly diagnosed LUTO patient had arrived. She'd rung and asked him to consult with a view to possible surgical intervention. He'd seen a few LUTO patients back home and had placed shunts successfully.

Of course, thinking about Callie was never a good idea. Things seemed to be fine between them, for which he was grateful, but fine was a long way from smoking hot and his body spent a lot of time remembering the smoking hot.

It was bloody distracting.

The light above the lift indicated it had reached his floor and he waited for the doors to open. Three people occupied the lift as he stepped in, pushed the button for his floor and then fell back against the wall. Opposite him the trio lined up against the other wall. A young, thin woman with a tiny baby bump evident beneath her snug T-shirt stood close to the two men but slightly separate. The two men, however, stood very close together, their arms brushing, their hips touching.

It was a comfortable stance—intimate, really—and Cade assumed they were partners. He smiled at them and, grateful to have a distraction from his thoughts of Callie, said to the woman, 'How far along are you?'

'Twenty-one weeks,' she murmured.

'Past the halfway mark,' he quipped.

The woman nodded and smiled but it seemed forced and the man closest to her reached for her hand and took it. Then the lift dinged and they all trooped out. And Cade was left alone in the lift with only Callie to fill his head.

Callie felt like throwing up when the knock sounded. Joe had paged to say they were on their way up and she was suddenly gripped with the urge to hide under her desk and pretend this wasn't happening. But she didn't.

She took a deep breath. 'Come in.'

The door opened and there he stood. Just as blond and

rugged and handsome as he'd always been. A little older but essentially Joe.

'Hello, Callie,' he said.

Relief, pure and sweet, flooded her system. A part of her had been terrified that maybe, despite the years and everything that had gone on between them, she was still in love with Joe.

A dozen different emotions flitted through her but none of them was love.

Callie nodded. 'Hello, Joe.'

Joe smiled at her then turned to the woman beside him. 'This is Raylene.'

Callie also switched her attention. She was a little startled to see the cute, petite blonde. Her hair was in a high perky ponytail and all her clothes and accessories were matching shades of pink. She looked like a cheerleader and so tiny that a puff of wind could blow her over. Even her bump was cute.

God, if this was what turned Joe on, no wonder he hadn't wanted her. Raylene was a girly girl to Callie's tall, athletic redhead. And pink definitely wasn't her colour.

Realising she was staring, Callie came out from behind her desk and shook the other woman's hand. It was a weird moment—for her anyway. Raylene didn't seem at all awkward or uncomfortable being in the same room as Joe's ex and Callie admired her composure—she'd been told she could be pretty intimidating.

'Have a seat.' Callie indicated the two chairs on the opposite of her desk. When they took them she said, 'Do you have the scans?'

Callie took a while reviewing the scans and the reports that came with them. She'd already spoken to the specialist they'd been dealing with, who had given her a thorough rundown. She asked the odd question as she went along but there wasn't a lot of chatter as she continued to familiarise herself with the case.

Eventually she lifted her head and addressed them both. 'I think you're a good candidate for a shunt. I've asked Dr Coleman, who specialises in prenatal surgery, to consult with me on this. I've also rung our top paediatric urologist and she's going to consult on the case. We might also need a renal physician, depending on the condition of the baby's kidneys.'

'So you can fix it?' Joe asked.

'I think so. But we'll know more after some more tests.'

'Thank you,' Joe said. 'I'm so grateful.'

Callie nodded briskly, uncomfortable with his gratitude. 'I'll just call Dr Coleman.'

Joe and Raylene waited while she placed the call. She hadn't told Cade it was Joe and she wasn't sure why—maybe she'd needed time to absorb it herself.

'Ready for you,' Callie said as Cade answered.

'Can you give me half an hour? Sorry, I just got caught up in Special Care.'

'No worries,' Callie said. 'I'll get the bloods done while we wait.'

Callie put the phone down. 'Okay. First step is to do some blood tests to rule out any chromosomal abnormalities. Take this to Pathology. It's on the second floor.' She handed them an already filled-out request form. 'Come back here when you're done.'

Raylene took the form. Joe said thank you one more time then they left. Callie sat staring at the door as it shut after them. That hadn't been too difficult at all. She'd always be angry with Joe and what had happened in their short marriage but it was good to know she could face him without falling apart.

As an equal.

Her inexperience had exacerbated her powerlessness back then. He was *Joe Rawlings*. The guy she'd dreamed about and built up in her head to be a saint, and when he'd turned out to have feet of clay she'd been too young, naive and unsophisticated to deal with his criticisms.

But they were on an even footing now. And he knew it, too.

Another knock broke into her musings—probably Cade. Her pulse spiked. The only other man who had caused her so much consternation. 'Come in,' she called.

The door opened and Joe stood there. 'Oh…Joe.' She stood. 'Everything okay? Did you get lost? It's a bit of a warren.'

He shook his head. 'No…it's fine. I was hoping I could…talk to you for a moment.'

'Oh.'

Callie didn't know what to say. She'd had a million questions crowding her mind since Joe had rung but she wasn't sure she wanted to open Pandora's box. Not right now. Not with Raylene likely to return so soon. Not with the bigger issue of his baby's condition, which they needed to focus on.

'Please, Callie. There's things I need to…tell you. Things you *need* to hear.'

A flash of anger flared through her veins. He wasn't running this show any more. 'Oh, you *need* to, do you?' she demanded. 'I *need* to? I gave you plenty of opportunity, Joe. I begged you to talk to me. But you chose to demonise me instead, remember? Or is it still *all my fault*?'

Joe shut the door behind him and advanced into the room.

'No,' he said softly, 'it wasn't your fault. I'm so, so sorry about the way things went down with us. The way I… treated you. You were lovely and innocent and so bloody sweet and I didn't deserve you. I know I certainly don't deserve your absolution or forgiveness or even time to hear me out but I *need* to make amends.'

'Again, it's all about you, isn't it?' Callie snapped, the wound he was picking at ripping wide open suddenly.

'No. I *wronged* you, Callie. It's my greatest shame…' He gave a half laugh. 'Ironically there are some back home who might not say that but I know. I know in here,' he said, bouncing a fist off his still impressively flat abdomen. 'I should have contacted you two years ago. Set things straight. I've been a coward.'

'*Two* years ago?' she hissed. *He had to be joking, right?* 'Try thirteen.'

Joe shook his head and Callie was struck by the absolute wretchedness of it. 'I was in denial until two years ago.'

She frowned. 'I suppose Raylene opened your eyes to how women really should be treated? Honestly, Joe, why did you marry me if what you really wanted was a peppy little blonde?'

Joe sank into the chair. 'Because what I really wanted was a guy called Paul, who was sensitive and arty and does yoga on the beachfront every morning and doesn't care what anybody else thinks of him. Unlike me.'

Callie blinked. She heard the words but she was having trouble computing them. *Was he saying what she thought he was saying?* She sunk into her chair. 'You're…gay?'

Joe gave a half smile. 'Apparently.'

Callie reeled from the admission. On one hand it was an overwhelming relief. On the other it was even more confusing. 'I don't think flippancy is called for here, Joseph,' she snapped, slipping back into old ways, old chastisements.

Joe placed his palms flat on her desk. 'Sorry… You're right.'

Callie took a breath. 'So you're gay but a woman called Raylene is having your baby.'

He nodded. 'She's a surrogate.'

Callie felt the doctor take over as the eighteen-year-old girly inside her shrank away and rocked in a corner somewhere. 'Are you the biological father?'

'Yes.'

'And your partner...?'

'Paul. He's going to be the biological father next time.'

'Okay.'

She didn't know what to say now. Everything made sense, knowing that Joe was gay. But there were still so many questions and she just didn't know where to start. As a doctor she could fire away but as the woman who had loved him to no avail, she was lost.

'I'm sorry,' Joe said. 'I've been denying my sexuality for years. I kept thinking if I just played some more footy, got pissed a little more at the pub with my mates, ploughed some more fields...got married, then it would go away. I come from a small rural town from farming stock. Where men are men and women swoon. I didn't want to be gay. I desperately didn't want to be a gay farmer in Broken Hill.'

'The only gay in the village?' she joked absently.

He smiled back. 'Something like that. It certainly felt that way.'

'So you married me.'

He nodded. 'Yes. And I really wanted to make it work. If only you hadn't wanted to *very inconveniently* have sex with your husband, it all would have been okay.'

Callie blinked. 'You're joking, right?'

Joe sighed. 'Of course.' He clasped his hands. 'I'm sorry, I didn't know what to do. I didn't want to be gay, but I didn't feel anything sexually towards you and that gave me incredible erectile dysfunction and I wanted to hide that from you—to protect you. But you were so sweet and earnest, trying to make it work, and it kept eating away at me until it was easier to push you away, to be a jerk so you wouldn't want to have sex with me.'

'You know you just could have told me, right?'

Joe shook his head and quirked an eyebrow. 'Really, Callie? I know I could have told the Callie sitting in front of me today, but telling the Callie who looked at me like I hung the stars, when I already felt so bad about myself? You were so…innocent. I didn't know how, where to even begin. And I'm not sure eighteen-year-old Callie would really have understood.'

Callie thought about it. He was right. Maybe she wouldn't have. 'Maybe not,' she admitted. 'But it's been thirteen years since we parted and, Joe, I've got to tell you, what happened between us really messed me up.'

He reached across the desk and held out his hand and Callie took it. 'I know, and I'm so sorry. If I could go back and change that, I would. But I hadn't even admitted it to myself until I met Paul three years ago when I was on holiday in Noosa. It's been a long road for me. It took me a year to finally admit it to myself then I had this clandestine long-distance relationship with Paul for another year before he said I had to make a choice. Telling my parents was the hardest thing I've ever done, besides leaving Broken Hill and screwing you over. They haven't come to terms with it at all. It's only the prospect of a grandchild that has kept dialogue open between us. Paul says it takes time, that they'll come round. I'm not sure he's right.'

Callie nodded. She knew how black and white things could be in the country. Of course there were open-minded people, too, but in an outback mining town they weren't exactly a dime a dozen.

'Paul sounds like a guy I'd really like to meet.'

And she realised it was the truth. A huge weight had been lifted from her shoulders with Joe's admissions. Sure, she'd come to realise through a full and active sex life over the years that she *was* a desirable woman but the old resentment she'd felt towards Joe for making her feel the opposite had never really fully gone away.

But confronted with him now all these years later, listening to his struggle, hearing him say he was sorry and truly believing it, was like an instant balm to her wounds. Her life was full and happy and so was his. It looked like they'd both come through their disastrous beginnings to a better life.

'He's outside. I know he wants to meet you.'

Callie was momentarily taken aback by the admission but, then, why wouldn't he? Paul sounded like the perfect partner. She nodded. 'Well, for goodness' sake, bring him in, then.'

And in less than thirty seconds she was being hugged by the man her ex-husband loved, and she could totally see why. He was handsome in a goofy way and very witty, which put her instantly at her ease.

'Joe has told me so much about you,' Paul enthused. 'He feels so awful about what happened in your marriage. He sings your praises every day. And while I regret the circumstances that brought us all together today, I'm so happy he got to make amends because I know how heavily it damaged him. You deserved better and I've been telling him that for three years. He needed to apologise.'

'Thank you,' Callie said. 'It means a lot that he has.'

'Does it?' Joe asked.

Callie nodded. 'Yes. You really hurt me, Joe. Knowing that you regret it…it helps.'

'I'm so sorry,' Joe said again. 'You're the last person I ever wanted to hurt and yet you're the one I hurt most.'

Callie walked into his arms then, her eyes welling with tears. 'Apology accepted,' she whispered.

'Please tell me there's someone special for you?' Joe asked, his breath brushing the hair at her temple.

Callie stepped out of his embrace, her thoughts turning to Cade. 'Not really,' she said, pushing them away. 'I haven't exactly been willing to make myself vulnerable to the whims of another man again.'

'Oh, no,' Paul said, and he grabbed her hands with passionate ferocity. 'We all need love, Callie. Don't shut yourself off from that. Never shut yourself off from that.'

Joe nodded. 'Loving Paul has been the most amazing thing I've ever done. It took courage I never knew I had but I am *thankful* every day that I did. Life's too short to be lonely.'

Callie could feel more tears queuing in her eyes. Knowing that her marriage breakdown hadn't been her fault was a huge weight off her shoulders. Were they right?

Joe had found love—why not her?

And in that instant she let the love flood in. The love she'd been holding in check behind barriers she'd erected a long time ago. She loved Cade. She'd been trying to pretend that it was lust. That what she felt for him was purely physical. But she knew that was nonsense.

He'd come into her life and been sweet and compassionate and understanding. It was like he understood her better than anyone ever had—even Alex. But it wasn't just compassion and gratitude and friendship she felt for him. Neither was it just blind, hot, searing lust and a thirst that couldn't be quenched. It was a feeling that she was meant to be with him, that their lives were intertwined, that they were destined to be together.

That she loved him. As much if not more than she had ever loved Joe in her foolish teenage flights of fancy. This wasn't some…crush. This was real. This was forever kind of stuff.

She looked at her ex-husband and his partner and even though part of her still couldn't take it all in, the other part was so grateful that she'd been given a second chance at love. *Real* love.

'You're right,' she said.

'There is someone, isn't there?' Paul asked.

Callie nodded. 'I'm not sure he feels the same way.'

Paul smiled at Joe and reached for his partner's hand. 'That's when you have to fight,' he said. 'You know how to do that?'

Callie looked at Joe when she said, 'I'm from the country, aren't I?'

Joe smiled. 'Damn straight.'

Cade was surprised when he hit Callie's office twenty minutes later that the trio who had been in the lift were now in her office. He smiled at everyone as Callie introduced them. 'This is my ex-husband Joe and his partner, Paul, and their surrogate, Raylene.'

Cade blinked. Callie had said that so casually he was glad he was sitting down. He searched her face for signs of stress but she seemed relaxed. 'Nice to meet you all,' he said, standing to briefly to shake both men's hands. 'I understand there are some bladder problems with the baby?'

The next couple of hours passed with information gathering and more appointments made for tomorrow to get a full handle on the situation. There was no time to ponder the bigger picture. Cade was as confident as Callie that the baby was a candidate for a shunt to be placed through fetoscopy but he liked to have all his i's dotted and his t's crossed.

When Joe, Paul and Raylene left two hours later, having

arranged to return in the morning, there was silence in Callie's office for a beat or two. 'Gay, huh?' he said eventually.

Callie looked at him and smiled. 'Apparently.'

'And how does that make you feel?'

Callie searched around for the right adjectives. 'Relieved. Vindicated. Sad that we both wasted so many years…hopeful.'

Cade frowned. 'Hopeful?'

Callie's heartbeat kicked up. From the moment Cade had walked into her office and taken everything in his stride, even more love had gushed into her heart and she knew she was going to take a risk.

Because she always called a spade a spade, said it like it was—that was the country way, after all. And now that she realised she loved him, she didn't want to waste another second.

Joe had found love—why not her?

'I'm in love with you, Cade.' There was that calling-a-spade-a-spade stuff again. 'It took me a while to realise that but Joe asked me if I had someone and I realised that if he could move on, forgive himself, find love, be happy, then why was I making myself miserable by denying what I know in my heart of hearts?'

Cade stood, horrified by her admission. Love was not on his agenda. 'Callie.'

Callie stood also. 'I know it's a lot to take on board,' she said. 'I know that you're going to need to think about it,' she confirmed. 'I just wanted you to know. *Needed* you to know.'

Cade couldn't believe what he was hearing. He raked his hand through his hair. 'I…' *I don't love you.* 'I…' Then he realised he couldn't lie to her or lead her on. For the longest time he'd wondered if he'd done that to Sophie and he wanted to be clear here. 'I'm not looking for love, Callie.'

Callie felt the rejection like bullets through her heart, and once upon a time she would have blamed it on herself but after today she knew this was about Cade and his issues and he needed time.

'I know. But I think you're scared. Like I was. I think there were a lot of times in your life when you weren't loved, weren't taken care of, and the times you were weren't exactly altruistic. I know what it feels like to want to be loved and have that denied to you. I know how that can make you feel like you're not lovable. But that's okay. I'm not scared any more and I'm not going anywhere, either. I love you, Cade, and I want to spend the rest of my life proving that.'

Cade took a step back as everything froze inside him. How could she love him? Especially after only a few months' acquaintance? The people who were *supposed* to have loved him in this life hadn't even managed that.

'You don't know me,' he said bitterly. 'I don't need anyone's love. And I certainly don't need yours.'

Callie held on in the face of his utter desolation. 'Okay. But *I* need yours. I've lived the last thirteen years without any love in my life and I thought that was fine, that I didn't need it. But I was wrong. I love you, Cade, and it fills me up and I want you to love me back.'

Cade shook his head as he backed away towards the door. 'You want too much.'

Callie swallowed a lump in her throat. Maybe she did. But she'd settled for less last time and she wasn't going to this time around. 'Yes.'

Cade shook his head. Sophie had wanted too much. He couldn't go there again. 'I can't,' he said. 'I just can't.'

Callie watched him turn and leave. Her heart bled for what could be. But she hadn't given up on Joe all those years ago so she sure as hell wasn't going to give up on Cade.

If the last few hours had taught her anything, it was that love was worth fighting for.

CHAPTER ELEVEN

WITH THE DIAGNOSIS of a posterior urethral valve blocking the flow of urine out of the bladder, and all the other tests coming back normal, Cade performed the shunting procedure with ultrasonic guidance two days later. After the baby was born he would need to go to surgery immediately to correct the problem permanently but a shunt was a good temporary fix.

Raylene was given intravenous sedation for both her and the baby as the pig-tailed shunt was inserted via fetoscope into the baby's bladder, through an incision low on the baby's abdomen. The tiny piece of plastic would be a conduit for the urine to flow out into the amniotic fluid, which had already decreased significantly. Thanks to the procedure, it would build up again and do its vital job of helping the lungs develop.

Joe had asked Callie to be there with them throughout. She was great, explaining everything as the procedure unfolded, which allowed Cade to get on with it. But she was wearing *that* dress and *vanilla* and to cap it all off her revelations from a couple of days ago were still swirling around inside his head.

She loved him.

Resentment bubbled in his gut as he worked. How dared she drop that on him? That wasn't the kind of relationship they had. They'd both known that from the beginning. And now she'd gone and changed the rules on him.

It was just like Sophie all over again.

He'd bet Callie wouldn't love him if she knew what had happened with Sophie.

How he'd been blazingly angry at her deception, at having fatherhood thrust upon him, at being taken advantage of when he'd specifically told her that fatherhood wasn't on his agenda. How they'd rowed and he'd told her he didn't want her or the baby. That she'd lied, tricked him into it and he hadn't wanted anything to do with either of them.

He'd been so furious.

And then she'd compounded everything by trying to kill herself and had forever cast him in the role of bad guy. He couldn't lie to himself. When he'd found out that she was okay but that the baby hadn't made it…the relief that whooshed through him had been like a drug buzz.

But what kind of a person did that make him?

He should have been grieving for his unborn child and part of him had been devastated at the loss, but, over-whelmingly, all he had been able to feel had been that he'd dodged a bullet. And he'd hated himself for that, the resentment growing and festering until the grief and the guilt, and the anger had become too much and he'd run away from it. Run from L.A. to New York. To Alex. To a whole new life.

And when it had eventually caught up with him there, he'd run to the other side of the world.

'Almost done,' Callie said to Paul.

Caught up in the past, Cade was startled for a moment to hear her voice. He tuned back in to the present, annoyed that he'd let his thoughts drift off his patient. He knew his hands and his brain could perform the procedure on au-tomatic pilot but it was no excuse.

Raylene and her baby deserved his undivided attention. And he was angry at Callie for that, too!

He finished up in ten minutes and was relieved when Callie volunteered to stay and monitor Raylene while she came round. She'd taken the day off to support Joe and Paul and he wanted her here with them, rather than anywhere near him, upsetting his equilibrium with her bloody vanilla essence and that damn pocket dress.

Had she worn them deliberately to mess with him? Because it was working. It had been days since he'd touched her, kissed her…and, God help him, he wanted more.

He slipped back a couple of hours later to check on Raylene's progress. She was sitting up in a cosy recliner chair with a cup of tea and some biscuits. She was still in her theatre gown but her drip had been bunged off and she was looking alert and relaxed.

'How are you feeling?' he asked, smiling at her, ignoring the delicious smell and sight of Callie in his peripheral vision.

Raylene smiled back. 'Good, thanks. A little bit sleepy still but no pain or anything.'

'That's good,' Cade acknowledged. 'How about we get you up on the bed and I'll do a quick ultrasound to check on things?'

Paul and Joe hovered around Raylene as they helped her up and she rolled her eyes at Callie. 'I *can* get out of a chair, you two,' she grumbled good-naturedly.

Cade turned on the machine, letting it boot up as he strode over to the light switch near the door and flipped it off. Callie reached over and pulled the blind down on the window, shutting out another spectacular Gold Coast day. The room darkened significantly. There was still light coming in from around the edges of the blind but it was dark enough to make the images easy to see.

Grainy snow soon flickered on the screen and Cade punched some information into the keyboard before picking up the warmed conducting gel and squirting it on Raylene's bared abdomen. 'Ready?' he asked.

'Yup,' Raylene said. Joe and Paul, who were standing next to her, also nodded.

He was very aware of Callie at the foot of the bed as he applied the probe to the blob of warm goo he'd squeezed on. She'd positioned herself for a good view of the screen—exactly as he would have done if their positions had been reversed.

The baby's image appeared on the screen and he noticed in his peripheral vision Joe reaching for Paul's hand.

'Hah! Look at that,' Callie announced, coming around the end of the bed towards him until she was standing close.

Within touching distance.

Part of him wanted to lean back into her, to have her slip her arms around his neck. To turn his face, bury it in her neck and take big deep sniffs of her.

How could he be angry with her and still crave her so badly?

'What?' Joe asked, looking at Callie then at Cade.

'The bladder has reduced significantly,' she said.

Cade nodded, ignoring Callie's tempting presence behind him, and did a quick set of measurements. 'By about half,' he confirmed.

Paul squinted at the screen. 'It certainly looks a lot smaller than in the last ultrasound.'

Joe let out a noisy breath. 'Thank God,' he whispered.

Paul hugged him, and Cade was surprised by the streak of envy that burned a path of destruction through his gut. Why he was envious he had no idea. Maybe it was the demons that Joe had overcome to get him to the place he was now.

Cade knew all about demons.

'There's the shunt,' he said, turning back to the screen.

They spent a few minutes watching. Looking at every inch of the baby again, listening to his heartbeat. Joe and Paul were keen to look as much as they could and Cade was happy to indulge them.

When they were done he wiped the glop off Raylene's stomach then got up and switched the light back on. Callie popped the blind up and for a moment, as the glare cut into the room again, it almost blinded Cade. He squinted against it and all he could see was her silhouetted figure in front of the window.

And what a figure.

He wanted her. It was irrational but it was there. He hadn't ever wanted anyone like this. But his needs were physical and she wanted more than that.

More than he could give.

Cade returned to the side of the bed, determined to be brisk and detached. To get through his standard spiel then get the hell out of the room.

'So, as I was saying yesterday,' he said, addressing all three and studiously ignoring Callie, 'there's a forty per cent risk that the shunt will dislodge, which is why it's important that you keep up the weekly ultrasounds through your care provider in Noosa.'

Joe nodded. 'We will.'

'But if it does dislodge,' Paul asked, 'is it just a matter of having another one re-inserted?'

Cade nodded. 'I once inserted four during the length of one pregnancy back in the States.'

'Four?' Raylene said.

Cade smiled at her and patted her hand. 'That's unusual,' he assured her. 'But I'd be prepared if I were you to have the procedure done at least once more.'

'Okay,' she said, her hand absently rubbing her baby bump.

'Do you want me to set up the first appointment with your care provider?' he asked.

'I'm going to do the first couple,' Callie said, stepping away from the window, her pockets coming closer.

'We've booked a unit for two weeks,' Paul said. 'We want to be sure everything's going okay before we head back home.'

'Oh,' Cade said, looking at Callie for long moments. 'Well, you're in very good hands, then.'

Joe laughed. 'Yes, we are.'

'Right. Well, I have surgery shortly so I'll take my leave. You guys are free to go whenever Raylene feels up to it. And I guess I'll be seeing you around the next couple of weeks.'

Joe held out his hand. 'Thank you so much, Cade,' he said as they shook hands. 'You have no idea what this means to us.'

Cade smiled as he shook Paul's hand, as well. 'Oh, I think I have some idea.'

Joe laughed. 'Yeah, I guess you must if you do this sort of stuff all the time.'

'It was my pleasure to be able to help. I'll see you later.'

Four sets of eyes followed Cade across the room. 'Man,' Raylene said, as the door closed after him, 'I envy the woman who warms his bed.'

'Amen to that,' Paul said.

Callie glanced at the frank appreciation on Paul's face. And on Joe's. She tried to remember if she'd ever seen that look directed at a man when they'd been married, and couldn't. Joe had been holding back his real self for too long—it was good to see him being *himself.* It was a crime that he'd waited so long to realise it.

And she didn't want that for herself.

She didn't want to pine away for Cade in secret because he couldn't handle the truth. Paul had been determined enough to fight for Joe—he hadn't taken no for answer.

And neither should she.

Not when she was fairly certain Cade had feelings for her, too. She wasn't going to give up on him without a fight. 'Excuse me,' she said. 'I'll be right back.'

Callie caught up with him at the lifts. 'Cade,' she said, drawing level with him. 'Thanks. For everything today.'

Cade shook his head. He didn't want her near him, clouding his judgement with all those damn pockets and her chocolate-cake memories. 'Come on, Callie, it's my job. No need to thank me.'

'Of course there is,' she murmured. 'This case isn't just any case to me and I really appreciate all you've done.'

Cade shrugged. 'All part of the service.'

The lift dinged and Cade sighed in relief. He waited for it to empty then stepped inside. The last thing he expected or wanted was for her to follow him in.

Cade pushed the door hold button and held out his other hand in a stopping motion. 'Oh, no,' he said. 'You do not want to get in this lift with me.'

'I...don't?'

He shook his head. 'You and those damn pockets need to stay the hell away from me.'

His gaze settled on her breast pockets and Callie felt the blast of heat from his gaze right down to the deepest muscle fibres of her belly. She lifted her chin. 'Well, that's too bad because I'm coming in,' she said, and she pushed past his hand until she was standing inside, a mere foot from him.

The doors shut behind them.

Cade's nostrils filled with the sweet milkiness of her. 'Goddamn it, Callie, vanilla?' he demanded. 'Were the pockets not enough?'

Callie's decision to wear both this morning had been deliberate but she'd forgotten she was wearing the vanilla oil, caught up as she had been in Raylene's procedure and recovery. She shrugged. 'I know you like it.'

Cade thrust a hand through his hair—'like' was such an insipid word. 'Like it? I want to push you against this wall, strip all your clothes off and sniff you all over,' he snapped. 'But you knew that, didn't you?'

Callie didn't think the rhetorical question required an answer and she doubted he'd like it anyway. If sex was the only way she could get through to him then she wasn't averse to using it, using his desire for her body to connect with him emotionally.

To start with anyway.

But that all went by the wayside as the heat in his gaze melted her common sense into a puddle of goo at her feet.

Callie leaned across and pushed the emergency stop button. An alarm filled the lift as it jerked to a stop, toppling her into him. 'So what's stopping you?'

Cade breathed heavily as her blatant invitation intertwined with her vanilla essence to reach down inside his pants. The air seemed to get heavier with each breath he dragged in, the alarm fading as desire washed everything else out.

'Oh, hell,' he muttered, seizing her upper arms, pivoting around with her until her back was against the wall.

He looked at her for long moment, his lungs drowning in her aroma now, craving its sticky heaviness. His gaze zeroed in on her mouth—her lips were slightly parted, welcoming.

'Cade,' she whispered.

Cade groaned as he slammed his mouth onto hers. Her immediate little whimper, the way her arms came up around his neck and her body aligned stoked the fire in his loins even higher. He flayed her mouth with his— probing her lips, commanding entrance, demanding her complete capitulation.

He just couldn't get enough.

Of her mouth, her taste, her smell, her belly-deep moans. Everything burned. Everything ached.

But he had to.

He wrenched his mouth away, his gaze raking her face, noticing her lips were wet and swollen from his punishing kiss. 'God, I wish I didn't want you this much.'

'There's nothing wrong with this, Cade,' Callie murmured, her voice husky as her hand stroked the hair at his nape. 'We can have this, we can have this all the time. Just let me love you.'

Cade stepped back on a groan. 'No, we can't.' And he jabbed viciously at the emergency stop button again.

The alarm ceased and the lift shuddered a little before moving again. He placed himself against the opposite wall from her—far away from the temptation of vanilla and pockets.

'Why?' Callie demanded. 'I know you want me,' she said. 'What's wrong with giving us a chance?'

Cade felt a hard lump rise in his chest. The same matted, twisted knot of pain he'd been pushing down for years. Since he'd been a little kid and he'd been powerless to stop his father beating Alex. It rose with all the old potency and hatred and self-loathing he'd ever felt.

'Because I don't deserve it,' he snapped. 'You don't know me. You think you do but you don't. Trust me,' he said as the lift dinged and he was so damn grateful he almost kissed the floor. 'You don't want any part of this.'

'So tell me,' Callie begged, racing against time as the lift doors opened. 'Let me be the judge of what I do and don't want to be a part of.'

Cade shook his head as he pushed off the wall. 'No,' he said, then strode out of the lift.

Five minutes later Callie's hands were still shaking from the confrontation as she hit a speed-dial key on her phone. She didn't wait for the greeting on the other end when it was picked up. 'Your brother is a jackass.'

'Callie? It's…three o'clock in the morning.'

Callie almost cried at the sound of Alex's comforting American accent, very different from his brother's. 'That doesn't alter the fact that your brother is a jackass.'

Callie could hear a sigh at the other end and then a voice in the background wanting to know who was ringing at such a God-awful hour. Alex's 'It's Callie' seemed to placate his wife.

And Layla's 'Say hi for me' made Callie smile.

'Layla says hi,' Alex said. 'Now, why don't you start at the beginning? What's happened?'

'He's totally incapable of love, that's what's happened,' Callie hissed into the phone. 'I mean, I get it—I know you guys had a seriously screwed-up childhood and that's got to give him trust and intimacy issues. Although, God knows, he seems to connect sexually *extremely well*—but he's not letting me in at all. I can help him with all that stuff. Why the hell won't he let me?' she demanded. 'God, he's as stubborn as you are.'

There was silence at the end of the line for long moments and Callie wondered if she'd lost the connection. 'Alex?'

'I'm here,' he said in a gruff, sleepy voice. 'Okay…so let me get this straight. What you're saying is…you're in love with Cade?'

'Yes, dummy, I'm I love with your brother. Hell, keep up.'

'Well, when the hell did that happen?' Alex demanded.

Callie waved a dismissive hand in the air. 'The last few months. After I bought him in a charity raffle.'

'Okay… I don't understand what that means and it's really late so I'm going to save all the what-the-hell questions for a more suitable hour. But if you want a tip to reach Cade, ask him about Sophie.'

'Sophie?' Callie frowned. 'Who the hell is Sophie?'

'Oh, no,' Alex said. 'It's up to Cade to tell you.'

'Some friend you are,' she grouched.

'You're welcome,' Alex said. 'I'm going now.'

The phone clicked in her ear and Callie stared at it for long moments. She'd forgotten that he'd fled here because of *woman issues*. It had totally slipped her mind. He'd certainly never had any *issues* with her. And the more she'd got to know him the more convinced she'd been that it was deep issues from his childhood that made him commitment-phobic.

But apparently a woman called Sophie held the key.

How could she compete with someone who might still have his heart on a string?

Cade was at his desk later that evening when his phone rang. The sun had just about set and darkness was closing in around him. He snapped on his desk lamp as he picked up the phone. 'Dr Coleman.'

'You may be my brother but if you hurt Callie I'm going to come and hunt you down.'

Cade wasn't amused. 'I thought you were supposed to be on my side.'

'Not if you're being an idiot. Are you being an idiot?'

'I'm not being an idiot,' he snapped. 'Callie, on the other hand, is acting like a complete idiot.'

Alex snorted. 'What's she done that's been so bad, bro?'

'She thinks she's in love with me. It's *totally ridiculous*,' he spluttered, outrage in his voice. 'We just don't have that kind of relationship. She didn't *want* that kind of relationship. I'm here for my career, not to…get involved with some mad woman who thinks she's in love with me. We hardly know each other,' he said.

'Have you told her anything about your past? Anything you haven't even told me?'

Cade remembered the virginity conversation. 'Some,' he admitted grudgingly.

'Then you've told her more than you've ever told anybody else. That means something, Cade. Trust me, I know.'

'Oh, God,' Cade grumbled. 'There's nothing more sickening than a loved-up reformed recluse.'

Alex laughed but it was short-lived. 'You haven't told her about Sophie.'

'It's none of her damn business.'

More silence. 'You've gotta stop beating yourself up about that, Cade. It's time to forgive yourself. Aren't you tired of running away from it? Stop running, man. Talk to Callie.'

Cade would rather stick himself in the eye with a hot poker. He wasn't about to admit to anyone else how badly he'd screwed up with Sophie. 'I don't recall asking for your advice.'

'Yeah, well, you're getting it anyway. Callie's the best and if you love her as much as she loves you then you'd be a fool to let her get away.'

Cade hated that Alex knew her better than he did. He hated hearing the affection in his brother's voice that hinted at a depth of relationship that he could only wonder about.

'Did you sleep with her?'

It was out before he could stop it. He knew it was none of his business but he had to know. Callie had said they'd only ever been friends but he knew what his brother had been like before Layla and he sure as hell knew how Callie had needed male affirmation almost as much as oxygen.

There was a hesitation on the end of the line. 'Alex, I said did you sleep with her?'

'I'm only telling you this because you and I made a pact when we patched up our differences that we would always tell each other the truth. Because really it's none of your damn business.'

'Oh, my God, you *did* sleep with her.'

'Yes, but—'

Cade slammed the phone down as a hot spike of jealousy burned like acid all the way up his oesophagus. He stood up so abruptly his chair crashed to the floor.

He didn't give a fig who or how many men she'd slept with in her past. She was an adult who enjoyed her sexuality—more power to her. But Alex hurt.

And he was going to go and tell her just that.

Callie had not long stepped out of the shower and was in her gown, pouring a glass of wine, when someone pounded on her door like there was a fire in the building. Her phone rang and she contemplated ignoring the door and answering it but another bash made up her mind. She picked up the phone, noticing she had several missed calls, and answered it on her way to her poor injured door. It was Alex.

'Oh, hi,' she said. 'Listen, just hang on a sec, there's someone at the door.'

She pulled the phone from her ear and used both hands to unlock the deadlocks and pull it open. Cade stood outside, glowering down at her, his tie yanked aside in its usual disarray. His hair looked like it had been raked through a thousand times.

'You slept with Alex.'

Callie's gaze locked with his. It wasn't a question or a demand. It was an accusation. Her heart rate picked up at the simmering frustration in his whisky eyes. She brought the phone back to her ear. 'I think I'm going to need to call you back, Alex.'

'It's Cade?'

Callie's gaze didn't waver from Cade's. 'Yes.'

'I'm so sorry,' Alex said. 'He wanted to know the truth so I told him. I've been trying to get hold of you to warn you.'

'It's fine. I'll deal with it.' She hit the End button then stood aside. 'You'd better come in.'

Cade had both hands planted wide on the doorframe. 'I don't want to come in,' he snapped.

'Well, I'm not having this conversation with you standing in the hallway so stop being a petulant child and get your butt inside.'

She didn't wait for a response, just turned on her heel and headed for her lounge room. By the time she was reaching for her glass of wine she'd heard the door click shut, and as the rich bouquet slid over her tongue, Cade appeared in her peripheral vision.

Cade shook his head at her as she turned to face him. She was wearing *that* gown. The woman was going to be the death of him.

'Well?' he demanded, as she calmly took another sip of wine.

'We had a one-night stand a few weeks after we first met. Nothing more. That's it.'

Cade felt the wind go out of his sails at her frank admission. He'd been expecting outrage and denial, like Sophie had expressed when he'd confronted her about her supposed contraception. But not Callie. 'Why didn't you tell me when I asked you?'

'Because it was none of your damn business, Cade. You and I weren't a thing then and Alex and I never have been. We've never felt romantic about each other. It was just a crazy, impetuous one-off.'

Cade snorted. 'Your speciality.'

Callie sucked in a breath at the insult. She wished she had a snappy comeback but she had nothing. Why was it that the people you loved were the ones who knew how to hurt you most?

Cade had shocked himself. He sat back on the arm of the lounge chair and raked his hand through his hair. 'God. I'm so sorry.... That was a complete knee-jerk reaction and totally unforgivable. I don't know what's the matter with me today.'

Callie felt her anger dissipate as quickly as it had risen. Cade looked so lost and confused. She hoped he was here insulting her because he loved her, but she wasn't sure if that was going to be an easy admission to extract from him.

She turned and poured him a glass of wine. As she handed it to him she said, 'I do. And I don't think it's got anything to do with me and Alex.' She'd made him think about his feelings and he was off kilter. 'Who's Sophie?'

Cade's hand stalled halfway between them and Callie pushed the glass the rest of the way into his hand. He stared into the red liquid. 'Alex has been talking, I see.'

Callie shook her head. 'No. All he said was to ask you about her.'

It was on the tip of Cade's tongue to say no, to go to hell, then to pass the wine back and just walk away. But the lump was there, hard and hot and bigger than ever, and he was so very tired of keeping things inside. The catharsis when he'd told her about his time in Beverly Hills had been profound.

'Sophie was a woman I had a fling with back in L.A. Before I went to work with Alex in New York. I don't know how it happened, how we ended up in a fling, because I was a total three-or-four-dates-then-on-to-the-next-one kind of a guy. But we were. I think her being an accountant had something to do with it. I could really get away from the pressures of work with her.'

'Makes sense,' Callie said.

'We'd been seeing each other for about six weeks. I was having a good time but I didn't have any serious intentions. And then she announced that she was pregnant.'

Callie blinked. 'Oh.'

'Yes,' he said grimly. 'Oh.'

'Weren't you using protection?'

'Of course,' Cade said testily. 'Condoms, and she was on the Pill. Or at least she told me she was on the Pill. So that one time we were caught out without anything, I felt okay about pressing on.'

'But she wasn't?'

'No. She never had been. And she admitted it to me. Told me that she loved me and wanted to marry me and now we could because she was having my baby. It was like some nightmare soap opera.'

'Oh, dear.' Callie had worked hard not to let any of the men in her life get the wrong idea but it had still happened and she felt for Cade.

Cade nodded. 'I totally freaked. I didn't want to be a father, not after my childhood. We argued, I told her I didn't want anything to do with her or the baby, to get out of my life.'

Callie winced. She could just imagine how awful the conversation must have been.

'Not my best moment.'

'What happened then?'

'Later that night she washed down a bottle of pills with a bottle of vodka.'

Callie gasped. She walked the three paces between them and put her hand on Cade's forearm. 'Oh, Cade, that's awful, I'm so sorry. Did she make it?'

Cade liked the feel of her hand on his arm. In fact, he wanted to pull her close and sink into her entire embrace. 'Yes. But the baby didn't.'

Callie shut her eyes briefly. Cade *had* been through the wringer. He may not have acted admirably at the time and that obviously weighed on him now, but he'd been dealt a massive whammy and he'd lashed out. 'I'm so sorry.'

Cade shook his head. 'Don't be, because all I could feel was relief. Just…overwhelming relief. Relief that she was okay but, more than that, relief that I didn't have to deal with an unplanned pregnancy.'

He looked down into his wine and swirled it around a couple of times before looking back at Callie—dear, sweet Callie who was looking at him like he was one of the good guys. 'How could I think that way?' he asked. 'What does that make me?'

Callie stroked his cheek with her spare hand. 'It makes you human.'

'No,' he insisted. 'It makes me awful. It makes me the bad guy.'

'Cade,' she chided gently, her hand coming back to rest on his arm. 'What do you tell mums when they're relieved when a severely deformed foetus is stillborn? Do you tell them they're awful and bad?'

'No.'

'And do you mean it?'

'Of course I do, but it's not the same thing, Callie.'

'Cade, you knew about the baby for, what, a few hours? Yes, you were angry. Yes, you argued, yes, you said some things that you plainly regret until this day. But you were entitled to feel all those things. You weren't to know that Sophie was going to act in such an extreme manner. You didn't have a crystal ball, Cade. You can't be blamed for her actions.'

'I shouldn't have been so harsh.'

Callie shook her head. 'So you think you don't deserve to be happy, to fall in love, have a chance at a future with someone because you argued with Sophie and she tried to kill herself? That being alone is your punishment or something?'

'You think I do deserve to be happy?'

Callie smiled gently at him and took a small step towards him. 'Of course I do, Cade. You are one of the most caring, compassionate people I have ever met. You had a bad night that had some terrible consequences, but you have to realise that you weren't responsible for her actions. Or the sequence of events afterwards. You have to forgive yourself.'

Cade sorted. 'That's what Alex said.'

Callie dared to take another step closer, her thigh brushing his knee. 'Then that's two concurring medical opinions,' she murmured.

Cade wondered if it could be that simple. He wanted it to be. And with Callie looking at him with love shining in her eyes, turning them a dazzling kaleidoscope of blues and greens, he thought maybe it could be.

'You're very wise in matters of the heart all of a sudden,' he said, his hand sliding to her waist and pulling her into the V of his open thighs.

Callie's hand slid onto his shoulder. 'I've had a crash course in love just recently.'

And in that moment Cade realised she wasn't the only one. Callie had stormed into his life and turned it upside down and he loved her for it. He hadn't been looking for love. In fact, he'd been hiding from it, but it had found him—she'd found him. His chest swelled with it.

He loved her eyes and her smile and that bloody gown and the way she'd been brave enough to take a risk on loving him even when he'd pushed her away.

'So have I,' he said.

Callie's breath caught for a moment and then she grinned. 'Really?'

Cade grinned back. 'Really.'

'So you don't want to...just be friends any more?'

'Oh, God, no,' he groaned, pulling her closer, his head level with her chest, his nose pushing the gown aside to nuzzle along her collarbone. 'That was a stupid idea.'

Callie shut her eyes. 'The worst.'

'I want to love you,' he said. He pulled away and looked at her. 'I do love you.'

It sounded strange for a moment. He'd never told a woman that before but telling Callie felt right. He knew it in his bones.

Callie's heart felt like it was going to burst from her ribcage as it swelled and soared. She took his wine and hers and placed them on the counter. Then she rushed back into his arms and kissed him. A kiss holding all the love in the world. A kiss to seal their commitment.

'I love you, too,' she said, pulling away, smiling down into his sexy face.

'I'm sorry it took me so long to get with the programme,' he said, staring into her beautiful face. How could he not have known when it was just there, humming away now in every cell? 'But I'm going to spend every day of my life proving it to you.'

Callie grinned. 'Oh, goody,' she said, planting her hand in the centre of his chest and pushing hard. He fell back, landing sprawled on the lounge behind him. She undid the belt on her gown and in one shrug of her shoulders it was off. 'You can start right now.'

Cade grinned. 'Yes, ma'am.'

* * * * *

A sneaky peek at next month…

Medical Romance™

CAPTIVATING MEDICAL DRAMA—WITH HEART

My wish list for next month's titles…

In stores from 6th December 2013:

❑ From Venice with Love – Alison Roberts

& Christmas with Her Ex – Fiona McArthur

❑ After the Christmas Party… – Janice Lynn

& Her Mistletoe Wish – Lucy Clark

❑ Date with a Surgeon Prince – Meredith Webber

& Once Upon a Christmas Night… – Annie Claydon

Available at WHSmith, Tesco, Asda, Eason, Amazon and Apple

Just can't wait?

Visit us Online

You can buy our books online a month before they hit the shops! **www.millsandboon.co.uk**

1113/03